CW01024905

Harry's Game

Sands of Time

Harry's Game

Sands of Time

Karl Jackson

Alpaca & Goose
2021

Harry's Game – Sands of Time is a work of historical fiction based on significant events that took place during 1942 - 1943. Any names, characters, places, events, or incidents within the story are either the products of the author's imagination or inspired by similar actual events and used in a fictitious manner. Any references or opinions related to any organisations or entities exist only within the fictitious realms of the story, and any resemblance to actual persons, living or dead, is purely coincidental.

Copyright © 2021 Karl Jackson

All Rights Reserved

All rights reserved. No part of this book may be reproduced or used in any manner without written permission of the copyright owner, except for the use of quotations in a book review. For more information, including reproduction, publication, or promotion requests, please contact the author:

karl@harrysgame.com

Book design & Illustration by Karl Jackson

First published – November 2021 by Alpaca & Goose

www.alpacagoose.com

First Edition

ISBN 978-1-9162651-5-8

www.harrysgame.com

'Friends'

Dedicated to those whose stories are lost

Chapter 1

Warm welcomes

"The Air Commodore will see you now, Squadron Leader Cornwall," the young Flying Officer said with a cheery formality, as he entered the dark and dreary waiting room where Harriet had been waiting for over an hour. She'd arrived in England the night before, after a long and arduous trip from Malta, which involved being chased across the Mediterranean by the Luftwaffe who, with a renewed vigour, were trying hard to sink the minelayer taking her west. Raid after raid chased and attacked, in between detours and slaloms to dodge the many Italian submarines lying in wait, detours which delayed their arrival in Gibraltar, and subsequently had Harriet arriving in London for her anticipated meeting with the personnel department much later than anticipated. She hadn't slept since leaving Malta, thanks largely to her living nightmare of being on a boat in the Mediterranean, and seemingly the sole target of the entire German and Italian war machine. The fear of being sunk any moment, combined with her recurring waking nightmares about what had happened to Cas, prevented her from making much use of the ship's facilities, which meant she hadn't had time for anything more civilised than a brief strip wash while changing uniforms in Gibraltar. To top it all, her smart blue best uniform fitted her starved and emaciated body like a bag. She was tired, angry, and sad, and didn't appreciate being kept waiting by some desk pilot who'd summoned her on a whim. "Ma'am?" the Flying Officer said, after standing awkwardly for a few minutes while Harriet continued to stare out of the window.

"Yes..." she replied, while shifting her tired gaze to him.

"The Air Commodore asked if you'd like to go through?" He gestured for her to follow him down the corridor, and she wearily pulled herself to her feet, then followed him to the office and stepped inside. "Squadron Leader Cornwall, Sir," the Flying Officer announced to the balding Officer sitting behind the large dark wooden desk. Harriet walked in and stood to attention, and the Flying Officer stepped out of the room after giving Harriet a difficult half smile, closing the door quietly behind him. The Air Commodore continued writing, not even looking up at Harriet, and forcing her to clear her throat impatiently after a few minutes. Something she did again, louder, after a dramatic sigh still hadn't elicited anything even close to an acknowledgement of her presence.

"Yes, I know you're there..." he said with an underwhelmed and tiresome tone, still without looking up. She rolled her eyes, then turned and headed for the door, while fighting hard not to let him have a piece of her mind. "Where on earth do you think you're going?" he asked, as she turned the handle and pulled the door open.

"Who? Me?" she asked, as she turned to look at him.

"Yes, you! I don't remember dismissing you, Squadron Leader Cornwall."

"I'm sorry, Sir. When you didn't acknowledge me, I thought you were expecting somebody else. So I decided to leave." She looked him in the eyes and waited for his response.

"I was busy writing, Squadron Leader!" He pointed irritably in front of his desk, and Harriet closed the door before returning to her place in front of him. "I don't know just how lax things have got over in Malta, but here in London we still have protocol, and as an officer of the Royal Air Force, you're expected to know it and follow it! Which means staying still and keeping your mouth shut in the presence of a superior officer! And don't you dare roll your eyes at me, young lady!"

"Yes, Sir..." she replied, while fixing him on her stare. Her words were dripping with disdain.

"I don't know what they were thinking sending for you, and I hope they know what they're getting into...!" he mumbled, while pulling a large brown envelope from the pile on his desk and holding it out to her, flicking it impatiently. "Your posting." She stepped forward and took it, before resuming her place and opening the envelope. "You may read it later, Cornwall." She resisted the urge to roll her eyes again, and held the envelope by her side while using every remaining scrap of energy to keep her mouth shut and not end her career on the spot. "For reasons best known to himself, the King of Norway has personally requested that you be given command a squadron of Norwegian pilots based up in Scotland. Apparently, they've been having a difficult time of things, though I can't imagine how that's going to be made any better by sending an impetuous young madam like you to join them."

"With respect, Sir, I'm a Squadron Leader in the Royal Air Force Volunteer Reserve, and whatever your opinions of me personally, I'd be grateful if you'd follow the protocol you're so fond of, and extend me the courtesy my rank deserves!" she said quietly and firmly.

"How very dare you!" he gasped.

"Will that be all?"

"No!" He stood and leant his hands on his desk while sneering at her. "I don't hold with the idea of women in uniform, Cornwall, even less so with the idea of letting them fly! You're nothing more than a poorly conceived experiment, made good by fairy stories invented to justify your continued existence in the service. Frankly, I think you should be ashamed to be part of it, especially the propaganda circus behind sticking those medals on your chest. It's an insult to all the men who won medals the hard way. Now get out, I can't stand to be part of those charade any longer!"

"Sir, if you were an officer, you'd respect my rank, and if you were a gentleman you'd respect me as a lady. However, as you're apparently neither, I'll tell you this. Whatever you may think of me, at least I can hold my head high and say I did my duty and looked the enemy in the eyes. I don't see many medal ribbons on your chest, or wings for that matter. Good day." She walked away and left him fuming behind his desk, and gave the door a hefty slam on the way out, staring sternly at the Flying Officer who was waiting nervously outside, and silently daring him to say something. She marched through the building like a whirlwind, carrying herself gracefully with her head held high, and a look in her eyes that challenged anyone to cross her. Despite the grace, she was furious, and shaking with rage. After all she'd been through, and all she'd risked, she was lost for words at the exchange she'd just had. She wanted to go back and rip into him, and let him know exactly how much of a circus she'd been part of; but she knew that her anger would come out as a fist on his nose instead of well considered words.

"Excuse my carelessness," a faceless voice said as their shoulder collided with hers. She swung around ready to give them a mouthful, and saw a familiar smile in front of her.

"Mister O'Kira..." she said, as she recognised the man she'd marched straight into.

"Squadron Leader Cornwall, it's a pleasure to see you again." He put his hands together and bowed while smiling warmly, something she mirrored. "How are you?"

"Honestly, I've no idea..." she replied with a frown. "I arrived from Malta this morning, and came straight here to be insulted by some jumped up personnel officer who called me a poorly conceived experiment belonging to a circus!"

"Ah, I suspect I know the officer you refer to," He sighed, and shrugged a little with disappointment. "You've arrived from Malta this morning, you say?"

"Yes, and I'm exhausted..."

"I have friends who served in Malta, I hear things are difficult?"

"You could say that."

"Worse, I hear that the tea is awful?"

"Beyond..." Harriet couldn't help but let out a laugh. Her biggest and most continuous complaint of her entire time in Malta was the poor quality of the tea, and the absurdity of her enduring mission to find fresh leaves, or recycle what she had. It had almost become an obsession.

"Then while you're in town, I'd be honoured if you'd let me buy you a cup of proper tea. Something to welcome you home more appropriately?"

"I..."

"If it wouldn't be too much of an imposition?"

"I'd love to." She smiled and nodded, and he led the way, taking her kit bags despite her protests. They walked a few minutes down the road to The Savoy Hotel, the centre of society for London's elite, and a place Harriet was both familiar with and happy to be visiting again. A table was found, and with remarkable speed and courtesy, the waiting staff brought a large pot of fresh tea, Fortnum's finest, which O'Kira insisted on pouring in an almost ritualistic manner. "Thank you," Harriet said, as she got comfortable and watched him pour. "I'd almost forgotten what civilisation was like."

"Perhaps from your conversation before we met, you'd prefer to be away from certain aspects of the civilisation we've come to endure."

"You're not joking. For all its faults, Malta was a great leveller." She took a sip of the tea she'd been presented, and immediately let out a contented sigh. "Oh my God, I can't tell you how good this tastes."

"There's more than enough, so please drink all you wish."

"It's very kind of you to bring me to tea, I wouldn't even have thought about it before we met."

"Perhaps a better option than crossing swords with somebody who doesn't appreciate your experiences."

"Quite..." She shrugged and frowned again as she thought of the conversation, and just how insulting the Air Commodore had been.

"There is much insecurity among some here in England, and I think that sometimes manifests itself in unfortunate ways."

"Insecurity?"

"Yes. It's understandable, and not unusual in times of war. Especially this war."

"How so?"

"You're one of the few who has had the opportunity to fight, Squadron Leader."

"Please, call me Harry."

"Of course, Harry," he smiled. "You've been on the front line almost continuously, through France and the Battle of Britain, not to mention Malta. You've faced our enemies, and your heroism is legendary in some circles."

"I wouldn't go that far," she said with an intense blush.

"My point is, that you are in the minority. The majority of the British population have had to sit and wait, and watch as the Germans bomb them indiscriminately, with no opportunity to fight back, or do the things you've done. There's been defeat and loss on every front, except in the air. Our pilots are heroes, and that makes some uneasy. They forget that everyone plays a part, that pilots need to be paid, their food needs to be procured and cooked, their uniforms made, their engines and aeroplanes built. That can make people feel insecure, and maybe even inadequate in their own contributions.

"That's ridiculous. I wouldn't wish what I've been through on anyone, and I'd never look down on somebody for not being a pilot..." She blushed a little more as she thought of her sharp words at the Air Commodore's lack of medals or wings.

"You don't need to; they so often do it themselves."

"I suppose I hadn't thought of it that way..."

"However, people's insecurities don't excuse how they treat others, and some people are simply pompous fools." He smiled at her mischievously, and she couldn't help but laugh again. "So, other than

14

picking fights with one of our less than pleasant officers, what brings you home from Malta?"

"The King of Norway, apparently." She lifted the envelope she'd been given and waved it half heartedly. "I'm being sent to Scotland at his insistence."

"May I?" O'Kira reached for the envelope, which Harriet handed over gladly while she topped up her tea. "Ah, yes, the Norwegians..." he said, as he read through her posting letter. "We've had a number arrive over the last few years, many having escaped Norway and travelled the long way around to get here, and after training them in Canada we've managed to form a few squadrons. They're good pilots."

"Spitfires?" Her eyes lit up with excitement.

"Not for you... Apparently you'll be flying Mosquitoes."

"Me?"

"You. You're to report there next week."

"Next week?!" She scowled

"Yes... There's a rail warrant, so it shouldn't be a problem."

"I was summoned from Malta immediately. I was supposed to be going on leave before coming home, but I was told there was no time."

"Perhaps you can enjoy some leave here in England instead? Visit family, maybe?"

"I suppose..." She thought of her planned leave in Cairo with Cas, then her heart sank again. If she'd gone as planned, she'd be as dead as him. She quickly snapped out of it and smiled, and thought of heading north and visiting aunt Mary instead.

15

"Though not right away. You're invited to dinner this evening," O'Kira continued, disturbing her daydream.

"Dinner, with who?"

"The King of Norway. He's dining here at The Savoy, and you've been invited."

"Oh..." Harriet slumped a little in her seat. She was exhausted, and a formal dinner was the last thing she needed, or wanted. If she had her way, she'd be heading out of London on the first train north.

"If I may, Harry?"

"Yes?"

"Why don't you stay here at The Savoy tonight? The Air Ministry regularly books rooms for visiting very senior officers, I'm sure something could be arranged?"

"I'm hardly a very senior officer..."

"You're dining with royalty; how much more senior do you need to be?" He smiled, then excused himself for a moment and left her to pour her third cup of tea. She tried to think ahead to visiting home for a few days, instead of thinking of the immediate future of a formal dinner, or further ahead to how the hell she was going to command a squadron of Norwegians. Neither did she want to think of the past. She'd been stuck on that particular subject since stepping onboard the ship in Malta, and sailing out of Grand Harbour into the black night of the Mediterranean. The Navy hadn't been quite as accommodating to her curious refusal to sleep in a cabin, despite one having been made available for her, the only woman on the voyage. They were annoyed if anything, and thought her eccentric or ungrateful, until one of the injured pilots heading home with her mentioned to a medical orderly that she'd been on the Santa Marija convoy. Once word had got around, she was given blankets and pillows, and allowed to sleep in a lifeboat. With nothing but the sound of the sea to distract her from the horror she was reliving in her head,

16

all she had was her memories of recent days, particularly of Cas. "It's done," O'Kira said as he returned to the table.

"What is?"

"Your room. I talked with the manager, and he was more than happy to arrange it for you."

"Oh... Thank you. That's very kind of you."

"It's the least I can do. Now, I must unfortunately return to the office." He looked at his watch, and Harriet nodded reluctantly, before standing to shake his hand. "It's been my pleasure to see you again, Harry."

"The pleasure's mine, and thank you so much for everything. I was seeing red when we met, and I daren't think what I'd have done if you hadn't brought me here to talk. I owe you, again."

"You owe me nothing, my friend. Good luck in Scotland, you're exactly the leader any squadron would be lucky to have."

"You're very kind, thank you."

"Goodbye, Squadron Leader Cornwall, and good luck." He bowed again, then her left her holding her cup and smiling warmly.

She couldn't help but smile as she finished every drop of tea in the huge teapot, which O'Kira had kindly paid for without her knowing, then she headed to the front desk to collect her room key. Much to her embarrassment, the gentleman at the desk was gushing with compliments, and couldn't be any more welcoming. He even asked for her autograph, which she obligingly gave with a polite smile and frown of suspicion. A bellboy was called to carry her bags and show her to her room, which was incredibly luxurious, with marble bathroom and a four poster bed, much more grand than anything befitting a scarecrow from Malta. She checked her watch, she had hours before dinner, but as tired and desperately in need of a bath as she was, she had somewhere she needed to go first; and after tidying herself up in the mirror, she headed out onto the streets of London,

17

and enjoyed the warm September sun as she walked along the busy pavements to the underground station. A short ride later, and she was standing at the door of her favourite tailor in Savile Row. She took a breath before going in, steeling herself for what was to come.

"Would you believe it?" her old friend said as she stepped into the shop.

"Hello, Ralph," Harriet said with a nervous smile.

"Harry, my dear girl. Wherever have you been?" He walked towards her, looking her up and down while smiling warmly.

"Malta..."

"Again?"

"Yes, it was something of an unexpected trip."

"Come in, can I get you a tea?"

"That would be nice, thank you." She followed him to his office, as he called for one of his staff to bring them tea. "You wouldn't believe how bad the tea was in Malta. Sweepings off the storeroom floor at best."

"Only the best here, Harry, you know that."

"It's why I come here."

"I notice your uniform is looking a little... Roomy?" he said as they sat at his desk.

"Yes. The tea wasn't the only thing in short supply."

"You poor thing, you must be starved."

"You get used to it... Ralph, I'm here to ask a favour..." she said shyly.

"Go on?"

"I've been unexpectedly invited to a formal dinner now I'm back in town, and I wondered if you could tidy my uniform up a little, maybe take it in a bit and make me look a little less like a scarecrow in a grain sack?"

"I think I can do something for you," he said with a chuckle. "when do you need it by?"

"Tonight," she replied awkwardly.

"Tonight?"

"Sorry..."

"Not to worry, I'll get you something to change into, and have the staff work on it right away." He jumped up and left with a smile, and returned moments later with a cricket jumper and some slacks, which Harriet changed into when he left the room again, before handing over her crumpled uniform and being measured by a seamstress. He brought a small plate of biscuits when he returned, which he put on his desk as he eased into his chair. "Not enough to build your strength I'm afraid, but they won't hurt."

"Thank you," Harriet smiled as she took one and dunked it in her tea before popping it in her mouth. Then quickly blushed at what she'd done.

"It's the only way," he replied with a wink as he dunked his own, instantly putting her at ease. "So, how long are you in town for?"

"Only a day or two, I'm afraid. The RAF are sending me to Scotland.

"Scotland?"

"Yes... A little different from Malta."

"And a little colder... At least we get to see you, however briefly. I'm very happy you called in, Harry. Even if it was to have your uniform taken in."

"My uniform wasn't the only reason I came to see you..." She frowned, and the joviality fell from the conversation. "I need to talk to you."

"Oh?"

"It's Cas..." She stared at him for a moment and his smile melted, as if he knew what she was about to say.

"How?"

"Shot down over the Mediterranean."

"I see..."

"He'd been hurt in a bombing raid, quite badly, and was being evacuated to a hospital in Egypt. Only, the flight never arrived. A distress call was picked up shouting about night fighters, but nothing after that. Aeroplanes went up to search the next morning, but it was useless."

"I'm sorry. Truly, I am."

"I thought it important you know. You're one of the few people who really knew him, and I know he thought a lot of you."

"As he did you, Harry. As he did you..." He leant forward and rummaged in his desk, then brought out a bottle of fine French cognac and a couple of glasses. "I think this calls for something a little stronger than tea, wouldn't you agree?" Harriet nodded as he poured them a drink each, and handed her a glass. "To Cas?"

"To Cas." Harriet clinked her glass against his, and they both swallowed it down. It burned her throat, but it was the best tasting thing she'd had in a while. Ralph poured another, then sat back in his chair and sipped, and Harriet did the same, feeling much less tense now she'd broken the news. "Thank you," she said timidly.

"When did it happen?"

"Just before I left."

"I don't imagine you've had much opportunity to talk about it?"

"Honestly, I've tried not to think about it at all, but the truth is I can't get it out of my mind. I was supposed to have been on the aeroplane with him... We were going to have some leave in Cairo, and relax a bit after a tough few months, at least that was the plan, assuming he recovered enough to leave hospital before I went back to Malta. Then I got my orders to report home, and my leave was cancelled. So, you see, I should have been with him, we both should have gone, and now here I am."

"That must be difficult for you to bear."

"In so many ways. Guilt included."

"Guilt?"

"For not being there with him. He was stretcher bound, and wrapped in bandages. Maybe I could have helped him if I was there? Get him out of the aeroplane or something. He couldn't have done it himself."

"You know that's no way to think, Harry. You weren't there, and you had no say in whether you were or not from what I understand. You can't feel guilty for that."

"Well, I do. Like I feel guilty for being here now, drinking nice cognac and having a nice uniform adjusted for me. Can you believe that I even have a room in The Savoy tonight? Finally, I get home to all these nice things, after dodging death more ways than you can imagine, and he's dead because a stray bomb injured him after he'd driven to the airfield to see me and make sure I was OK."

"It's human, you know, the feelings you're experiencing. Survivor's guilt, I think it's called. However, as normal as it is, it's important you understand that none of what happened was within your control." He gave her a warm smile, which she returned through teary eyes while nodding a little. "I've known Cas a long time, as you're well

21

aware, and I like to think I've got to know him reasonably well over the years. As well as he allows anyone to get to know him, that is; and if I know anything at all of him, I know he'd be telling you exactly the same right now. In addition to telling you that you can't dwell, and you must focus on what's ahead. As difficult as that may be."

"I know..." She sniffed and wiped her tears on the silk handkerchief he passed her. "It's just hard."

"It will be, and for some time. Though you're a strong young woman, Harry. You'll get through this, and you'll keep moving forward. It's what he would want."

"Thank you, Ralph." She nodded and forced a smile through her tears. "I'm sorry, I'm just tired. I haven't slept for days."

"Don't apologise for having emotions. The fact you can still feel them is a good sign, I suppose. It means the war hasn't broken you just yet."

"It's tried hard enough."

"I can't even imagine. There were stories in the newspapers about Malta, it sounded horrific."

"I had it better than most there, I suppose, but things weren't easy. No fuel, no ammunition, and no food. You're taking my uniform in because there wasn't enough food to feed everyone on the island, so they just kept cutting and cutting the rations. Some days it was a couple of boiled sweets, a couple of hard biscuits and tinned jam, and a bowl of some sort of watery grey stew with a couple of pieces of potato and something they said was meat."

"For dinner?"

"For the day."

"That sounds terrible."

"It was better than nothing, and those that have been there throughout the siege have lived that way for years now. Even the water was tainted. The processing plant could only be run a few hours a day due to fuel rationing, and the water always tasted salty and metallic, and sometimes of fuel after it had been stored in old petrol cans before being boiled for tea."

"Makes England seem like the lap of luxury."

"I suppose." She smiled again, and took another sip of her brandy. "I'm so sorry, I wasn't expecting to sit here wittering on."

"Not at all, it's what friends are for."

"I'm happy we're friends."

"Me too. I'm grateful you thought of me, Harry. While it's terrible news, I prefer knowing than not; and if anyone was going to tell me, I prefer it to be you."

"I'm sorry we couldn't have met again under better circumstances."

"As am I, though I'm still happy to see you, and I hope that with a little time you'll feel better, time and a lot of food." He pushed the plate of biscuits to her, and she took another without hesitation. "Let me go and check on your uniform for you, make yourself at home." He left her to her thoughts for a while, knowing it was the right moment to let her have some space to cry and compose herself. It was the first time she'd really talked about what had happened with anyone. She'd stayed with Robbie while she waited for her boat home, and had intended to let her know about Cas with the same stoic approach as she'd told Ralph, but instead she'd ended up sobbing, then sleeping, and hardly uttering a word, other than to say he was dead. Talking about it had been hard, but helpful. Ralph had talked a lot of sense, and his warmth and kindness allowed him to be there for her, while at the same time processing his own emotions. It helped that he knew Cas well enough to be friends. It made it OK to be upset, though the tiredness was making it worse. She looked at her watch, the rare Omega that Cas had bought in Switzerland in his days as a pilot, and loaned to her when they first met in France. She smiled as she rolled her wrist and watched the light dance off the face, reflecting the pearlescent pinks and turquoises hidden on the ivory white face. For a moment, she felt bad about having it. Thinking that maybe he'd have survived if he'd had his watch. He'd always told her it was lucky, and that it would keep her safe, and it had. She'd lived on the edge and been close to death so many times, and somehow sneaked through when really she should have been dead ten times over. Without it she'd be dead, maybe, but Cas would maybe be alive. Every fighter pilot she'd met was superstitious in some way or another, more so the further they were into their operational tour, so she knew she wasn't alone in thinking that way. Maybe they were onto something.

More tea came when Ralph returned, and they talked about Malta, and London, and how England had been since she'd been away. It had been a difficult place to live, apparently. There were still bombing raids, though nowhere as near as many as there had been, and people were sick of rationing. Food, clothes, almost everything was rationed, except vegetables and fish. To top it all, there'd been nothing but bad news since Dunkirk. The army in the western desert had been chased back and forth by Rommel, Greece had fallen, Singapore had fallen to the Japanese, Egypt was in the balance, and the Americans had taken a beating at Pearl Harbour. It all made for a terrible tale. People just didn't have anything to hope for. Malta's ferocious refusal to yield was about the only success story, and even that wasn't much. A tiny island in the Mediterranean with a starved population and no real importance in the war, at least in the eyes of most.

A couple of hours had passed before Harriet's uniform was ready, taken in perfectly with temporary stitches that Ralph showed her how to remove as soon as she was able to build herself up again, and he'd had some new blouses made up for her, and some new stockings were acquired too, though he refused to say where he managed to procure them with the rationing. The uniform had even been cleaned and pressed, and was looking as good as new. Harriet blushed when she saw herself in the full length mirror. She looked how she wanted to again, smart, not like a scarecrow in a bag, and her uniform fit perfectly. She thanked Ralph profusely, and as usual he refused a penny in payment, instead putting it on her bill for when the war was over. He also thanked her for visiting and telling him of Cas. He knew it wasn't easy for her, which made him all the more grateful that she'd done it.

Chapter 2

Heading North

Harriet let out an exhausted sigh as she slumped into her seat in the busy compartment on the packed train north, having fought her way past the many businessmen and service personnel filling every scrap of space. The morning had been a rush, right from the persistent alarm call that finally roused her from the deep and dreamless sleep that she'd crashed into after dinner with the King and his entourage. It was the first proper sleep she'd had since leaving Malta, and both her body and mind were demanding more, having finally had a taste of something so desperately needed, and missed. She'd just had enough time for a breakfast of toast with butter and marmalade, accompanied by as much tea as she could take onboard, before heading across London to King's Cross station to catch her train north. She rested her head against the window after the train lurched into life, and watched the world pass by as the carriages snaked through the bombed and rubble strewn suburbs of north London. While keeping her gaze outside, she was acutely aware that the other passengers in her compartment were looking at her questioningly, as though her apparent tiredness was the result of a late night in London's nightclubs, dancing and drinking into the early hours. Something RAF pilots had developed quite a reputation for. The truth couldn't have been any further away, and as Harriet closed her eyes with the gentle rocking and clicking of the train on the tracks, she thought back to the previous day, and night.

After leaving Ralph's exclusive and very welcoming shop in Savile Row, Harriet had made the most of being in London; and following what she'd developed as a tradition in her visits to the capital, she headed to Fortnum's to do some shopping. Rationing made things difficult, but not insurmountable, thanks largely to her apparent celebrity status among some who worked there; those who'd met her previously and followed her story, including her death defying low level pass in her Spitfire during the Battle of Britain, for which she'd been presented a very nice hamper. It made her blush when staff talked to her as though she was a star of stage and screen, but it helped when the management made a point of finding ways for her

26

to do her shopping almost unhindered. She never took advantage, never taking more than was fair, and always paying the full rate despite management's protestations, and this visit was no different. She bought tea, mostly, and some tinned goods she knew were hard to come by in most places. Tinned meats and fruits, biscuits, jams, and a few other bits and pieces. Nothing excessive, but following the starvation of Malta, she couldn't help slipping in a few treats to help her build up her strength. After Fortnum's it was to Harrods for toiletries and new underwear, and a few other essentials, including some more of her favourite Chanel perfume. Then it was back to the hotel, where she promptly fell asleep in a bath which quickly chilled, leaving her to wake with a stiff neck, pruned fingers, and shivers which made getting ready for her meeting with the King all the more challenging; a meeting which she was already late for thanks to her unscripted sleep in the bath.

After arriving late for dinner, which had the RAF attaché in fits having spent quite some time apologising on her behalf, and inventing excuses for what could possibly be delaying her, the King engaged her like a long lost friend, much to the surprise of both her and the attaché. By his own admission, the King had made a nuisance of himself at the Air Ministry since their first meeting, calling, sometimes in person, for updates on her career; and now he had her captive at dinner, he demanded details of how his brave Norwegian Skaldmaer, or shield maiden as he explained, had fared in Malta. He was as proud of her as he would be a daughter, and he explained that when a newly formed Norwegian Mosquito squadron had been decimated by the Luftwaffe in its first month of operation, losing a number of aircrew over the North Sea and the Norwegian coast, including their Commanding Officer, he'd insisted she was given command. The RAF had initially said no, naturally, not liking to be told what to do by somebody else, especially when they already had plans for a replacement from one of the Norwegian fighter squadrons; but the King's persistence changed their minds, an inevitable outcome when he recruited the support of his British counterpart, and subsequently the Prime Minister. The King's theory was that her experience as a combat leader and reputation as a pilot would inspire the squadron and pick up their morale. Although she smiled politely throughout, Harriet was less than convinced. Given the choice, she'd much rather not have the pressure, though she couldn't really say as much in the face of the King's excitement. She tried to explore whether the man whose job she was taking would be insulted, but she was reassured that he hadn't yet been promoted, and neither did he have any twin engine experience. He would still be leaving his squadron, but had a conversion course to go through before they'd let him anywhere near a Mosquito. Something Harriet found ridiculous compared to her own experience of being thrown in it and taught on the job, as had happened with every single aeroplane she'd flown other than the old Nieuport she'd learned to fly in, when great care was taken to give her years of very close tuition. At the end of the evening, the King insisted that she call him direct if she needed anything at all, and made her promise that she would, and then he left her to return to her room and crash into her bed and straight into a deep sleep.

Having been unceremoniously nudged from her dreams by the conductor when her train finally arrived in York, Harriet had jumped an eastbound train, and stopped off at her old air station on her way home; where she stood on the edge of the dispersal and watched as a Mosquito circled the airfield having given quite a display. She smiled as the pair of Rolls Royce Merlin engines vibrated the air with their familiar and unmistakeable sound, but as warming as it was to see the Mosquito cruising effortlessly across the autumn sky, there was also a degree of apprehension. The last time she'd flown a Mosquito, she'd ended up in a ball of flames some way from the end of the runway, and feeling lucky to escape with her life. She'd enjoyed flying the Mosquito, and had fond memories of flying it as an instructor, despite its best efforts to try and kill her, and she'd long since accepted that the accident was something she was going to have to put behind her if she was going to continue flying, or at least she'd tried to accept.

It was impossible for her not to hold her breath when the Mosquito's wheels came down as it gently descended on its final approach to the runway. Losing an engine on final approach was second only to losing one on take off when it came to helping the crew get their harps, and even watching made her a little apprehensive. It touched down lightly and without incident, much to her relief, and slowed along the runway before taxiing over to the dispersal and coming to a halt. The engines cut and propellers stopped spinning, then the hatch opened, and a bag was thrown to the ground, followed by a body which swung from the airframe long before the ground crew got the steps to it. Harriet's heart jumped as the pilot pulled off their flying helmet and straightened their tussled blonde shoulder length hair while picking up their flight bag. She watched, staying stationary and resisting the urge to run forward, until Nicole finally looked over and saw her. She stopped in her tracks, staring mouth open in surprise for a moment, then quickly bursting into a sprint.

"My God, is it you?" Nicole asked, as she jumped at Harriet, and wrapped her in a tight hug.

"If it's not, you're assaulting a stranger," Harriet replied with a giggle, trying her best not to let her emotions get the better of her.

"Or a ghost!" Nicole kissed her on each cheek, then hugged her tight again before letting go and standing back to look at Harriet. "I went to school with you, so I know that you know how to write, albeit badly. Couldn't you have let me know you were coming home?" she ranted, her French accent becoming all the more pronounced.

"I didn't know myself until the last minute."

"Then you could have written to let me know how you were. I haven't heard from you in ages!"

"I did write, didn't you get my letters?"

"Not for a long time... Though we both know that the mail can be slow, I suppose, especially getting out of Malta."

"It sounds like you missed me..."

"Don't be ridiculous." Nicole shrugged in her characteristically dismissively way. "It's been quite nice not having to live through the chaos that seems to follow you." She smiled, then hugged Harriet again. "I'm so happy to see you, Harry. I've heard stories from Malta, I've been so worried about you. Welcome home."

"I missed you..."

"Of course you did, I'm delightful," she laughed, as she finally released Harriet again. "Shall we go to the Mess? I need a coffee!"

"Let's..." Harriet laughed, and they walked arm in arm to the Mess, via the dispersal so Nicole could check in and leave her parachute, and Harriet could collect her bags. "Where's Archie? Harriet asked as they walked. "When I arrived, they told me you and he were up on a flight."

"We were. He has a meeting in London, and a new Mosquito to collect, so I dropped him at Northolt and came back myself. I think he's planning to meet with his fiancé, so will likely stay overnight."

"Typical... I've just come from London! If I'd known you were there, I'd have got a flight home with you, instead of taking the train."

"If you'd told me you were in the country, I'd have collected you."

"I've already apologised for that."

"They don't have phones in London?"

"You know, I'm really not sure I missed you after all..." Harriet rolled her eyes

"Lies," Nicole replied with a smirk. "You know you love me."

"Unfortunately..."

"So, why are you back in England?"

"Do I need a reason to come and visit the girl I apparently love?"

"No, but the RAF doesn't recognise love. It recognises orders, and ridiculous routines that make no sense, other than in the mind of some stupid old man somewhere."

"You haven't changed..."

"My point remains. The RAF don't just send people home, especially not you, not from Malta." She frowned at Harriet. "Are you hurt? Is that it? Did they send you home because you're unwell?"

"No..." Harriet smiled reassuringly.

"Are you sure? You look thin, like you haven't seen a good meal in years."

"I had one last night at The Savoy, thank you."

"The Savoy?"

"Yes."

"The exclusive hotel in London?"

"Yes..."

"Nice for a Squadron Leader... Anyway, I'm quite sure they have telephones at The Savoy."

"I'm quite sure they do, and I'm sorry I didn't call. I'd literally just got off a boat from Malta, and was thrown into a meeting before heading north. I didn't even think, and I really am sorry, I just wanted to come and see you. I really have missed you."

"I'm happy you came." Nicole smiled and squeezed Harriet's arm. "You still didn't tell me why the RAF let you escape Malta? I don't think things have improved there since we visited?"

"They're much, much worse."

"Which is why you're so thin."

"Yes..."

"Is that why they sent you home? Because you're too thin?"

"No..."

"Are you going to tell me?"

"If I must..." Harriet sighed.

"Well?"

"Well... The King of Norway requested that I be brought home to command a Norwegian Mosquito squadron up in Scotland... There, now you know!"

"You're serious?"

"Told me himself."

"Only you, Harriet Cornwall... Only you."

"What?"

"Who else could escape the most brutal war zone in the world, on the whim of a King who also happens to be a personal friend."

"Shut up! It's not like that."

"Then how is it? Anyone else would still be in the baking heat, and drinking that terrible water. It is still terrible, isn't it?"

"Worse. There's so little fuel they can only run the water treatment plant a few hours a day, and they still use petrol cans to distribute it out to the airfields. It's a bit like what you remember, but with more salt and petrol."

"I imagine Cas was delighted that your royal friend helped you escape, while he has to stay in the heat. How is he? Still being faultlessly kind to you, despite the lucky star you repeatedly sail under, I imagine?"

"He's dead..." Harriet's heart squeezed tight, and her stomach flipped as the words fell out of her mouth without warning. She knew the conversation was coming, but she didn't think it would be so early after they were reunited, or so blunt. Nicole stopped in her tracks and turned to face Harriet, whose eyes were already filling with tears. "I'm sorry... I didn't mean to say it that way."

"Harriet... How?"

"He'd been hit in a bombing raid. They were getting so frequent, much more so than when you were there." She forced a half hearted smile, which Nicole wasn't able to return, not seeing the pain in her friend's eyes. "He survived, though, despite the odds, but he was pretty beaten up, and the doctors decided to send him to a hospital in Egypt, somewhere he could get better treatment and recover properly." She looked up into the sky and fought to keep herself from totally falling to pieces, again. "Then..." She looked back to Nicole, and into her big eyes, which were damp with tears. "Then they got him, German night fighters that is. The Sunderland he was evacuated on never got as far as Egypt." Nicole didn't say a word, instead she just stepped forward and hugged Harriet while they both cried. Cas had been a wonderful friend to both of them, and the news of his death was devastating. He'd been the one that had made their life in the RAF possible, and the one that had fought for them, and for their right to fly and be part of the RAF. He'd had such an impact and been such a friend, that his untimely death was difficult to process.

"Let's go," Nicole said after a while, and Harriet nodded in agreement, again forcing a smile.

"I didn't mean to tell you like that, I'm sorry."

"Don't be, you needed to tell me."

"I did, but I hadn't intended to just blurt it out. I've been thinking about it all the way here. How to tell you, I mean. I suppose that's why I didn't call you from London... I wanted to, but I knew that as soon as I heard your voice, I wouldn't be able to stop myself from telling you, and I wanted to do it in person."

"How long are you staying?"

"A few days... I have to be in Scotland next week."

"Then forget the Mess, we'll go home."

"Home?"

"Yes. You haven't been gone so long that you forgot where you live, did you?" Nicole smiled sweetly, making Harriet feel warm knowing she was with her. "Your aunt will be happy to see you, and you need your family around you for a while."

"Yes, mum."

"See what happens when I'm not around to look after you?" She ruffled Harriet's hair a little, then took her arm again and continued to the Mess, and to her room, where Harriet was left to sit on the bed while Nicole got out of her flying kit. She smiled as she watched Nicole pull on her tie, and struggle as she always did to and fasten it neatly.

"You never could fasten a tie properly," she said as she stood and pulled the tie apart, then fastened it properly while Nicole pursed her lips in frustration.

"It's because they're stupid pieces of clothing! You know that the Chinese say a necktie strangles creative thought, don't you?"

"I've known you most of your life, and you haven't met one Chinese person."

"That doesn't make it any less true!" Nicole lifted her nose in the air, then turned and checked herself in the mirror. "Perfect. Come, let's take you home." Harriet smiled, and followed Nicole through the Mess, and out to an immaculate looking Aston Martin in the car park outside. "Let's put your bags in the back."

"Since when do you drive an Aston Martin?"

"Since Archie agreed to let me use it when he isn't around."

34

"I can't imagine he dared argue..." Harriet smirked, and helped Nicole squeeze her bags into the back of the car, then they climbed in as Nicole started the rumbling engine, which sounded very much like an aeroplane. "When did you learn to drive?" Harriet asked nervously, as Nicole let off the brakes and the car launched into life.

"I've been able to drive for a long time."

"Since when?"

"Grandpa let me drive his truck all of the time."

"Again, I practically lived with you. You drove your grandfather's truck when he wasn't there to catch you, and when he did catch you, you were grounded. Repeatedly."

"But he showed me how."

"Eventually, and even then it was only to stop you killing yourself, or me, when I was stupid enough to go along with you."

"So, I'm right, grandpa taught me, and I drove regularly in France. It was a good enough story for the British government to give me a licence, so it's good enough for me."

"I'm not sure it's good enough for me..."

"You'd rather walk?"

"How far is it again?" Harriet laughed as Nicole rolled her eyes, clearly unimpressed, then she narrowly avoided the Station Warrant Officer as she whizzed out of the main gate, receiving a mouthful of hardly distinguishable curses as she left him standing in a daze. "Friend of yours?"

"Mister Thompson? Oh, we have an understanding."

"I don't doubt that." Harriet raised her eyebrow as Nicole smirked, then took off onto the open road. The roaring Aston Martin made short work of winding roads and undulating hills, before dropping

35

down the long descent towards home. Harriet smiled as she saw the barrage balloon filled smog of Hull in the distance, it was a reassuring sight in the late afternoon sun, and made her feel safe to know she was home. "Do the Germans still come?"

"Sometimes, but not as frequently as they did, and only ever at night."

"Good..."

"Mostly they're after the docks, but sometimes their bombs land on the city and cause problems. It's not too bad, though."

"It sounds like heaven compared to Malta."

"How bad did it get?"

"I can't even describe it... Ten times worse than when we were there together, at least. They mostly focused on Grand Harbour and the airfields. Valletta and the three cities were rubble, and they wrecked Floriana. They'd come day and night, with hardly a few hours rest between raids sometimes; and between the bombers, the fighters would sweep the island and have a go at anything moving... They got Robbie in one of the raids."

"No?"

"Yes, she's OK, just about. A few broken bones, but it was a lucky escape. She had to be dug out of the rubble of her building after it was hit."

"It sounds terrible..."

"It was. Lissy and Anj said to tell you hello. They miss you, though I can't imagine why." Harriet laughed as Nicole scowled playfully.

"The poor things had to put up with you alone? This is why they missed me. I was the delight that made you tolerable."

"I thought it was something like that."

"I'm happy you made it out safe, it sounds like you were one of the lucky ones."

"Yes... I was flying Photographic Reconnaissance Spitfires most of the time, safely away from the daily grind in the combat squadrons." Harriet gave a half smile, not wanting to share just how deadly her assignment had really been. It wouldn't do any good to scare Nicole more, she didn't need to know the details.

"I'm happy you were safe."

"I'm sorry about Sully... I wish I'd been able to tell you in person."

"It was hard to hear the news. I was grateful you got a message to Archie asking him to tell me, instead of just sending me a telegram. That would have been harder."

"I wish I could have done more, but there was nothing else to tell. You know how it is over there, sometimes people just don't come back."

"I know... It seems Malta took a lot from both of us."

"It did. I still love the island, and the people, but I'm in no rush to get back." The car rolled through the gates of Aunt Mary's house, and up the gravel drive. Nicole honked the horn a few times before coming to a stop. "Like to announce your arrival?"

"The kettle won't put itself on," Nicole laughed, then turned off the engine. "Shall we?" Harriet nodded, and the pair got out of the car and removed her bags.

"Aunt Mary, look what I found," Nicole said, as she led Harriet into the kitchen.

"Oh my God!" Mary gasped from her seat at the table. She sat gobsmacked for a moment, stunned by the sight of her niece standing before her. "Harriet..."

"Hi, Aunt Mary," Harriet said shyly.

"She turned up on my airfield looking lost, so I thought I'd better bring her home," Nicole said, as she wandered across the kitchen and looked in the food cupboard. "Do we have any biscuits?" Mary ignored Nicole's grumbling, and walked over to Harriet and gave her a warm hug.

"Welcome home!"

"Thank you," Harriet whispered, trying not to cry.

"Why didn't you tell me you were coming home?"

"She forgot how to write," Nicole shrugged, as she tried another cupboard. "Are you sure there aren't any biscuits?" Mary and Harriet smiled at each other, and Harriet felt a huge sense of relief wash over her that she hadn't anticipated.

"Nicole Delacourt, do you ever stop think about your stomach?" Mary asked.

"I'm hungry."

"Well, I don't have any biscuits, I'm afraid. Not until I bake some."

"I can save you the effort," Harriet said, as she put one of her bags on the table, then produced a tin of biscuits from Fortnum's, and a caddy of finest Assam tea.

"My God, proper biscuits..." Nicole gasped from across the kitchen, and hurried over the seize the tin, which Mary quickly pulled from her hands. "Hey!"

"Not until you've both been and washed up. I'll put the kettle on, and we can have tea and biscuits out on the patio and enjoy the sun while we still have it." Nicole frowned while Harriet giggled. "Off you go!"

"You know that we are fighter pilots in the RAF?" Nicole said with the frustration of a scalded schoolgirl. "Officers, no less! We're used to being the ones giving orders."

"Not in my house. Now, go and get cleaned up and out of those uniforms, or there'll be no biscuits."

"They're your biscuits," Nicole said to Harriet. "You could support me in this."

"And argue with Aunt Mary? Not a chance! Come on, let's go do as we're told." Harriet picked up her bags, and walked through the kitchen with a big smile in her face.

"This is ridiculous!" Nicole complained, as she traipsed behind Harriet through the house and up the stairs.

"See you in a few minutes," Harriet said, as she opened her bedroom door and stepped inside. The sun was glaring through the window, casting a golden silhouette of the frame on the wall. She dropped her bags and walked around the room slowly, touching the furniture, and smiling at the warmth she felt in her heart. She couldn't stop herself from crying tears of all kinds, of joy, of sadness, of relief, and exhaustion. She gazed out of the window as the golden September sun lit up the garden, and she cast her mind back to Malta and all that had happened. She thought of Robbie, and of Cas, and the smile he'd given her before being carried onto the Sunderland that was supposed to be flying him to safety. Then she thought of that last moment when she thought she saw his face at the porthole, however briefly. She'd thought of little else since she'd left the island, and regardless of the talk she'd had with Ralph about her guilt, she still felt it. Her mind had even played desperate tricks on her for a while, and every now and then she'd think that maybe she didn't see Cas on the Sunderland because he wasn't on it. Maybe they'd taken him back to the hospital at the last minute, or he'd refused to get on and was still in Malta. The thought would excite her for a brief moment, and just for a few minutes she'd feel happy and excited, and she'd need to get back to Malta to tell everyone where he was hiding. Then the reality would hit her like a tidal wave, and knock her flat again. It was a cruel fantasy, but still better than her beating herself up for what had happened, which was the other competing thought. If she hadn't been cross with him, he wouldn't have driven to the airfield to clear the air and apologise, and he wouldn't have been caught out in a bombing raid heading back to work afterwards. That was one of her demon's favourites to torture her with.

"Have you even moved?" Nicole asked, as she came into Harriet's room.

"What's that?" Harriet asked, as she blinked out of her daydreams, and turned to see her friend standing in the doorway wearing a beautiful green summer dress. "Sorry, I was a little distracted..."

"Are you OK?" Nicole walked over and stood in front of Harriet, looking at her with concern.

"I'll be fine. I'm just tired, that's all..."

"When did you sleep last?"

"Properly?"

"Here, let me help." Nicole unbuttoned Harriet's tunic and pulled it off, then gently helped her out of her uniform. "Harry, you're so thin..." she gasped softly, as she saw Harriet's ribs and collar bones protruding from her tight tanned skin. Next she unfastened Harriet's tight bun and let her hair fall around her shoulders, then helped her step into her blue dress before running a brush through her hair and tying it with a ribbon. "There, better. My pretty girl."

"Thank you," Harriet whispered.

"Let's go and have tea and biscuits." Harriet nodded, and they went downstairs to join Mary on the patio.

Tea and biscuits were followed a couple of hours later by an evening meal of rabbit stew made with carrots and potatoes, and real meaty rabbit. It was nothing like the grey fatty mystery meat meals she'd been fed in Malta, that the cooks optimistically described as rabbit stew, but was nothing of the sort. Most weren't even sure there was

40

any rabbit in it, especially as nobody had seen a wild rabbit on Malta in months. Or many of the native feral cats, for that matter. Mary and Nicole wanted to know all about Harriet's exploits, though Nicole kindly steered the conversation away from anything she knew would be difficult for Harriet, which was greatly appreciated. Instead, Harriet talked of flying her blue Spitfire, Vixen, high above the Mediterranean, and searching for convoys or taking photos of enemy installations, before outrunning their fighters and escaping home in time for bad tasting tea. She made it sound much more romantic than it was, and significantly less dangerous. She turned the tables after a while, and asked after Nicole's career. Things had gone well, apparently, and Archie's small team of instructors had developed into a unit of experts who knew everything there was to know about the Mosquito fighter bomber, and they ran regular courses to up skill squadron instructors and pilots in all aspects of operation, from advanced handling, to precision gunnery and bombing. They'd just finished their most recent course, and Archie had stood them down while their aeroplanes were serviced and refitted, and they were taking some time to rest before topping up their own skills ahead of the next course starting in October. Nicole had taken to the job like a duck to water, and she'd developed a well deserved reputation for being a tough instructor who got the best from her students, and often received thank you gifts at the end of the course. She'd also been a welcome guest when she visited front line squadrons to fly missions for a few weeks and keep her skills sharp, which was an expectation of all the instructor pilots. It had taken some getting used to at first, certainly for the male pilots not used to a female turning up and flying with them, but their own squadron instructors had often already been through training with her, and knew her well enough to warn their pilots to treat her as they would any other pilot, and to not get on the wrong side of her.

Harriet eventually excused herself, after her eyes had closed mid way through the conversation for the third time, and having made her way to her room she fell into her bed as the last light of day danced across the sky outside. It was wonderfully peaceful, no bombing raids or scrambling aircraft, just the song of the tweeting and singing birds drifting through the open window from the garden outside. She daydreamed for a while, thinking mostly of how nice it was to be home; and despite the difficulties being experienced by the local

41

population, she loved how normal home felt compared to Malta. She felt truly safe for the first time in months. As the light faded, to be replaced by a sky of deep blue and dark orange, the door opened, and Nicole came into her room.

"What's wrong?" Harriet asked.

"Nothing," Nicole replied, then pulled off her dress and climbed in bed beside her. "Move over."

"I'm quite sure you have a bed of your own," Harriet sighed, then shuffled to a cooler place on the sheets, as Nicole wriggled and got comfortable, snuggling next to Harriet, and putting her head on her shoulder.

"Shut up," Nicole replied, and gave her friend a squeeze. "I've missed you."

Chapter 3

Up Where the Air is Clear

It was nice to be home, and after a couple of days lounging in the garden, eating stew and anything else substantial, and revelling in the excitement of getting water straight from the tap and it not tasting of salt or petrol, Harriet was starting to unwind and feel like herself again. The nightmares continued, much to her distress and disappointment, and despite her mock complaints she was grateful for Nicole sharing a bed with her, and holding her in the night when she'd wake crying, or gasping for breath, having been haunted by terrors of the desert, or the tanker. She'd survived both experiences, somehow, but they'd left physical and mental scars; from the burned skin and badly blistered feet from her time in the desert, to her sore lungs from the oil and flames of the convoy, and the many red marks left on her body from the burning hot spent brass bullet cases from the machine gun she took control of, that would fall around her neck and down her blouse, trapping themselves between her skin and tightly fastened life jacket. Despite the pain and discomfort, the physical injuries were easier to deal with. Now she was home she was able to soothe her skin with cold wet towels, and walk around in the garden barefoot to let the blisters heal properly. The mental damage was a little harder to manage, and in addition to the nightmares, she had to contend with being irritable with the most innocent of niggles, and at times consumed by the darkest thoughts that made her wish she'd been on the Sunderland with Cas regardless of the outcome. Aunt Mary helped a lot, and spent lots of time with Harriet, mostly just being herself and making things normal. Looking after her, cooking good meals, washing her clothes, and taking her for walks in the countryside to get some air. Looking after was exactly what Harriet needed, and after an initial resistance, she responded it to well.

Nicole had to work most days, much to Harriet's disappointment, mostly doing test flights and helping catch up on the administration while the unit's aircraft went through major servicing and refit, but she came home each evening and spent time with Harriet, sleeping by her side and hugging her when the night terrors came.

"You should come with me to the airfield tomorrow," Nicole said, as they lay in bed and watched the sky turn through the different colours of sunset through the bedroom window.

"Why?" Harriet asked.

"Archie wants to see you."

"Why does he want to see me?" Harriet frowned as she tried to think of what she'd done, or what he was going to ask her to do.

"Because he's your friend, I suppose," Nicole shrugged and rolled her eyes. "Why else?"

"Nothing I can think of," Harriet let out a giggle.

"You're hard work. Get some sleep, and I'll drive you tomorrow."

"I'm not sure that particular thought is as relaxing as you think..."

"How did you ever make it as a fighter pilot?"

"I was a fighter pilot before you."

"By luck, no more. Anyway, you're welcome to the job. I quite enjoy what I've been doing. Being an instructor suits me."

"You mean because you get to tell people what to do?"

"Yes, and they have to do it!" They both laughed as they snuggled. It was Harriet's fourth night of being home, and she'd started to have thoughts about how she could extend her stay, while feeling increasingly jealous about Nicole's job. She'd love to do the same, and she regretted having to give it up, even though she had thoroughly enjoyed most of her trip to America, and would take another posting there in a heartbeat. The more she thought about it, the more reluctant she was to go to her new posting in Scotland. It was a repetitive thought that annoyed her, mostly because she knew

44

the RAF well enough to know she didn't stand a chance of changing the plans.

"Ah, here's trouble! Welcome back to England, Harry Cornwall!" Archie said excitedly as Harriet walked into his office, and he jumped from his chair and rushed around his desk to greet her. "Is it me, or did both you and your uniform shrink simultaneously since I last saw you?"

"Malta rations," she replied with a shrug.

"Well, at least you got a tan out of it."

"There is that..."

"Harry... It's so good to see you again. I couldn't believe it when Nicole said you were back in town."

"Only temporarily, unfortunately. I'm heading to Scotland shortly."

"Yes. Yes, I'd heard. A Norwegian squadron?"

"Yes, newly formed."

"You should fit in, being an undeniable native of the Norse homeland."

"Funny..." Harriet rolled her eyes and gave a half smile at his mischief.

"We haven't had them through here, I don't think?" He looked over to Nicole, who shook her head.

"Though she doesn't want to go," Nicole added. "Despite being requested by the King of Norway personally."

"Oh? Why's that?' Archie asked.

"I'm just starting to get used to being home, that's all," Harriet replied. "Anyway, how are you?"

45

"Couldn't be better!"

"And that evil sister of yours?"

"Distinctly more evil by the day..." he sighed, making Harriet laugh as he glanced upwards in mock prayer. "You think I'm joking. She's currently teaching WAAFs how to march and salute, and causing more trouble and making more enemies than you ever did when you had the job."

"She took over from me?"

"Yes. What a mistake that was! Your friend the Station Commander didn't want to risk getting another one of you through the door, so took the approach of better the devil you know. Sadly, for him at least, he didn't quite know that particular devil as well as he thought, and she's been turning him grey ever since. Looks like some of your bad influence rubbed off on her."

"Me? We didn't work together that long!"

"I notice you didn't try and tell me you're not a bad influence."

"Would you have listened?"

"Other than Nicole, I've known you longer than most in the RAF..."

"Meaning?"

"Meaning I know full well what a bad influence you are." He gave her a wink, which she couldn't help but smile at. "Look, Harry, there's no easy way of saying this, but Nicole told us about Cas, and we were all pretty beat up about it."

"Yes, he was a good man."

"Very much so. Sully, too. Seems pilots of our vintage are becoming a rare breed."

"Do you keep in touch with any of the others?" Harriet asked, trying to move the conversation on to those that are living, and away from the darker side of things.

"Max and I have drinks every now and then, the old rogue is still doing well; and I called in to see Singh a while ago."

"Singh? How is he?" Harriet's eyes brightened as she remembered her old commanding officer.

"He's alright, considering. He was badly burned, as you know, and had to go through a lot of experimental plastic surgery with the Guinea Pig Club. He doesn't fly anymore, he can't due to his injuries, but he does a lot to support burned service personnel as the RAF's liaison officer to the Guinea Pigs. We talked about you quite a bit when I visited."

"Me?"

"Yes, you and Nicole, the troublesome terrors who brought chaos and mayhem to our peaceful little squadron."

"Harsh..." Harriet frowned, while Nicole rolled her eyes.

"He's very proud of you both, you know? He's followed your careers closely, and even boasts that he's the one who discovered your talents."

"I'm not sure it's anything to boast about," Harriet said.

"Some less others," Nicole shrugged.

"So, when do you head to Scotland?" Archie continued.

"The day after tomorrow. I'm going on the night train. It takes longer, but they're less susceptible to delays. Or so I'm told."

"I see... Mosquito squadron, you say?"

47

"Yes, a new Norwegian squadron. They've had a tough time of things recently."

"It's why they're sending her," Nicole added. "So, they know that no matter how bad things have been, they can always get worse."

"How do you tolerate her?" Harriet asked Archie, who simply laughed in reply.

"When did you last fly a Mosquito?" he asked.

"Right before I crashed it at the end of your airfield."

"That was a while ago, can you remember how?"

"How to crash? Oh yes, I'm an expert."

"Well, I was going to ask you if you want to get a bit of practice in on one of ours before you go, but you're not exactly filling me with confidence."

"Really?"

"I have an instructor with nothing better to do." He smirked as he nodded towards Nicole.

"Not me?" Nicole asked.

"Well, Grumpy's away on detachment, and the others have duties assigned..."

"In that case, I couldn't be happier to," Nicole said with a wicked smile, as she jumped from her perch on the edge of the desk.

"Thanks..." Harriet said to Archie, who simply smiled and winked. "Now?"

"No time like the present."

"I haven't got my flying kit."

"I put it in the car for you," Nicole said.

"Now it is..." Harriet sighed. "If we end up in a ball of flames again, it's not my fault. Neither of you can complain."

"I won't be sitting beside you; I'll be fine." Archie looked at Nicole and raised an eyebrow mischievously. "Thank the lord for volunteers... Right, you'd better get on and make the most of the sunshine." Harriet and Nicole left his office and headed to the changing room, where they got into their flight kit. Nicole had even kindly remembered to bring trousers for Harriet, which she wore under the flying overalls she'd been loaned, and soon they were strapping themselves into Nicole's Mosquito, with her sitting in the navigator's seat while Harriet took the pilot's seat and went through her pre flight checks.

"You remember where everything is?" Nicole asked.

"Yes, thank you," Harriet replied.

"You're sure?"

"Quite sure..."

"It's been a while."

"It'll be longer if you don't shut up and let me get on with it!"

"There's no need to be so tense."

"You know, I can probably fly it by myself if you'd rather watch from the ground?"

"With your history on Mosquitoes that may be safer."

"You know where the door is."

"I do, and I'll be ready to jump if you try to kill us."

"Keep talking and I'll try harder." She started one engine, and then the other, and quickly started her taxi to the end of the runway, doing her checks as they rolled.

"In a hurry?"

"Habit." Harriet checked around, ran up the power, then let off the brakes. The Mosquito jumped into life and raced along the runway, pulling hard with the torque, and needing a heavy push on the rudder bar to keep the nose straight. Remembering her last take off, Harriet pulled back on the controls and felt the wheels lift from the ground. Seconds later she'd retracted them, and was heading at speed into the pale blue autumn sky. Her tummy flipped as it always did as the two powerful Merlin engines dragged the Mosquito upwards, and she couldn't help but smile as she soared high over the still furrowed ground where the last Mosquito she'd flown had come to its end. "So, where to?" she asked as she looked over to Nicole.

"Let's go east and look at the coast."

"East it is. Here we go, hold on." Harriet banked hard and pulled back on the stick, feeling the g forces pulling her tight into her seat as the Mosquito turned tight and she pointed it to the east in a powerful climbing turn. She almost laughed to herself she enjoyed it so much, and even Nicole couldn't help smirking, once she'd accepted what type of ride it was going to be.

"Are you trying to lose me out of my seat?"

"Being a flying instructor slowed you down?"

"Enough to want to enjoy it in safety until the end of the war!"

"You've got old."

"I'd like to get older."

"So, what have you got to show me, instructor?"

50

They headed out over the coast, and once Harriet had stopped playing with Nicole while she got used to the Mosquito again, Nicole put her through her paces. The instruction was clinical and demanding, and Harriet was soon skimming the waves so low that a flinch would be enough to lose concentration and crash into the sea. She was lost in her job, focusing on every instruction Nicole gave her, from how to get the most from a climb or a dive, to how to really throw the aeroplane around to evade flak or a pursuing fighter. That done, when Nicole was satisfied that Harriet was sweating enough, it was down to the gunnery range to shoot up some low level targets, where once again Nicole gave precise guidance on how Harriet could improve her aim and attack, before finishing off with low level glide bombing runs, throwing the bomb forward onto the target as the Mosquito pulled up and rolled away to avoid the blast. They went around a few times, getting low and getting the approach right, and then they moved on to dropping the bombs and getting them on target. The instruction and the techniques were far in advance of what Harriet had done herself when she was training pilots, and she was excited and proud of Nicole for becoming such a skilled pilot. It was blatantly obvious why she'd been welcomed into front line squadrons to fly with them.

"OK, that'll do for now," Nicole said, as they passed two hours in the air. "Let's head home for tea."

"Yes, Ma'am!" Harriet replied, and after finishing a low level approach over the sea, she pulled up over the army pillboxes on the cliffs, and skimmed the trees as she headed home.

"How was it flying a Mosquito again?" Nicole asked.

"Exhausting," Harriet replied. Her muscles were sore, as was her emaciated behind from sitting on her parachute for two hours; and her head was tired from the precision instruction, and having to respond exactly as she was told again and again. Listening and learning while flying wasn't something she was used to, certainly not at the intensity she'd just experienced.

"You're out of practice," Nicole laughed. "You've been too long enjoying the sun of Malta, and living the high life."

"Yes, that's exactly what it is..." Without warning, Harriet bulled back on the stick, then started a slow roll that caught Nicole by surprise and made her squeal. "Oops!" she giggled.

"I don't remember telling you to do that!"

"I don't remember you telling me not to."

"Let's go home, and try not to kill us on the way." Nicole rolled her eyes dramatically, then smiled as she turned to look out of the window at the passing countryside. "You did well, considering..."

"Considering what?"

"That you've been out of it for a while."

"You do know that I was actually flying in Malta, don't you?"

"You weren't flying a Mosquito." Nicole shrugged casually.

"I suppose... You did well too, considering."

"Considering what?" Nicole scowled.

"Considering what a terrible pilot you used to be. You really did a good job today, you're not a bad instructor."

"You're rude."

"You love me."

"I tolerate you, because nobody else would."

"It's OK, I know you're shy. I promise I won't tell anyone you did a good job."

"When do you leave for Scotland again?"

"Why? Are you going to miss me?"

"Doubtful... Anyway, you should be paying attention to your flying. You need the practice." They laughed as they rocketed over the Yorkshire countryside. Harriet had been nervous before flying the Mosquito again, her mind had made it into a much more challenging memory than it needed to be, exaggerating the swing on take off to the point where she'd almost over corrected a little, until Nicole cleared her throat in an unsubtle nudge for Harriet to watch what she was doing. It was an understandable exaggeration though, considering the last time she'd flown a Mosquito she'd almost died. She was happy that Archie had suggested taking a flight so she could iron out her nerves before joining her new squadron, it would have been embarrassing to turn up and crash on the first sortie. She was grateful for Nicole's instruction, too. While it had only been a couple of hours, it had sharpened her skills more than she'd expected, and part of her wanted to go again for another lesson. Unfortunately, the greater part of her was the one feeling sore and tired, and that's what won the argument. After approaching the airfield and joining the circuit, she scrubbed off the speed and came in for her final approach, drifting over the boundary fence before touching down as light as a feather, and rolling down the runway. She corrected the torque and added just enough pressure to the rudder pedal to hold off the swing as she taxied to the dispersal, where she came to a halt and went through her shut down routine and checks. "Better control of the swing than on take off," Nicole said with a shrug.

"Thanks..." Harriet replied, as she pulled off her flying helmet. "I mean it, thanks for today, you've really helped. I can't believe how much I'd forgotten, or how much I didn't even know. You've learned a lot."

"Of course."

"It's hard to like you sometimes!" Harriet frowned, while Nicole laughed as she pushed the door open, then threw her kit to the ground and swung out after it. Harriet couldn't help herself, she sat and smiled for a moment as she thought through the last couple of hours of flying, and tried to remember the key points of Nicole's tuition before they escaped her tired brain.

"Are you coming?" Nicole shouted up through the hatch. "Or did you go to sleep?"

"Coming!" Harriet replied, and threw her kit out of the hatch, narrowly missing Nicole; then following her gymnastic prowess, she took a hold of the doorframe and swung out. Unfortunately, her arms gave way and her grip slipped before she could control her landing, and it took Nicole's quick reflexes to jump forward and catch her. "Thank you," Harriet said as casually as she could, while nose to nose with Nicole, and staring into her eyes, as though the entire routine had been planned. "You can put me down now."

"The Norwegians are in for a big surprise," Nicole said, as she lowered Harriet to the ground and let her go from her grip. "Between your flying and your not being a Norwegian, they'll have every reason to mutiny."

"At least it won't be because I'm a girl, for once."

They headed to the dispersal office, then got out of their flying kit before heading back to Archie's office, where he whisked them off before they could sit, piling them into his car and driving them to the pub in the local village for a drink.

"So, how was it?" Archie asked, as they raced down the country lanes. "You didn't kill each other, so that's a good base to start from."

"She's a good instructor," Harriet replied.

"She's an alright pilot," Nicole added.

"Good compared to how she was as a pilot, that is," Harriet retaliated.

"I'd forgotten how much hard work it was having you both together," Archie sighed, making Harriet and Nicole smirk at each other. "Anyway, I've got some good news for you, Harry."

"Oh?" Her mind raced around the potential options, number one being that she wasn't going to Scotland after all.

"Yes. You won't need to get the train to Scotland." Her heart skipped as he talked. "It seems pointless when we have Mosquitoes sitting here doing nothing, so I thought Nicole could run you up there the morning you're due to report. Give you an extra night in your own bed."

"Oh. Oh, that's great. Thank you." She forced a smile, and tried her best to be light hearted. Nicole looked her in the eyes, she could read her like a book, and she knew all too well what she was thinking.

"So, how does it feel going to command your own squadron?"

"Like I'm some sort of imposter waiting to be found out."

"Accurate," Nicole shrugged.

"That's normal," Archie said, ignoring Nicole while Harriet scowled at her. "I'd say you've more than earned it, though. You've lasted longer than most fighter pilots who have been on ops as long as you, and you've done a bloody good job of it."

"Thank you." Harriet's uncontrollable blush started, no matter how hard she tried hard to fight it.

"No need to thank me, it's true."

"The only person I know who complains about being given command of a Squadron," Nicole muttered, as they pulled up outside the pub. "Drinks are on you."

"Do we drink with junior officers?" Harriet asked Archie with a half smile on her face. "Or did we bring her to watch the car while we go inside?"

The three had a drink and talked about the war, and their old friends. Harriet lost herself in the conversation, and the laughter, and for a moment she let herself believe she was back in the squadron. The old days had been so exhausting, but despite the hardships and the losses, and the near constant exhaustion of combat over Kent, they had

55

lived. They flew four or five times a day, risking death each time, sometimes getting shot from the sky, and sometimes friends didn't come back, but they lived fast and loved life. She thought of the many nights in the Mess, drinking, dancing, singing, and even the Mess rugby which Harriet and Nicole had fully involved themselves with, and put up a good fight against the men. They stayed late into the evening, enjoying each other's company, and ended up being bought several drinks by the locals, including the detachment of Home Guard who turned up. Harriet was even convinced to play the piano, and at one point the whole pub was singing along to the popular tunes she'd heard on the radio, and somehow managed to play by ear with no sheet music or practice. It was a riot of a night, leading to Harriet sharing Nicole's bed in her room in the Mess, where she slept like a log thanks to the strong local beer, and bootleg whisky the landlord had hidden behind the bar for special occasions. It had been the most fun that Harriet had enjoyed in a long time, and as the drinks flowed, her inhibitions left, and she stopped thinking so much about the bad memories, and instead just lived in the moment.

The next morning, Harriet and Nicole made their way to the hangar and the oxygen bay, where a sympathetic airman, who couldn't help blushing in Nicole's presence, made sure they had a bottle of oxygen each to help soothe their hangovers. Nicole was subdued, but functioning. Harriet, however, felt like she'd died somewhere in the desert. She hadn't had much to drink in Malta, certainly not enough to make her tipsy, and the night they were recovering from was so many stages beyond tipsy. After their hangar visit, where they drained a bottle of oxygen each to try and cure their hangovers, they had a breakfast of bacon and eggs, before meeting with Archie to find that the day's weather report was so miserable that he'd decided to stand Nicole down for the day. A blessing that saw both of them back at Aunt Mary's house, drinking hot sweet tea while lying in bed.

"It's a shame you have to go to Scotland so soon," Nicole said, taking Harriet by surprise.

"Going to miss me?" Harriet asked with a laugh.

"Yes," Nicole replied, almost solemnly.

56

"What's wrong?" Harriet frowned as she put her empty teacup on the bedside cupboard, and turned to look at Nicole as she snuggled down under the blankets and out of the cool air, and rested her head on the deep feather pillow.

"I'll just miss you, that's all." Nicole forced a smile as she put her own cup down, and snuggled the same, facing Harriet. "It seems we only ever see here for brief moments, and it's not the same, not after we spent so much time together."

"I always miss you."

"Really?"

"Yes, of course. Why wouldn't I?"

"I don't know. Maybe the great Harriet Cornwall has other things in her life these days."

"You don't really believe that?"

"Maybe?"

"You know, I lost count of the times in Malta that I wished you were there with me." She smiled as Nicole's eyes opened wider. "Things got bad over there, in lots of ways, and whenever I thought I couldn't go on, I thought of you. If I'm honest, there were times I just wanted a hug. You always looked after me, and you always made it OK when I felt bad. I missed that, and I always do."

"I'm sorry I wasn't there with you." Nicole moved close and wrapped her arms around Harriet, the way she always had when her friend was feeling low.

"Me too. Though in a way I'm happy you weren't, as much as I missed you."

"Why not?"

"My friends didn't last long over there... I'm not sure I could cope if I lost you as well."

"You won't lose me."

"I hope not... Let's talk about something else, I think of Malta enough already."

"Scotland?"

"No. Not that either."

"Then what?"

"After the war."

"What about it?"

"What will we do? The war can't go on forever, and whether we win or lose, we'll have to do something with the rest of our lives. We can't just go on fighting, not forever."

"I haven't really thought about it..."

"Never?"

"I try not to. I've thought of going back to France, but to what? We were going to be nurses, but I don't think that's an option, not after all we've done."

"No. I certainly don't want to be a nurse!" Harriet smiled for a moment, and thought of all the nurses she'd met, especially Emily. She hadn't seen her for so long, or even had a letter, though that wasn't really a surprise. She hadn't had many letters on her travels.

"All I've thought of is going back to France and seeing my grandparents. I imagine seeing their faces, and spending time with them, but nothing else."

"Nothing at all?"

"I daren't."

"What do you mean?"

"What if we don't win? Even with the Americans in the war, things aren't going well. If we lose, I may never get to go back to France."

"I suppose... We can't think that way, though. We've got to think we'll win."

"And then what? If we win, and we survive, what's to say my grandparents will still be alive? What's to say France isn't in ruins? There are stories, from those that have escaped. The Germans are looting the place, and shooting anyone who gets in their way. I heard that in one village twenty people were shot in reprisal for the Resistance shooting one German. I love France, and I want to go home, but it scares me to think that home won't be there anymore, or home is no longer what I recognise... What about you? What will you do after the war?"

"I don't know. Travel, maybe? There's so much of the world I'd like to see, preferably while people aren't trying to kill me."

"I like that. Where shall we go?"

"Maybe not Malta."

"Maybe not right away, but I'd like to see Lissy and Anj again."

"Maybe we can get them to come to us? I'm really in no rush to get back."

"Where else?"

"America."

"You've been there already."

"I can't wait to go back. You'd love it there, Nicole, it's so different to anything. The food, the people, the weather even. We should go, that should be the first thing we do. I'll show you New York, then we'll go to California, and then Hawaii."

"If you say it now, we have to do it."

"I promise."

Chapter 4

Take the High Road.

Harriet smiled as she flew over the colourful Scottish hills, the heather shining purple and green in the golden sun of the late September morning. She'd reluctantly accepted her fate, and her posting, and after saying goodbye to Archie and Grumpy, who'd arrived from his detachment in time for farewell drinks the night before, she'd won the argument with Nicole to fly the Mosquito to Scotland. They took off just before first light, and raced north in time to see the sunrise over Edinburgh, before skipping over the beautiful hills and rolling forests towards their destination close to the east coast. They'd planned their flight the day before, after another training session where Nicole put Harriet through her paces, and pushed her to her limits in handling the Mosquito, and Harriet had navigated her way flawlessly through the darkness and the dawn while Nicole slept next to her. As she approached the air station, with the vast North Sea pitching and rolling to the east, she pulled up into a roll and shocked Nicole awake, much to her amusement, and Nicole's shock, then joined the circuit ready to land.

"Idiot! Why would you do that?" Nicole blasted. Harriet had tears in her eyes, as she tried not to laugh too hard at Nicole's shocked and disturbed state.

"Sorry..." Harriet replied, with all the sincerity she could muster. "I tried to wake you, but you were in a very deep sleep." She'd done no such thing, and the roll was an impulsive act she just couldn't resist.

"When I said I'd miss you, I was lying, trying to make you feel better!" Nicole continued to bluster, while trying hard to keep her own smile in. It's exactly what she'd have done if the roles were reversed.

"Time to land."

"Already?"

"Ahead of time. There's a strong south westerly wind behind us, so you'll have a slower drag back home."

"At least it'll be a stable flight home." She rolled her eyes. "Anyway, pay attention! I don't want you to kill me when we land. You know what you're like." They both smirked, and as Harriet circled the airfield ahead of her landing, she saw the Mosquitoes lined up on the dispersal, with ground crews going about their work preparing them for the day. There were a number of other aircraft scattered around the station, including a squadron of twin engine Bristol Beaufighter torpedo bombers, and a number of Spitfires, Sunderlands, and a collection of other aircraft. It looked like a busy place to be, and the formal structure of the air station with its neatly lined aircraft and ring of anti aircraft defences made Harriet feel nervous. After the craziness of Malta, she wasn't sure how she'd fit in with such organisation. She was used to being left alone to get on with things, and it didn't seem like there would be much hiding from the normality of the RAF in Scotland. After sighing to herself, Harriet lowered the wheels and made her final approach to the runway, then touched down lightly with hardly a bump. Nicole gave her a smile of approval, and with a push on the rudder bar she corrected the swing while throttling back, before turning off the runway and heading for the dispersal by the control tower. "Not bad," Nicole said, as they came to a halt, and Harriet went about shutting down her engines.

"I had a good teacher," Harriet replied.

"This is true."

"Of course..." Harriet pulled the lever to open the bomb day doors so she could retrieve her kit bags, then finished off shutting everything down. Nicole had already opened the hatch, and was in the process of throwing herself out into the cool air. Harriet smiled, and followed behind her, landing on the concrete and pulling off her flying helmet so she could smooth her hair and put on her service cap before heading over to the control tower.

"Coming?" Harriet asked Nicole, as the fuel bowser rumbled towards them.

'I'll wait here and make sure I get refuelled properly; I don't want to end up walking home," Nicole replied. "I'll get your bags out for you."

"Thank you. I knew there was a reason I brought you."

"You're funny."

"I know." Harriet smirked, then walked over to the tower. The wind was cool, but not unpleasant, and made her grateful she'd worn flying boots and her sheepskin Irvin jacket. It wasn't long ago she was racing around the skies above Malta in her shorts, blouse, and plimsolls, all of which were frequently soaked through with sweat. Being back in England in September had taken some adjusting to, being in Scotland as the leaves were already starting to turn was going to take a lot more. "Squadron Leader Cornwall," she said as she faced the duty officer.

"Sir?" the young officer replied, as he stood from his desk.

"Ma'am," Harriet replied, much to the sniggering amusement of the WAAF sitting across the office.

"Ma'am?" he repeated, looking more confused.

"Pilot Officer?"

"Davison. Philip Davison." He held out his hand and smiled brightly, making Harriet roll her eyes in dismay.

"Pilot Officer Philip Davison, I'm Squadron Leader Harriet Cornwall."

"Oh..." His eyes widened as the realisation hit. "Oh. Ma'am." He pulled his hand back and stood smartly to attention.

"I'm told you're expecting me?"

"Ma'am?"

"Mister Davison, it's going to be a very long day if you don't wake up and start paying attention."

"Squadron Leader Cornwall is the new Commanding Officer of the Norwegian squadron, Sir," the young WAAF said as she stood beside Davison and handed him a file.

"What?" he asked. "Yes. Yes, of course." He took the file and looked back to Harriet, who gave the WAAF a smile and a nod of appreciation. "Welcome, Ma'am."

"Thank you. I'm assuming you have plans for me now I'm here?" she continued, while he fumbled with the folder. "I'll be disappointed if I've come all the way here from Malta for nothing."

"Ma'am? No. No, Ma'am."

"I think Groupie wanted to see Squadron Leader Cornwall when she arrived," the WAAF added.

"Ah, here it is," Davison said confidently. "Squadron Leaser Cornwall expected on the ten o'clock train from Edinburgh, transport required, report to the Station Commander on arrival."

"Well, I'm already here, so you probably don't need to collect me from the train station," Harriet said. "Perhaps you can just get me to the Station Commander?"

"Yes, Ma'am. Of course."

"My pilot, Flight Lieutenant Delacourt, is outside with our aeroplane. We haven't had breakfast yet, and I wondered if the Mess was open to visitors?"

"I'll give them a call, Ma'am. Groupie is in a briefing, and not due out for another half hour or so. I'll have a truck take you to the Mess, and let him know you've arrived."

"There, all sorted," Harriet said with a firm smile. "We'll be outside." She turned and left, giving the helpful WAAF another nod of gratitude, and leaving Davison looking as confused as when she'd first arrived. She pulled her sheepskin collar up around her neck as a cool breeze sent a shiver down her spine, suddenly feeling colder than a few minutes earlier. She was starting to regret being in Scotland. Being mistaken for a male officer didn't help anything, and she felt that was only the start of a posting having to fight to be recognised as a woman. Again.

"Everything OK?" Nicole asked.

"If you call being mistaken for a male officer OK, then yes, things are going swimmingly."

"You can hardly blame him." Nicole shrugged casually, making Harriet frown. "You need to eat more, you're so skinny it's easy to think you're a boy."

"Didn't Archie say to get back home before that weather front comes in?"

"He did, but the weather front isn't due until this afternoon, and I'm hungry."

"In that case, you'll be happy to know I've arranged breakfast for us."

"You have?"

"Yes. In fact, here comes your carriage." Harriet pointed to the truck, which was rumbling into life outside the control tower.

"Well, you can put your own bags in the carriage. You may be a Squadron Leader, but I'm not your servant."

"If I wanted a servant, I'd have one that didn't give me such a hard time."

"It would be difficult to find somebody who wouldn't."

The truck pulled up, and Harriet threw her bags in the back while Nicole climbed in, then once she'd joined her they went on their way, leaving the ground crew to refuel Nicole's Mosquito and prepare it for its return flight. It was a quick journey to the Mess, where they left their flying jackets, hats, and Mae Wests on coat pegs, and tidied themselves before stepping into the dining room, which was scattered with a few officers here and there, while the waiting staff busied themselves tidying. They took their places at the table, and were served with hot fresh tea and a plate of bacon and eggs each, along with a rack of toast cut into triangles, and a pot of butter and another of raspberry jam.

"Breakfast is nice," Nicole shrugged, as she tucked into her bacon.

"That's something," Harriet replied, feeling frustrated that her first encounter at her new home was less than encouraging; and while she wasn't exactly missing Malta, she wasn't looking forward to what came next.

"At least it's not Malta," Nicole added, as though she'd read Harriet's mind.

"No. No, that's true. It's certainly colder than Malta."

"You don't seem happy to be here."

"I'm not..."

"It'll be OK. You know that. When you have leave you can even come home to visit, it isn't far."

"I'm sure I'll be fine. It's just that I don't feel like I belong."

"Here?"

"In the RAF. At least not this version of it." She looked around at the Mess dining room, with the smart stewards going back and forth, and the silver cutlery and fine china plates.

"You're just used to being a scarecrow and doing as you like."

"Shut up."

"Harry, old man!" A familiar voice called from across the room, and Harriet's head whipped around to see her old friend Group Captain Alastair Saltire at the door, and a smile immediately broke onto her face. She and Nicole stood as he marched purposefully across the room. Moving chairs in his path and dodging stewards. "My dear Harry, how wonderful to see you!" he gushed as he stood before her. "And Nikki! The old gang's back together. Sit, sit!" He gestured wildly and theatrically, as he always did everything. "You don't mind if I join you?" he asked as he pulled out a chair.

"Please, Sir," Harriet replied with a warm smile.

"Oh, come on Harry old man. I think we can make it Alastair! I rushed over as soon as they told me you were here."

"You're the Station Commander here?" Harriet asked, and immediately kicked herself at the apparent stupidity of her question. "I mean... I didn't know."

"What? Yes. Yes, of course. Though only just, I took over a few weeks ago. Welcome to my command!" He laughed, while waiving the steward over and ordering. "Jacob, would you mind getting me a coffee, and if you could, I'd be obliged if it was the good stuff you have hidden away, none of that Air Force issue dust. One for Nikki, too." He gave Nicole a wink as the steward quickly left. "I know you French don't like our coffee, and frankly I don't blame you. I have some of the proper stuff sent up from London when I can, it makes the war more tolerable."

"I may ask for a posting!" Nicole replied with a big smile.

"If I could get you, I would. Where are you these days?"

"Hiding on a specialist Mosquito training unit in Yorkshire," Harriet replied for Nicole, rolling her eyes as she did.

"A Mossie training unit you say?" Alastair replied, fixing Nicole in his mischievous gaze. "Interesting..."

67

"It's a good job," Nicole said. "We teach advanced handling and ground attack techniques. I was surprised we hadn't had your Norwegians visit us when Harriet told us she was coming here."

"That's probably because we haven't had chance to send them to you yet. Though to be fair, they've only just converted to Mossies from their Beautfighters a couple of weeks ago, so it's all a bit new. I should be interested in knowing more about your outfit though. Who's your CO?"

"Wing Commander Russel."

"Not Archie Russel from back in the day?"

"The same."

"Oh wonderful! Good on him! I'll drop him a note in due course. Are you staying for long, or is it just a flying visit? If you'll pardon the pun."

"Just dropping off some baggage," Nicole replied, while nodding in Harriet's direction, and getting a frown in reply.

"Dropping off baggage! Fantastic!" Alastair laughed, then turned back to Harriet. "I can't tell you how excited I was to know I was getting you, Harry. It was like a load off when I read the posting notice. I'd only just got here myself, and there's quite a job to do. Knowing I have somebody with your experience on the team makes things significantly easier."

"Thank you," Harriet forced a smile through her blush. "It was something of a surprise to me too."

"Oh? How's that?"

"I was in Malta a couple of weeks ago, and got the notice about my posting out of the blue."

"Malta? Really?" he gasped.

"Yes..."

"I didn't know. Have you had any leave?"

"A few days at home with her," she nodded at Nicole. "So not really."
It was Nicole's turn to receive a disapproving scowl.

"Wonderful!" Alastair laughed again. "Well, at least you've had
something. I hope you brought your long underwear with you, if
you'll pardon my familiarity. Having been in India on my last
posting, I can confirm from bitter personal experience that Scotland
is a little cooler than Malta."

"I've brought everything warm that I own!"

"Good! Good, you'll need it no doubt. Especially now we're heading
into the colder months. Still, it's a beautiful country, and I have no
doubt you'll enjoy it here!" The coffee was delivered, and he took a
sip before letting out a contented sigh while relaxing into his chair.

"This coffee is wonderful," Nicole said as she sipped hers.

"Worth the effort getting it here. This war's dragging on and
becoming rather tedious, I'm sure you'll agree, and it's important we
still enjoy the nicer things in life when we can."

"Having just got back from Malta, I couldn't agree more," Harriet
said.

"Quite! A few of the boys we have in the Beaufighter Squadron spent
some time in Malta earlier this year. They said it was awful, and they
didn't care for the lack of food and the off tasting water, when they
could get it."

"I can believe that." Harriet's mind went back to the foul tasting
water, and how much of a relief it was to get her hands on it when
her mouth and throat were parched dry.

"Right!" Alastair started, as he drained his coffee cup and put it on
the table. "Why don't you come up and see me when you've finished

breakfast and seen Nikki off, and I'll take you to your squadron and introduce you to your chaps." He stood and straightened his clothes. "Lovely to see you again, Nikki. Send my regards to Archie, won't you? And let him know I'll be in touch soon."

"Of course. It was nice to see you, thank you for the coffee," Nicole replied with a smile.

"My pleasure. See you in a while, Harry." He marched off as excitably as he'd arrived, leaving Harriet and Nicole to finish their breakfast, which they did hungrily. Harriet filled easily, but it didn't stop her finishing every last crumb, and washing it down with so much tea she felt it sloshing in her stomach when she and Nicole walked out to the truck that was waiting to take them back to the dispersal, where Harriet escorted Nicole back to her Mosquito.

"I wish I was going back with you," Harriet said as she stood with Nicole by the open hatch.

"I think things just improved here," Nicole replied with a warm and genuine reassurance. "Alastair is a good boss."

"I suppose."

"Will you come home and see me? When you're on leave, I mean?"

"Whenever I can."

"Take care, Harry, and stay safe."

"You too." Harriet stepped forward and gave Nicole a tight hug, which they finally had to break with the sound of the ground crew approaching, who'd come to see Nicole off.

"Make sure you eat more, boy!" Nicole said with a smile, then turned and ran up the short flight of steps into the cockpit. Harriet smiled to herself, then walked off to the grass so she could watch Nicole leave. Despite the sun, the wind was getting cooler, and she pulled her collar up around her ears again as she waited and watched, as first one engine started, and then the other. Once everything was as it should be, Nicole set off and taxied to the runway, where she stopped for a moment before racing off at speed, and climbing quickly into the sky. She circled, and passed low to give Harriet a wave, then with a waggle of her wings she turned south and roared out of sight. Harriet's heart sank a little, despite the half smile on her face, as her friend left her once again. She stood for a moment, watching as the Mosquito quickly became a dot in the southern sky, then she went back to the control tower and got a ride to Alastair's office.

"How much do you know about what do here, Harry?" Alastair asked excitedly, as Harriet took a seat in his office, having made her way there straight from the dispersal. She nodded politely as she took the welcoming cup of tea from the smiling WAAF and made herself comfortable.

"Not a lot... I was just told I was coming to command a Norwegian Mosquito squadron. Apparently they've had a tough time of things."

"Well, that's the essence of it, I suppose." He frowned for a moment, an uncharacteristic mannerism for the usually jovial character. "I suppose I should fill you in on what goes on here, before I get to your squadron." He smiled as the fire came back to his eyes while he walked over to the large map on the wall of his office. "The Germans are in desperate need of the many minerals mined almost exclusively in Scandinavia, much of which they use to harden steel for weapons or armour plating, among other things, which I'm sure you'll agree we'd rather the Germans didn't have that much of these days. Anyway, since they marched into Norway, the efficient German industrial machine has been loading all of the freshly mined goodies onto merchant ships and sailing them down the coast to Rotterdam in Holland. From there it's put on barges and distributed to factories across the Ruhr and beyond. Once unloaded, the merchant ships are then reloaded with coal from German, French, and Polish mines, and taken back to Norway to fuel the industry; and so the cycle continues."

"So it seems..." Harriet said, as she joined him and looked at the maps.

"The merchant ships usually travel in convoys escorted by flak ships. Requisitioned trawlers mostly, loaded to the gills with anti aircraft guns of all calibres. Absolute buggers they are. Anyway, it's our job to intercept these convoys and disrupt the supply lines. Less minerals from Norwegian and Finnish mines means less hardened steel and less armour plating in tanks and aircraft, which makes fighting against them a lot less dangerous; and less coal heading the other way reduces their success further."

"Sounds simple enough."

"Oh, it is. The difficulty is actually sinking the ships." He sighed as he returned to his desk, and Harriet went back to her seat and her cup of tea. "Coastal Command have been at it for a couple of years, and the price is high. Between the fighter squadrons on the coast, and the flak ships in the convoys, along with the occasional destroyer or other Kreigsmarine vessels, the losses to our bombers has been horrific, to say the least." He sipped his tea while Harriet swallowed hers, hard. It seemed like the bad news she'd been waiting for was being delivered at last. "I was sent here with orders to try and turn things around, and that's where you come in!"

"Me?"

"Yes. Our Beaufighters are excellent torpedo bombers, when they get through, but they're slow. Compared to German fighters at least, and can be a little sluggish in manoeuvring when fully loaded. We managed to get hold of some Mosquitos, eight currently with more on the way, and the theory is that with their speed and firepower, they'll be able to take on the fighters and flak ships, and change the nature of the battle. Working in conjunction with the Beaufighters, who should have a better chance of getting through to the cargo ships once your Mossies have done their work, it should be quite a potent force for our German friends to think about."

"I see... How do we find the convoys?"

"Reconnaissance. We have a couple of PRU types attached to us who go looking for trouble. As soon as they do, the Wing of Mossies and

Beaufighters will go up and do their job. It's a new and untried system, so we're going to have to figure out how we make it work."

"I saw Beaufighters in action in the Mediterranean while flying reconnaissance myself, and I've seen what they can do to a convoy when not bothered by fighters."

"Good, so you'll know what we're up against."

"Yes..." Her mind drifted for a moment, back to Malta and the missions where she'd circled after finding a convoy, taking photos of the damage after watching the bombers do their work. A lot of bomber crews had been lost raiding convoys, and it made her feel uneasy to think that was her new job. "And the Norwegians?" she asked, after bringing herself back into the room.

"Viking warriors each and every one!" Alastair smiled for a moment. "They trained over in Canada, a place near Toronto so popular with them they named it 'Little Norway'. They arrived up here in the late summer. They got right to work on Beaufighters, and they've done a good job, but they've had a devil of a time. They're good pilots, you see, and keen as mustard to get stuck into the Germans, they just don't have that much experience in combat, and the German Focke Wulf 190 fighters have bloodied their noses a bit. They lost their skipper, adjutant, and both senior flight commanders a few weeks ago, four crews lost on one mission, eight men altogether. That's why they sent for you."

"With respect, Alastair, I'm not sure what I'm going to be able to do. I'm just me, and I haven't exactly been a team player for a while. I'd be much more use to you in a PRU Spitfire."

"Nonsense. These men need a leader. They need somebody with experience, and a good head for combat in the air, and they need somebody with a connection to their own country."

"I think we both know that I'm about as Norwegian as this teacup." Harriet frowned, as she put the empty cup on the desk between them.

"I don't know, you're Norwegian enough to get the King of Norway on your side. I dare say that if you're enough for him, you're enough for them." He smiled at her, and his eyes twinkled again. "Though, if I'm honest, I couldn't care whether you were Norwegian, or an Apache. The truth is, Harry old man, you're a damned good leader, and an even better pilot; and before you argue with me, remember that I was your CO during the Battle of Britain! I saw what you did there, and how you inspired those around you. A bit of that could make all the difference around here." Harriet forced an uncomfortable smile and nodded. "Right, we'd better get you down to your squadron, so you can say hello. I've arranged some digs for you in the local village, and I'll see if I can rustle up a vehicle that you can borrow until something more permanent comes available."

"I don't suppose you have a spare motorcycle lying around anywhere?"

"I think we can arrange that. Come on, let's go say hello." He gave her a wink and grabbed his hat, and she followed him to the door. "Leave your bags if you like, I'll have them dropped at your digs this morning." Harriet nodded, and joined him walking outside to his staff car, which he drove sedately and casually through the air station, pointing out places of interest and importance that she knew she wouldn't remember, before stopping at the dispersal hut outside one of the hangars. A neat row of Mosquitos stood outside, but there didn't seem to be much going on other than a few ground crew tinkering here and there. "They usually have a flight of two on standby, just in case the reconnaissance types find anything between missions. Though I'm going to stand your squadron down for a few days, so you can get settled in and have time evaluate the situation. See what you need to get them in fighting shape and all that."

"Am I likely to need much?"

"You tell me. Anything you think you need, you've got a direct line to me. Ask and it shall be given. Within reason, of course..." He gave her a wink, and she smiled warmly in reply. She was more accepting of the situation knowing that Alastair was looking after her. Anywhere else she'd be terrified, and while she was still nervous, his presence was more reassuring than she could have hoped.

"Well, no point in delaying it..." she said as she reached for the door handle.

"One thing, Harry."

"Yes?"

"As tough as they've had it right now, they need a leader, not a friend." He looked at her for a moment. She could see in his eyes what he was saying, and she gave him a nod of understanding, before stepping out into the cool air. She was still thankful for her sheepskin lined flying boots, and if she wasn't going to meet her pilots for the first time she'd be wrapped up in her flying jacket, too, but she felt they needed to see her in uniform. If for no other reason than to let them know she was female. Her arrival encounter had stuck firmly in her mind.

"Gentlemen," Alastair said as he entered the room. The collected crews quickly stood smartly to attention, and one who was wearing his cap saluted, which Alastair casually returned. All eyes fixed on Harriet as she closed the door and stood by his side. They were all young men, none looking older than her, a mixture of pilots and navigators wearing RAF blue trousers, brown flying boots, and the new, shorter, battledress flying jackets that stopped at the waist, instead of the more traditional long tunics usually worn in the RAF. "Gentlemen, I'd like to introduce your new Commanding Officer, Squadron Leader Harriet Cornwall." A gasp went around the room, with a little indistinguishable muttering at the back. "Squadron Leader Cornwall fought as a fighter pilot in France and the Battle of Britain, and has two operational tours in Malta under her belt; and she's got more kills to her name than every pilot on this station combined. You'll listen to her, and you'll learn from her. She was requested by your King personally, so I expect you to make her feel at home." He looked around, then gave Harriet a nod. "Dinner at seven, Squadron Leader. I'll leave you to get to know your team. Lieutenant Pietersen has been holding the reins for the last couple of weeks." He pointed to a tall young man with dark hair, firm cheekbones, and piercing blue eyes. He nodded smartly in acknowledgement as Harriet saluted Alastair before he left. Her heart was racing, and as she turned to look at the gathered crews again, she immediately wished she was facing the same number of Germans in combat.

"The Group Captain has stood us down for a couple of days so we can get to know each other, " she announced firmly, and confidently. "I'd like to start with an evaluation flight this morning, so make sure your aeroplanes are ready to fly. Lieutenant Pietersen, I'd like a word in my office."

"Yes, Ma'am." He gestured to the office at the end of the room, and she walked past the still staring eyes, and past the sparking black potbellied stove that warmed the hut, then stepped into the office and closed the door, before making her way to her chair and gesturing for Pietersen to take a seat. "Welcome to the squadron, Ma'am," he said as he got comfortable. "May I ask where in Norway you're from?"

"No..." She looked him in the eyes, suspecting where he was going with his question. "How are the squadron performing?"

"Very well, Ma'am."

"Is there anything we need to work on?"

"No, Ma'am."

"So, we're an effective unit."

"Yes, Ma'am."

"Good. In that case, you can take me for a spin around the local area and show me the sights."

"Ma'am?"

"I assume I have an aeroplane assigned to me?"

"Yes, Ma'am."

"Well, lead the way." He stared at her for a moment, then stood and led her from the room as quickly as they'd entered, grabbing his jacket and flying helmet on the way. There was silence in the hut as Harriet pulled on her sheepskin jacket and followed him outside, towards the lined up Mosquitoes. Pietersen gave the nearby ground crew a thumbs up to signal they were leaving, and then turned to climb the ladder into the cockpit. He stopped as Harriet coughed, leaving her to walk past him and up the ladder. He raised an eyebrow, then followed her in and strapped himself into the navigator's seat.

"I thought I was showing you around, Ma'am."

"You are. I don't know the area, so once we're up you'll need to give me an idea of the landmarks." She went through her pre flight checks, then with a shout out of the window to warn the ground crew, she started one engine, then after settling it, started the other. Seconds later she'd waved the ground crew and chocks away, and she was taxiing at a fast pace towards the runway, going through her checks on the way. At the end of the runway, she checked the power and her instruments, then turned to Pietersen. "What's our call sign?"

"Viking."

"Of course." She called the tower. "Viking one requesting scramble."

"Claymore replying," the tower replied. "Clear, Viking one."

The very second the clearance message finished, she opened the throttles and launched the Mosquito down the runway, pushing hard on the rudder bar to fight the swing and keep the nose straight. Then, she pulled back on the controls, and the pair of mighty Merlin engines pulled them into the sky. The undercarriage came up quickly as she turned into the circuit, before heading to the coast, and out towards the North Sea. The Mosquito shot out low over the cliffs, to the excited waves of the anti aircraft gunners. She waggled her wings in reply, then pulled up hard into a steep climb, taking Pietersen by surprise, and throwing him tight into his seat. She levelled, then turned tight, and raced back down to the wave tops in a dive twice as steep as her climb, skimming the water as she finally pulled straight

77

and level, and flew at full speed parallel to the coast. Pietersen formally and obligingly gave Harriet instructions on landmarks as they flew around the area. He didn't say much, and the distanced and defensive attitude he'd started with in the office wasn't shaken, despite her throwing the Mosquito around the sky so expertly.

"Look, Pietersen, I'm not sure what I've done to earn the cold reception, but I'm here to stay and we're going to have to get on," Harriet said as they headed back in the direction of the air station as they completed their tour.

"Yes, Ma'am."

"So, you can start by telling me how the squadron is really doing. The Group Captain told me you've had a tough time recently."

"No tougher than other units, I'm sure."

"That doesn't answer my question."

"They're brave men, they know their jobs."

"You can speak freely, Pietersen. If that's what it takes for you to talk."

"Very well…" He looked at her for a moment, before continuing. "We have had a bad time, that's true. Every one of us has risked our lives to get to England, so we could fight for the families and friends we've left at home in Norway. Since we got here, we've been thrown at convoys relentlessly. We've lost lots of friends, and our leaders, and for what? A few boats, that's all, and still the Germans are winning the war."

"Is that everything?"

"No. We're a close Squadron, like family, and none of us much like a newcomer coming into our squadron, especially not one like you."

"Because I'm female?"

"Because you pretend to be Norwegian when you're not."

"Is that really your problem?"

"You asked," he shrugged.

"I did... Now it's my turn. I'm here at the insistence of people I'm not going to win an argument with, so we're stuck with each other; and we need to find a way of making it work, before the squadron suffers any more needless losses. I can assure you that having managed to get through Malta, I'm in no hurry to get myself killed in Scotland! So, regardless of your feelings about me personally, or the state of the war, you need to do what I say, and when I say it; and as the senior pilot I'm expecting you to make sure the rest do the same. Understood?"

"Understood, Ma'am."

"Good; and in return I'll do all I can to make things better than they were. Oh, and for the record, my grandfather was from Norway. Take that how you will."

"Get out of here," he said nervously.

"Excuse me?" Harriet asked as she looked over to him with a frown.

"Quick, get us out of here. Look, Germans!" He had a startled expression on his face. She followed his gesturing out of the window, and saw the twelve Junkers 88 twin engine bombers rapidly approaching the air station. They were a few thousand feet below, and skimming the waves and flying in three diamonds of four, one diamond behind another, just like so many had done in the past.

"I don't think so," Harriet replied. "I'm assuming the guns were loaded before the flight?"

"What? You're insane! It doesn't matter how many bullets we have! We can't take twelve of them on, their gunners will cut us to pieces!"

79

"Hold tight! Viking leader to Claymore Control. Bandits coming in low and fast. We're going to intercept, so tell your gunners to keep their eyes open!" She looked over to Pietersen, who was sweating in horror. "Ready?"

"You're serious..."

"Tally Ho!" Harriet pushed the nose down and started a dive, calculating her trajectory carefully, to put herself right in front of the bombers, the perfect place to break up the raid. Or so experience had told her. Her heart started to pound as the Mosquito gathered pace, and the speed indicator quickly wound up, as the aeroplane responded to her light touches on the controls while the altimeter quickly unwound. She searched the sky to confirm there weren't any fighters, not that she was expecting them so far from home, but she'd become so accustomed to seeing a swarm hovering over a bombing raid that checking was instinct.

"What are you doing?" Pietersen gasped, as badly aimed spirals of glowing red tracer started to reach up towards them. The bombers had seen them, and knew they were coming, but continued to hold their formation without wavering, as Harriet had come to expect of the disciplined Luftwaffe pilots.

"Breaking them up! Hitting a raid head on is the only way, you're far too vulnerable coming in from behind, especially on a raid like this. Hold on." She pulled back on the stick, feeling the Mosquito fight her a little as she dragged it out of the dive in front of the lead bomber, and no sooner had she levelled out, she took aim and pushed the fire button. The four cannons and four machine guns thundered into life simultaneously, and long white streaks of smoke threaded out towards the oncoming bomber like lances. It felt like an age waiting for the impact, but in reality it was a split second from firing to seeing the mix of high explosive and incendiary shells explode through the cockpit of the 88, sparking and flashing, and starting fires around the sprays of blood from the executed crew. It immediately dived straight into the sea, throwing up a towering plume of spray, forcing those behind and to each side to splinter to avoid a collision with the fast moving Mosquito heading towards them. Harriet pulled back on the stick a little, and hopped over the oncoming formation, which had limited options in terms of escape, due to the very low height they'd been flying in at to try and avoid being seen by the chain of radar protecting the British coast. She passed through the spray, and the mesh of tracer coming up from every angle, then pulled into a steep and tight turn, ready to come back for another go. Pietersen's knuckles were white as he gripped tight to hold himself in place, while Harriet's mind was automatically running the many calculations required to get her in place; speed, angle of turn, enemy speed and position, direction, trajectory and fall of her shots, it was a lot, but to her keenly trained and experienced mind it was something she hardly had to give consideration to, she just did it. Coming out of her turn, she fired into a space that a bomber flew into, clipping its wing as it pulled into a climbing turn to escape and head back out to sea. Harriet had done her damage, the bomber's engine shot out a long jet of flame as the propeller vibrated to a standstill. There was nothing more she needed to do to it, the damage was enough to make sure that it would either go straight down, or crash into the sea on the way home. The rest of the bombers had scattered in every direction as they crossed the coast, releasing their bombs in the water and on the cliffs, and heading back out to sea as fast as they could. Harriet searched the sky for the next target, and on seeing that there was nothing inland, she pulled up and around, and gave chase to those running for home. All she could think of was shooting another down, and another, and her mind was racing, thinking of how many she could get. She'd been overtaken by instinct, the automatic need for survival that had been hammered into her through combat after combat over Malta was surging through her veins, reminding her that the only way to win, to survive, was to knock as many down as possible, and make sure they couldn't come back again. She closed on a straggler, and the gunners started to fire in the desperate hole of holding her off. Pietersen flinched a few times in his seat, as he sat defenceless and almost helpless as Harriet gently slipped left and right to stop the gunner getting on target, teasing almost, toying with him as a cat would its prey. Once in perfect position, she pushed the fire button, and sent the deadly mix of cannon shells and bullets into the tail empennage of the 88, severing it cleanly before dropping to the waves as the 88 stood up on end and pointed the nose straight up, before it flipped and followed the tail into the sea, spraying the Mosquito in a tidal wave that shook Harriet in her seat, and pulled her out of the haze of battle she'd been trapped in. She continued her circle as the remaining bombers raced into the distance as fast as their engines could drag them. For a moment she considered giving chase, she knew she could get one more at least, but the reality of her situation started to break through to her rational brain. There'd been a lot of return fire from the bomber formation, and there was no telling if any of it had hit home and done some damage. Developing problems out over the North Sea didn't sound appealing, so she turned back towards land and started going through her checks. "Are you OK?" she asked as she looked over to Pietersen. He looked at her and nodded, forcing a half smile through the nerves. Harriet nodded in return, then lined up on her approach. Speed scrubbed off, throttle back, wheels down, flaps down, and she glided in for a perfectly soft landing. Kissing the runway lightly, before slowing and taxiing back to the dispersal and shutting down.

"I'm sorry," Pietersen said as they pulled off their helmets and sat in the creaking quietness of the cockpit. "For questioning you up there, I mean. I'm not a coward, I just wouldn't know where to start attacking a large formation like that. I've never done, or even seen, anything like it."

"You know, the first time I was in Malta, there'd be two of us to intercept a raid of one or two hundred bombers and fighters, sometimes more..." She paused for a moment, as she thought back to the days when she and Nicole would fly into battle in obsolete old biplanes, turning, diving, and spinning, and never getting away from seeing the enemy in front, behind, and chasing from every direction. "There's nothing to be sorry for, Pietersen. You can't help what you don't know. It's my job to teach you, if you'll let me, and give you the skills and confidence to take on whatever you're thrown at."

"Teach me to do what you just did, and I'll follow you anywhere." He offered his hand, which she shook firmly.

"Right, I want a list of our aircrews, their proficiencies and skills, and any deficiencies we have in terms of equipment or personnel."

"Yes, Ma'am."

"And I suppose you'd better let me know who my navigator is, unless you're thinking of taking that seat permanently."

"Not me, I'm a pilot, I love flying too much. You have a choice though, there are more navigators than pilots at the moment."

"Your recommendation from those not currently assigned?"

"Eikemo. He's young and needs a little guidance, but he's keen and loves his job."

"OK, I'll see him when we're back inside. Is there anything else I need to know about before we go back in?"

"Yes, the paperwork is in a terrible state since we lost our Adjutant. We don't have a clerk. One of the mechanics has been trying to help out, but I don't think his heart's in the job; and I've had one of the spare navigators, Ericsson, acting as Adjutant. He's a flyer though, not an administrator, and despite his best efforts, he hasn't a clue about RAF procedures."

"OK, I'll look into it. Thank you." She gave him a smile and a nod, and he opened the hatch and climbed down the steps, leaving her in the cockpit by herself. When she was sure he'd gone, she let the tension out of her shoulders and slumped into her seat for a moment, and shook the tightness from her hands. The trip had been significantly more eventful than she'd anticipated, and a local familiarisation flight had quickly turned into a bloody battle, which she hardly remembered. She'd gone into an automated state, a blur where she functioned instinctively, and put everything she knew into turning back the enemy raid. Fleeting memories of flying through waterspouts and seeing enemy bombers burn passed before her eyes, and for a moment she frowned in concern that she could slip into such a state.

"Everything OK, Ma'am?" A Flight Sergeant from the ground crew asked, as he looked up at Harriet through the hatch. He had a noticeable Norwegian accent.

"Yes. Yes, thank you," she replied with a smile. "No snags to report, she flew very well."

"Thank you, Ma'am. We do our best." He beamed proudly as he replied.

"Better than that, I think." She handed him her kit, then climbed down the steps into the cool air. "I'm Cornwall, the new CO." She offered her hand, which he shook after a moment of hesitation.

"Chief Olsen, Ma'am. The boys call me Ollie."

"Nice to meet you, Ollie. Is there anything the ground crew need?"

"Not much, we're well looked after. Though we'd be happy to see the Germans out of Norway, Ma'am. If you can help with that?" he replied with a smile.

"I'll see what I can do." She smiled as she walked slowly towards the dispersal hut.

"Three cheers for the CO, a true Norwegian warrior!" Pietersen shouted, as Harriet walked through the door. "Hip hip!" The gathered crews cheered excitedly, much to Harriet's surprise and embarrassment. Once the cheering was over, they clamoured to shake her hand and congratulate her on her success in the air. Pietersen gave her a nod, which she returned subtly and politely, before entering her office and throwing her flight kit on the hat stand, then sitting at her desk. "Ericsson, Ma'am," Pietersen said, as he showed a confused looking young officer into her office.

"Thank you. At ease, Ericsson," Harriet said. "Right, what's the paperwork situation?"

"Frustrating," the young officer replied. "My English is good, but I'm not quite sure I understand half the paperwork I have, and I don't have a clue about the RAF policies for processing the other half that I do understand."

"OK, well you'd better leave it on the desk." She pointed to the empty desk across the room. "I'll have a look through it and see where we start. How do you feel about the Adjutant's job?"

"I'd rather swim back to Norway and fight the Germans bare handed."

"Let's hope it doesn't come to that." She nodded to her in tray, and he dropped a pile of papers he'd been carrying on top of what was already mounting up. "I'll see if we can get you flying soon."

"Yes, Ma'am. Thank you!" He saluted and left, giving Pietersen a nod and a smile on his way out.

"Better send in Eikemo," she said to Pietersen, who nodded before going to collect the young Navigator, who appeared at the door a minute later.

"Eskimo, Ma'am," he said excitedly, with a smart salute. He was short, shorter than Harriet, with a mop of sandy hair, and bright blue eyes.

"Eskimo?"

"It's what the others call me. I was given the name by the Canadian instructors, and it stuck."

"Well, come in." She gestured to the space in front of her desk. "I'm told you're a good navigator?"

"The best in the squadron, Ma'am."

"I hope so, because you'll be flying with me from now on. I need you to be sharp and accurate, and to be able to lead us to our target and back without hiccup. Understood?"

"Yes, Ma'am!"

"Good. I want a course to the training area north of here. We'll go via the gunnery range up the coast. We leave in an hour, so you'd better get over to meteorology and check the weather out."

"Ma'am!" He ran from the office like an excited puppy, something that made her fight a smile that was threatening to break our across her face.

"Pietersen, brief the crews. Wheels up in an hour. I want to see how they handle their aeroplanes and what their shooting's like. Have someone call through and let the range know we're coming, and see if you can find me a cup of tea." Pietersen nodded and left, closing the door behind him, and leaving Harriet to let out a sigh. She'd got through her introduction to her new squadron, so far at least, but she was finding it hard channelling the best of her CO from Malta, Singh, Flash, and Barnes, with a bit of Archie and Cas thrown in for good measure. She'd had some very good commanding officers, and now she was a stranger in charge of a squadron of new faces, she was grateful for what she'd learned from all of them. From the adventurous excitement of Malta, to the hard faced bluster of Flash. She was using something of each of them, and it was exhausting. A cup of tea to compete with American efforts appeared after a while, and she sipped at it with disappointment, while looking through the mountain of paperwork that had been dumped on her desk. There was everything she could imagine, and more. Requisitions for kit and equipment, requisitions for new pilots, posting papers for ground crews, combat reports, mission reports, inventory reports, inspection reports. It was as though nobody had actually done any paperwork in weeks, instead just hiding it, and hoping for the best. She sorted it while she drank her tea, trying to make sense of at least some of it, and quickly realising that it was going to be a full time job she'd have to tackle on an evening after flying duties.

An hour and a half later, and Harriet was circling over the gunnery range and watching each of her pilots go in to attack the targets. They flew bravely and confidently, but not enough to get low and close to their targets, and not urgent enough in their pulling up and taking evasive action. Something repeated when she snaked them through the valleys to the north to test their handling skills. They were good, but they'd be easy targets for enemy fighters. They were too slow, and their reactions weren't sharp, meaning their manoeuvres were subdued and not urgent, confirming Harriet's thoughts that they'd be sitting ducks. She was reassured by the overall quality of their flying, though, which meant there was a good foundation to build on. Overall, it was a useful flight, and she'd made mental notes throughout, including on the abilities of Eskimo, her navigator, who'd done exactly as she'd asked without fault. He didn't even flinch when, to finish off the assessment, Harriet threw her Mosquito around the valleys so low she set the sheep stampeding. Soon enough it was over though, and she reluctantly led her squadron back to the air station, back to the ground, and her mountain of paperwork.

After lunch, and a full debriefing of her crews, she gave an impromptu lesson in handling, and the principles of gunnery, she scheduled the training sessions for the following day, and explained what she was expecting, and what study and preparation work would need to be done that evening. Pilots and navigators alike took notes and asked questions, and they all had a spark of life about them, when the transport was ready to take them to their accommodation after a long day. She waved, as she watched the truck roll away, then looked over to the line of Mosquitos and their ground crews. It had been a mixed day. For a moment she thought she was going to be in trouble, and stuck in a fight with a squadron of aircrew she had very little in common with, something that was saved by the Luftwaffe's sneak low level raid that gave her the opportunity to show what she was capable of, and that she wasn't just some passenger they'd been lumbered with. She smiled to herself, then frowned a little as she tried to piece together the battle again. There was still nothing more than a blur in her mind. It had happened sometimes during her first visit to Malta, when she'd been up four or five times in a row to take on relentless waves of enemy aircraft, but never on a single sortie. Her wondering was broken by the arrival of Alastair's black staff car, driven by a WAAF. She'd been sent to collect Harriet to take her to her accommodation, much to Harriet's surprise, but she didn't hang around. Grabbing her flying kit, she jumped in the passenger seat and was driven off the air station, and along the narrow country roads bordered with wildflowers and thistles, all bathed in the golden glow of the late afternoon sun. It wasn't overly warm, but Scotland was beautiful, and she was in love with the surrounding nature already.

She was dropped at a picturesque country pub in a small village not far from the air station, and told by the driver that she'd arrived at her digs. She raised an eyebrow and smiled, then said her thanks before heading inside. A large open fire crackled and sparked, but there was nobody to be seen, leaving her to wander around shouting 'hello'.

"You must be the wee Squadron Leader we've been told to expect," an older, and quite austere lady, said as she stepped through a door from the back of the pub.

"Harry Cornwall," Harriet replied, offering her hand, which the lady shook gently. "I'm told I'm staying here?"

"Stuart's the name, Maggie Stuart, and not quite..."

"No?"

"No... Come with me, I'll show you." She led Harriet through the pub, and out the back to a large and very well kept garden, following a stone path through sweet smelling roses to a small orchard, which led to a thatched roof cottage, with a thin smudge of smoke squiggling up from the stone chimney. "This is you," Maggie said. She put the key in the lock and turned the handle, then led Harriet into the cosy lounge.

"You're sure?"

"Why wouldn't I be?"

"I don't know, it seems very nice."

"I'm happy you think so. Mister Saltire said it would be ideal for you."

"Better than."

"It's our guest house. We used to let it to people holidaying up here on the coast, but the war seems to have got in the way of that to some degree. Fortunately, your Royal Air Force pays well."

"Yes..." Harriet looked around excitedly, not quite believing her luck.

"There's a kitchen through there, we've stocked it with the basics, and the bedroom's through that door. Unfortunately, the toilet is outside, though it's quite well maintained, and you shouldn't have any problems. Just make sure you take a light if you go at night, it can get dark out."

"Thank you, I'm sure I'll be fine."

"Breakfast will be in the pub, as will dinner. Which, I should add, is an hour from now. There's some hot water boiling on the stove, it should be enough for you to wash up."

"Dinner?"

"Yes. Your evening meal, of course."

"Of course… It's just that I'm meant to be meeting Group Captain Saltire for dinner this evening."

"And you are. He'll likely be here in a while, so I'll leave you to get on." She breezed out of the door, leaving Harriet to wander around smiling. Her bags had been put in the bedroom, where a large double bed was covered in heavy blankets and scattered with cushions. A neat parcel wrapped in brown paper and tied with string sat next to her bags, with a note from Alistair saying, 'something for the cold'. She frowned curiously as she looked at it, then let herself smile as she pulled at the string and opened the package, revealing an ecru colour sailor's woollen roll neck sweater. She felt the softness of the wool in her hands, then brushed it against her face for a moment, it was a very welcome gift. Her friend, 'Ships', a Fleet Air Arm pilot attached to her squadron in the Battle of Britain, would wear his roll neck when flying in the autumn before she left, and she'd always been jealous of how warm he looked. She'd tried to get her hands on one, but they were exclusively navy issue, and hard to get hold of if you didn't have the connections, and by the time she'd finally asked Ships for his help sourcing one, she'd been posted to Malta. The last place she needed a warm woollen sweater. She had an issue sweater of course, but it wasn't the same. It was too long, too baggy, and designed for a very different type of flying in a very different war; and the cricket jumper Cas had 'loaned' her was fine for summer and autumn flying, but it was lightweight at best, and not designed for winter at twenty thousand feet. She put the sweater in a drawer, along with some of her other clothes, and the rest she hung in the large free standing wardrobe, including the uniform she pulled off her weary body.

After exploring the cottage, dressed in the aloha shirt and denim shorts she'd brought back from Hawaii, she stepped out into the garden to make sure she could find her way to the outhouse, just so she knew where it was when the time came. The garden was simply beautiful. Perfectly kept, with flowers and shrubs of all sorts, and aromatic light violet roses by the door that made the air smell of sweet perfume and strawberries. She could easily have got lost in the moment, and she would have if she didn't have dinner to go to, so she reluctantly dragged herself back inside and poured some water from the large kettle on the range into a tin bowl, then had a strip wash to remove the sweat from the day's unexpected combat.

After watering the roses with her washing water, she returned to her room and got dressed in her newly adjusted best uniform, which fit like a glove thanks to Ralph's expert tailoring. She tidied her hair and tied it into a tight bun, then checked herself in the mirror. Her eyes were still dark and sunken following her Malta experience, and her cheekbones still drawn, but she was otherwise presentable in her own over critical mind. It was only dinner with Alastair, she reminded herself a couple of times, and that seemed to be enough to settle her.

"Harry, old man!" Alastair boomed from the large dinner table, as Harriet walked into the side room in the pub. "How was your first day?"

"I've had worse days," she replied, trying to be casual and nonchalant in the face of Alastair's theatrical greeting.

90

"Good. Good! Have a seat." He gestured to the seat across the table, and waved for a beer to be brought through. "Now, what's this I hear about you upsetting the neighbours?"

"I..." Harriet raised her eyebrows in surprise, not sure who she'd upset, or how, and immediately started to worry about just how much her new Norwegian friends had been humouring her.

"Three Germans on your first day. I've got to say, Harry, it's given me something to smile about knowing you've picked up right where you left off. Absolutely first class!" He laughed and took a swig of his beer, encouraging Harriet to do the same.

"She always was a show off..." a familiar voice said from the doorway, startling Harriet so much she choked on her beer, and ended up spitting some of it back into the glass. She stood and turned to see AP standing before her, smiling, and looking smart in her best uniform.

"That's Squadron Leader show off to you, Flying Officer Kaye!" Harriet replied sharply, fighting the smile that was making her cheeks hurt.

"Yes, Ma'am. Of course, Ma'am," AP replied with heavy sarcasm and a mischievous smile.

"What on earth are you doing here?" Harriet asked, her eyes wide open with shock. Then she quickly turned to Alastair. "What's she doing here?"

"You don't think you're the only female pilot we have, do you, Harry old man?" Alastair winked, while AP moved to a seat at the table.

"Still think you're special, I see," AP added.

"I can't believe you're here..." Harriet said, looking AP up and down, and smiling at the sight of her friend.

"Who do you think flies our reconnaissance missions?" Alastair asked. "Anyway, more about reunions later. I'm starving and ready to eat, sit down won't you?"

91

"You're a photographic reconnaissance pilot?" Harriet asked AP as they sat. "That's amazing!"

"They didn't want me on a fighter squadron. Apparently, they'd had enough of you in Fighter Command, and couldn't bear the thought of having another woman fly with them." AP shrugged casually, then took a sip of the beer that was quickly delivered to her. "I started on Spitfires, then moved on to Mosquitoes when we got them a month ago." AP rolled her eyes while Harriet simply stared in amazement. It was the last person she'd expected to see.

"AP's been with us a while," Alastair said. "One of our resident superstars, and an absolute favourite; even though I'm not supposed to have them, of course..." He waved towards the landlady excitedly, signalling it was time to eat. "You can keep your eyes off her, Harry. I know what you're thinking, and it's a no!"

"What?" Harriet asked innocently.

"She's mine, and she reports to me. I can't afford to lose her to join your little flying circus."

"I'm not a horse to be traded," AP said sternly.

"Oh behave, AP. You know full well I wouldn't be giving you up in a hurry," Alastair reassured.

"You're assuming I want you," Harriet shrugged, getting a stern look in return from her friend.

"So, Harry, how did you find the squadron? Didn't give you any trouble, did they?" Alastair asked.

"Nothing I couldn't handle," Harriet replied as casually as she could.

"They probably heard she punches people that cross her," AP added. "She does that, you know. All sweetness and light until you get in her bad books, then she's like a demon."

92

"Don't be rude," Harriet said with a frown.

"What's it going to take to get them in shape?" Alastair continued. "There's something in the pipeline for next month, and we're going to need you to be ready to go."

"It wouldn't hurt if you could talk with Archie, and see if you can get us to the front of the queue for a week or so training with his team. The pilots are good, but their handling and gunnery could do with some fine tuning, and Archie's team do a good job."

"I'll call him in the morning. Anything else?"

"The clerk is a mechanic, and hopeless, I need a new one who knows what they're doing."

"Done."

"The red haired WAAF in the control tower seemed on the ball when I arrived. I don't know her name, but if she's free?"

"She can be. Is that all?"

"Not quite... There's one more thing I need."

"Name it."

"I need an Adjutant. A proper one, somebody that knows how the RAF works. Without one, I'll be spending most of my time sitting at my desk all day buried under paperwork, and I'm not sure that's what either you or I want."

"That should be easy enough, I'll have a think about it and see what I can do."

"I have a few ideas..."

"Not AP. I told you, she's out of bounds." Before Harriet could reply, he turned excitedly as the landlady and her husband appeared carrying the food. "Bravo! Thank you so much, could I trouble you for three more beers? Put them on my tab."

"Meat," Harriet said, as the plate of fresh roast meat, mashed potatoes, and carrots was put down in front of her.

"Venison, to be precise," Alastair said. "They roast it wonderfully here, and the carrots are glazed with local honey, and taste simply divine."

"You've seen meat before..." AP said.

"Yes... Just not so much, for so long. You won't believe what I had to live on in Malta."

"The best thing about being posted to Scotland, Harry," Alastair said, while he started to cut at his own chunk of venison. "Is that the beautiful countryside is packed full of wild deer. So many, in fact, that they can be an absolute hazard at times. I'd say you'll be sick of it in a month, though I just can't imagine that happening to a person." He popped the meat in his mouth and dramatically rolled his eyes. "Heaven."

Harriet cut a piece of the meat and ate it. She hadn't tasted anything like it, not even in The Savoy. She tried to eat slowly, so as not to fill up too quickly, at least that was the theory, but by the time she was halfway through the meal, she was full to bursting, and had to admit defeat. Malta was going to take a long time to get over. She filled quickly when she ate, and if she pushed through and kept eating, her stomach would let her know about it with terrible cramps and urgent toilet distress. Instead, she sipped on her beer and enjoyed her conversation with Alastair and AP, mostly explaining how she'd managed to get through Malta. They were intrigued and kept pushing for more and more, neither believing just how bad it had been, or how desperate. They also talked about the joys of Scotland. There was lots of rain, of course, it's what Scotland was notorious for, but both were more than content with their posting. Beautiful countryside, warm and friendly people, and all the meat and fish you could eat. The Germans rarely visited, apparently, and Harriet's earlier run in had been a stroke of bad luck, or good luck, depending on the perspective. It was explained that they came at night, if they came, and the raids were few and far between. Occasionally they'd show up in the daytime for a hit and run before heading back to their bases in Norway, but it was rare, and likely to become more so in Alastair's opinion, following Harriet's timely intervention. They talked until their meals were gone, and the post meal whisky was finished, then Alastair said Goodnight and left Harriet and AP to go through to the main bar, and sit beside the roaring open fire with another rather large whisky.

"I can't believe you're here," Harriet said again.

"It was a surprise when Alastair told me you were on your way," AP replied with a warm smile. "We weren't sure you'd get here, and I didn't want to let myself believe it until you'd actually arrived." Her smile faded a little as she talked. "Though now I'm sitting here looking at you, there's a piece of me that wishes you weren't."

"That's a little harsh..." Harriet frowned jokingly.

"I mean it," AP said, looking at Harriet sternly. "It can be dangerous around here."

"What do you mean?" Harriet's heart squeezed a little.

"The squadrons have taken a bit of a beating for not much return. We've lost a lot of crews, and I'm not sure I like the idea of you going the same way."

"Don't worry about me, I'll be fine!" Harriet said after a moment, casting off the darkness that was threatening to ruin her day, and smiling confidently. "As I was leaving, it was said that Malta was the most bombed place on earth. If I can survive that, I'm quite sure I can survive Scotland." She gulped down her whisky and stood. "Another?" AP smiled and finished her own drink, before handing Harriet the glass to get refilled at the bar. "You were heading off to train as a pilot the last time I saw you," Harriet said, as she returned with two more large whiskies. "How was it?"

"Awful," AP replied. "They made me start from the beginning, principles of flight, everything. They totally ignored the fact that I already had a pilot's licence!"

"Oh dear..."

"Originally, I was supposed to train with your friends from the ATA, but when they found out I was coming from a ground role and hadn't flown the same types as them, they held me back until there were other females to train from scratch. It wasn't a long wait, fortunately, but there's really no reason I couldn't train with the others."

"The RAF can be like that, I suppose."

"I see you've learned that much at last."

"I had no choice!" They both laughed between sips.

"It wasn't all bad. The wait meant I got to train with Daisy, and it was good to have her around. It made the tedious bits all the more tolerable, and I was able to help her with some of the more technical aspects of ground school."

"Daisy? How is she?"

"Good, the last I heard at least. We write regularly, and she'll be happy to know you're doing well."

"Did she pass?"

"What? Yes, of course she did! She's down south flying liaison aeroplanes with army cooperation. She loves it."

"I'm happy for her. For both of you in fact. You've both done so well."

"So have you..." AP pointed her glass at the rank on Harriet's cuffs.

"I wouldn't go that far."

"Well, they don't promote just anyone, or give medals away for no reason, either."

"Shut up. We both know I only got either is because there was nobody else stupid enough to give them to."

"I didn't want to say... Anyway, in all seriousness you should be proud of yourself. You've come a long way from that scruffy girl that fell out of a smoking Hurricane and straight into a war."

"In all seriousness, I'm not sure it's been worth it."

"Don't be ridiculous."

"I'm not. Sometimes the price is just too much, you know?"

"What do you mean?"

"All the people we've lost. I sometimes think it'd be easier if I hadn't met them. If I hadn't got in that Hurricane I wouldn't have been here now, I'd probably be in Switzerland with my parents, and I'd never have had to lose people."

"You can't think like that. You've made a big difference, and I'll kill you if you ever tell anyone I said this, but you've made a big difference to those you otherwise wouldn't have met, me included. No Harriet Cornwall, no AP flying Mosquitoes. If you've done nothing else, you've done that. You put girls in aeroplanes, and upset the boy's club on the way. That's got to be worth it."

"I suppose," Harriet smiled.

"As much as I could sit here catching up all night, I should be going shortly. I have to fly before first light."

"Where to?"

"Norway. I'll probably be home before you've even had your breakfast."

"I'll think of you while I'm wrapped up warm in bed."

"Forget the nice things I said about you."

"Where do you live?"

"In the Mess." She checked her watch, then gulped her whisky and stood. "The transport will go without me."

"I'll walk you out," Harriet said as she gulped her own whisky, and felt it burn all the way down. The night air made her head swim a little, and she had to grab AP's arm to steady herself.

"Time hasn't helped you handle your drink any better I see," AP sighed.

"Shut up," Harriet replied. "I haven't had the opportunities."

"Too busy shooting Germans?"

"Something like that." The bus from the air station rumbled down the road, the slits of its cat eye headlights glowing dimly in the early evening darkness.

"It really is good to see you, Harry," AP said, then gave Harriet an unexpected hug. "Look, why don't you come up with me tomorrow morning? It's a milk run, nothing exciting, but it'll give you a chance to have a look at the Norwegian coast. I can have you back in time for breakfast."

"Really?."

"Why not?"

"There's no reason, I suppose."

"I'll send the duty driver for you in the morning. Three o'clock alright for you?"

"Not really..."

"I'll see you in the morning. Goodnight, Squadron Leader."

"Goodnight."

Chapter 5

Norse

After a night in a bed so soft she didn't ever want to leave it, Harriet had managed to drag herself out into the cold morning air that made her bones shiver. She couldn't remember when she last felt so cold, and after boiling some water to wash and drink tea, she quickly dressed, long underwear included, and pulled on her new sailor's roll neck sweater under her sheepskin jacket and flying boots, before heading out to stand on the side of the road and wait for the duty driver, who turned up after a few minutes in a rickety truck which bumped and rumbled along the narrow lanes.

"Morning!" AP greeted Harriet, as she stepped out of the dark, and into the dimly lit Photo Reconnaissance hut. She was uncharacteristically chirpy, her smirk giving away her enjoyment of seeing Harriet's bleary eyed tiredness."

"Morning? It's still the middle of the night!" Harriet muttered in reply.

"Here," AP handed her a mug of hot sweet tea, which Harriet sipped at quickly.

"Do you have any biscuits?"

"There's a war on, you know?"

"That doesn't make me any less hungry."

"In the tin." AP gestured to the small barrel by the hot water urn. "And don't eat them all, they're for the whole flight."

"I maybe haven't been in the RAF as long as you, but I worked out pretty quickly that a Flying Officer doesn't give orders to a Squadron Leader," Harriet grumbled, as she dipped the biscuit in her tea, then quickly pushed it into her mouth before it fell apart.

"Apart from when the Flying Officer is the Captain of the aeroplane being flown, and then the Squadron Leader does as she's told."

"We'd better hurry up and get in your aeroplane in that case, before the Squadron Leader has something to say."

"Well, I've been waiting for you..." AP shrugged, as Harriet joined her looking over the map on the table. "These fjords are where we're heading." She tapped on the virtual rabbit Warren of jagged coves and inlets on the map. "Norway has thousands of miles of coastline, counting all the islands and fjords, which can make it difficult to track the German ships until they get out into the North Sea. We got a message from the Norwegian resistance recently suggesting that some German merchant ships are hiding out in one of these fjords while they wait for their escorts. If we can confirm it, we can maybe arrange a surprise for them."

"What's the plan?"

"The meteorology types are thinking there's some miserable weather coming from the north with lots of low cloud, so I want to get there before daylight and try to find the ships, then use the cloud for cover on the run home."

"Flak?"

"The Norwegian resistance hasn't reported any in that area."

"Fighters?"

"More than likely. We'll cross the coast within range of a troublesome fighter airfield, the same lot that gave your squadron a hard time recently. They have the new Focke Wulf 190s, and they're a menace."

"I've heard about them, but haven't come up against them yet."

"They're fast and manoeuvrable, and well armed. You'd better hope we don't come up against any."

"I'll keep that in mind..."

"Right, got your parachute?"

"Will I need it?" Harriet asked as she tapped the parachute bag.

"Let's hope not. I don't fancy swimming home, but it doesn't hurt to have one just in case." They finished their drinks and left the hut, walking side by side through the cold dark air towards AP's turquoise blue Mosquito, which looked as black as coal in the night. The ground crew were busy tinkering and preparing, and AP greeted them warmly, for her, and checked there was nothing she needed to worry about before climbing up through the hatch in the floor of the cockpit. It was a different type of Mosquito from that Harriet was used to, modelled on the bomber version, with a clear Perspex nose for easy observation, where she was used to seeing her cannons and guns, and a hatch underneath instead of to the side. She followed AP inside, and took her seat in the navigator's position, making sure her parachute straps were tight before she fastened her harness and got comfortable. "Ready?" AP asked, as she looked at Harriet with a smile that could only just be made out in the glow from the instruments that softened the darkness of the cockpit.

"When you are."

"Let's get moving in that case." AP started one engine, and then the other, and went through her checks in the careful and calculated way she did everything, then released the brakes after calling chocks away, and followed the red light on the back of the tractor out in front as it led the mosquito to the end of the runway, where she went through her final checks. She called the control tower, and seconds later the runway was lit up ready for her to push the throttles open, and the Mosquito leapt into life. She held the swing expertly as the Mosquito charged along the runway, and Harriet smiled to herself as the aeroplane jumped into the sky with ease, and the lights were extinguished, returning the world below to darkness.

They passed over the cliffs and headed east, out over the North Sea. It was dark and murky, with thick cloud above, and a rolling sea below, and it was difficult to see where the water ended and the sky started, which made the glowing instruments more important than ever. Harriet was used to flying at night, but it was usually in the Mediterranean with a clear sky and a million stars to guide her, nothing like what she was currently experiencing. She looked over at AP, who was wearing her trademark frown of concentration as she expertly guided them through the still air, just a few hundred feet above the sea, making Harriet smile again at the sight of her friend, so capable and confident. All the fights they'd had just to be allowed to be pilots would have been avoided if a senior officer had just sat where she was and watched AP fly.

"What?" AP asked, after Harriet had been looking at her for a while.

"Nothing," Harriet replied with a giggle.

"Then stop looking at me!"

"Am I making you nervous?"

"You're making me paranoid!"

"I don't know how."

"By staring at mc. And don't say you're not, I can see you!"

"You should be concentrating on your job; we don't want to crash into the water."

"I don't crash..." She looked at Harriet and gave her a confident wink. "We'll stay at this altitude until we're about one hundred and fifty miles from the Norwegian coast. The German radar, Freya, has a range of about one hundred and twenty miles, but we like to drop early just to make sure we don't let them know we're coming."

"Does it work?"

"Mostly, yes. You've got to watch for their flak guns, though. If they're awake and watching, we're right in front of them and a perfect target as we cross the coast. Most are fixed, fortunately, so we kind of know where they are; but they have a mobile unit as well, and they can turn up anywhere, so you'll need to keep your wits about you."

"I'll keep it in mind."

"You should. The flak can get rough sometimes, it's not the same as swanning around in a Spitfire, like you're used to."

"What do you think I did in Malta?"

"Swanned around in your Spitfire, didn't you?"

"A Photographic Reconnaissance Spitfire, and I can assure you I saw enough flak."

"If you say so..."

"Didn't fancy fighters yourself?"

"I wasn't allowed."

"What do you mean?"

"Don't you know?"

"Know what?"

"Following your little run in with the new AOC's Chief of Staff down in Kent, somebody high up put a hold on female pilots flying in Fighter Command."

"I didn't know..." Harriet's stomach squeezed. She'd thought it was all done with when she'd first been sent to Malta, and didn't think for a moment it had rumbled on in her wake. The thought made her uneasy."

"Alastair told me. It was an embarrassing moment for the higher ups, and they thought the best way to deal with it was to pretend it didn't happen, which naturally meant they'd rather not have female pilots hanging around to remind them of what had gone on. Especially not the types that grab newspaper headlines. Anyway, they didn't want us, Bomber Command were adamant they wouldn't take us, on the grounds of it being tantamount to heresy to have a woman command an aeroplane crewed by men, apparently. God forbid they'd ever think the best person to command an aeroplane was the best skilled and qualified, and not dependent on what they had between their legs. So, it was out of sight out of mind, Coastal Command, Army Cooperation, or out of the country."

"I don't know what to say. If I'd known I'd..."

"You'd what?"

"I don't know. If I'd known they'd behave that way, I'd have kept my mouth shut in the first place."

"I'd have lost all respect for you if you did. From what I hear, they had it in for you, and us, anyway, so it wouldn't have made any difference. Besides, we're flying, aren't we?"

"I suppose..." Harriet shrugged unhappily. She was annoyed that despite everything, there was still a desperate attempt in the corridors of power to stop women from flying. It didn't make her feel great about all she'd done, and all the risks she'd taken. She knew she'd done what she had through duty, but it left a bad taste in her mouth knowing she was still less valuable than a male pilot in the eyes of some, just because of her gender.

"Honestly, I don't know if I could have done what you and Nicole did in fighters anyway, I'm not sure many of us could, and maybe not being sent to a squadron in 11 or 12 Group could have saved my life."

"Don't be ridiculous, you're a good pilot."

"I know I am, but it took miracles for you to get through it, and you had experience behind you. I'm not sure the rest of us would have been as lucky. Especially with the losses fighter command sustained over the winter after you'd left. It's only rumours, but they say we lost more pilots flying sweeps over France than we did in the Battle of Britain."

"I heard that too..."

"I didn't get to fly fighters, but I got to fly the fastest Spitfires ever made and take photos, and now I do the same in a Mosquito. It has its risks, but it could be a lot worse."

"I suppose... It's still not fair that you should be treated different."

"It's not fair that any of us should, and it goes both ways. The boys get sent to the front line to fight it out, it's not fair on them that we don't. Still, there's no differences where we are now. Alastair works us girls the same and treats us the same, and has the same expectations of me as he does any of his male pilots."

"I'm pretty sure he doesn't let his male junior officers call him by his first name, or invite them to dinner for that matter."

"That's different."

"How?"

"We're old friends, apparently."

"Apparently... Wait. What's that?" Harriet asked as she caught a glimpse of something on the water ahead of them. She squinted in the darkness and made out what looked like a boat.

"Where?" AP asked. The fun dropped from her voice, and she instinctively scanned all around.

"On the water, eleven o'clock." Harriet pointed and AP focused for a few seconds as the murky shape came out of the darkness. Her adrenaline was flowing in an instant, having not expected to see anything in the darkness she was instinctively expecting to receive a burst of gunfire from the unexpected boat.

"Idiot!" AP said as they passed over the boat.

"What?"

"You had me worried."

"It's a boat."

"It's a float!"

"A what?"

"Seriously, how did you make it this far in the RAF, let alone make it to the rank of Squadron Leader?"

"You're really not helping!" Harriet blustered with a frown.

"It's an Air Sea Rescue float. There are a few dotted about, they're on the map." AP reached over and tapped the map on Harriet's leg. "They're moored below common crossing routes for downed air crews. There's supplies and a radio on board, and they're checked regularly by the rescue launches. You know what rescue launches are, don't you?"

"Yes..." Harriet rolled her eyes, making AP smirk in reply.

"There are three fast ocean going types attached to our air station. They're based just along the coast, and tend to be out and about if something big's going on, just in case."

"That's reassuring to know. They had a couple of launches in Malta. They pulled a lot of pilots out of the drink, and saved quite a few lives."

"I wouldn't be that reassured, especially not this time of year. They estimate you'll last no more than fifteen minutes if you ditch in the water. Longer if you get in your life raft, assuming the shock of the cold doesn't kill you outright."

"You're full of all sorts of good news."

"Well, it's not the Mediterranean."

"I'd worked that out, but thanks..."

"Anyway, if you do go down, try and get in your life raft as soon as you can. If you're close to a float, even better. Approach from the back, there's a slope for you to crawl up."

"I'll keep that in mind."

"Good luck. I've no intention of going in, so you're on your own."

"You know, the bombing never stopped in Malta," Harriet said after a moment of reflection. "Most days they'd come three, four, or even five times, and there'd be the fighter sweeps in between, where 109s would come over the island at low level and shoot up anything that moved... Then, just when we thought it was safe to go to bed, they'd come back at night and bomb us some more."

"Sounds fun..."

"Yes, and I never thought I'd miss it until I got trapped in a Mosquito with you."

"You've missed me..." AP checked her watch, then looked around outside. Dawn was just starting to lighten the eastern sky, bringing the faintest distinction between the sea and the sky. "Right, time to pay attention and drop to the surface." She gently nudged the nose down, and they were soon skimming the waves, racing towards Norway so low that one flinch or distraction would be enough for them to hit the water, so Harriet stayed quiet for a while, and let AP focus on the task ahead. "Better keep your eyes open."

"Are we in range of their fighters?"

"We will be shortly, but I'm more worried about us hitting a trawler."

"You're not funny!" Harriet frowned, then settled into a routine of checking the sky for fighters, and the sea for things they'd crash into; while occasionally glancing at the compass and map, and checking her watch to estimate when they'd make landfall. She smiled as the Norwegian coast came into sight at exactly the time she'd estimated, and AP guided them expertly through the entrance of the fjord, passing between the steep cliffs either side. Harriet's eyes opened wide in surprise, as they quickly came upon a line of five merchant ships moored in a neat line in the centre of the fjord. "That was fortunate!" AP nodded in response, while keeping the Mosquito at wave top height, and skimming the surface of the water as she passed the ships. "They're low in the water..."

"Must be ready to set off."

"Have we got what we need?"

"Yep, let's go home." AP pulled up and skipped over the cliffs, keeping low as she turned and headed west. She opened the throttles and pushed the engines to the maximum. Even if the sentries on the ships hadn't seen the Mosquito, they'd certainly have heard it, and there was every chance that they'd already be letting their fighters know they had visitors. Harriet's heart raced with excitement, and she spun her head side to side, up and down, searching the sky for unwelcome guests. "How's your morse?"

"Rusty..."

"You only need to send the code word and coordinates," AP instructed, and Harriet nodded and went about sending her message. She tapped slowly as she spelled out first their callsign, and then the code word for finding the ships in the first fjord. She waited a while, then sent it again when she hadn't had a reply. "Well?" AP asked, a little impatiently.

"Shut up and focus on the flying!" Harriet barked, then went back to the morse key. AP pulled up hard and climbed for the heavy grey cloud base that was outlined by the first light of dawn, and shortly before they were enveloped, Harriet received the confirmation message from control. "Done!"

"Good. Now, let's make sure we get back and don't get lost in this cloud."

"You know, you really need to work on your motivational speaking."

After a happily incident free run home, which AP timed, navigated, and flew perfectly, they broke cloud not far from the Scottish coast, then touched down just after dawn and rolled to the Reconnaissance Flight's dispersal, before shutting down and stepping out into the cold damp air. The ground crew went to work removing the film from the cameras so it could be developed and rushed to the interpreters, while Harriet and AP made their way to the control tower to meet Alastair and report their mission.

"How was it?" Alastair asked, as they entered the control room.

"Piece of cake," AP replied. "We got the photos, and got out of there quick before the fighters turned up. The clouds helped keep us hidden."

"Good show. We'll find out shortly if it's paid off. I sent the Beaufighter boys in anticipation of your confirmation, and they shouldn't be far off the Norwegian coast." He gave AP a warm smile, then turned to Harriet. "So, Harry, how do you like Norway?"

"I'll let you know," Harriet replied with a smile. "I'd better get to work."

"No you don't!" He looked directly at Harriet, making her frown in confusion. "Breakfast first." He gave her a wink, which made her smile again. "We'll go over in a few minutes, I just want to hear the score..." Harriet and AP nodded, and he looked over to the WAAF sitting by the radio with her headset firmly in place so she could listen for news from the bombers.

"How long?" AP asked.

"Anytime… Why?"

"I'm hungry." She shrugged.

"Of course!" He laughed and slapped her on the shoulder. "I don't blame you! Must have been the middle of the night when you two were up and about." At that, the WAAF waved and called his name, letting him know a message was coming through. She scribbled quickly, then tapped an acknowledgement much, much quicker than Harriet could, making her frown in disappointment at her own morse skills. "Four merchant ships are now significantly lower in the water than they were designed to be," Alastair explained as he read the message excitedly. "By several hundred feet, I would imagine." Harriet and AP smiled at each other, and Harriet felt a glow of success inside, which quickly tempered as she thought of her own experience on the tanker, and imagined how terrifying it must have been for the crews. "Good work, ladies! It looks like the drinks are on me tonight!"

"Can we go and get breakfast now?" AP asked.

"Absolutely! Oh, and I have some good news for you, Harry. Our old friend Archie has agreed to squeeze your chaps into his training schedule. They leave for Yorkshire tomorrow, and start the hard work the day after."

"Really?" Harriet replied excitedly.

"Yes, they'll only be down there for a week, it's all Archie could spare, and even then things are going to be tight! Look, Harry, it's your call of course, but with things as they are it's not entirely necessary you go along with them. After all, you already know your stuff."

"I understand... She smiled, though felt conflicted at his words. She knew that the training schedule would be busy, and that the crews needed the time much more than she, but at the same time she wanted to go to Yorkshire again, and see Nicole and the others."

"I don't doubt you, Harry old man. Are you OK?"

"What? Yes. Yes, thank you so much. For arranging it, I mean. It'll do wonders for the crews."

"Don't mention it. Anything to help and all that. Oh, and there's a little surprise for you when you get to work."

"What sort of surprise?"

"It wouldn't be a surprise if I told you, would it?" He laughed theatrically. "Oh, you are a card, Harry. I have missed having you around. What sort of surprise indeed!"

After breakfast, Harriet made her way over to her dispersal, while going through her choice to stay behind in her mind. It was still early, much earlier than she expected to see anyone, so it was a surprise when she opened the door to see the WAAF from the control tower standing by the stove and trying to keep warm.

"Good morning..." Harriet said with a smile, as she started to hope this was her surprise.

"Good morning, Ma'am," the WAAF replied. "Group Captain Saltire said I'm to report to you from now on."

"Yes, sorry about that. I need somebody organised and used to the RAF's way of doing things, and I asked for you."

"Me, Ma'am?" the WAAF blushed as a look of surprise came over her.

"You. I'm working on getting a new Adjutant, but for now I have a mountain of paperwork which needs sorting, processing, and preparing, so whoever I get for the job doesn't die of a heart attack on their first day. Think you're up to it?"

"Yes, Ma'am. I'll certainly do my best."

"Good. Hang your coat, and I'll get you a cup of tea."

"Ma'am..." the WAAF smiled as Harriet went over to the flask.

"What's your name?"

"Olivier, Ma'am."

"First name?"

"Chloe. Ma'am."

"I like that. I'm Harry Cornwall," Harriet introduced herself as she handed Olivier a cup of tea.

"I know, Ma'am." She smiled warmly, and Harriet felt herself blush a little.

"Right, let's get you to work." She led Olivier to her office, and showed her the mountains of paperwork not only on her own desk, but spilling untidily over the others in the room. "I'm told there's more, but this should keep you busy for now. You can use my desk until you've made a hole in the work and cleared a space across the room."

"Ma'am..." Olivier nodded.

"I suppose we should set some ground rules before the others get here..."

"Yes, Ma'am."

"OK, so first of all you don't need to call me ma'am every five minutes, not when there's nobody else around." Olivier nodded and smiled. "Second, you're now a member of the squadron, and once you've settled in we're going to rely on you to know what's going on. You report direct to me, and I expect you to be straight with me, and let me know if you need anything, you're struggling with anything, or something or someone is giving you a hard time. Understood?"

"Got it."

"Also, you and I are the only females on the squadron. If anyone takes advantage or behaves inappropriately towards you, you're to let them know immediately, and then let me know."

"I've been here a year; I'm used to it and can hold my own."

"Good. In that case, I'll leave you to get to work. It'll probably be overwhelming at first, so don't feel you need to get everything done right away. Take your time to work out what needs doing." As she talked, a truck rolled up outside, and the unmistakeable clang of a tailgate rattling as it was dropped open heralded the arrival of the crews. A minute later they were traipsing into the dispersal hut, chattering amongst themselves excitedly. "Let's go and say good morning." Harriet gestured to the door, and Olivier followed behind her, then stood at her side as the crews fell quiet and turned to look at them both. "Good morning, gentlemen," Harriet started, receiving a polite chorus of 'good morning, Ma'am' in reply. "This is Chloe Olivier, she's our new Squadron Clerk. She's here to help us get on top of the paperwork, and she reports direct to me. So, do all you can to make her feel welcome, and to make her life easy so she can help us focus our time on flying." The crews nodded and smiled warmly. "OK, now we've got the introductions done, I have some news for you. Tomorrow you'll be heading south for a week, to a training unit in Yorkshire who are going to put you through our paces on the Mosquito." The crews looked at each other excitedly. "I won't be coming with you, unfortunately. Lieutenant Pietersen will lead, and I expect you all to give one hundred percent while you're there. The pilots on the training flight are my friends, and they're the best there is. Listen to them, learn from them, and make the most of your time there. That said, today I want you to prep your aircraft and make sure they're ready to go. Once everything's done, you can stand down and go get your kit packed. It's going to be a busy week, so don't take anything unnecessary. You won't be socialising. Any questions?"

"What type of training, Ma'am?" Pietersen asked.

"Low level bombing and gunnery, and a bit of advanced handling. I've been through the training myself, and it's hard, but it'll improve your chances of surviving the next fight we get into." The crews nodded. "OK, if that's everything, get yourselves to work. The sooner you're sure your aircraft are ready, the sooner you can knock off." There was a stampede as the excited pilots and navigators crashed through the door, nudging each other out of the way and emptying the room in seconds. "Well, that got them moving..." Harriet said with a shrug, then looked to Olivier, who nodded and smiled in reply. "The peace and quiet will give us chance to get on top of that paperwork.

After working with Olivier to make a start on sorting the mountain of reports, requests, and everything else, and prioritising the more important stuff that urgently needed a signature, a task that took the rest of the day, Harriet made her way back to the village on the RAF blue Norton motorcycle that had been delivered to the dispersal with Alastair's compliments, and had an evening meal by herself in the pub. She'd called the photo reconnaissance dispersal before leaving to see if AP wanted to join her, and was disappointed to learn that she was due to go up on a twilight mission, and wouldn't be back until late, so she was left with her own company, and thoughts. It wasn't a bad thing, though she'd really wanted to spend more time with AP. It had been such a long time since they'd seen each other, and Harriet had missed her friend, and wanted to spend as much time as she could catching up. She was exhausted, though, from the early start and the seemingly unending hangover from Malta, and not having company meant that she didn't even bother with a whisky, and instead went straight to her cottage and got out of her uniform, before collapsing into bed. Despite the exhaustion she didn't go straight to sleep. Her mind raced through all that had happened since she'd arrived in Scotland. It had been a whirlwind introduction to her new command, and she was hoping that wasn't a sign of things to come. Then, as had happened at every bedtime since Malta, she thought of Cas. The waking nightmare didn't get any better. A few times she'd wished he'd just been killed outright by the bomb. The thought of him being dragged down into the blackness of the sea with the downed Sunderland, trapped, wounded, and unable to escape, left her in tears every time. She'd tried not to think about it before bed, which almost guaranteed that she would. She had no choice. Bed, darkness, thoughts, tears, in that order, followed by some bargaining and praying, before finally going to sleep, where nightmares of varying intensity waited for her. A current favourite being trapped in her aeroplane as it sunk in Pearl Harbour. Feeling the cold and darkness, and the desperate pressure in her chest before she drank the water down in an attempt to hasten her end and stop the suffering. A nightmare which merged with Cas, and had her waking gasping for breath and trying to reassure herself. In Yorkshire it had helped having Nicole to hold her and soothe her, Scotland was going to prove more difficult.

Chapter 6

Over the Rainbow

Harriet and Olivier stood on the edge of the dispersal and watched as seven of the eight squadron Mosquitoes took off, formed up, and headed south. An hour earlier the spare crews without an aircraft had been loaded onto an old Armstrong Whitworth Albemarle bomber that had been converted to a transport, and flown south with ground crews and kit bags, leaving the squadron almost deserted, except for Harriet, Olivier, and a few others. Harriet was conflicted as she watched her Mosquitoes leave, and become small black dots in the southern sky. She wanted to go with them. A week at home with Nicole would have done wonders for her, she knew that much, but she also knew that she'd be wasting valuable training time by going along. Alastair had left the decision with her, as was his way, though she knew that he knew she would make the right one. As difficult as it was. As the last speck disappeared out of sight, and the rumble of engines faded into the distance, they went to Harriet's office and got stuck into the mountain of paperwork that couldn't be avoided. Olivier had done a fantastic job the previous day, and got the majority sorted into appropriate piles of priority, but there was still a lot to get through, and despite her previous experiences running a squadron, and Cas' patient instruction on how to process the paperwork, there was lots of stuff she didn't have a clue what to do with, even when she had signed it. Some of it she didn't even recognise, but signed anyway as it seemed like the right thing to do at the time.

"Chloe, are you enjoying yourself?" Harriet asked, as she looked at her watch. It was gone eleven in the morning, and they'd been working continuously since the squadron had left, stopping only to pour tea which, while not Malta or America standard, was still not particularly good.

"Ma'am?" the young WAAF replied with a little surprise in her voice, both at the question, and being called by her first name.

"This is the least interesting work I've done for ages."

"I'm used to it, Ma'am. It's what I do..." Chloe shrugged politely.

"Don't you get bored of it?"

"I don't know. Sometimes, maybe, but it's all for a good reason. If we get this done, the squadron will run better and be more effective, which means we'll win the war quicker."

"That's one way of looking at it..."

"What other way is there?"

"Wouldn't you rather be doing something else?"

"Like what?"

"WAAFs do lots of jobs."

"We don't really get that much choice in it. We get sent where the RAF need us, to jobs they think we'd be good at. I have a good level of education, and they said I'd make a good clerk. So here I am."

"Well, I'm bored of it."

"Begging your pardon, but of course you'd get bored of it. You're a pilot! I'm a clerk, though, this is what I do."

"Yes, I am a pilot!" Harriet smiled, then stood from her desk. "Let's have a break!"

"A break?"

"A break." Harriet picked up the phone and called the stores. "Squadron Leader Cornwall, 373 Squadron. I need some flying overalls, size small, a small flying jacket, helmet, and..." She looked at Chloe. "What size shoes are you?"

"Five..."

"Boots in size five. Yes, yes, put them on this squadron's issue. What? Wait..." she frowned and rustled through her papers again. "Hansen. Yes, he's a new navigator. I need them right away, if you have anyone that could run them over? My clerk will sign for them. Thank you, I'm grateful." She put the phone down and smiled at Chloe. "Want to go for a ride?"

"Ma'am?" Chloe looked at Harriet with a raised eyebrow of confusion.

"Come on." Harriet grabbed her sheepskin flying jacket and marched out of the office, with Chloe running behind and pulling on her greatcoat.

"Where are we going?"

"As far away as we can get from paperwork." Harriet smiled mischievously, and led Chloe into the hangar. "Ollie?" she shouted, as she saw the Flight Sergeant standing beside her Mosquito, and talking with one of his mechanics.

"Ma'am?" he replied with a smile, as he dismissed his mechanic.

"How come she's in here? Is something wrong?" Harriet asked, while pointing at her Mosquito.

"Quite the opposite, Ma'am. We brought her in yesterday for an upgrade."

"Upgrade? What upgrade?"

"This..." He led her to the side and pointed up to the nose, and the orange fox's head painted on it, in addition to the Squadron Leader's pennant that was painted just above the door to the cockpit. "The Group Captain told me the fox was painted on your aircraft in Malta, and asked if we wouldn't mind adding it, along with your flag. I hope you don't mind?"

119

"Not at all..." Harriet replied, as a big smile stretched across her face, though she did wonder how on earth Alastair would know about what she did in Malta. "Is she ready to fly?"

"Yes, Ma'am. Are you going up?"

"Yes... I need to go over to meteorology first, but maybe in half an hour?"

"I'll have her pulled out and made ready."

"Thanks, Ollie." She then looked to Chloe again. "Let's go." They marched over to the meteorology unit, which was headed by a civilian from Edinburgh university, an older and quite eccentric man who lived for all things to do with the weather, and was curiously named MacLeod, which Harriet had been told, much to her amusement, was pronounced MacCloud. Harriet had only met him once, briefly, and in the short time they were talking he talked excitedly about rainbows and ice crystals, which despite not being prepared for, Harriet found fascinating. Cas had told her about the rare phenomenon of icebows, something he'd experienced when flying near the Alps in Switzerland. He'd talked so passionately about them that she'd felt transported there, and again when MacLeod mentioned the phenomena she'd been lost in her imagination once again. MacLeod was teaching a pair of junior officers about weather fronts when Harriet and Chloe arrived. They looked like their heads would explode any moment, and they seemed to welcome the distraction Harriet brought when she called in to ask what the weather was looking like for the coming hours. Scotland's climate was changeable at best, and AP's advice on day one was to always check with meteorology before going up, as it was possible to take off in perfect blue skies and sunshine, and half an hour later be weathered in with heavy rain, clouds down to the ground, and zero visibility. MacLeod was clearly enjoying educating his captive audience of new meteorology officers, and only broke briefly to let Harriet know the forecast, winds included, and to warn mischievously of a chance of rainbows with the approaching cold front sinking from the north. It was a twenty minute briefing that Harriet thoroughly enjoyed, while Chloe stayed quietly fascinated. The short briefing also gave the young officers time for a tea break so they could decompress their heads, something they appeared to be grateful for. As a favour, McLeod had asked if Harriet could take up a camera, and try and get a few shots of the clouds on the edge of the weather front, photos which would help his research if she got close enough. Harriet agreed, and he gave a brief demonstration of how to use his own personal small automatic thirty five millimetre camera. Once this was done, and with a cheery goodbye, Harriet and Chloe headed back to the dispersal hut, where Harriet's Mosquito was waiting outside with the orange fox head painted proud on the side. A sight which she couldn't help smiling at again, and for a moment she wished she'd gone south with the squadron, so she could show off to Nicole. She also let her mind go to her parents for a moment. She hadn't seen them since before the war, and while there'd been some annoyance with her father about her career choice, he'd apparently grown to accept it, or so her mother's letters suggested, and Harriet couldn't help but wonder what he'd say if he saw a Mosquito carrying her own markings. Her thoughts were broken by the almost perfect timing of an airman arriving from the stores on his bicycle, carrying a large package wrapped neatly in brown paper, which Chloe signed and carried inside. "Right, get yourself dressed, and we'll get going as soon as you're ready," Harriet said as she opened the package to see the flying clothing she'd ordered, and pushed it across the desk to Chloe.

"You're serious?" Chloe asked.

"Have you ever flown?"

"Never..." Her eyes opened wide

"Well, that's something we're about to change. Better go to the bathroom before we leave, I don't know how long we'll be."

"Yes Ma'am!" came the excitedly nervous reply. Harriet smiled, then headed back out to go through her pre flight checks.

Half an hour later, after Ollie had strapped Chloe into her parachute, and Harriet had strapped her into the navigator's seat, they were roaring through the air and following the cliffs north. Harriet had got them off the ground quickly, and decided on taking a scenic low level ride along the coast, waggling her wings at coastal defence positions as they passed. She glanced over to Chloe occasionally, who was transfixed with excitement, wide eyed at the view and smiling in a way that only those who loved flying could. It was enough to make Harriet smile herself. It was a small thing, taking her clerk for a flight, but she remembered her own first flight and knew how much it had meant to her. It had changed her life in so many ways. She didn't need to say anything to Chloe, and she didn't want to, she knew there were times when it was best to stay quiet and not ruin the moment. After following the coast for a while, Harriet took them up high, well above twenty five thousand feet, where the temperature dropped like a stone, then headed inland and over the mountains. The views were incredible, and between the black and white clouds hanging in the deep blue sky they saw what MacLeod had warned them of, scattered patches of rainbows, or icebows as Cas had called them. They hung in tattered intensely colourful waves, as the sun reflected through ice crystals and made them stand out against the dark blue sky. It was beautiful, and quite mesmerising. It was the first time that Harriet had seen anything like it, and for the first time in as long as she could remember, she was at peace. Her mind was empty, and her heart was calm as she flew the Mosquito in graceful sweeps, marvelling at the sight and feeling as close to heaven as she thought possible.

"Were you paying attention when MacLeod showed us how to use the camera?" Harriet asked. Chloe looked at her and nodded, her eyes smiling as she recognised what Harriet wanted her to do. "I'll get us in the right position, you do your best to get some good photos."

"I'll do my best..." Chloe replied, as she took the camera from the brown leather case she'd kept slung around her neck, and fumbled with it to get it ready, while Harriet swung around and put the Mosquito on the perfect approach, so they could see the icebows highlighted almost perfectly by the clouds and blue sky, setting up Chloe for the perfect shot.

"Ready?"

"Ready..." Chloe took aim and clicked again and again as they passed, then took a few more shots as Harriet banked around and came back closer, this time flying nose first at the closest and largest icebow, until they were enveloped and passed through the transparent layer of ice crystals which made the sky seem milky once the colours had faded.

"I think that'll do us. Let's go home," Harriet said, and Chloe gave her a nod, then packed the camera away again as the Mosquito was taken for one last sweep of the clouds, before diving away to the south, and back home to the air station. They joined the circuit, and after calling in to control, Harriet put the Mosquito gently on the tarmac and taxied back to the dispersal, where Ollie was waiting for them. "Did you use all of the film in that camera?"

"Not quite. There's a few photos left; I think."

"Good. Do me a favour, would you?"

"I think I owe you more than one, so name it."

"If I stay up here, would you take a photo from outside?"

"Happy to!" Chloe smiled, and after Harriet's help unfastening her harness, she climbed down the steps that had been put against the cockpit by Ollie. She quickly made her way around the nose, then took out the camera and took a couple of photos while Harriet posed. Minutes later, Harriet had joined her, and after enlisting Ollie's help, she and Chloe had a photo taken together by the Mosquito.

"So, how was flying?" Harriet asked as they walked to the dispersal hut.

"I don't know what to say, I'm not sure I have the words..."

"You enjoyed it, though?"

"More than anything I've ever done."

"More than paperwork?"

"My God, yes!" Chloe laughed. "You've changed me, and if I'm a terrible clerk in the future, it's because I'll be dreaming of flying. Ma'am..." she added, as she remembered who she was talking to.

"I hoped that would be the answer," Harriet said with a smile. "Why don't you get off and go get some lunch while I take the camera back to MacLeod? You may as well have a long break; I think you've earned it."

"Thank you... What should I do if anyone asks where I've been?"

"What do you mean?"

"I don't know, was what you just did even allowed? Taking a clerk for a flight, I mean? I want to tell the world, but I don't want to get you into trouble."

"Tell anyone you like," Harriet smiled. "I needed a volunteer to crew for me on a meteorological flight, and as the squadron are all away on training, you were it."

"You're sure?" Chloe bounced with excitement.

"There have to be some benefits to working on my squadron, and I'm so bad at paperwork you're going to need every benefit we can offer!"

"I really can't thank you enough, Ma'am. I mean it, and I know you said not to call you Ma'am when there's nobody about, but it feels right. I respect you."

"I'll let it go this time," Harriet winked. "Besides, you wait until you get stuck into that paperwork. You'll hate the day you heard my name."

"I doubt that," Chloe laughed. "What shall I do with the flying kit?"

"Keep hold of it, you'll probably need it again. Besides, Hansen won't miss it. Apparently he was posted to Canada last month to instruct at the Norwegian training unit." She smirked as she talked. "One of the benefits of poor paperwork is that nobody knows he left yet. The beauty of it is that he won't even get billed for it, it'll just be added to the Norwegian government's tab. Better keep that part between us, though. I could probably get into trouble for that, especially with him..." Harriet pointed to Alastair's car as it pulled to a halt at the dispersal door.

"The secret's safe with me." She handed Harriet the camera with a wink.

"Good. Get yourself off, and I'll see you this afternoon."

"Good afternoon, Sir," Chloe said politely, yet formally, as she passed Alastair.

"Good afternoon..." he replied with a frown of confusion, as he watched her march away in her flying kit. "Harry, if I'm not too much mistaken, that looked remarkably like young Olivier. Your clerk..."

"She's been helping me out with a few things..."

"Things must have changed since I flew regularly, but I don't remember needing a clerk in the cockpit... Not to worry, I'm sure you'll tell me what you're up to when the time comes."

"Nothing untoward."

"No doubt. Is that a camera you have there?" He looked to the small brown leather case Harriet was holding.

"Yes," Harriet smiled as she looked at it. "It's Mister MacLeod's. He asked me to do some meteorological photography to help his forecasting research while we were up on an air test."

"Sounds interesting."

"Very... In fact, I was wondering if we could order a couple of cameras for the squadron? I know we have the photographic

125

reconnaissance flight, but they're usually tasked with much bigger projects. Having a camera handy may be useful."

"It's worth asking. I'm not sure what we'll be able to get hold of any, almost everything useful in terms of camera equipment has been sent to those who do photography for a living. I'll certainly see what I can do, though. No promises."

"Thank you."

"Good flight?"

"Incredible. I got some good photos of the weather front coming in from the north, hopefully they'll be helpful."

"Good show! Anyway, I suppose you're wondering why I turned up unannounced?"

"Not really, I thought it was a social visit."

"Oh Harry, you do make me smile; and yes, of course, I do intend to be a regular visitor as and when. However, I did have a reason to call in."

"Oh?" Harriet felt her stomach squeeze nervously for a moment, unsure of what to expect.

"Yes, it's a good job you didn't set off with your squadron, I have something of an errand for you."

"An errand? I'm not sure I understand."

"You will, Harry. You will... I need you to nip down to Northolt and collect a package."

"What sort of package?"

"A vital one, Harry. Something that's going to make a big difference to what we do here. You can probably get down there this afternoon if you go straight after lunch." He patted her firmly on the shoulder.

"Where did you find flying kit for Olivier? You've only been here five minutes..." He looked in the direction that Chloe had walked off into, still in her flight kit, reluctant to take it off until everyone she knew had seen her wearing it.

"Oh, it was just lying around. Left behind by one of the Norwegians who was posted out to Canada before I got here, I think."

"How very fortunate." He gave Harriet a knowing smile. "Give you a ride to the Mess for lunch?"

"Can we stop by meteorology so I can give MacLeod his camera?"

"I think we can do that."

After lunch, and a check of the charts to plot her course, Harriet was back in the air and heading south. The safest place for the journey was at altitude, up in the ice blue sky and far above the scattered light cloud. It was cold, but beautiful, and for a moment the brilliant blue and golden autumn sun had Harriet's mind flashing back to Malta, though the temperature prevented her from getting fully lost in the thoughts. It was cold, and despite the sheepskin boots and jacket, long underwear and sailor's roll neck pullover, the frosty air still nibbled a little when it got in through a crack somewhere. The air was clear, though, and there was no turbulence to distract from the smooth ride south with only the hum of the engines for company. It was an easy flight, and by running the engines within the parameters, but maintaining as much speed as possible, she was approaching London in the mid afternoon, and descending to pick up the landmarks, so she could find her way to RAF Northolt, a station she knew very well from her first steps into the RAF, when she was assessed for proficiency following her interview with the then AOC of 11 Group. Two years had passed since he'd put his faith in her, and given her a chance to prove herself as a pilot. It felt like a lifetime ago. Despite what had happened in France and at Dunkirk, she was still so innocent. She didn't know what she'd got herself into, and was trapped in a whirlwind of desperation, with the only focus being doing her part to stop the invasion, and prevent Britain going the same way as France and the Low Countries, and falling under the boot of the German war machine. Things had changed since, though the desperation was the same. Invasion seemed less likely, especially since the Russians were keeping German eyes to the east, though still not an impossible eventuality. Everything was on a knife edge, and the loss of North Africa, which she knew was imminently close, could change everything. For now, though, she had other things to think about, like collecting Alastair's package and getting back to Scotland before the cold front sunk lower across the country, as it was forecast to do, and brought some murky weather with it. The sooner she could get back, the sooner she could focus on her part in the war as it was, and try to slow down German coastal shipping.

After a smooth circuit watching a squadron of Spitfires take off and scurry in the direction of Kent, Harriet brought her Mosquito in for a gentle landing, before rolling to the line of visiting aircraft near the tower and shutting down. After going through her checks, she extracted herself and jumped down to the ground, where she straightened her hair and clothes, put on her service hat, then walked over to the tower to check in.

"Squadron Leader Cornwall, 373 Squadron," she said to the duty officer. "There's a package for me?"

"Yes, Ma'am," came the polite reply from the young Pilot Officer.

"I'll need fuel, I'm not staying."

"I'll arrange it, Ma'am." He nodded to the Sergeant, who disappeared to take care of it, while he picked up the phone. "Squadron Leader Cornwall has arrived from Scotland. Yes. Very well." He put the phone down and looked to Harriet. "If you'd like to take a seat, Ma'am, we'll have your aeroplane refuelled in no time."

"I've been sitting down all the way here; I need to stretch my legs. Is there anywhere I can get a cup of tea while I wait?"

"I'm sure we can make that happen, Ma'am."

"Thank you, and where's the bathroom?" She'd been crossing her legs for the last thirty minutes of her flight, and was desperate for the toilet. She'd thought back to her flight on the DC3 in America, and how amazed she'd been that there was a toilet on board, not to mention how shy she was at using it. Terrified she'd fall through the bottom of the aeroplane with her pants down, or worse, in her mind at least, the door would open and expose her to the main cabin. The duty officer gave her directions to the tower toilet, and after thanking him she went away to relieve her bladder, while thinking how different her visit was to the first time she'd landed, when a sullen and miserable duty officer had refused to take her seriously just because she was female, though he didn't treat Cas any better, much to his annoyance. She smiled at the memories. They were dangerous times, but better somehow. She was still fresh and new, and not the still tired and bony looking wretch she saw looking back at her in the bathroom mirror, with dark rings around her sunken eyes from endless months of fatigue. Rings which she was sure would remain a lifelong feature, as they weren't going anywhere fast despite the more settled sleep she'd had. After splashing her face and drying herself off, she returned to the watch room and collected a tin mug of warm tea, which she was very grateful for, then went outside to pace and stretch her legs in the warmth of the afternoon, while she waited for her package to arrive. "What on earth are you doing here?" Harriet exclaimed, as she turned and was faced with an unexpected sight that made her heart squeeze with happiness.

"Section Officer Russel reporting for duty, Ma'am." Ginny replied formally, with a smile and a salute.

"Stop being ridiculous!" Harriet replied sternly. "And answer my question. What are you doing here?"

"Going to Scotland, apparently..."

"What?"

"I was told to pack my bags and get down here right away, because some troublesome Squadron Leader requested me as their Adjutant. Don't act like you didn't know."

"I'd asked, but didn't expect I'd get what I wanted."

"Looks like you have friends in high places."

"Or your CO has had enough of you giving him a headache, and jumped at the chance to pack you off to the frozen north." Harriet couldn't stop herself from smiling, she was very happy to see her friend again.

"I had a good teacher... So, how do we get there?"

"In that," Harriet smirked as she pointed to the Mosquito.

"Oh..." Ginny's eyes opened wide, as she tried not to look too perplexed by the large fighter bomber in the near distance. "I didn't realise they had passenger cabins?"

"They don't. Your bags can go in the bomb bay, and you'll fly up front with me..." Harriet looked her up and down and frowned. "If you have trousers and long underwear, I'd probably go and put them on. It can get cold up there, and a skirt is hardly going to be comfortable." Ginny's eyes widened more as she nodded. "We'll get off as soon as they've finished refuelling her. I want to get back before dark, if I can."

"I'll be right back!" Ginny replied, then grabbed one of her bags and ran inside the tower, leaving Harriet to smile warmly to herself. She'd asked Alastair for Ginny; it was the only name she could think of when it came to organisation and knowing how the RAF worked. She'd hoped, but hadn't imagined it would happen. She smiled and made a note to thank Alastair with a large drink in the Mess. He'd worked wonders for her in the few days they'd been together. Her squadron were getting specialist training, she had an efficient clerk, and now she had an accomplished officer to run the show for her on the ground. Scotland had been a whirlwind so far, but it was all starting to come together, and her initial misgivings were a long way behind her. A thought came to her as she paced, and she quickly followed Ginny to the bathroom, where she stripped off her soft woollen roll neck pullover and gave it to her to wear for the flight. She had a sheepskin jacket to keep her warm, and while she'd be cooler without the pullover, Ginny would be even colder if she didn't have it. It was a small gesture, but one she hoped would help, and a few minutes later they both went back outside. Ginny looking every bit the part with the pullover under her tunic and greatcoat.

"All refuelled and ready to go, Ma'am," the duty officer said as he stepped outside to join her.

"Thank you," Harriet replied. "We'd better get going."

"Begging your pardon, Ma'am, but I thought it would be worth knowing that there a cold front coming down from the north, and bringing some weather on its leading edge. I thought it worth mentioning as you may want to hang around a while." Harriet looked at him, and to the sky. "We can arrange accommodation in the Mess?"

"Thanks, but I think we'll be OK. Worst case we can stop off in Yorkshire on the way home. I appreciate you letting me know."

"Ma'am." He saluted and smiled politely, then Harriet picked up one of Ginny's bags and started walking towards her Mosquito.

"I know you've flown before, Ginny Russel," Harriet called back. "But just in case you'd forgotten, the way it works is the aeroplane moves, not the airfield, so you need to be on it..." She smirked to herself as she walked, then glanced back to see Ginny rolling her eyes as she picked up her other bag and hurried to catch up.

"I hope I don't regret this."

"Regret what? I'm the one that asked for you, remember?"

"Regret being your friend..."

After loading Ginny's bags into the bomb bay, they climbed into the cockpit and Harriet strapped her friend into the navigator's seat ready for the flight home, something Ginny was particularly thankful for when they ran into the rapidly sinking leading edge of the cold front coming down from the north, which had reached northern England much quicker than had been forecast. The headwinds had strengthened, making progress a little slower than anticipated, but that was the least of the challenges the Mosquito had to face, as Harriet guided it through an unexpected storm that had enveloped them almost from nowhere. The cold front had collided with the warm moist air in the south, and the result was a rapid moving wall of black clouds that overtook the Mosquito and bounced it around like a ping pong ball, as the rain outside fell so heavy that it was impossible to see through the windscreen, and drips were finding their way through the cracks and into the cockpit, making Ginny worry increasingly, while Harriet fought hard to keep the aeroplane flying, at the same time as doing all she could to remain calm and appear as though there wasn't a thing to worry about. The truth was something significantly different. Harriet had flown through bad weather before, but the unexpectedly fierce clash of fronts was amongst the most dangerous and terrifying she'd experienced. She tried climbing to get above the clouds, without much luck, then considered trying to get under them, if she could, but she was over the hills of northern England, where the clouds would often descend into the valleys, meaning there was every chance of her flying the Mosquito straight into the side of a hill. Mid way through giving climbing another try, they passed out of the rear of the clouds, with the blackness disappearing behind them as fast as it had arrived, leaving them in cold and blustery, but otherwise clear skies.

"Being your friend isn't the only thing I regret..." Ginny said as she took a deep breath of relief.

"Stop being dramatic," Harriet replied with a casual shrug and a roll of her eyes. "It was only a rain shower..." She gave Ginny a wink, while smiling to herself and trying hard not to show how scared she'd been. To] maintain a positive exterior, she kept one hand on the stick and one on the throttle for a while, just until her hands stopped shaking.

Chapter 7

Blooded

By the time the squadron had returned from their training, Ginny and Chloe had processed and cleared the entire backlog of paperwork, quickly leading to the squadron increasing in efficiency almost overnight. New aircraft had been requisitioned, and new aircrews were on their way, with the promise that the squadron would be up to full strength by the end of October at the latest. In addition to the administration being back as it should be, the training that the aircrews had received at the hands of Archie and Nicole had given them a newfound confidence. Nicole and Archie had even flown north with them when they returned, so they could report back to Harriet on their performance, and have an impromptu drunken celebratory meal with Alastair, AP, and Ginny. The brief visit ended with some heavy hangovers, and a recently dispatched deer. which Alastair had acquired from a farmer who supplied the local pub, being loaded into the bomb bay of Archie and Nicole's Mosquito. It was very black market, and there would be trouble if they were found out, but it was agreed by all that one of the many deer that roam the Scottish hills wouldn't be missed too much. Nicole had promised Harriet that Aunt Mary would receive enough to keep her in stews, and Alastair had found a very nice bottle of scotch to thank Archie with. All in all, it had been a visit that everyone had enjoyed thoroughly, except for the hangovers.

Harriet had put the squadron through their paces on their return, and she was impressed at the vast improvements in handling and gunnery shown by all of the crews. The pilots and navigators themselves were proud, and all of them walked much taller than they had when she'd first arrived. It had only been just over a week, but the squadron was hardly recognisable from the one Harriet had found on her arrival, and she couldn't help but smile when she visited Alastair, and reported that they were now operational and ready to fly. An announcement which got them a mission to fly the very next morning, when Alastair intended to put his new strike force into action for the first time against a convoy that the Norwegian underground had reported to be gathering in the fjords, something confirmed by AP in an early evening reconnaissance flight.

After a sleepless night, during which Harriet had tossed and turned while trying hard not to think ahead to the mission, a forlorn attempt that had only led to her thinking of it more, she got up much earlier than she'd planned and got dressed in her warm flying clothing, before heading to the dispersal hut to have a cup of tea, and go through the flight planning again. She'd already spent all of the previous afternoon, and evening, going over the navigation, the plan, the routes, the weather, and every minute detail of what could be expected, so there wasn't really that much to check.

"You're here early," Ginny said, as she and Chloe arrived in the dispersal hut. They'd stopped via the Mess and collected flasks of hot tea and coffee for the crews to drink while they were briefed and prepared for their mission, along with a tray of homemade oat and honey biscuits that one of the chefs had prepared at Alastair's request. Something to keep them warm on a cold morning.

"I wanted to go over things one last time."

"You went over things one last time last night..."

"It doesn't hurt to be sure." Harriet looked over her chart again, while Chloe poured her a cup of tea and brought it over with a biscuit.

"Of course... Have you had breakfast yet?"

"Not yet."

"Are you going to?"

"Probably not."

"Why?"

"You're my adjutant, Section Officer Russel, not my mother." Harriet sighed and rolled her eyes as she sipped her tea and took a bite of her biscuit.

"It's the most important meal of the day."

"No, it isn't. That's a myth made up by an American woman to help sell breakfast cereals."

"What?"

"It's true, I learned it from a friend while I was over there. I even read the original article. She was a dietitian, or something like that, and had written it in a journal while she worked for Kellogg, the man who made the cereals..."

"Well, I never knew that."

"You learn something new every day."

"Well, fact or fiction, it can't hurt for you to eat before flying, can it?"

"You'd have to ask my navigator what he thinks."

"Why?"

"Because eating breakfast before a mission makes me sick, and I'm not sure how he'd feel about being covered in vomit."

"Charming..."

"You asked... Anyway, I'm off over to meteorology to check the morning's weather. I'll be back soon." Harriet shrugged and gave the frowning Ginny a smile. She headed out into the cold dark air, and sauntered through the silence with her hands in her pockets, her mind still focused on what lay ahead, and her desperate hopes that she'd done enough to prepare her crews for what was coming.

"Ah, Squadron Leader!" MacLeod greeted Harriet with a twinkle in his eyes, as she entered the meteorology office. She hadn't seen him

135

since the day he'd asked her to take a few photos of the cold front for him. He'd been called away to consult on a weather matter of some importance, leaving his students and assistant to advise in his absence.

"Good morning, Mister MacLeod. Do you have the morning's forecast for the Norwegian coast?"

"I do, and please call me Christopher."

"I will if you call me Harry."

"Of course, Harry. Now, before we get to the weather, there's something else I'd like to discuss with you..." He stood with his hands on his hips, and frowned in a way that made Harriet nervous.

"Yes?"

"The last time we talked, you were going to take some photos for me..."

"Oh... Didn't they come out? We did our best, and I'd hoped we'd got some good shots for you."

"They certainly did come out..." He gave a slow nod as he opened a folder. "As luck would have it, the camera was loaded with very expensive and very hard to get hold of colour film. Frankly, the stuff's like rocking horse droppings to get a hold of." Harriet started to blush as she remembered the impromptu photo shoot she and Chloe had indulged in after the flight, and wondered exactly how much she'd cost him in his expensive colour film. "Without it I'd never have seen such incredible sights." He burst into a smile, as he pulled out a large photo of an icebow standing bright on a blue sky. "Absolutely amazing!" he continued, as he showed her more photos. "I really can't thank you enough, Harry, you've helped my research no end, I'm indebted to you."

"My pleasure," she smiled with relief at his excitement, having expected a telling off.

"Though I'm hoping these will go some way to rewarding you." He gave her a knowing smile as he handed her another file, which she opened to reveal copies of her photo shoot, both colour and black and white, along with a few copies of the better shots of her icebows. "I made a copy each for you and your observer, and a couple for you to send to family."

"Thank you!" Her smile stretched across her face as she looked at the photos. "Really... Thank you so much."

"My pleasure. It's a minor misuse of Air Ministry resources, but if you need any more copies, just ask... Now, your weather report."

"We'll be off before first light, hoping to hit the Norwegian coast around sunrise."

"Well, there doesn't seem to be too much to worry about, other than the absence of cloud to hide in. There's a relatively strong easterly wind blowing and whipping up the sea, though it shouldn't cause you much of a problem, unless you plan on doing a spot of swimming while you're out and about."

"I'd rather not."

"Should be fine in that case, I've written up a report you can take back to your chaps. Good luck."

Harriet returned to the now bustling dispersal hut, and her office, where she left her photos in her drawer before briefing the aircrews on the mission and the weather report, and going through the route one last time with Eskimo, her navigator, and the lead navigator for the mission. Then, after a visit from Alastair to wish everyone good luck, and a phone call to the Beaufighter squadron to confirm they were ready for the off, it was to the aeroplanes to go through the checks and make sure all was set. Harriet sat tight in the soft glow of the instruments and checked her watch repeatedly, waiting impatiently until the hands finally swept into place for her to start the engines, which she did one by one. After checking the gauges, and satisfying herself that everything was as it should be, she led the squadron to the end of the runway, and then into the dark inky blue

137

moonlit sky, where she circled before forming up and heading east, with the Beaufighter squadron due to follow not far behind.

Eskimo navigated them through the darkness perfectly, keeping a keen eye on his watch, the compass, and his map, and making allowances in timings for the wind. AP's familiar call sign, Valkyrie, sent them a short morse code message shortly before the Norwegian coast was scheduled to come over the horizon, giving them a course correction that would put them right on top of the convoy, and warning of six flak ships escorting as many well loaded merchant ships sitting low in the water. Harriet followed the coordinates until the convoy was given away by the smudges of smoke from the funnels, squiggled into the distant sky, making her stomach tighten as she prepared herself for what would come next.

"Viking squadron, combat positions," Harriet instructed, then watched left and right as the Mosquitoes split into a line abreast of four loose pairs, the attack formation Harriet had taught them, and Archie's team had drilled into them. "Work in your pairs, and focus on one ship at a time, aim for the guns and try to keep their focus off the Beaufighters." Call after call of 'Wilco' came from the other aircraft, confirming her instructions. "OK, here goes. Valkyrie, you'd better get out of here, things are about to heat up. Broadsword squadron, follow us in, and we'll try to keep them busy. Tally Ho!" They raced towards the ships, skimming the waves as they closed on the front of the convoy which, to Harriet's surprise, hadn't caught sight of the approaching Mosquitoes. She felt every muscle tense as she waited for what she knew was coming. She'd seen it in Malta, both from the air and from the sea, and she knew that any second the world was going to explode. The black hulls of the ships came closer, and right on cue the sky lit up as lines of green tracer from the leading flak ship arced towards them. To get more guns on the approaching raiders, the pitching and rolling flak ships turned left and right, and the sky quickly turned into a mesh of anti aircraft tracer crisscrossing in every direction, but not quite getting low enough to intercept their attackers. Harriet had pulled her squadron so low that spray from the rolling waves was soaking her windscreen, making them a difficult target. As the ships rolled, their gunners could get on target, however briefly, and glowing lines of tracer converged on Harriet's Mosquito. She didn't flinch, just kept the ship in her

138

sights, and as soon as she was in range she pushed the fire button, and felt the vibrations through her seat as the four cannons and four machine guns buzzed into life. Round after round slammed into the ship both above and below the waterline, while miraculously the enemy anti aircraft fire danced all around, but not one of them were able to get her in their sites. "Now!" She shouted at Eskimo, as she pulled up to avoid crashing into the flak ship, and immediately he did as he was taught, and released the bombs from the open bomb bay, slinging them at the black hull of the ship. Seconds later, the Mosquito was rocked as the dim early morning sky was lit by a glowing orange light, and huge geysers of water were thrown into the air as the scattering of bombs destroyed the flak ship, sending shrapnel in every direction. Harriet had to pull hard on the controls to keep the Mosquito upright, as the tail lifted and rolled, trying to flip the aeroplane over. As she pulled up and away from the blast, another of the flak ships was more successful in targeting her, and a hole was blown in the side of the cockpit, sending a scattering of shrapnel into her leg and hand, and blowing the window out to her right, the shell narrowly missing Eskimo on the way. She released the pressure on the controls for a moment as she opened the throttle, and the Mosquito instinctively rolled, pulling the nose hard right, and in line with another flak ship that was turning tight to get as many guns as possible on the raiders. She pushed the fire button again and strafed the decks, hitting a couple of the gun positions, and putting one entirely out of action, before she pulled hard on the controls again and climbed over the ship, drawing its fire, and keeping the gunners from focusing on the other Mosquito coming at it low and fast from out of Harriet's shadow. She kicked hard on the rudder bar and pushed the controls the opposite way to where they wanted to go, and started a shallow bank just in time to see the Mosquito throw its bombs at the ship. They straddled it, sending huge plumes of water into the sky, and knocking a hole in the side while simultaneously starting a fire as the Mosquito pulled up and over, shooting all the time. As she continued to bank and climb, she got a good view of the convoy, the Mosquitoes were among the ships and causing chaos with the escorts, keeping low and moving in fast and unpredictable ways, desperately trying to avoid the mesh of tracer. It was deadly, but it was working, and the defenders didn't see Broadsword, the squadron of torpedo laden Beaufighters, as they raced into the fray. Two of the six merchant ships went up in flames almost immediately, and another blew apart in such a ferocious explosion that Harriet felt the shockwaves, as she fought to keep her already battered Mosquito from falling out of the sky. She noticed one of the flak ships was getting the range of a Beaufighter, and quickly pushed her Mosquito's nose down and ran at it, raking the decks from tip to stern with cannons and machine guns, hitting one of the anti aircraft guns, and ravaging the bridge as she passed overhead, and distracted the crew long enough for the Beaufighter to make its escape.

"Look out, bandits coming out of the sun!" AP's voice cut through the noise on the airwaves.

"Viking squadron, bandits coming out of the sun! Break, break, break!" Harriet repeated, and the Mosquitoes immediately went into action, turning nose to the sun and ready to face what was coming down, which Harriet soon recognised to be Focke Wolf 190s, the fast, heavily armed, and agile German fighters that had been running rings around allied aircraft since they'd arrived in the war, and made previous versions of the Spitfire obsolete overnight. She pushed the throttles fully open as she climbed to meet them, with another Mosquito coming up on her left wing and joining her in the climb. "Valkyrie, get the hell out of here!" she shouted at AP, as she saw the blue Mosquito high above them.

"On my way!" AP replied.

"Viking squadron, don't hang around too long, break and home as soon as you can! Tally Ho!" She pushed her fire button as the leading 190 let loose with a stream of tracer that zipped past her cockpit, close enough to singe the paint to the left of her head. The Mosquito next to her hit home, and the same 190 exploded in mid air, and Harriet had to roll hard right to avoid the glowing engine as it shot downwards like a meteorite, followed by a shower of other shrapnel. A 190 passed in front of her and she severed its tail with her still blasting cannons and guns, sending it spinning into the sea as she sped under the others following close behind it, too tight to adjust their angles of attack to get their guns on her. The other Mosquito had broken left at the same time, and both came around in a wide arc to have another blast at the remaining four 190s, who had continued their dive into the fray, but were already quickly being overwhelmed by the fast and powerful Mosquitoes, while the Beaufighters dropped to the waves and ran for home. What remained was a very one sided battle, and after another 190 was knocked down, the remaining three turned tail and fled with a pair of Mosquitoes chasing hard behind, determined to catch at least the one that was already trailing smoke behind it. "That's enough!" Harriet shouted. "Break off, and head home!" Both Mosquitoes responded immediately, and rolled away from their chase, leaving the lucky three to speed back to their airfield in Norway. Harriet joined them after circling once more to make sure the enemy had genuinely had enough for the morning. "Are you OK?" Harriet asked Eskimo, as she satisfied herself nobody was going to come back for round two.

"I think so," he replied breathlessly. His oxygen mask had been slashed by the shrapnel, as had his Mae West, though there was no sign of any blood. "Are you?"

"I'm fine," she said, as she looked at the bloodied flying glove covering her left hand, and the holes in the left leg of her trousers, which were now damp with blood. Both were out of sight for Eskimo, and she thought it best not to worry him. She was hurting, but not worried. The bigger concern was the Mosquito's handling. It had taken a battering, and it was becoming a hard fight to keep it level, keeping MacLeod's quip about swimming home close to the front of her mind. The concern didn't get any less when the left engine started to overheat, and she had to back off the throttle, before finally having to shut it down and slow down her run for home, which left her a long way behind the others, who quickly became dots in the distance.

"Will we make it?" Eskimo asked nervously, unable to keep the worry from his voice.

"Yes," Harriet replied confidently. "Mossies can fly well enough on one engine. We'll be fine, just a little late." She looked over to the left engine as the propeller windmilled uselessly in the airflow, while the remaining engine did its best to get them home. Her adrenaline had been flowing on overdrive since they'd spotted the convoy, and it wasn't easing. Her heart was pounding as a hundred and one thoughts went through her head, mostly planning for how she'd ditch, and how they'd survive. The wind was strengthening, and the sea was very bumpy to say the least, which had helped the attack on the convoy, particularly in making it hard for the gunners to target properly as they pitched and rolled, but the weather was now becoming more of an enemy than friend, as she considered how hard it was going to be to land on the water without tipping over and drowning them both. One of the Air Sea Rescue floats passed below, bobbing in the waves, and she gave a thought to whether she should press on, or put down close to it, knowing at least they'd have a chance. She didn't go through with it though, the one engine was still doing a good job, and by Eskimo's calculations they were about half an hour from the coast, helped along with a strong back wind pushing them through the air to safety. Finally, after what felt like hours, the Scottish coast came into sight, and Harriet started going through her checks. Her arms, shoulders, neck, and back were tight from fighting the controls all the way home, and her injured leg was cold and shivering, making it hard to keep pressure on the rudder bar. It was going to be hard work landing, and she didn't feel like she had the time or strength to do a circuit, so she called up the tower and told them she was coming in on one engine. She scrubbed off all the speed she dared, then guided the Mosquito onto the runway, shutting off the power and fuel as soon as she was sure she was safe, determined not to have the two mix if she landed heavy and came to a crushing halt. The fire crew and ambulance were at the ready, and followed her to the dispersal, where Alastair and AP were waiting for her, along with the rest of her squadron. "There, told you we'd make it," she said with a wink to Eskimo, who nodded and gave her a big smile in reply, while pushing the hatch open and unfastening his harness. "Go on, I'll be out in a minute," she said, and he quickly removed himself from the cockpit, having thrown his flight bag out first. The moment he was gone, Harriet pulled off her flying helmet and rested her head against the rest, closing her eyes for a moment and taking a few deep breaths, before looking around at the holes in the cockpit. The adrenaline was starting to wear off, and she was exhausted and shaking, though she wasn't sure whether it was the cold or the fear that was causing it.

"Everything OK?" Alastair asked, as he popped his head in through the cockpit door.

"What?" Harriet replied, as he startled her from her thoughts. "Yes..." She gave him a forced smile, then fiddled with her harness, and let out a gasp as a stabbing pain cut through the cold of her left hand.

"What's up, old man?" He climbed into the cockpit and looked at her. "Bloody hell, you're hit!"

"No... No, I'll be OK," she protested, then tried to lift up, and let out a Yelp as she felt a searing pain in her thigh.

"You will be!" He backed out of the cockpit and shouted for the ambulance, then came back to help her out of her seat, and gently moved her to the cockpit door while stepping down the ladder, and guiding her down with the help of AP, Pietersen, and a few of the others who'd arrived to see what was wrong.

"What happened? Are you OK?" AP demanded, as Alastair and Pietersen stood either side with their arms around her, holding her upright while she gasped at the pain. "Is she going to be OK?" she asked Alastair, before Harriet even had a chance to answer.

"I'll be fine after a cup of tea," Harriet replied with a wince and a half laugh, though she was well aware that the laugh was for the audience, and not entirely convincing.

"Go with her to the medical centre," Alastair said to AP, as the ambulance pulled up and she was loaded inside. AP nodded and jumped aboard, sitting beside Harriet as the doors were slammed closed and she was rushed to the medical centre, where the Station Medical Officer was waiting for her.

"What happened?" the SMO asked, as Harriet was carried into his clinic. He was a gruff older man, with steely eyes, and a sharp Scottish accent that made is words all the more cutting, even when he was being pleasant. Harriet had met him briefly in the Mess and found him very intimidating. Tall, with short grey hair and matching moustache, he reminded her of an angry headmaster, and even though she didn't really know him, she'd given him a wide berth.

"She was hit by flak," AP replied.

"I see. Well, get her on the bed and let's have a look at the wounds. Nurse!" The orderlies lifted Harriet from the stretcher and laid her on his inclined operating table, then quickly left as a pair of nurses got busy cutting away the left thigh of her trousers and long johns, and the brown leather glove from her left hand.

"Has she lost consciousness?"

"I don't think so, she managed to fly all the way back."

"I see... Did she report any loss of movement or feeling?"

"You know, I am able to talk for myself," Harriet said through gritted teeth, as the cold of flying a Mosquito with large holes in the airframe at over three hundred miles per hour through the wind and sea spray thawed a little, and the pain of the wounds started to bite, more so as the nurses cut and pulled at the fabric that had stuck to her flesh as her blood had dried.

"Well?"

"Well, what?"

"Did you hit your head as well?"

"What? No!"

"Then did you lose consciousness, or any feeling, or movement?"

"Numb from the cold, that's all..." She looked to AP, who rolled her eyes casually and shook her head. "Though it hurts a bit now."

"Good. Right, thigh first. Let's make sure we haven't hit an artery. Nurse, clean up that hand and I'll get to it in a moment." Harriet looked to her hand, it was bloody with shards of metal sticking from it, but not as bad as her thigh, which was slashed and cut with a stubble of shrapnel sticking out along the left side of her leg from hip to knee. She winced as the second nurse handed him a syringe, and he injected her close to the wound, then poured a saline solution over the cuts and gashes, which stung and made her bite her tongue until the anaesthetic did its job and numbed her flesh. The SMO then took some forceps and gripped a sliver of metal, then wiggled to release it before pulling it from her thigh. It had gone deep, and despite the pain being dulled, she felt her spasming muscle grip it tight and fight to stop it being removed. Finally, with a sickening, sucking pop, it was out. The SMO held it up so she could see it. It was longer than her finger, and almost as thick, and covered in thick, dark red blood. She felt a little dizzy and laid her head back, as he smirked and dropped it with a metallic clang into the tray the nurse was holding. He then prodded and checked, to make sure the long piece of sharp metal hadn't nicked an artery, then he moved on to the next piece, and the next. She felt sick, and started to shiver as the shock set in. AP stood with her hand on Harriet's shoulder, comforting her as best she could. Harriet grabbed her hand as a particularly well lodged splinter was removed from her flesh, after grinding against her thigh bone as the SMO wiggled it free.

"It's alright, not much more..." AP said. "Do you think we could get a blanket?" she asked. As she noticed Harriet shivering.

"Nurse, blanket," the SMO instructed, and a thick white woollen blanket was wrapped around Harriet's torso. "Right, I think that's all of it. Clean and close." He moved up to her hand, and first looked into Harriet's eyes and gave her a warming wink, then started prodding at her flesh. "This shouldn't be as bad," he said, then gave the wound another shot, and a spray of saline, then with his pliers he removed a wide sliver of metal from the middle of the back of her hand with another sucking pop. "An inch higher, and a little either way, and you'd have lost a finger," he said casually. "A few inches lower and it would have got your artery, you were lucky!" Harriet nodded, and bit her tongue as her hand and thigh throbbed in unison. The cold was deep in her bones, or so it felt, and a deep nausea set in, alongside a tiredness that made it a struggle to keep her eyes open. The SMO continued his work, while the nurse expertly cleaned her thigh and stitched the gashes, before moving up to do the same for her hand while the SMO got out of the way, and the second nurse moved close and started to dress the cleaned and sutured wounds. "There, done... How are you feeling?" he asked as he returned to Harriet's side.

"Cold and sick," she replied.

"Yes, I expect you would. That'll be the shock kicking in. You know, you were pretty lucky, young lady." He showed her the tin container holding a mesh of bloody metal and wood slivers and splinters. "Any one of those could have nicked an artery, and a few were damned close, and you'd have bled out long before getting home. As it is, there's just a bit of soft tissue damage as far as I can see. It's going to hurt like hell for a few days, and it'll take a while for you to be able to use your hand properly, not to mention the limp you're going to have, but I don't imagine there's any permanent damage."

"Thank you," Harriet gasped, then laid her head back against the inclined table, taking a deep breath to stop the dizziness that was taking over her.

"Not at all. Buy me a whisky the next time we're in the Mess, and we'll call it even." He gave her another wink, and Harriet forced a smile through her discomfort. "The nurses will finish patching you up. I'll see if I can rustle up a cup of sweet tea for you, that should sort the chills and nausea, then we'll see about getting you bedded down." Harriet nodded as he left, then she looked up to AP.

"Thanks for staying with me."

"Don't be stupid, where else would I be?"

"I don't know..."

"There you go, then!" She gave Harriet a stern look, then a half smile that turned up just the corners of her mouth. "Anyway, I wanted to make sure you were OK, so I could kill you myself!"

"What? What did I do?" Harriet protested, her head still swimming with waves of dizziness.

"Flew like a maniac and almost got yourself killed, that's what!"

146

"Sorry..."

"I mean it! I watched you go in at that ship, you got so close you put your bomb right down the Captain's throat!" She frowned at Harriet, who couldn't help smiling at the image. "You didn't have to take the paint off to get a good shot."

"I wanted to make sure..."

"Make sure of what?"

"Make sure I was on target."

"Is that all?"

"And make sure the squadron saw me do it, so they would be confident when it was their turn. If a girl can do it, anyone can, right?"

"You're an idiot!" AP hissed, as she squeezed Harriet's shoulder warmly. "It wouldn't have given them confidence if you'd been hit, would it?"

"It would have shown them I wasn't afraid," Harriet shrugged.

"You've got to have brains to be scared. They haven't known you as long as me, and don't know that you've got nothing between your ears except hot air!"

"Shut up..." Harriet let out a laugh, which somehow caused a pain in her leg that made her gasp as the nurses finished dressing her wounds.

"Seriously, are you going to be OK?"

"Yeah... You heard him, could be worse."

"I suppose..."

147

"Did everyone else make it back?"

"Surprisingly, yes. A few got shot up a bit, but nothing serious. They were full of themselves when they landed, until they realised you weren't with them. They wouldn't leave the dispersal, even when Alastair tried to stand them down, not until they knew you were safe."

"They need to stop doing things like that, they're too soft!" Harriet frowned in discomfort at the thought of people waiting for her and worrying for her. "You all do. I'll be fine, I always am."

"Yes, you look it..." AP looked at Harriet's now dressed wounds with a raised eyebrow. "Anyway, you don't get to choose who cares about you, so stop complaining."

"Shut up... Anyway, it would have been worse if you hadn't warned us about those fighters. I hadn't seen them, and they'd have been on us if you hadn't shouted."

"Happy to help."

"You know that you shouldn't have even been there, though. You were unarmed, and had no business hanging around in a battle, especially when fighters were getting stuck in."

"I'm fine."

"This time."

"Don't try and turn this on me, you're the hot head who flew headfirst into a wall of flak, not me. I stayed up high where it was safe."

"Don't you have somewhere to be?"

"Not really..."

"Good..." Harriet smiled, and reached up and squeezed AP's hand again. "I'll try not to be as hot headed in the future."

148

"Good luck."

Chapter 8

Jolly Hockey Sticks

"What are you doing here?" Ginny asked with a frown, as Harriet limped slowly into the dispersal hut. Her trouser leg was in tatters, held together with safety pins, and wrapped in a bandage, and her left hand was bandaged and in a sling.

"I work here," Harriet casually replied.

"I'm quite sure you're supposed to be in hospital."

"I'm quite sure I don't care."

"Harry!"

"Ginny!"

"Seriously, are you well enough to be here? Alastair called and said you'd be staying in the medical centre overnight while you recuperate."

"I got bored."

"That doesn't answer my question!"

"Still don't care... Now, how about a cup of tea? It's freezing out there."

"You're incorrigible."

"Thanks."

"It's not a compliment."

"It feels like one."

"I despair."

"What were the results?" Harriet asked, as she lowered herself into one of the deep leather armchairs in the otherwise abandoned dispersal hut.

"Three of the six merchant ships went down, with two more badly damaged, along with four of the flak ships sunk." Ginny smiled as she gave the news, while pouring Harriet a cup of tea from the urn. "Alastair's over the moon with the results."

"Losses?"

"Not one. A few of the Beaufighters were shot up, but nothing to write home about." She handed Harriet the cup, then sat opposite with her own. "It was a huge success, a report's already gone up to Coastal Command HQ."

"Good." Harriet smirked to herself contently as she sipped the tea.

"Apparently, somebody put the fear of god into the Germans, and whipped our little gang of Vikings into a frenzy," Ginny said casually, with a raised eyebrow. Harriet shrugged and continued smiling, pleased with the outcome, and proud of having done it right.

"Where is everyone?"

"Alastair stood them down. A Flight are down at the Mess on thirty minute standby, just in case anything pops up, but he gave the rest the day off. Besides, some of the planes were shot up and need some work before they go up again, and it seemed pointless keeping the boys hanging around."

"Aeroplanes."

"Yes, those. So, how are you? Other than being in need of some new trousers?" She nodded at Harriet's leg, making her blush as she looked down to see the mess she was in.

"I've been worse..."

"Somehow, I believe that. Anyway, I'm happy to know you're safe. Your navigator was pale when he got back. Said something about you being a devil. At least that's what I think he said. Parts of it were in Norwegian, which isn't my strong suit, so it could have been anything, I suppose."

"That all sounds a little bit excessive, you were probably confused."

"Of course, not being Norwegian I tend to struggle with words like devil. Though I'm not a fighter pilot either, so it could be a technical term I didn't pick up when learning to fly in my old Tiger Moth... Oh well, want me to order you some new trousers?"

"I suppose..." Harriet looked down at her bandaged leg and shrugged. "I'll get you the address of my tailor, he has my measurements."

"I'll get it sorted while you sleep."

"While I what?"

"Sleep? You were up in the middle of the night and flying this morning, isn't the usual routine to go and sleep it off?"

"I'm fine. I have a mission report to write, among other things."

"Are you sure it can't wait until tomorrow? There's nothing much else that needs doing that I can't do for you, and you should really get some sleep..."

"Well, Section Officer Russel, you don't get to tell me what to do, so you'll have to put up with me a little longer," Harriet smirked smugly. A smirk which was quickly replaced by a frown as the door opened, and Alastair strode into the dispersal hut.

"No, but he does..." Ginny replied with an innocent smile.

"Ah, there you are, Harry old man! You naughty thing!"

"You told him I was here?" Harriet narrowed her eyes as she stared at Ginny, who simply shrugged in reply.

"I thought you'd head here! The SMO told me his patient discharged herself as soon as his back was turned, so I had young Ginny on standby!"

"The medical centre was making me feel nauseous, it was that clinical smell which seems to hang around," Harriet replied, as Alastair stood between them with his hands on his hips.

"I do get your meaning, old man, I'm not a fan of the place myself. Though that doesn't excuse you being a poor patient."

"I'm fine, really," Harriet protested innocently.

"Yes, the SMO said you'd say that. The wonders of modern medicine, apparently."

"I had a few scratches, that's all. I hardly think that's enough to keep me in a hospital bed. Besides, you know how bossy nurses can be."

"I do, and I know how bossy I can be when the mood takes me. Come on." He held out his hand, which Harriet frowned at before taking, and being pulled from her chair.

"Where are we going?"

"If you won't stay in the medical centre, you can stay in your digs. You too, Miss Russel. You can stand guard, with my personal authority to tie her to her bed if she tries to leave before breakfast tomorrow."

"Happy to, Sir," Ginny replied politely, as she stood and went to get her coat, giving Harriet a sly smirk on the way.

"I don't know why I asked for you," Harriet scowled.

"Oh, don't be like that, Harry. You'll be glad of her when the drugs the SMO gave you wear off." He helped her limp out to her car, and with Ginny's help got her onto the back seat, despite her leg quickly stiffening and making it difficult to bend. "Right, take the Squadron Leader back to her digs, and no stopping on the way. No matter what she says!" he said to the driver. "Well done today, Harry. You did a sterling job!" He gave her a warm smile which melted her frown a little. "Get some rest, you've earned it." He then looked to Ginny. "Remember, tie her to the bed if she gives you any trouble, my orders."

"With pleasure, Sir." Ginny smirked at Harriet, who rolled her eyes in reply.

"I'm not entirely sure you can tell her to do that," Harriet added with a sigh.

"Of course I can!" Alastair laughed. "I'm a Group Captain, I can tell her to do anything I like. Now, no more delaying tactics, off you pop!" He slammed the door closed and tapped the roof, then watched as the WAAF drove them away, through the station and out along the winding country roads.

"I can't believe you took his side," Harriet said to Ginny.

"You heard him, he's a Group Captain, what could I do? I was hardly going to say no when he called the dispersal and told me to keep an eye out for you. He'd have sent me back down south to torment the WAAFs, and that wouldn't do."

"Wouldn't it?"

"Not really. The old Station Commander didn't really take to me, though he was quite clear in saying it wasn't my fault. Apparently I was doing just fine until I met you."

"This again? I'm not sure what I did to get up his nose so much."

"You're not?"

"Not entirely..." Harriet smirked a little, as did Ginny. "Thanks..."

"For what?"

"Taking Alastair's side and telling him where to find me."

"He knew all too well where to find you, I'm just happy you didn't decide you were going flying before he got there. That would have been awkward."

"There's a thought..."

"Foot down, driver!" Ginny instructed, and the young WAAF smiled at her in the rear view mirror.

"I don't see why I couldn't have stayed at the dispersal," Harriet complained, as Ginny helped her through the door of her cottage.

"I don't see why you'd want to. You apparently live in the most beautiful cottage in Scotland, and you want to sit in a tobacco stained dispersal hut that smells of pipe smoke and aviation fuel," Ginny replied with a frown as she looked around.

"I could have written my combat report..."

"You know the squadron had been stood down, and nothing was going to happen, don't you?"

"I know..."

"Just checking. Right, do you want a hand getting out of your uniform?"

"Not necessary."

"You're sure?"

"Quite. Don't worry, I won't climb out of the window and run away."

"Should I stand guard just in case? You know Alastair gave me permission..."

"Behave!" Harriet laughed. "The range should be warm; you could make us a cup of tea if you want something to do? I brought some of the good stuff with me from Fortnum's."

"In that case, I'll get busy. Don't be long, or I'll need to send a search party." She gave Harriet a wink, then went through to the kitchen while Harriet limped uncomfortably into her room.

"Don't be long..." Harriet muttered to herself, while biting her lip as she closed the door and leant against it for a moment. Her leg was aching deep to the bone, it was more uncomfortable than painful, but the discomfort was nagging and continuous, until she tried to use her leg normally by putting pressure on it, and then the pain had a direct line to the centre of her brain. She took a breath, then pulled off her uniform one piece at a time, while getting frustrated with not being able to use her hand properly. She dumped it all in a corner, except her long white woollen socks, which she kept on as the floor was cold, then she pulled on a dress before shuffling her way to the living room, where Ginny was relaxing in one of the soft leather chairs and sipping her tea. "Get lost in there?" she asked with a mischievous smile. "I was about to send out a search party."

"Shut up!" Harriet barked, as she lowered herself uncomfortably onto the couch. "Getting undressed with one hand isn't as easy as you'd imagine."

"I'd imagine it to be awkward."

"It was..."

"I put a couple of logs on the fire, it should warm up soon."

"Thank you, and for the tea." Harriet lifted her cup and sipped at it, feeling the hot tea warming her insides and refreshing her mouth, which had a distinct metallic taste since she'd landed.

"You're welcome. You've got good taste in tea, I'll come here again."

"I'm grateful for you getting me home... Now I'm out of my uniform, I'm starting to realise how tired I am."

"Why do you do it?" Ginny asked after a while, the mischief gone from her voice, and replaced with a soft genuineness that was rarely heard.

"Do what?"

"Push yourself so hard... Archie told me what it was like when you and he used to fly together. He said you were unstoppable, always leading from the front, and always the last to give up and go home, even when you were exhausted."

"Archie exaggerates, you know what he's like," Harriet replied with an uncomfortable smile.

"I do know what he's like, and I know what he meant when he talked about you. I'd see it when we worked together at the training depot. I'd just assumed you had a strict work ethic, and liked to do a good job where others would cut corners and take it easy, but seeing you on the squadron is different. It's more than that, isn't it? More than just doing your job properly?"

"If only it was that simple," Harriet sighed. Her brain was starting to slow as she finally let herself relax.

"What do you mean?"

"How many female Squadron Leaders do you know of?"

"Just the one."

"Exactly. There aren't that many more female pilots of any rank. Like it or not, we need to do it better and sharper than anyone else. If we don't, they'll stop us."

"I know... Still, you can't keep going all the time, not like this. Even machines need switching off sometimes, or they'll burn out."

"I'm wearing a dress and woolly socks, and laying on my couch with my feet up at lunchtime, how much more switched off do you think

I need to be?" Harriet let out a long sighing yawn as she finished talking, and stretched her arms out wide.

"A little more, apparently," Ginny giggled.

"Apparently..." Harriet yawned again, as a wave of tiredness hit her like a wall, and forced her to slump down the couch and lay her head on the soft feather pillow.

"Tired?"

"A little, yes..."

"Why don't you have a snooze?"

"I think I will, just for a short while."

Having been made acutely aware of the dangers of raiding a convoy, mostly by the nagging pain in her thigh and hand that she downplayed as much as possible, Harriet spent her enforced recovery time with her head buried in the books, crunching numbers, and using her mathematical prowess in an attempt to reduce the chances of being injured the next time they went into battle. It was the only thing she could do to stay sane. Alastair had been quite firm in grounding her until she was recovered, and the SMO had given his personal authority to fly again, something he'd withheld for a week despite her best efforts to pretend the wounds didn't hurt. Despite being injured, and grounded, the squadron still had a training programme to follow, more low flying, and visits to the gunnery and bombing ranges to help prepare them for the mystery job Alastair had briefed her about when she'd first arrived. To help her keep control of the squadron, and the schedule, while keeping her out of the cockpit of a Mosquito, Alastair had put an Anson and pilot at her disposal, and she spent many hours sitting high above the training areas and watching the Mosquitoes perfect the training they'd started in Yorkshire, while she gave instructions over the radio. She took Ginny and Chloe with her most of the time, so they could help spot and keep track of the training, and when she could, she'd take the ground crews up too, giving many of them a rare opportunity to see the aeroplanes they worked so hard to maintain in action.

As part of her number crunching, Harriet had several conversations with the intelligence section, a team of specialists who spent most of their time analysing AP's reconnaissance photos, and they were able to give her the details of the anti aircraft guns the Germans were using. Mostly they were a mix of quad mounted 20mm guns, single 37mm guns, and the occasional very deadly 88mm, a gun used to throw heavy explosive shells six miles into the sky at a rate of fifteen rounds per minute. Following her intelligence gathering exercise, she met with the commander of the local anti aircraft battery and learned all she could about effective distances, rates of fire and reload times, before sitting down with all of her new information and a pencil and paper, and working through the calculations which would give her the answers she needed. Once done, she'd twisted Alastair's arm to give her permission to fly, and then have the anti aircraft guns on the coast target her and fire in anger while she tested her theory which, to her relief, showed that if she circled two and a half miles from the British equivalent of the 37mm guns, the shots would fall off and miss, and the same would happen with the 20mm at a little over a mile. This left only the 88mm to think about, and in her experience it was pointless worrying about that, the reload and firing rate was lower than the others, and there weren't that many of them on flak ships, and most importantly, if it hit you, you wouldn't know a thing about it. Once she was sure of her calculations, she led the squadron in a live firing training mission to prove her theory and settle their nerves, a mission Alastair asked to accompany her on as her observer; and to her smug satisfaction the Mosquitoes circled safely while flak flew at them just out of range. Despite the apparent danger, Alastair didn't stop smiling the entire time.

Shortly after proving her theory, the squadron was tasked on another raid against a convoy that was making a run down the coast, under the cover of some changeable weather. AP had found them hugging the coast, after the Norwegian resistance had sent a radio message announcing their departure from the fjords; five heavily laden merchant ships escorted by eight flak ships, and four torpedo boats, along with a rarely seen destroyer of the Kriegsmarine for company. The Germans were obviously keen to avoid another savaging, and hoped the extra guns would do the job. AP had also reported seaplane patrols circling above the convoy, watching for incoming raids, and no doubt in contact with a swarm of fighters waiting to spring into action, two of which had appeared from nowhere and chased AP halfway home, getting in a few shots which rattled her fuselage and made it a close run thing. Despite the increase in escort ships, Harriet's plan paid off. After making sure they'd been seen approaching, she led her Mosquitoes into a circle two and a half miles out, as the entire German convoy erupted into life, exactly as they had done the previous time, with every gun firing in a desperate attempt to put up a wall of flak and keep the raiders at bay. Then it happened, just as Harriet had calculated, the guns slowed to a chatter as they needed to reload, and that's when she gave the signal. She'd timed it perfectly, and the Mosquitoes were among the convoy and tearing up the flak ships before the guns could get going again in any sort of coordinated way. Cannons, guns, and bombs ripped the escorts to pieces, and while they were kept busy, the Beaufighters raced in and set their sights on the merchant ships, releasing their torpedoes at short range, and sinking ship after ship. The sky was soon thick with black oily smoke, which was lit by the red and green flashes of tracer rounds as the remaining escorts did what they could to maintain a defence, and in the chaos it had been difficult to see the swarm of Focke Wulf 190 fighters joining the mix at low level, having skipped over the cliffs, and approached as low as they dare, to make it difficult to be seen. Difficult, but not impossible, and Pietersen had caught sight of them just before they reached the battle. The raid broke off and away just in time. The Beaufighters had already made their escape under the cover of the mayhem caused by the Mosquitoes, turning and running as soon as their torpedoes were gone; and with Pietersen's warning, the Mosquitoes were able to make use of their speed and skim the waves westwards towards home before the majority of the 190s could get amongst them.

What remained of the convoy had turned and ran back to Norway under the constant umbrella of fighter protection, while the majority had been sent to the bottom, giving what Alastair had taken to calling his 'Strike Wing' their second success in a row, and changing Coastal Command's fortunes in the North Sea. After two years of being mauled for very little return, there were a lot of congratulations flowing from Coastal Command HQ, and further afield from the Air Ministry, and even Government. It hadn't been without loss, though, much to Harriet's displeasure. She'd lost one of her Mosquitoes to an

88mm shell in the raid, which had blown it apart on their first run in; and another had been badly damaged once the flak got going again, and had been picked off by the 190s when running for home. Four men gone. Four of her men. It was a painful blow that took her right back to Malta and her crew, Bill and Art. The Beaufighters had taken losses, too, with one of them being caught by flak as it pulled up from its torpedo run, and a couple of others being shot up and their crews injured. The losses took the shine off the success for Harriet, and left a bitter taste in her mouth, and once she'd stood the squadron down, she spent the afternoon writing to the families of those who'd died. She knew full well that the letters wouldn't go to Norway, at least not until the war was over, but it was something she needed to do, and at least she could get them, and a full report of the squadrons efforts and their bravery, to the Norwegian government in exile.

The success of the raids was recognised and built on, with both squadrons working together to practice their tactics, including Harriet's circling technique, and working their timing precisely so the Mosquitoes could get amongst the defences before the gunners had a chance to reload. The operations continued into November, when the weather permitted, and the strike wing raided and destroyed another five convoys for very few losses. The losses did come, though, despite the training and the improvements, and the German reluctance to change their strategy from opening fire with every gun they had as soon as the Mosquitoes got close, and across the five missions another two Norwegian crews were lost, with one picked up out of the sea worse for wear, and another three of the squadron were injured badly enough to put them out of the war for a while at least. Each loss hit Harriet hard, and every letter she had to write to a family who wouldn't know for years, if ever, that their son was dead, was painful to write. One of the worst moments was when AP came back trailing smoke, having been set on by three 190s who made her fly like a demon to get away. She was OK, but her observer lost his leg from the knee down to a cannon shell. It had been a close thing, too close for Harriet's liking, or AP's, and the two had more than a few whiskies that night.

Harriet kept smiling, despite the heartache of the losses, and focused on keeping the squadron busy so she, and they, didn't have time to dwell. Training missions for low flying and gunnery, attacks on the bombing range, and lectures on dogfighting, meteorology, and everything else she could think of that would be helpful. She also kept her eyes on the social needs of her squadron, and made sure there were regular parties in the Messes, and lots of sports to keep her crews fit. She'd even joined in the station's hockey tournament, taking the honorary role of captaining the WAAF team, and leading them to victory against teams from the squadrons and support services, all male teams, and she soon got a reputation for being as deadly with a hockey stick as she was with an aeroplane, as she shoulder barged and held up men twice her size. One or two even got themselves flattened when she got into the game a little too much. Off the pitch, there was a massive party organised by Alastair to reward the station for their hard work, and all the on pitch scuffles were quickly forgotten, and Harriet was bought several celebratory drinks, in addition to being asked if she'd like to play for the station rugby team. A step too far that Alastair put a stop to, despite Harriet's keenness to accept, justifying his decision by reminding her that the RAF needed all the pilots they could get, and he didn't want to deal with the fallout if she injured another station's aircrews by playing rugby the way she played hockey.

Chapter 9

There Be Dragons

"Harry old man, do come in!" Alastair said as Harriet stood in his doorway, knocking politely, and wondering why she'd been summoned. She'd just landed from a patrol where she was showing two new crews around the local area, and putting them through their paces on the gunnery range and low flying loop, when Ginny had met her by her Mosquito and told her she'd been summoned to report to Alastair's office right away.

"You sent for me, Sir?" Harriet replied questioningly, wondering what was so important that he'd asked to see her the moment she landed. A summons which had kept her overthinking mind occupied from the moment Ginny had told her.

"Close the door and take a seat. How are your new crews?"

"Not bad, but they'll need sharpening," she replied while taking a seat. Knowing they needed a lot of work to get them combat ready, certainly more than a bit of sharpening, and she was hoping she could talk Alastair into sending them down to Yorkshire for a week.

"We'll get to that. First we need to talk about a little job we need doing."

"Oh?"

"Yes. Orders from Command HQ, so it's a must do I'm afraid."

"That sounds ominous..." Harriet replied uncomfortably, hoping she was misreading the atmosphere.

"Quite..." He frowned for a moment, making Harriet's stomach flip. There'd been rumours around the station for weeks about something big coming, he'd even suggested as much when she'd arrived, though October had been and gone with nothing out of the usual. Most of the recent rumours she'd heard were suggesting a raid on the Tirpitz,

163

Germany's main battleship, which was stationed in Norway to terrorise the convoys taking supplies from Britain and the USA to Russia. Its huge guns could wreak havoc on a convoy without even coming close to being within range of the escorting Royal Navy destroyers and cruisers. "I won't beat around the bush, Harry, we've got a big job on. The Norwegian resistance have been in touch to let us know that one of Germany's major warships is planning on making a run for home from Trondheim."

"The Tirpitz?" Harriet's heart was racing.

"No, that particular thorn in our side is currently tied up and under maintenance in a fjord close to Trondheim. Our target isn't much smaller, though. She's a pocket battleship, or heavy cruiser in our language, and just as much trouble as the Tirpitz. If we can get her, we'll do a great deal to ease the lives of our chaps running the convoys to support the Russians." He stood and walked over to the large map on his wall, and Harriet followed, standing at his side as he tapped his finger on Trondheim, up on the northern Norwegian coast. "We're expecting her to make a run for it sometime tonight, and slip down the Norwegian coast before heading past Denmark, and into her home port at Wilhelmshaven on the German coast. If we get our timing right, we can nail her before she gets there."

"OK..." Harriet replied. Her heart and mind were racing in unison, as she tried to think through what she was facing, and how to do the job. "What are we facing?"

"That's the thing..." He looked her in the eyes, and for the first time since she'd known him she saw fear in his eyes. "I'm addition to her main battery of six eleven inch guns, and secondary armament of eight six inch guns, her anti aircraft battery is going to make her a hard nut to crack." Harriet felt the hairs on the back of her neck stand up in anticipation. "Six 88s, four twin 40mms, and twenty eight 20mms."

"Bloody hell..." she muttered, as she imagined the giant ship carrying more guns than an entire convoy. All under central control, and all operated by experienced Kriegsmarine gun crews. In an instant she knew this was going to be different to anything else she'd done, and while she'd never attacked a battleship before, she didn't need much of an imagination to know it wasn't going to be a picnic.

"Yes, that's one way of putting it," Alastair replied with a smile. "Think your chaps are up to it?"

"We'll give it our best shot," she said as confidently as she could, while doing everything possible to hold in the fear.

"I have no doubt. We'll have reconnaissance kites scouring the area for her, and once we have a reasonable idea of where she is, AP's going to lead you in, as she always does. Get your Mossies in, and do everything in your power to keep their guns busy, so the Beaufighters can make their run and get their torpedoes off." He paused and Harriet nodded to confirm she understood. "Now, as soon as AP has eyes on, we'll have a squadron of Wellington bombers heading in behind you, so do what you can, but once the torpedoes are in the water, get yourselves out of there. Understood?"

"Understood..."

"Any questions?"

"Will they have any escorts?"

"Honestly, we don't know. If they do, it'll likely be destroyers or torpedo boats, or both. Something fast enough to keep up with her."

"OK..."

"Better get your chaps briefed, and be ready for wheels up before sunrise. We're going maximum effort on this one, Harry. Let's get it done, and subject to nothing urgent coming in, I'll see if I can get the squadron away on a few days leave afterwards to let their hair down."

"They'll appreciate that," she smiled as she headed for the door, pushing the mission to the back of her mind for a moment.

"They've more than earned it in the last few months. You've done a good job with them, Harry."

165

"They've done the hard work while I do the paperwork."

"Oh, here. From London." He pulled a small, tinned Fortnum's fruitcake from his drawer and threw it to her. She nodded and smiled, then walked through the door. "I'll see you in the morning."

Harriet's mind was more than occupied as she went about her business. Before leaving headquarters, she called the dispersal and had Ginny get the squadron together, calling in those already stood down ready for a briefing. In the meantime, she headed to meteorology, where MacLeod informed her it would be a full moon and clear sky through the night, with a fog forming before dawn. Not ideal weather, but not good for the battleship either. With a full moon making it hard to hide, she hoped the reconnaissance flights would find it and track it before it got lost in the morning fog. Timing would be everything, as it always was. The full squadron were assembled, ground crews included, when she finally got back to the dispersal. She didn't waste any time in briefing them, and after listening to their gasps and answering their questions, she stood them down and sent them to their beds with strict instructions to lay off the booze. It was going to be an early start and a tough fight, and she needed them as sharp as they could be, especially the new crews who had hadn't even had chance to fire in anger yet, and would now be going up against a battleship.

"Hey," AP said as she entered Harriet's office, where she and Ginny were going through some paperwork.

"Hey," Harriet replied with a smile.

"You've heard about the job then?"

"Yeah..."

"Not going to get some rest?"

"Soon. Ginny and I were just going to have a cup of tea, do you want one? We can share this." She pulled out the tinned fruitcake and AP smiled.

"I suppose." She pulled up a chair, while Ginny went through to the main room to pour AP a cup of tea. "I've come to ask a favour..."

"Go on."

"You know I lost my observer, Tim?"

"Yes, how is he?"

"He's short of a leg, but otherwise OK."

"That's something."

"Yes..." She smiled and thanked Ginny for the tea, while Harriet opened the small tin and cut them a piece of cake each.

"So, what's the favour?"

"Well, with it being a big job, everyone's allocated, and there aren't any spare bodies to crew with me. I was going to take one of the photographic interpretation boys, but their boss has said absolutely not. They're needed, apparently."

"What do you need?"

"I was wondering if I could borrow your clerk, Olivier? I know you and I have both taken her up a few times, and she's got keen eyes... She doesn't have to do much, ballast mostly, but I could do with her observation skills."

"It's going to be a rough trip."

"Not for me. I'll be staying well out of the way once the shooting starts."

"I don't think it's a decision I can make," Harriet said with a frown, which was mirrored by AP. "Olivier!" Harriet shouted, and a few seconds later Chloe's quick footsteps heralded her arrival.

"Ma'am?"

"Chloe, there's no right answer to this, and I won't judge you either way," Harriet started. "Flying Officer Kaye needs an extra pair of eyes on a flight tomorrow, and wondered if you'd be up for filling the righthand seat?" Chloe's eyes opened wide. "Before you answer, you should know it's going to be a rough one, and no matter how good of a pilot Kaye is, she can't guarantee your safety."

"Yes, Ma'am! I'm in, Ma'am!"

"You're sure?"

"Positive."

"You'd better get off and get some sleep in that case. Be here for four tomorrow, and have a hot drink and something to eat first."

"Ma'am!"

"Oh. Here..." Harriet cut her a piece of fruitcake, which Chloe took happily. Her smile beaming ear to ear as she ran off to gather her kit. "Make sure you bring her back in one piece!" Harriet whispered firmly to AP.

"I remember when you were as fresh and keen as her," AP replied with a smirk.

"She was that innocent?" Ginny asked, while Harriet rolled her eyes. Choosing to shovel a chunk of fruitcake into her mouth instead of replying.

"Oh, yes. You should have met her in France, all polite and quiet. Butter wouldn't melt."

"What happened?"

"Hey!" Harriet mumbled through her mouthful, then swallowed the cake quickly. "I met her is what happened!" she pointed at AP. "Who, I should add, didn't even give me the time of day. Wouldn't talk to

168

me, wouldn't smile, wouldn't even acknowledge I was alive. The only time she did talk to me, she shouted at me and told me off."

"What for?" Ginny asked excitedly.

"Everything!"

"She was a little naive," AP said casually. "Needed toughening up a bit."

"I'll show you tough in a minute, Flying Officer. How do you fancy a posting to Balloon Command?"

"Good luck, Squadron Leader. I report direct to a Group Captain, and he likes me."

"At least somebody does."

They laughed and talked, while enjoying their tea and cake, then Harriet and AP left Ginny to her paperwork and headed to their beds, AP in the Mess, and Harriet riding her motorcycle back to her cottage, where she spent several hours staring at the ceiling and thinking of everything that was about to come. Sleep evaded her, and no matter what she tried, her brain wouldn't be quiet. So, instead of tossing and turning she got up again and wrote letters. To her parents in Switzerland, with the hope it would get there one day, and to Bunny in America, in addition to Aunt Mary, Robbie, and Nicole. She was sure of at least two getting where they were going, the other three relied on a space on a ship, or a flight getting through. She told them of the weather in Scotland, and wished them all well. It was enough to make her smile with positive thoughts of them all, thoughts which helped quieten her mind a little, enough to get to sleep at least, with the help of a cup of bitter cocoa.

"How are you always here before me?" Harriet asked, as she walked into the dispersal to be greeted by Ginny, who was standing with a smile on her face and a cup of tea at the ready.

"I like to be up early," Ginny replied with a shrug and a smile. She handed Harriet the tea, which was warming, and just what she needed following the short, but bitterly cold ride to the air station on her motorcycle. "Besides, somebody has to be here to help you get ready for the day."

"I like to think I'd manage," Harriet replied with a frown, while warming her hands over the stove. "Any updates?"

"Nothing much different since you left. I checked in with Ops on my way in, and they haven't had anything from the reconnaissance flights searching through the night. The Norwegians saw her leave yesterday evening, but they lost her after dark. Apparently the fog came in much earlier than anticipated."

"Great..." The door opened and she turned to see Chloe wrapped in her flying kit, and wearing a smile bright enough to light the darkest of nights. "Morning!"

"Morning, Ma'am. Is it still on?"

"What?"

"The raid. Is it still on?"

"You're keen."

"Yes, Ma'am."

"She's been spending too much time with you," Harriet frowned at Ginny, who simply smiled in return, while pouring Chloe a cup of tea. "Make sure you do exactly as you're told today," Harriet continued, returning her stare to Chloe. "It's going to be rough up there." Chloe nodded and smiled.

"Ready?" AP asked, as she opened the door and popped her head in. Chloe looked questioningly at Harriet, who gave her a nod of approval.

"Remember what I said, AP," Harriet said as Chloe stepped through the door.

"I remember everything you say..." AP winked and smirked in reply. "See you up there, good luck!"

At that, the transport truck pulled up outside, and the tailgate rattled open, and as AP disappeared into the darkness, the crews were filing into the dispersal hut almost silently. Alastair arrived shortly after to see them off, and to confirm that the battleship was in the fog somewhere, though he was still convinced that the ship would be where they expected it to be, based on its known speed and the weather conditions. He was sure that if it wasn't, it would be because they'd been tricked and the battleship had doubled back up and over Scotland, and out into the Atlantic. Apparently, the worst case scenario, as it would cause devastation to the convoys coming from America and Canada. The briefing was detailed, with map coordinates, radio frequencies, timings, and an update on the weather conditions; and once all questions had been answered, Harriet sent her pilots off to their aircraft. Then, after saying goodbye to Ginny, she and Eskimo went out into the dark to their Mosquito.

After going through the pre flight checks, Harriet started her engines, then led the squadron to the end of the runway. AP had long gone, she'd heard her Mosquito climbing into the moonlit sky while she was briefing the squadron, and the way AP flew, she knew they'd be a long away ahead before the squadron got in the air. Especially as her photographic reconnaissance Mosquito was unarmed, giving her more speed to race out to sea ahead of the pack. Once up, Harriet circled as planned, and formed the squadron into their four flights of four aircraft, as briefed, then led them low over the cliffs and out to sea. The black sky was lit by the silver light of a large full moon that sat quite low in the sky, and for a moment she let her mind wander back to her flight to Egypt from Malta. She'd been excited at the time, and had no idea of the adventure in the desert that lay ahead of her. An adventure that had left her with a tan that was only just starting to lighten after months in the cool rain of Scotland. It had also left her with scars that weren't in a hurry to heal, both physical and mental. She snapped herself out of her daydreams and checked her instruments, and her watch, and fiddled with the cockpit heating vent as she waited for the engines to heat enough for it to scoop some warmth from the coolant running behind the air intake on the wing, and channel it to the cockpit. It was a useful and efficient device that made flying in the depths of a Scottish November much more tolerable, though she still needed her long underwear and sailor's roll neck. She glanced left and right, and back over her shoulders. Her flight of four were in two loose pairs, one forward and one behind, staggered to give them all clear visibility forward. Everyone was where they needed to be, which was reassuring, and helped her keep her mind off the tightness she'd had in her chest since hearing of the mission. A tightness that she knew came from her inescapable fear of taking on a battleship. She'd even changed her battle plans from those successfully employed against previous convoys. Sitting around circling at two miles distant would be a death sentence for her crews, especially with all the larger calibre guns the battleship carried, so instead she was relying on the element of surprise.

Halfway to the target, a message was received from a Sunderland flying boat confirming a sighting of the mighty German battleship, reported to be slipping in and out of fog banks some way from the Norwegian coast, and much closer than had been anticipated. About the same time as the message came through, a thin blanket of fog started developing below, sitting maybe fifty feet above the water, and glowing silver in the moonlight. Harriet kept her eye on it as it thickened, and the distant easterly sky lightened from black, to royal blue, to a light silvery purple. It was going to be a beautiful day, if she got to see it. She went through her checks again, then felt her tummy squeeze as AP called up and confirmed the sighting, giving a course correction, and warning of an escorting destroyer hiding in the fog ahead of the battleship, only visible by its mast passing through the fog banks. She also warned Harriet to be careful, as she took station at thirty five thousand feet, about as high as she could, sitting to the west of the target and hiding in the still dark sky; far enough away to stay hidden, while still keeping the German convoy in sight.

"Viking squadron, hold your positions," Harriet said, as she checked her altimeter. They were around fifteen minutes from the target, and the fog was stretched as far as she could see, like a shimmering silver blanket. It gave her an idea. She pushed the control yoke forward a little, dipping the nose ever so slightly and starting a slow descent, watching the altimeter unwind as she went. The gauges weren't always incredibly accurate at low levels, and every fifty feet that fell off was done slowly and gradually, until she got the wings into the fog, which was so thick that the propellers did little more than whip it up a little, as it settled just below her windscreen. One hundred feet exactly. There were patches higher, she could see them in the distance, but they were few and far between, and significantly thinner and relatively easy to navigate. "OK, Viking squadron, spread into attack formation and bring it down to one hundred feet exactly. Do it slowly, and don't go below." She glanced to Eskimo, who nodded with nervous excitement. "Any lower and I'd have to dangle you out of the cockpit on a piece of rope, and pull up when you scream," she said mischievously, trying to break the tension that was threatening to make her chest explode.

"If it's that or going back to not flying, give me a rope," he replied, making Harriet smile to herself.

"Keep your eyes open once the shooting starts, watch for fighters and let me know if I'm doing anything stupid."

"Like flying at a hundred feet above the sea, in the fog, and heading towards a heavily armed German battleship?"

"Yes, if you catch me doing something stupid like that, just let me know."

"Will do!"

"Oh my God..." Harriet gasped, as the giant black superstructure of the battleship came over the horizon, climbing out of the fog like a huge dragon, bristling with armoured scales in the ghostly dawn light, as fingers of fog wound around the masts and towers.

"That's big..." Eskimo said.

"It's huge," Harriet replied, as she fought to comprehend the scale of the huge battleship ahead of them.

"Stand by, they're launching their reconnaissance seaplanes!" AP warned, breaking through the atmosphere of the moment.

"Understood," Harriet replied, snapping out of her trance. "Viking squadron, two minutes out. Guns and bombs hot, and watch for escorts in the fog." The squadron checked in one at a time, confirming they were ready for action and on station. Not wanting to take her eyes away from front and centre, to make sure she didn't drop into the fog and end up in the water, she glanced briefly left and right out of the corners of her eyes, seeing the cockpits and propeller tips of mosquitoes each side. Then, pulling her head and her attention to the left, she noticed a mast passing just off of the tip of her wing. Had she been any lower, she'd have hit it. Another ship in the fog. As she looked forward again she saw the battleship was making smoke, lots of it, and her already racing heart stepped up a few gears as she realised that meant the enemy knew they were coming. She squinted and frowned as a rapid succession of yellowy orange lights sparkled through the smoke and across the ship. For the briefest of moments, her mind raced to explain the lights, first wondering if the Wellington squadron had arrived early, and then very quickly coming to the realisation of what was happening, when a glowing red shell the size of a large post box passed just above her cockpit. The noise was deafening, even above the noise of the engines, sounding like a freight train howling past. The Mosquito was bounced up and down by the shock wave, and Harriet's mouth dried instantly, as a torrent of sweat started to run down her back. "Viking squadron, hold position and push the throttles through the gate to maximum speed. Here we go, Tally Ho!" She pushed her own throttles forward as she spoke, forcing the pair of merlin engines to their maximum, hoping the increase in speed would throw off the ship's targeting, in addition to getting her there quicker so the big guns couldn't target her. A few seconds later there were more sparkles, and her peripheral vision lit up as a shell found home somewhere to her left, blowing a Mosquito out of the sky in a blinding explosion. They passed the two mile perimeter, and the swirling fog and smoke was lit up and glowed as lines of green and orange tracer from the 40mm and 20mm cannons snaked into the sky in the direction of the Mosquitoes. Then, without warning, other snakes of tracer shot up from all around, below them, behind them, it was as though the entire North Sea was shooting at them.

"Torpedo boats!" AP yelled over the radio. "They're all around you, get out of there!"

"Too late!" Harriet replied as she pulled back on the controls, narrowly missing a stream of flak which passed under the belly of the Mosquito. Eskimo opened the bomb bay and held on to the bomb release as Harriet fought to drag them up steep enough to avoid the superstructure. "Release!" she shouted, as the bridge of the giant battleship loomed in front of them. She simultaneously pushed the fire button, and raked the metalwork with cannons and machine guns, making sparks dance across the grey paint as she found home.

"Bombs gone!" Eskimo replied, and the black bombs were catapulted towards the battleship, hitting the top of the mast, and blowing away the gun position and observation deck, just as Harriet pulled up and over it, and took a cannon shell through the outer right wing. She rolled as she climbed, trying to make herself a hard target as the guns on the port side of the ship now had something to fire at. Double and quad 20mm guns opened up, and streams of tracer zipped all around, flashing by the cockpit continuously, with one passing through the rear of the cockpit and shattering the roof. Harriet looked over her shoulder as she reversed her roll, and saw the Mosquitoes passing through the smoke and fog, as explosions sent huge plumes of water into the sky, while one bomb at least found its mark, and exploded on the beast's deck. As Harriet banked around to her right, she came across the destroyer AP had warned her about, which was now turned broadside and firing at her and anything else in the sky with everything it had, and another couple of hits rattled her fuselage. She quickly pushed the nose down to avoid the aim of an 88 firing from the battleship, just as the destroyer passed through a thinning patch of fog. She took aim and fired along the deck, hitting an anti aircraft gun, and rattling the main armament, igniting the ammunition with a lucky high explosive shot from her cannons. The turret glowed red and jumped from the deck, sending burning shards of metal up through Harriet's right wing as she banked away into a long, wide turn. She kept low and skimmed the fog, keeping the destroyer between her and the battleship to protect herself from its guns. She fired again, raking the water, and drawing a neat line up the side of the destroyer and into the bridge. As she pulled up and skipped across the destroyer again, she got the full sight of the battle. Mosquitoes swarmed, passing in and out of the thick mix of fog and smoke which was now the only thing keeping them alive, while the giant battleship lit the sky up with an unrelenting barrage of flak. Over to her left she caught a glimpse of the Beaufighters coming in, they were higher than the mosquitoes, and already they were being engaged by the torpedo boats hiding in the murk below. She pointed her Mosquito at the front of the battleship and opened the throttles, determined to draw at least some of the fire and give the Beaufighters a chance. She saved her ammunition for when she knew she was in range. There was no point in firing at the main turrets on the great armoured beast, she knew that much, though even they had anti aircraft guns perfected on top of them, so she took aim at the bridge and fired, then gently eased the rudder and swung right, running bullets and cannon shells into the flak gun to the right of the bridge, then skipped over it, and ducked back down into the fog as other guns targeted her with more glowing streams of tracer which raised splashes from the sea, showing her exactly how low she'd got. The battleship's main armament opened fire as she passed, making the fog and smoke glow red and orange, and she felt instantly like she was in the heart of hell. As she gently eased the rudder to turn the Mosquito in a low, wide turn ready for the next pass on the battleship, a torpedo boat came out of the fog directly in front of her. Her heart almost stopped, she was so low that all she could do to avoid it, or clipping the water with her wing, was to push opposite rudder and pull up. The mast struck the starboard wing hard, making the whole Mosquito shudder, and worrying Harriet that the wing would come off in its entirety. The mast snapped before the wing, fortunately, and being part of a torpedo boat, it was narrow and relatively flimsy. Had she hit anything on the battleship, or even the destroyer, it would have been a very different story. As it was, they were still in the air somehow, though the controls were hard work, and the equally as surprised torpedo boat crew had flinched long enough to miss their chance to blow her out of the sky with their anti aircraft guns. She pulled up above the fog and out of their view, and straight back into the chaos. Her head was spinning as she tried to anticipate what to do next, while calculating how much ammunition she thought she had.

"Home!" Eskimo shouted again and again, then punched Harriet in the arm hard enough to get her attention. "Torpedoes gone, let's get out of here!" He shouted as she stared at him briefly, letting his words filter through the battle her brain was busy fighting. "We need to get out of here. The torpedoes are gone, we need to get away while we can!"

"Yes..." She nodded and checked her compass, before dropping back into the fog and skimming the waves again. "Viking squadron, break and home. I repeat, break and home! Watch your tails for fighters." She looked to Eskimo, who gave her a nod of relief before she pulled up again and opened the throttles fully, racing high and fast while slipping and skidding left and right, determined to make it difficult for the tracking gunners to anticipate her altitude or position. The battle was quickly behind them, though they were reminded that they weren't quite safe when another freight train shell from the main guns passed so close Harriet was sure she could feel the heat from the glowing red metal. She turned tight as she climbed, changing her position to make sure the next shot would have to be more than a slight correction to hit her, then she stood the Mosquito on its tail and flew straight up to twenty thousand feet, where she levelled and turned back to survey the scene. The battleship was surrounded by a huge cloud of black smoke and thick fog that covered it entirely, and extended in each direction to cover the destroyer and anything else within a mile at least. The cloud continued to erupt with gunnery of all sorts, and Harriet watched as the shots fell among the retreating Mosquitoes and Beaufighters as they desperately tried to escape. She then caught sight of one of the battleship's spotter planes, it was circling not far away and giving fire control instructions, allowing the gunners to fire blind with remarkable success. She was on it in less than a minute, and her remaining ammunition put an end to its mischief making, taking off the left wing and sending it spinning downwards. She scanned the sky, spinning her head left and right as she searched for the second seaplane. She knew it had two, but she couldn't see it anywhere. She watched for a moment and the gunnery eased a little. More shells were fired in the same direction, but it was clear they were now truly firing blind, so she turned west and headed home.

The controls were sloppy at best, but the Mosquito was flyable, and most importantly both engines held and kept the aeroplane cruising at full speed through the pale blue skies towards home. It was morning, the sun had risen, and the further west they got, the less fog there was on the surface. There was haze, but Harriet was able to see

177

other Mosquitoes heading home, and Beaufighters, though not many. It was normal that the squadron would scatter and make their own way back at different speeds and from different directions. Once they got stuck into a fight, they could be anywhere when they were called off, and the rules were that you didn't wait around. You pointed west and opened your throttles until you were out of danger, hoping that a swarm of 190s weren't chasing you home. Eskimo kept them on track, and both were relieved when land came into sight, and shortly afterwards they were lining up with the runway. The relief quickly evaporated when a red flare was fired from the control tower, sending her around again.

"Viking Leader to Claymore, what's wrong?" she called the tower, irritated that she'd been waved off. She was ready to be on the ground, the sloppiness of the controls was getting worse, and she wasn't convinced she could keep them in the air much longer.

"Claymore here," came a friendly reply. "Your undercarriage is still up, go around again." Harriet felt herself blushing with embarrassment, then quickly frowned.

"I did put the undercarriage down... Didn't I?" she asked Eskimo.

"I thought so..." he replied.

"Me too..." She quickly worked the switch again, but nothing. "Viking Leader here, do you see my undercarriage?"

"Claymore here, only one leg. It looks like your left is stuck..."

"Great..." Harriet's heart sank. She fiddled with the switch a few more times, hoping to loosen the left wheel and encourage it to drop. "Anything?" she asked.

"Negative, recommend passing the tower and we'll have a look."

"Wilco." Harriet scrubbed off as much speed as she dared while in the circuit, then came in low over the tower, banking away as she did and giving the collection of blue suits now gathered on the balcony, Alastair included, a good view.

"Claymore to Viking Leader, you've a hole in your wing where your left landing gear should be."

"Understood. Clear the runway, I'm coming in hot." She pulled the Mosquito out to sea while letting others land, and when she was told they were clear, she scrubbed off speed and headed back in for the runway. "Tighten your harness and brace yourself," she said to Eskimo, who nodded compliantly. "Claymore, this is Viking Leader. Shutting down now." She cut the fuel and feathered the propellers, then switched off the electrics, not wanting to risk electrical sparks and aviation fuel mixing if the landing went badly, then she held up the nose as she brought the Mosquito in, just to the left of the runway. The tail touched first, and seconds later the nose was pulled down to the grass, and dirt was thrown in every direction as the propellers and fuselage dug in, and Harriet and Eskimo were thrown into their straps. Once on the ground she released the controls and used one hand to brace against the control panel, while holding the other over her face. The Mosquito groaned and creaked as it bounced and scraped along the ground, until finally it came to a halt. "Are you alive?" she asked Eskimo, as she pulled off her helmet and reached up for the remains of the escape hatch, much of it having been blown away in the battle.

"I think so..." he replied. He was pale and shaking, but nodding excitedly.

"Out you get, then. Don't hang around." She pointed to the hatch, and he jumped up and pushed the remains open, then dragged himself out while Harriet released her harness. Her heart was racing more than she dared show, and her hands were shaking so much she couldn't get the harness open. Memories of the last Mosquito crash came flooding back, and all she could think of was how long she had until the flames reached her. "Come on... Come on!" she muttered as she fought with the harness.

"Are you coming?" Eskimo asked, as he popped his head back down into the cockpit. Looking at him gave her the focus she needed, and the harness snapped open.

179

"Here," she held up her flight bag and maps, which he took from her as she stood on her seat and followed him out of the jagged hatch. Once outside, she stood on the remains of the nose and looked back at her Mosquito, expecting to see the roaring inferno of the last time, and was surprised when it wasn't there. The wreck was smoking, but there was no sign of fire, much to her relief. She then turned to the noise of the ambulance and fire truck as they raced to their aid, and she couldn't help smiling as she followed Eskimo in jumping down to the ground; while at the same time Alastair stepped off the fire truck's running board with a slight stagger to stop him falling, as he'd stepped off too early, while the truck was still moving a little faster than he expected. "Careful," she said with a mischievous smile.

"You're one to talk!" He looked at her, then Eskimo, then the smoking ruins of her Mosquito that the firemen were already damping down with foam.

"I think the Chief's going to have his work cut out putting that one back together."

"Rather that, than us having to put you back together. Again... How are you both?"

"Alive, remarkably."

"How bad was it?"

"A battleship, a destroyer, and there must have been half a dozen torpedo boats or more. We were lucky."

"The Wellingtons are on their way in, they should be hitting any minute."

"Good luck to them. What about us, how did we do?"

"I don't know yet, it's too early to say."

"You mean they're not all back?"

"Not half." He winced as he told her, he could see the sadness in her eyes.

"Why don't you go and get yourself a cup of tea, and get out of your flying kit?" she said to Eskimo, who was standing by her side looking exhausted and scared. "You've more than earned it."

"Ma'am." He nodded and smiled, then headed off in the direction of the dispersal.

"Well done up there today, Eskimo," she shouted after him. "I was lucky to have the best navigator in the squadron with me." He turned and grinned, and gave her a thumbs up. "His navigation's fantastic, and he's got a very cool head," she said to Alastair as they watched him leave. "Not bad for somebody so young."

"You're not exactly old yourself, Harry," Alastair said warmly.

"I feel it...'

"Shall we head to the tower and watch them come in?"

"No..." Harriet shook her head and smiled up at him. "I should be with my squadron. I'll wait there until they're all home."

"I'd do exactly the same in your place. Come on, I'll walk you over." He put his hand on her shoulder, and they walked together in the direction of the tower, pausing briefly to watch a Beaufighter come in.

"I don't think they'll be buying us many pints in the Mess."

"What makes you say that?"

"From the brief glimpses I saw, they were slaughtered. We were so busy fighting for our lives that we didn't have time to keep them safe."

"You mustn't think that way, Harry old man. Sometimes things just don't go to plan, but you were still there doing your part. Had you not been, I imagine slaughter wouldn't go close to describing what

181

would have happened. It's probably hard to accept now, but you'll come to it." He gave her shoulder a squeeze, and she smiled back at him, struggling to find anything useful to say. She continued to squeeze her hands to try and stop them shaking, while glancing up at the sky every now and then. Another Mosquito came in as she arrived at the squadron dispersal, the right engine was smoking, but it landed without a problem, and Harriet felt a little relief. She knew she couldn't stand to watch one crash in front of her, not at the best of times, but certainly not with the way she was feeling. She'd acted on instinct throughout the battle, and once again she had blurred recollection of the details, as her subconscious brain had taken over. Now she was on the ground though, the adrenaline was starting to ease, and she was struggling to hold things together. She felt cold. Colder than the icy wind that was blasting over the airfield. She felt sick, too, and no matter how hard she tried, she couldn't stop her hands shaking. "Here we are," Alastair said as they arrived at the dispersal. A couple of the crews were standing outside smoking and drinking tea, and scouring the sky. Ginny was waiting in the doorway, she looked Harriet in the eyes and gave her a smile that told her she knew what she was feeling, and that she'd be OK. "I'll catch up with you later, Harry. Your chaps did a wonderful job today, despite the opposition. You should be proud of them." He gave the crews a respectful nod, having talked loud enough to make sure they heard his praise.

"I am," Harriet replied. "Thank you, Sir." She stood smartly to attention and gave him a formal nod, and got a wink and smile in reply as he turned and left.

"How are you?" Harriet asked the crews outside. They nodded and smiled, and confirmed they were as well as could be expected, and asked how she was. Then, after a few minutes of talking, she walked in through the door and past Ginny, who simply smiled and followed her to her office and closed the door behind her. Harriet threw her flying kit in the corner and pulled her gloves off, all while looking out of the window and biting her tongue.

"We've had nine back so far," Ginny said. Harriet nodded, but still didn't talk. She felt numb, while at the same time her head started to spin as patches of memories flashed before her eyes. She jumped when Ginny walked over and put a hand on her shoulder. "Are you OK?"

"Not really..."

"What is it?"

"I thought I'd had it this time."

"Fortunately not."

"Not fortunate for those that won't be coming back. I saw one of ours get, from B Flight I think, blown out of the sky by an eleven inch shell as big as a post box. The only saving grace is that they wouldn't have known a thing about it."

"Nine came back so far. Eighteen people, you included. Whatever happened out there, that's still good news. The day's not over, either. There's time for the others." She turned Harriet to face her, and looked in her eyes. "I know this isn't professional, and it isn't done, but you'll just have to put me on a charge afterwards," she said firmly, making Harriet frown with confusion. Ginny then stepped forward and hugged Harriet, taking her by surprise and making her go rigid for a moment, before relaxing and almost melting into her friend's arms. It wasn't what she wanted, or was expecting, but it was exactly what she needed, and by the time she heard the sound of Merlin engines circling outside, she'd managed to relax enough to reduce the shaking in her hands to a mild vibration, and untangle some of the more difficult thoughts running through her head. "Go watch them in, and I'll bring you a cup of tea." She let Harriet go and gave her a smile, and after checking herself in the mirror, Harriet headed out to stand with the others and watch a pair of Mosquitoes come in one after the other. It was a reassuring sight. Eleven out of sixteen aircraft. Ginny joined her and gave her a cup of tea, it was sweet with extra sugar, and had a lingering taste of rum that Harriet didn't question. The station intelligence officer arrived after a while, and started taking reports from the crews. Harriet remained outside, watching and waiting. Bargaining in her head with any god listening, negotiating for just one more. The tea did its job, and she even felt herself enjoying the drifting tobacco smoke as it hung in the wind, while pilots and navigators chain smoked as they talked through their experiences. As the crews finished the reports she stood them down, but none wanted to leave, not until they were beyond the cut off. The time the missing Mosquitoes would have left based on their remaining fuel. There was a heavy atmosphere when five minutes passed after the cut off, and then ten. Then, at thirty minutes past the cut off, and just as they were gathering their kit to head to the Mess, a rough sounding Merlin buzzed in the distance. They all dropped everything immediately and ran to join Harriet, standing beside her to watch as a Mosquito came in on one engine. It was in a bad way, but the pilot, Pietersen, guided it down perfectly, and taxied it to the dispersal, shutting down just as the fire truck and ambulance arrived. Neither of which were needed, mercifully. It was enough to make Harriet smile. Twelve back, three quarters of her squadron, with only a handful of minor injuries among them, and two serious. It was sickening, but it was enough. It was better than it could have been. After welcoming Pietersen back, and finding out his shot up engine helped his fuel go a little further, and get his wrecked aeroplane back, she congratulated them on their efforts and sent the, all to the Mess.

"I can call the duty driver and get you a ride home, if you like?" Ginny said, as she stood by Harriet's side and gave her a fresh cup of rum laced tea. "I mean, if you're too tired to ride your motorcycle back."

"Maybe later," Harriet replied with a smile.

"Not now?"

"Not now... I have letters to write."

"You know, that could wait until tomorrow at least."

"I won't sleep until I've done it. You can get off, though. You've been here since before me, you must be exhausted."

"I'll wait."

"For what?"

"For you, of course."

"Don't be ridiculous."

"I'm not, it's my job."

"I'm not sure you fully understand the role of adjutant."

"I'm thinking more about my role as a friend." Ginny shrugged and Harriet blushed, then rolled her eyes and headed to her office.

"You can stay, but stop putting rum in my tea. The letters need to be legible." They laughed a little, and Harriet went to her desk and started writing, while Ginny went about her post mission paperwork, reporting losses and damages, and requesting replacements of equipment, aircraft, and aircrew. It was solemn work, but like the letters, it needed to be done. She'd put them in front of Harriet every now and then to be signed, between letters, and when she made another cup of tea, she laced it with more rum than before, much to Harriet's faux outrage that didn't stop her drinking it gratefully.

"That's everything..." Ginny said, as she and Harriet sat by her desk. The letters were written and ready to be sent to the Norwegian government in exile, and all reports and requisitions were written and signed. "I'm assuming you're not going to find another excuse not to go and get some sleep?"

"Want to come with me?"

"Home?"

"I need a good drink after today, something without tea in it, and I'd rather not drink alone. I'm not that sad and broken, at least not yet."

"In that case, if you don't mind me stopping by my room for a few things, I'm in!" They both stood and got their things together, then left the office to be faced with Alastair standing in the doorway of the hut.

"What is it?" Harriet asked, her tummy tightening instinctively. She knew there was something wrong, and her brain ran through the many possibilities, including the decision to send them up for a second go at the battleship.

"AP isn't back..." he replied, giving a simple yet painful frown.

"What?" She'd heard him, but his words felt like a knife through the heart.

"She hasn't been heard from for a while, and she's beyond her fuel cut off. We've called around the local airfields she could have reached, but nothing."

"I don't understand... I thought she was back already. She should have been. She should have left the battle long before us." Harriet's mind was spinning again.

"Harry, I wanted to be the one to tell you."

"No," Harriet replied firmly, and threw her things down on a table, before pulling her flying jacket on again and fiddling with her Mae West.

"Harry..."

"Not today!" Harriet bellowed. "I'm not losing her, not now. Not today."

"Where are you going?"

"To the hangar to find an aircraft."

"Harry..."

"I'll call the Chief," Ginny said as she ran into Harriet's office, while Harriet continued to get ready.

"This isn't wise, old man. You're in no fit state."

"They've got nothing," Ginny said as she returned to the room. "Every one of ours that came back is full of holes and needs work. The Chief says he can get one ready for early evening if he puts everyone on it."

"Not good enough," Harriet replied, then turned to Alastair. "I need the Anson. Please."

"No..."

"Please, I can't lose her. I have to try."

"The Anson won't do you any good."

"Alastair!" She felt tears in her eyes.

"I can do better than that," he said with a sparkle in his eyes, then walked past her to the office and made a phone call before returning to Harriet and Ginny. "Right, let's go." He walked to the door, with Harriet close behind.

"Where are you going?" Harriet asked, as Ginny followed.

"With you, and you know the answer if you say otherwise."

"You'll need your coat," Harriet said, as Alastair led them to his car, which he drove like he was being chased, to the control tower and the steel blue PBY Catalina seaplane sitting in front of it with engines turning. Harriet's eyes lit up. She'd flown to Hawaii in a Catalina, they had great range and weapons, and it was the ideal tool for search and rescue. "That beats an Anson."

"Told you..." He gave her a wink as he stopped the car and jumped out. A WAAF was waiting for him, holding his flying jacket and boots, which he quickly changed into. "They called in an hour ago on their way north from their station in Fife. They've been having trouble with one of their engines, but the pilot reckons it'll be OK for a test flight now we've changed the plugs for him." He led Harriet and Ginny to the door, and they were showed in by a gunner. Ginny was taken to a seat in the rear of the fuselage, while Harriet and

Alastair went forward to see the pilot. "Thanks for the ride, chaps," Alastair said as he stood behind the pilots.

"Our pleasure, Sir. Where are we heading?"

"One of our reconnaissance kites is missing somewhere between here and Norway. Squadron Leader Cornwall here will give you coordinates." He stepped aside and pushed Harriet forward. She handed the co pilot her map and pointed out the routes she'd taken in and out of the battle.

They flew for hours, zigzagging back and forth along the route and scouring the sea for a life raft, or even signs of wreckage, while also keeping a lookout for German fighters. There was nothing though, just mile after mile of a sea that was getting greyer as the minutes passed, and clouds rolled in on the stiff breeze from the southeast. Then the penny dropped. As the pilot announced they were going to have to return to base, Harriet asked him to make a diversion to the northwest. The weather had been quite still during the battle, but as she ran for home she remembered the strengthening wind pushing her north as she fought with the sloppy controls. She kicked herself for not remembering, though it gave her a glimmer of hope. The pilot was obliging, and turned north, as the seas started to roll, and the dark clouds gathered. They zigzagged again, searching, flying low and scouring the dark water with its increasingly frequent white wave tops.

"There!" Harriet shouted excitedly, as she leant forward between the pilots and pointed at the red and yellow Air Sea Rescue float pitching and rolling in the sea. "The flag's up! There's somebody home!"

"Bloody hell, she's right!" The co pilot muttered. "What do you say, skipper? Can we land?"

"It's going to be rough. The sea's about at the limits, but we'll try. Better get back and strap in," he said to Harriet, who immediately nodded and moved as quickly as she could through the aeroplane to the rear cabin, to the large gun blisters either side of the aeroplane. Ginny and Alastair were waiting, they'd been looking out of the blisters with the crew, and searching the sea tirelessly.

188

"Hold on, we've found them!" Harriet said excitedly, as she braced herself for landing, just before the lumbering great Catalina swooped out of the sky and skimmed the waves, sending metallic shudders through the floor as they bumped against the swell. Harriet was quickly on her feet as the gunner swung his gun and opened the blister window. "I'll go!" Harriet said. He looked at her for a moment, then nodded and handed her a loop of rope, which she quickly fastened around her.

"Harry..." Alastair said as he stood beside her.

"I'll be fine. Hold the rope tight." She gave him a smile, then stepped out of the blister and stood on the ledge as the pilot tried to manoeuvre close to the long boat shaped metal float. He tried again and again, but couldn't get close. The rising swell was bumping the giant seaplane away, and he was reluctant to get too close in case the pointed front of the metal rescue vessel collided with the Catalina and holed it, putting them all in trouble. Harriet was getting frustrated, and after another failed attempt to get close she kicked off her flying boots, then pulled off her jacket before tying the rope around her again and diving headfirst into the North Sea before anyone could stop her. It was ice cold, and the shock made her gasp breathlessly as she surfaced, and an icy pain stabbed deep into her brain. She felt the rope being pulled and realised what was happening, they were going to pull her back in, so she put her head back in the water and started swimming hard, kicking and flailing her arms as she pulled through the rolling waves with all of her strength until she finally reached the back of the float and crawled aboard. The pitching and rolling seemed so much worse than when she was in the Catalina, making it difficult to make her way up the slope, gripping the freezing cold and slippery metal rungs to steady herself, while bashing her knees against the metal, and feeling the sharp stabbing of the cold shoot through her body. She was shivering as she continued towards the hatch at the top of the steps, and it hurt her hand to hammer on the metal door. She hammered again, then gripped the handle and turned it, before pulling it open and looking inside, down into the depths of the float. In the darkness she saw two bundles wrapped in blankets. "Wake up!" She yelled, but neither moved, so she descended into the metallic hull, which was roaring with the noise of the waves hammering it repeatedly, and the thundering rumble of the Catalina's engines. "Wake up!" she shouted again, as she kicked the nearest bundle, before bending over and pulling the blanket back to see AP and Chloe, huddled together, pale and lifeless. "No, no, no," she muttered, as she knelt and put her fingers on the side of AP's neck to feel for a pulse. Her skin was cold, almost icy, and her lips were blue, but the hard prodding as she tried to find a pulse made AP stir and half open her eyes. "AP, I need you to wake up. OK?" She shouted over the noise. AP nodded and smiled, then lay her head down again and closed her eyes. Harriet grabbed her by her sheepskin collar and pulled her up, shaking her eyes open again at the same time. "Don't you dare go to sleep! Now get up!"

"Ma'am..." Chloe whispered, and Harriet looked over to see the equally as pale and cold looking Chloe.

"Chloe, get up. Get up now!" she ordered, and the young clerk nodded, then forced herself upright. She looked like death, but she was functioning and responding to instructions, and that's all Harriet needed. "Help me get her outside." Chloe nodded and helped Harriet pull AP to her feet, and then up to the deck. Harriet tied the rope around AP, fastening it under her arms and making sure it wasn't going to slip. "Chloe, I want you to wait here. I'll be back, OK?" Chloe nodded. Her pale blue lips and drowsy red ringed eyes made Harriet's heart squeeze as the girl sat quietly and compliantly, slumped against the now closed hatch of the float. Time was of the essence, so Harriet dragged AP into the water, then held her from behind to keep her head above the surface and gave a thumbs up to the PBY crew, who pulled the rope and reeled them in as fast as they could, dragging them up to the blister and taking AP inside. "Give me the rope," Harriet demanded, as she hung onto the ledge. She was shivering almost uncontrollably, and could hardly feel her fingers, but she managed to get the rope around her again before she lowered herself into the water and started swimming back to the float. It wasn't such a shock this time, as she was already cold, but that wasn't necessarily a good thing. She felt her energy draining with each powerful kick through the water, and rode the rolling waves that lifted her and carried her forward. She was exhausted by the time she clawed her way up the deck the second time, where she found Chloe slumped and her eyes closed. Harriet shook her hard, and Chloe instinctively nodded and moved, as if operating under somebody else's control, and Harriet was able to get the rope around her and drag her down into the water, where another thumbs up led to another drag through the waves. This time Harriet held tight to Chloe, knowing she was losing her grip and would be lost if she didn't, and Chloe instinctively grabbed back. Salt water filed their mouths and shot up their noses, but it was enough to keep Harriet fighting, and soon both she and the young clerk had been dragged into the Catalina.

"That's it, Skipper, we've got them!" The crewman shouted, and while Harriet lay shivering on the floor, the Catalina powered into life and quickly leapt into the sky with several large and uncomfortable bumps, leaving the increasingly rough sea behind them.

Harriet was struggling to focus. Her eyesight was dull and blurred, and the pain in her hands and feet was immense. She couldn't feel anything she touched, and at the same time it felt like red hot needles were being stuck deep into her fingers and toes. If that wasn't enough, she had a headache that made her feel as though her skull would crack open, and she was shivering so hard she found it hard to breathe. The crew pulled at her wet clothes, then quickly stuffed her into a sleeping bag and carried her to one of the forward cabins, and laid her on a bunk before strapping her in. Through her bleary eyes she could see AP and Chloe, each in sleeping bags in other bunks that she passed on the way to hers. Alastair and the crew were piling them with blankets and trying to feed them warm cocoa from a flask, desperately trying to get some warmth into them.

"Move aside," Ginny said, as the wireless operator piled a blanket on top of Harriet. "Get her a drink of something warm, I'll take it from here." He nodded, and Harriet watched as she pulled off her greatcoat and tunic, throwing them to the other side of the bunk, then kicked off her shoes before pulling open the sleeping bag and climbing in alongside her. It was a tight squeeze, but Harriet instinctively grabbed her when she felt her body heat, while Ginny reached over and pulled her greatcoat over the top of the sleeping bag and blanket, and pushed her folded tunic under her head, lifting her off the pillow a little, and letting Harriet rest her head on her shoulder. She rubbed her hands vigorously over Harriet's ice cold back, using the friction to warm her skin a little, until the wireless operator returned with a tin mug of coca, which Ginny took and carefully held to Harriet's lips so she could sip.

"Are they OK?" Harriet whispered through her chattering teeth.

"They will be," Ginny replied. "Now stop worrying about them, and make sure you stay awake. OK?" Harriet nodded, and Ginny gave her another sip of cocoa. "Tell me your name."

"What?"

"Your name. Tell me your name."

"Harriet..."

"No, it isn't! Tell me your name! Come on, think!"

"Harry..." Harriet looked up at Ginny and smiled weakly. "Harry Cornwall."

Chapter 10

Ungentlemanly

"Harry, do come in," Alastair said, as Harriet knocked on his office door. "This is Major Carlyle." He gestured to the army officer sitting to the side of his desk, and smoking a cigar that filled the room with a fragrant blue smoke.

"Squadron Leader," Carlyle greeted Harriet with a firm handshake, after jumping from his chair. He was in his forties, and very well spoken, with just a hint of an accent that she couldn't quite place. She smiled politely in reply, then looked at Alastair questioningly. After landing following the morning's patrol, she'd received a message from Alastair's office summoning her to a meeting, and suggesting she should be in best uniform. It had been frustrating to say the least. She didn't like being rushed, and finding out as soon as she landed that she had to get home, get tidied up, and get changed, before racing back for some unannounced meeting had left her annoyed. Especially as she hadn't had chance to have a proper breakfast yet, instead having to make do with tea and biscuits, hardly a sustaining meal, especially as she'd been hungrier than ever for every day of the two weeks since her swim in the North Sea. It had taken over a week to recover from the severe hypothermia that had hit her still emaciated body. Even though she'd been back from Malta a few months, she still hadn't put on that much weight, and hadn't the fat stores to help protect her from the extreme cold of being plunged into the ice cold North Sea while already exhausted. She'd only just got back to flying, and while she was mostly recovered, she was continuously hungry.

"Did you get a chance to eat yet?" Alastair asked, as Harriet closed the door and took a seat in front of his desk.

"Not yet..." she replied. Trying hard not to seem as irritated as she was.

"Right, well we'll make this as short and painless as we can. I'll call the Mess and tell them to have a decent breakfast ready for you when we're done."

"Thank you, Sir," Harriet said with a smile, keeping it formal, as she had no idea who the Major was, or what he was doing there. Knowing she would still be getting a decent meal changed her mood almost instantly.

"Not at all." He picked up his phone and gave the instructions, then leant back in his seat and smiled. "Harry, Major Carlyle flew in this morning from London. He's come to talk to you about something you may be able to help with."

"I'm not sure what that could be, but I'm happy to try," Harriet replied with a slight shrug and a pleasant smile.

"Harry..." Carlyle started. "I can call you Harry, can't I?"

"Why not?" Harriet shrugged again; not entirely sure what else she would say. She was trying to size him up. He was wearing an army uniform, but the badge on his service cap and the buttons on his tunic were of the General Service Corps, a catch all group for anyone who didn't fit with a specific regiment or unit, so it was hard to work him out just from his uniform. He was also powerful and athletic looking, not the usual desk job type that spent the war fighting paperwork, so her guess was that he was in active service in some way.

"Good. In that case you can call me Carlyle. Everyone who knows me does."

"Thank you..."

"First things first, Harry, I must remind you that as an officer of the Royal Air Force, you are subject to the Official Secrets Act, and as such anything discussed today isn't mentioned to anybody out of this room, on pain of something very nasty happening..." He looked at her with a menacing smile, which suggested his playful words and demeanour were a very loose veil covering something much more sinister.

194

"Naturally," Harriet replied casually, trying hard to match his demeanour, and not show that his threats of something nasty had any impact on her at all. Despite making her a feel little uneasy.

"Harry, I'll cut to the chase, as I know you're hungry after your morning flight, and probably thinking more about your breakfast than some old man talking to you about secrets." His menacing smile flickered again as he talked. Both intriguing Harriet, and making her squirm a little. "I work with what some like to refer to as the Ministry of Ungentlemanly Warfare, and I've been reading your file."

"My file?" Her heart raced a little. Had somebody finally found out that she'd been nothing more than an English schoolgirl living in France when the Germans invaded, with absolutely no military training, and no right to be in a uniform and pretending to be a pilot? In a brief second her mind raced.

"Yes... Apparently you speak fluent French?"

"Some would say otherwise, but yes. I lived there half my life."

"I know... Your family's quite well known to us." He took a puff on his cigar as Harriet's stomach tensed. "Nothing sinister," he continued, as if he could read her now panicked thoughts, while smiling again in a less than reassuring way. "How fluent are you? Have you lost much in your time since leaving France?" He asked in almost flawless French, with a hint of a Parisienne accent.

"I'm not sure, I don't get to talk in French that often. Why don't you tell me?" Harriet replied in French.

"A hint of Reims, I like it," he said warmly, switching back to English and taking Harriet by surprise. "Almost perfect. It wouldn't fit if your accent was flawless. In my experience, something of a regional dialect always lends a little authenticity."

"Thank you... Though you have me at a loss, Carlyle. You seem to know a lot about me, but I don't know anything about you; and I'm still not sure what you want with me, or how my speaking French is of any consequence?" She remained as calm as possible, while desperately hoping her nerves and doubts about what was happening weren't showing.

"Of course, I'm getting to that. The French part is vitally important, if you were rusty it would have been pointless going any further." He gave Alastair a nod, then turned his gaze back to Harriet. "Now, your commanding officer has already agreed to release you to us, but we only take volunteers, so you'd need to add your agreement, if that wouldn't be a problem?"

"Agreement for what?"

"To work for us. Temporarily, at least. I mean, there is a war going on, and you could be ordered, but where would the point be in that? A volunteer is worth ten pressed men, and all that. Besides, in our line of work you kind of need to want to be there, if you get my meaning?"

"Not at all... How am I supposed to agree to something, when you haven't told me what the something is?" She frowned, and Alastair smirked in a way that was both reassuring and irritating.

"I'm afraid I can't tell you until you agree to work for us."

"Let me get this straight, you want me to agree to do something before I know what it is?"

"Precisely. It involves flying, if that helps?" He shrugged, and looked over to Alastair as he did the same.

"Go on, then," Harriet said, trying not to roll her eyes too much.

"You agree?"

"I suppose."

"You agree?"

"I agree!"

"Wonderful! In that case, sign here." He pushed a document in front of her which read similarly to the Official Secrets Act, though with apparently much more punitive terms for breach. She took her pen from her pocket and signed, then pushed the document back to him. She was intrigued, and nervous, scared even, but something about the situation made her want to know more. "Harry, I want you to go to Switzerland for us. Geneva, to be precise. Which is why your French needs to be of a high standard, understandably."

"Understandably..." Her heart raced as she processed what he was saying.

"As you know, timekeeping is vitally important in everything we do, from timing operations to allowing pilots and navigators to fly against the enemy with the precision we've come to expect." He nodded to the Omega watch on her wrist, the one Cas had given her, that she'd worn every day and in every flight since. "We get parts from Switzerland as often as we dare through diplomatic pouches, but we need something more specific collecting. You see, there are certain tools we need to build precision watches, tools that only the Swiss have. We've lost three sets so far in our attempts to get them to England. Intercepted packages, a crashed aircraft, and a ship sunk, to be precise, so we thought we'd send somebody to collect them in person, and make sure they get back in one piece."

"I see..." If Harriet's mind had been spinning before Carlyle's revelation, it was now moving so fast she was struggling to string more than a couple of words together.

"You'll fly to neutral Sweden on board a civilian aircraft, then take flight from Sweden to Geneva. Once there, you'll meet with our Swiss watchmaking friends, and collect their little gift for us before returning to Sweden, and then back here. Remarkably simple, really."

"So it seems... I have just one question?"

"Yes?"

"How?"

"Excuse me?"

"How am I supposed to do all of that?"

"I just told you..."

"I'm a pilot in the RAF, don't you think somebody would notice me walking around Europe? I don't know much about the legalities, but I'm not sure neutral countries would allow that either. Not to mention what their German neighbours would think."

"Good observation, Harry. Which is why you'll be going as Amelie Faucon, a Swiss banking representative working in their New York office."

"Who's Amelie Faucon?"

"An unfortunately young lady who died in 1921, shortly after she was born. It's OK, we've done the hard work, before you ask." He opened his case and passed her a Swiss passport, complete with Harriet's photo. She looked at it, then at him. "We like to be prepared, just in case..."

"Apparently."

"You'll be in Geneva a couple of days at the most, your hotels and flights are booked, and you'll have an allowance to spend while there. If anything, it'll be something of a holiday for you. Alastair's been filling me in on your recent exploits in the air, and you can probably do with a few days off."

"I'm not entirely sure it's that simple," Alastair said with a suspicious frown. "Perhaps you and I should have a chat about it, Harry? Before you decide... We can always withdraw your agreement and keep you on base until Carlyle has found somebody else."

"I'll do it!" Harriet said, before she had a chance to talk herself out of it, which she was already doing a good job of. "Somebody's gone to a lot of effort already, even going as far as making me a passport, so it feels like it's important."

"Tell her..." Alastair said firmly, fixing Carlyle in an icy glare that was all the more forceful coming from somebody she knew to have such a kind nature.

"Tell me what?" Harriet asked.

"If you should fall into German hands, and they see through your cover story, you'll be shot as a spy." Carlyle's mischievous demeanour dimmed as he spoke.

"A spy?" Harriet was still fighting to remain calm, though inside she was starting to feel sick.

"Yes. Ministry of Ungentlemanly Warfare, remember?"

"I'm hardly a gentleman."

"You should be OK in that case... Look, I won't dress it up for you, you're smarter than that and wouldn't appreciate it if I did. The fact is, we're desperate. Sending a young woman with an almost native command of French could be our way in. There's lot's hanging on this, you're right. I can't give you details, but if you can get the watchmaking tools back here to us, it'll have a significant and almost immediate impact on the war effort. Time is everything in war, Harry, as you well know. The more high quality and accurate timepieces we can get on the wrists of our combat leaders, the more efficient we're going to be. I can't tell you more, so if you do this you'll just have to trust me."

"I assume you can tell me when?"

"What? Oh, yes. Yes, silly me. You leave today."

"Today?" Harriet's eyes opened wide in surprise.

"Yes, why? Did you have plans?"

"I..."

"Oh, you'll need civilian clothes. Do you have any with you?"

"Nothing appropriate."

"Not a problem, we anticipated as much, and had a few items put together for you.

"OK..."

"Right, that's about everything for now. I'll meet you at lunch for a full briefing, give you time to get your breakfast and try on your clothes." He lifted a large leather holdall and put it on the desk, then stood and offered his hand, which Harriet shook firmly while looking him in the eyes. "Welcome to the Special Operations Executive."

"The Mess will be expecting you, Harry, I'll have a room made available to you on station to save you a trip back to your digs," Alastair said reassuringly. "Don't worry about the squadron, I'll make sure they're looked after in your absence."

"Thank you. Will that be all?"

"Yes, get off and get your breakfast."

"Oh, Harry. There is one other thing," Carlyle said.

"Yes?"

"You don't mention this to anyone outside of this room. Please stay in the Mess until it's time to leave, and be dressed and ready to go when we collect you. I'm sure we can have lunch brought to your room?" He looked at Alastair, who nodded in agreement.

After an unusually full breakfast of bacon and eggs, black pudding, toast, and lots of hot tea, Harriet went to her allocated room in the Mess, where she threw off her uniform and laid on the bed for a while. She had a lot going through her mind. She knew she'd been struggling after the raid on the German battleship, which despite making it to the safety of Wilhelmshaven, had been beaten up badly enough to make sure it would be staying there for quite some time. It was a successful raid, or so Alastair had tried to reassure her. The battleship was out of the fight, torpedoed and bombed, and ravaged with gun and cannon, and the destroyer had been sunk, along with a couple of torpedo boats, but in Harriet's mind it had been a terrible and terrifying failure. She'd lost a quarter of her squadron, eight men in all, though the Beaufighters had it worse. Of the twenty aircraft they put up, eight didn't come back. If she was honest with herself, she was struggling before that. She hadn't really recovered from Malta, she hadn't had time, and then she'd jumped straight into a new way of fighting that she wasn't used to. Her shaking hands had started long before the hypothermia, she'd had them for weeks. Her nerves were frayed, and she knew it. She also knew that she shouldn't be flying, let alone leading a squadron, but she just couldn't say it out loud. Not to Alastair, or AP, not to anyone. She had her duty, she'd been trusted with commanding the squadron, and she didn't want to let anyone down. Not the King, or Alastair, but most of all not her crews. She'd grown very fond of her Norwegians, and they'd accepted her, despite their bumpy start, and she didn't feel she could leave them. She knew the time was coming, though. She'd either lose her edge and be shot down, or lose her grip and break down. The shakes, the memory blackouts, they were all signs. She knew that's why she took the job with Carlyle. Somehow the threat of being shot as a spy wasn't as bad as getting back into a Mosquito and flying another shipping raid.

After spending too much time in her own mind, she pulled herself away from her bed and opened the holdall to see what clothing delights the army had managed to put together for her. She cringed as she unfastened the zip. She'd seen the issue underwear the WAAFs were given, it was horrendous, and she couldn't imagine any other item of clothing being much better if that was the standard. To her amazement, she unravelled a beautiful and perfectly packed royal blue skirt and jacket, with an ivory white silk blouse. As she looked closer, she saw the labels, Norman Hartnell. Tailor and designer to the Royal Family. Her eyes opened wide. She'd heard of his clothing, and seen the high society photographed wearing it in the newspapers, and she knew that the suit of clothes she was looking at would cost several months of her pay, even as a Squadron Leader. A matching overcoat and a pair of stunning heeled black shoes finished off the outfit, along with a hat that looked a little like a man's fedora, though more feminine. To her amazement, there were also boxes of underwear and silk stockings in the bag, along with fine Egyptian cotton towels monogrammed with her new initials, AF, and a makeup bag with everything she could ever have asked for from the Chanel counter in Harrods. Even a small bottle of her favourite perfume. The dark thoughts that had been swirling around her mind quickly deserted her, and she hurried to pull on the clothes, desperately hoping and praying that they fit. She wasn't disappointed. Everything fit as though it had been made for her, they'd even got her shoe size right. She looked at herself in the mirror, the clothes were perfect. She smiled, a lot, and after carefully undressing again and hanging the clothes on the empty locker, she headed for the bath, which she filled with hot water and scented bath oil from the bag she'd been given, before climbing in and relaxing, determined to be as pampered as possible before she went to meet her firing squad.

The morning passed quicker than Harriet had hoped, and after a sandwich and tea were delivered at lunch, she dressed in her new civilian clothes and did her hair and makeup. She almost didn't recognise herself when she was done. She couldn't remember the last time she'd been dressed up in such a way. She'd been out on the town in her uniform, but that was different. Even her trip to the Air Ministry in the clothes aunt Mary had bought her wasn't the same. She checked her watch and gave herself a spray of perfume, before checking herself in the mirror once more until a knock on the door pulled her away.

"Can I come in?" Carlyle asked, as he stood in the doorway looking her up and down.

"Yes..." Harriet stepped aside and invited him into her room. He was carrying a large and expensive looking suitcase, which he laid on her bed before opening.

"This is your case for the trip. It has a false bottom for the package you're to bring home," he explained, while showing her how it worked. "You can pack your things in there, towels and all, it should bulk it out enough and make it look like you're authentic." He stepped back and let Harriet look at the case, then pack it with her towels, make up, night dress, and spare underwear, before closing and locking it. "Your wallet," he said. Complete with business identity and enough money to stay comfortable, American dollars and Swiss francs. Remember that it comes from the King's treasure chest, so don't get too carried away..." He gave her a wink as she checked inside, and quickly closed it immediately when she saw how much money was inside. "Your tickets for your flights to and from Geneva." Then he pulled a small silk purse from his pocket. "This, Harry, is to remain a secret strictly between us." He opened the purse, then took her hand and emptied a small mound of shining and sparkling diamonds into it. "You're to give these to our Swiss friends, and we don't tell a soul, our side included. Understood?" Harriet nodded slowly as he took each diamond in turn and popped them in the bag, then tied the top and handed it to her. "Hide them, keep them safe, and make sure they get to where they need to be."

"Anything else?" Harriet asked, trying to be as nonchalant as possible.

"Yes." He handed her a midsized handbag which perfectly matched her outfit, then pulled a Walther P38 pistol from his pocket. "The pistol is German, and remarkably deadly."

"I know, I've used one before..." She looked at the Walther, and checked the ammunition and safety catch, just as she had with the pistol she'd used back in France, having been given it after her first victories in combat. Carlyle raised an eyebrow.

"It wouldn't be unusual for a young professional woman travelling alone in a war to have one. Use it only if you must, it'll draw attention." She nodded and slipped it into a pouch in her purse. "Then there's this..." He opened a small tin and pulled out a small oval rubber pea.

"What is it?"

"An 'L' pill..."

"A what?" She took it and rolled the rubber between her finger and thumb.

"A suicide pill, the L stands for lethal. Take it from the rubber sleeve, pop it in your mouth, and bite with the back teeth. Seconds later your heart will stop from a lethal dose of potassium cyanide, and the game's over." He looked at Harriet, who stared at him in disbelief. Her heart started pounding so quickly that she didn't think she'd need a pill to kill her. If it kept going, it was likely to explode all by itself. "I'm not being dramatic when I say don't let the Germans take you alive. If they find out you're a spy, they'll torture you until you convict your own grandmother, before hanging you in a public place somewhere as an example to others. Keep the pill on you at all times, and if things aren't looking good, you know what to do."

"I..."

"It's quite painless, I'm told. Anyway, you won't need it." He smiled, then rummaged in his pocket once again. "Last but not least, something for you." He handed her a box containing a pair of beautiful diamond earrings. "The diamonds are real, and worth a fortune. They're your insurance, a way to buy your way out of trouble instead of taking that pill." Harriet nodded, then went to her mirror and put them in. They were incredible, and they sparkled in the light in a way only a diamond could. "You certainly look the part. Right, I'll give you a couple of minutes." He left her to finish packing and getting dressed. She looked at the dreaded 'L' pill, and thought for a moment she'd accidentally leave it behind, then quickly decided against it. As much as the idea of using it filled her with horror, she didn't appreciate the idea of torture either. She'd heard the stories, and narrowly avoided a very personal experience at the hands of the Gestapo before escaping from France, so she reached back and pushed it deep into her tight hair bun, securing it so it wouldn't move, then tidying the hair and forgetting about it. A last make up check, thick woollen coat on and fastened, and hat on and pulled to one side. The girl in the mirror wasn't somebody she recognised, but she liked her, and immediately wanted to spend more time with her. She grabbed her case and opened the door, leaving her uniform and everything of her other self packed in a bag ready to be collected by Alastair. "This way, Mademoiselle Faucon." Carlyle gave her a wink, then took her case and led her down the hall and out of the fire escape, then down the steps to Alastair's staff car, which he was leaning against and enjoying a cigarette while waiting.

"My God..." Alastair said as he saw her.

"Bonjour," she replied confidently.

"Harry, is that you?"

"Of course," she shrugged, lifting her nose in the air dismissively as she talked, channelling her best impression of Nicole. He nodded and smiled, then opened the door for her and saluted as she climbed in, doing her best not to smirk. Carlyle climbed in after her, and Alastair jumped in and started the engine.

"Your identity discs?" Alastair asked while driving. He held his hand over his shoulder, and Harriet passed them forward. "You don't have anything else that identifies you?"

"I don't even recognise myself in the mirror, I think we're safe." She smiled at him in the rear view mirror as he sped them to the runway, and along it, far out of sight of the buildings where a Mosquito was waiting. It was painted in camouflage, though different to her squadron's, and with red, white, and blue striped markings along with a civilian registration written in large letters.

"A Mosquito?" Harriet asked.

"A civilian version belonging to a civil airline, the British Oversees Aviation Corporation. The Swedish would impound a military aircraft for breaching neutrality rules, so we can only use a civilian aircraft flown by civilian crew."

"I see..."

"There's a life jacket and blanket inside for you, and a flask of cocoa and some biscuits." Alastair stood by the steps and offered his hand. "Good luck, Harry."

"Thank you. There's a letter back at the cottage, just in case..."

"It won't be needed."

"Better get on board, you've a schedule to keep," Carlyle cut in, shaking Harriet's hand firmly. "See you in a few days." She nodded and forced a smile, then turned and climbed up the ladder, finding it much more challenging in high heeled shoes than it usually was in her flying boots, then popped her head into the cockpit and looked at the pilot's seat.

"Welcome aboard..." AP said with a smirk. She was wearing a dark uniform with gold braid on the cuffs, and civilian wings on her chest. Her hair was tied up tight and smart, clipped into place and looking like she'd had a haircut. "Ma'am," she added, with more than a hint of sarcasm.

"What are you doing here?" Harriet asked.

"I'm your pilot, George Johns."

"George?"

"I was told when I volunteered for the BOAC that it needed to be something suitably ambiguous, and I thought a girl's name that could pass for a boy would fit."

"Of course... Volunteered?"

"I'm assuming the same way you volunteered to get dressed up in clothing inappropriate for a cold flight to Sweden."

"Probably..." Harriet looked at her skirt, and the harness, and quickly started to agree. Alastair passed her suitcase up through the hatch, which she stowed in front of her, then waved as he closed her in.

"There's a parachute on the back of your seat, pull the harness on and you're ready to go." AP smirked as Harriet irritably pulled up her skirt while shuffling in her seat, then fastened the parachute and safety harnesses. She'd felt like a film star when she walked to the aeroplane, now she felt like a turkey all tied up for Christmas. AP finally passed her a blanket, while letting out a giggle. "For your modesty."

"Thanks!"

"Let's hope you don't need the parachute. We should be faster than most things around, it's why we're OK to go in daylight. We don't have any guns though, so hopefully we won't run into a 190, otherwise we're toast."

"I have faith in you."

"You should, I'm a good pilot."

"I know, you can even land on water..."

"Shut up, that was different."

"Shall we get going? You need to get the engines warmed up, my legs are cold, and I'll need the cabin heat."

"Then you'd better be nice, and stop mentioning the sea incident."

"You're the boss."

"I know. She handed Harriet a helmet and oxygen mask, which she put on after carefully removing her hat and placing it on her knee, much to AP's amusement. "Don't mess your hair up."

"Don't you have some driving to do?"

"OK, stand by. We'll get the engines started, and we'll be taking off shortly. Make sure you're strapped in, and your oxygen is working."

"I'm sitting right here; do you have to be so formal?"

"Understood, ready when you are," a man replied over the radio, startling Harriet in the process.

"You didn't think you were the only passenger on this flight, did you?" AP asked with a smirk.

"Where the hell is he?" Harriet looked around the small cockpit, wondering if she was missing something.

"There's a bed in the bomb bay, complete with oxygen, harness, and hot drinks."

"You're serious?"

"Yep. A gentleman with a large heavy briefcase is heading to Sweden to buy ball bearings with the gold he has stashed inside. When I drop you off, I'm taking as many as we can buy back with us."

"It's quite some enterprise."

"You're telling me. Apparently we can't produce enough, and we need them desperately, the Germans are the same and need them just as much, so everyone looks the other way while aircraft from both sides fly in and out of Sweden. Or so that dubious Major from the SOE said."

"Carlyle?"

"That's him. I don't trust him, he's suspicious looking."

"I know what you mean..."

The flight was surprisingly smooth, and not long after taking off, the engines were running warm and AP has the cockpit heat set to a comfortable level, which kept both her and Harriet happy as they raced across the North Sea. The Mosquito was fast anyway, but without the armament and ammunition it was even slicker, and the ride was comfortable all the way to Sweden. Harriet and AP talked the whole way, enjoying each other's company as they reminisced about the old times. Harriet came close to telling her how she was feeling, about her stress and her worries, but she thought better of it. She had other things to do, and she knew she didn't need dark thoughts getting in the way. The only time they stopped talking was when they approached Stockholm in the early evening. The lights glowing in the darkening evening sky made them both smile. They'd lived through blackouts for so long that it was almost unthinkable to see a city lit up at night. It made Harriet think of America, and her friends who she missed. It also made her feel excited and nervous; she had no idea what she was getting into, and no idea what was going to come next. As they descended to a well lit runway, at an airport littered with civilian marked transport aircraft of all types, she started to worry that she'd made a mistake. The relaxed enjoyment of her flight with AP was quickly ebbing away, and her stomach was turning. She stared out of the window at the lights as the Mosquito touched down lightly, and AP followed instructions from the tower to park on a row of visiting aircraft.

"Are you OK?" AP asked.

"Yes..." Harriet replied after a minute. "Yes, fine." She forced a smile.

"Look, Harry, I don't know what you're doing out here, all I know is that I have to pick you up the day after tomorrow; but if you want to come back with me right now, I'll do it."

"No. No, it's fine."

"You're sure? We can make up an excuse, say things looked awkward, maybe?"

"I'm sure. It's OK. I'll be OK." She took a deep breath, then unfastened her harness and started to straighten her clothing. AP nodded reluctantly, then released the hatch in the floor and dropped the extending ladder.

"I'll go and let our passenger out, and give you a few minutes to tidy up. Wrap up warm." She leant forward and gave Harriet an unexpected hug, then disappeared through the cold blast and down the steps, pulling on her peaked service cap as she left. Harriet took the mirror from her bag and checked her makeup and hair, to her relief she still looked presentable, and after wriggling and crouching above her seat while she straightened herself out, she started nervously down the ladder, taking care not to slip in her heels as she pulled her suitcase and handbag down after her. It was cold, icy cold, and the stiff Scandinavian wind breezed up her skirt and made her miss her trousers and flying boots. Yet another regret. She checked herself again at the bottom of the steps, then pulled on her black leather gloves and picked up her case, just as AP reappeared in front of her. "Ready?" she asked an increasingly nervous Harriet.

"Ready... Where do I go?"

"That way, I think." she pointed in the direction their passenger was heading, towards a brightly lit concrete building. Harriet nodded, and they walked side by side.

"I'm Swiss French," Harriet whispered as they approached the main doors, which were guarded by Swedish soldiers wrapped up in long thick white coats with fur collars, and warm looking white fur hats.

"What?" AP replied.

"I'm Swiss French. I thought you should know; in case anyone asks. I'm visiting from America."

"You could have mentioned that before now."

"I didn't think..."

"Unusual for you."

"Shut up."

"Just be careful, whatever you're doing. If anyone asks, I'll stick to the basics and say you didn't talk much on the flight."

"OK."

"Good luck and be careful." She pulled the door open and gestured Harriet into the terminal hall, where she was waved over to a grand looking desk by a uniformed official, while AP was waved over to a desk marked 'visiting pilots'.

210

"Good evening, miss," the official said in warm, heavily accented English, while looking Harriet up and down. "Your passport, please." He held out his hand patiently.

"Bonsoir, Monsieur; and it's Mademoiselle..." Harriet replied, again channelling her best impression of Nicole, and adding a casual French accent to her own English. She pulled her passport and flight tickets from her bag and confidently handed them to him, while glancing around, nose held high, as if surveying her domain. Her heart was racing, but she knew that if she was to complete her mission, she had to put on an act that would be believable to most.

"Of course, Mademoiselle Faucon," he replied, while stamping her passport before handing it back to her, along with her tickets. "You're just in time, your flight is scheduled to leave shortly. I'll have one of our staff see you outside."

"I'm grateful." She gave a nod and a hint of a mischievous smile. The official snapped his fingers and waved a young man over, then said something in Swedish that she almost recognised from the Norwegian she'd picked up on the squadron. The young man hurriedly picked up her suitcase, then beckoned she follow him. "Thank you," she said to the official, giving another smile, then turning on her heels and following confidently and casually, turning the heads of soldiers, officials, and travellers alike as she passed through the hall. AP watched her, glancing from a distance, and just catching her eye long enough to share a smile before Harriet was led back outside into the cold, floodlit night. The young man talked to her in Swedish, nodding and smiling as he did, but he talked so fast that she didn't have a clue what her was saying, so just continued with her nonchalance while occasionally giving him a look which seemed to make him blush a little. She worried she was agreeing to something questionable, but he seemed pleasant and quite harmless, and if anything, just keen to impress and do his job. He jabbered on about something, then pointed to a large silvery grey four engine aircraft with the word 'Lufthansa' written on the side in large letters, along with a civilian registration, and a huge Nazi swastika on its red tail. Harriet's heart almost stopped. She looked at the young man, who nodded and smiled, and encouraged her along as she slowed her pace nervously. "Suisse," she said, as she pointed to her tickets. "Suisse, Schweiz." She tapped the ticket again.

"Schweiz, Schweiz." He nodded and pointed to the German aeroplane while waving her along. She looked around as a hundred thoughts passed through her mind. Had she fallen at the first hurdle? Had it been a trap? Did they know she was coming? He waved her along, and she had no option but to follow. She was committed, or so it seemed. If she made a scene she'd blow her cover, if she made a run for the Mosquito, she'd blow AP's too. She had no option but to straighten her back, walk tall, and deal with whatever happened next. Her mouth was starting to dry, and despite the cold wind she was starting to sweat. The young man shouted something in Swedish to the official waiting at the steps around the other side of the aircraft as he led Harriet.

"Fraulein," the official said as he greeted Harriet, holding His hand out for her papers.

"Mademoiselle," Harriet corrected, almost dismissively. Determined to maintain her confidence, even if it was a facade that had her shaking violently on the inside.

"Of course, excuse me," he replied, in very good French. "You almost missed us. Please, take a seat and I'll have our bag brought taken board. Enjoy your flight."

"Thank you." She took back her papers, then walked up the steps and in through the door, where she was met by a stewardess dressed in white tunic and black skirt, looking every bit the image of Germany. Her golden hair was wound in intricate bunches each side of her head, and her big blue eyes lit up the cabin. She greeted Harriet in French, then showed her to a single seat by the window, facing another, and across the aisle from two double seats set up the same way. The older man sitting opposite stood politely, bowing almost as she took her seat, and the two couples sitting across the aisle, all looking in their thirties or forties, smiled politely.

"Francais?" The older man asked as they sat.

"Suisse," Harriet replied.

"Ah, of course," her replied in very good French. "Do you fly often?"

"Every now and then." Harriet looked around as she talked, and watched as the cabin crew went about preparing for flight, and the first of the four engines was started, dimming the cabin lights as it did.

"It's civilised, I like it. I try to fly as much as I can, but don't get the opportunities these days. You know how it is."

"Yes..." Harriet smiled politely, she couldn't believe she was on a German aeroplane and talking to a German, when it wasn't two weeks ago that she was trying to sink a German battleship while trying hard not to be shot out of the sky.

"Now it's between cities, up here to Sweden for business, but that's all. What about you. Where do you fly?"

"America."

"America?"

"Yes. I work in our office over there. They fly lots between the states."

"I went to America once, before the war. To New York, do you know it?"

"A little. I had the best steak in a restaurant not far from Times Square."

"Ah... Yes... I do miss travelling, and steak. You're lucky you still get to enjoy both away from the war. I envy you." He pulled out a cigarette case and offered her one.

"No, thank you."

"Good. I'm told these things will kill me, but it think perhaps there are a few things ahead of the queue." He laughed loudly as he lit his cigarette and blew out a cloud of blue smoke. "What do you do in America?"

"I work for the bank."

"Of course, you're Swiss. What else would you do?" he laughed again, as did Harriet.

"And you, if I may ask?"

"Manufacturing. My machines need ball bearings, and the Swedes have them by the cart load. I come here every now and then to collect a new order." He leant forward and half whispered. "I extend my stays a little, so I can enjoy the food and beer, and escape the war for a while." He winked, then laughed again before sitting back as the aeroplane started to move, and start its taxi to the runway end. Harriet took off her coat, then fastened her lap belt and got settled, before the four engines roared loudly and started the sprint down the concrete. "My favourite part of flying!"

"Mine too!" Harriet said with a big smile, as the large transport aircraft jumped into the air. She was nervous still, but a little less than before she'd boarded the aeroplane. Once in the air, she had her face almost pressed to the window, watching the lights of Sweden as they were left behind, and then turning to the silvery light of the moon dancing across the scattered clouds. It was beautiful, and so peaceful. Or it would be if it wasn't for the fact that she was on a German aeroplane and surrounded by Germans. She felt strangely safe though, and as she chatted with Hermann, her new friend from Bavaria, she just had to remember her cover story, and stick firmly to French. One slip up, one English sentence, and she could quite easily give herself away. She just had to play the part. Much to her surprise, the flight was over before it had really begun, and no more than two hours after taking off they were coming in to land. The silver moonlight lit up a sprawling metropolis below, a city much bigger than she expected of Geneva, though her rapid calculations told her that even in a stripped down Mosquito she wouldn't get to Switzerland from Sweden in two hours. "The heart of the Reich..." Hermann said as he gazed out of the window at the passing streets.

"Excuse me?" Harriet asked, feeling her heart start to race again as they came in to land, and she saw the sign on the terminal, 'Berlin'.

"Berlin." He looked at her with a shrug. "Being a devout Bavarian, I don't care for the place myself."

"Why are we landing in Berlin? I thought this aeroplane was heading for Switzerland?"

"You may have flown lots, my young friend, but maybe not so much in Germany. There aren't that many civil flights these days, and those there are often transit through Berlin."

"I didn't know..."

"We're going the same direction. Stick with me, and I'll show you the way." He unfastened his lap belt as they rolled to a halt, then put on his coat before helping Harriet into hers, and together they joined the short queue of passengers bustling slowly towards the exit, and the steps out into the night. She pulled her collar high and her hat low as she walked into the terminal building. Her nerves were quickly becoming frayed, and she felt her chest tighten so much she could hardly breathe when she saw the guards of the SS, the Schutzstaffel that formed the Nazi party's own private army, standing at their posts around the building, wearing their smart yet incredibly sinister black uniforms, and holding polished rifles. They looked like giants, with steely eyes staring straight ahead, scanning everyone as they guarded against those looking to make trouble. "Kettenhunde," Hermann whispered to Harriet. "Chain dogs... You see the breastplate they wear, hung around their neck on a chain? The mark of the military field police, nasty pieces of work at the best of times, but these belong to the SS and are much worse." Harriet nodded and swallowed hard, while all the time trying her hardest to remain graceful, though feeling quite sure she stood out like a sore thumb, and that it would only be minutes before they found her out. She stopped for a moment to look in her bag for her passport, making sure she waited long enough for Hermann to be a safe enough distance from her not to be implicated when they grabbed her. He'd been nothing but pleasant, but her experience of the Gestapo in France suggested his friendliness would get him in hot water when they found out he'd been making friends with a spy. She continued to look in her bag, while glancing at the other passengers out of the corner of her eye as they were processed. Once she was sure Hermann was far enough away, she pulled out her passport and continued walking towards the official at the desk.

"Halt!" a man called out from behind her, and the hairs on the back of her neck stood on end as she continued to walk, praying he wasn't talking to her. "Fraulein, halt!" he repeated, and Harriet slowly came to a halt, then with a deep breath to try and compose herself, she turned to face an SS Officer. He had a deep scar down his cheek and pale washed out eyes that made him look all the more terrifying in his black uniform, and on his cap was a less than thrilling silver skull and crossbones. "You dropped your ticket..." he said in sharp German, as he held it in his hands and glanced down at it for a moment, while Harriet stood frozen to the spot. Her mind was a mess of confusing thoughts, and stalled as she tried to translate his words from German, into English, and then prepare her response in French.

"Ah, my ticket, thank you," she replied in French. Then, trying hard not to mess it up, she talked in German, with a French accent. "My tickets."

"Your passport?" He held out his hand, and she immediately obliged, smiling the best she could. "Swiss..?"

"Yes."

"Bank?"

"Yes..."

"Come with me." He marched across the room, the heels of his highly polished black boots clicking on the floor as she walked at his side, unwillingly but unable to do anything other than follow his instructions. He led her past the other passengers, who were waiting patiently to have their papers checked, each of them looking away as they noticed her, desperate not to make eye contact and suggest any sort of familiarity which would have them dragged out of the line to join her. Even Hermann looked down at his shoes, after doing a double take when she passed. The officer stopped at the front of the queue and handed Harriet's passport to the official, who simply stamped it and handed it back. "Welcome to Germany," he said, much to Harriet's surprise, giving her a smile which made him look even more sinister, if that were possible. "It's important that we look after our Swiss friends. Please, take a seat in the waiting area and enjoy a drink. You'll be called when your flight is ready." He handed over her passport and tickets. "And please be careful, tickets aren't easily replaced. Good evening." He clicked his heels and gave a short, sharp bow, then turned and marched away, leaving Harriet fighting to control her shaking limbs. The official looked up and pointed to the waiting area, and she smiled a little in reply before walking away and heading to the first bathroom she could find. Where, after making sure she was alone, she bent over a toilet and retched, before telling herself to 'get a grip, then cleaning herself up with cold water and a soft towel, and redoing her makeup. She looked at herself in the mirror. She looked good, considering, but felt terrible. She wanted to cry, and wanted to go home. Berlin wasn't even mentioned, it wasn't part of the plan. She could just about handle the trip, but not the SS. She tidied her hair and checked the 'L' pill was still where she'd left it, and for the first time since the whole escapade had started, she thought she would have to use it. She didn't want to die, but she didn't want to be tortured and executed either, and now she was in the heart of Nazi Germany, she appreciated having the pill and an easier way out, should she need it.

Having spent a terrifying hour in the airport's bomb shelter, where she sat tightly squeezed in with passengers, officials, and a scattering of senior officers while the RAF bombed a Berlin factory district not too far away, Harriet was grateful to be escorted outside to a Swissair DC3, the same type of twin engine aeroplane she'd travelled around America in. The cabin wasn't quite as luxurious, but wasn't far off, and as soon as she was seated she sat gripping nervously at the arm rests of her chair, while praying the pilot would hurry up and get moving. She'd had her fill of Berlin, and couldn't wait to be gone. There'd been talk in the terminal of British bombers lurking in the dark skies above, waiting for transport aircraft so they could take them down, but it was a risk Harriet was willing to take. She knew with a degree of confidence that bombers didn't tend to hang around after dropping their bombs, and if they did, it was her logic that flying would be better than staying where she was. Besides, she had her pill. She'd be dead before the wreckage hit the ground if they were shot down, and given her current predicament, that was strangely reassuring. The cabin was only half full, so when the doors closed and the engines started, she relaxed into her seat and breathed a sigh of relief knowing she wouldn't have anyone sitting with her and asking her questions. Her head was tired. Exhausted with fatigue, and with the intense period of living a double life, where every word to leave her lips had to be carefully chosen, and delivered in the right language, with the right accent, and in the right way. She was acutely aware that her safety was incredibly fragile. No longer was she sitting in a heavily armed aeroplane, behind an armoured glass windscreen and with armour plating below and behind her seat. She was a young woman in an expensive suit, with only her mind to keep her safe. She had a pistol and a suicide pill, neither of which were going to keep her alive. She was learning quickly what it took to stay alive on the ground, where you stood face to face with your enemy, instead of swooping around in the air and shooting at a machine. It was different, and it was terrifying.

Chapter 11

Tick, Tock.

Harriet looked from the window of her hotel room, and out over Lake Geneva. It was mesmerising watching the lights of the city dance off the dark water. She sipped on her wine as she watched, and tried to stop the shaking that had almost entirely taken over her since Berlin. The stewardess on the DC3 had even checked on her a few times, and brought her a brandy to steady her nerves, after Harriet had to fake a severe bout of airsickness, and spin a story about how much she struggled with flying. It wasn't a million miles from the truth. Flying had made her feel nauseous and shaky with increasing frequency in recent times, so it wasn't a huge stretch to suggest it was the flight causing her problems, and not the terror of what she was doing. The crew were sympathetic all the same, as were a very pleasant and polite Swedish couple returning home from an appointment in Berlin. They'd helped Harriet with her bag after they'd finally landed, and shared a taxi with her to make sure she got to her apparently quite exclusive lakefront hotel safely.

The room was quite luxurious, certainly on a par with The Savoy, and the hotels she'd stayed in while in America, and the staff had been very welcoming with complimentary wine, and a tray of Swiss cheese and fresh baked crusty bread being delivered to her room shortly after arrival. She couldn't face either at first. The only thing that could calm her was getting out of her clothes and taking a hot shower, and scrubbing herself with the scented soaps from her travel bag. It helped settle her a little, and by the time she was wrapped in her warm dressing gown, the tiredness started to hit her. She was exhausted. The stress had sapped her energy, and she was more than ready for sleep, but relaxing a little had also reminded her how hungry she was, and she quickly destroyed the entire crusty baguette and plate of cheese, along with half the bottle of wine. It was all she needed. On top of the exhaustion and the hot shower, the food and wine were enough to knock her out, and after slipping her pistol under her pillow, she dropped into a deep and disturbed sleep of endless nightmares.

219

Harriet dragged herself from her bed the following morning, and after wrapping herself in the robe once again, returned to the window and looked out at the lake. She was excited to see what it looked like in the daylight, and smiled as she looked out of the long patio style windows. The lake was shimmering blue in the golden sunlight, framed beautifully by the snow capped mountains in the near distance. It was a view she made the most of while enjoying her breakfast of meat and cheese with fresh baked bread, and a large pot of fresh coffee. She'd ordered room service, thinking it was the better option as it would help her avoid unnecessary conversation, which had the potential to trip her up. Once finished, she showered and dressed, and took her time doing her makeup and hair ahead of her morning meeting with the watchmaker. An engagement that was playing on her mind, and making sure her nerves wouldn't have the opportunity to settle, and the longer she sat waiting and looking at her watch, the longer she had to think of the many different ways her mission could go wrong. The more she thought, the more nervous she became, and the more she started to notice her fingers shaking again, not to mention the return of the nausea in her stomach. Before she could get any worse, she packed her handbag and case, made sure her pill was secure in her hair, then headed out for a walk, hoping the cold air would help her clear her mind. She walked the short distance to the lake, and followed the shore while watching the swans and geese, as they paddled around the lake that stretched endlessly into the distance. She soon reached the centre of the town, and all the large buildings and department stores with their hoardings advertising fine Swiss goods overlooking the picturesque lake. The town was busy, with people going around their daily routines, and it felt like a million miles from war torn England. She stopped for a coffee and a pastry, having walked past numerous bakeries with incredible looking wares in the window, including a multitude of macarons in a variety of colours and flavours. She wanted to put her French to the test before going to her meeting, and thought a casual exchange in a bakery would be as good as anywhere else, and despite conversing perfectly with the lady serving her, she still felt like an imposter. There was nothing she could do about it, though, the time of her meeting was fast approaching, and there wasn't a great deal she could do to practice her linguistic skills before the big moment.

"Mademoiselle Faucon, it's a pleasure to meet you," the man said in the most formal French as he stood to greet her. She'd been very well received in the watchmaker's headquarters, and shown immediately to a boardroom occupied by a balding middle aged man wearing a sharp suit and wire rimmed glasses that has almost perfectly circular lenses.

"Good morning," Harriet replied. "Thank you for seeing me, I'm sorry I'm a little early."

"Not at all, it's my pleasure. How are you finding our beautiful city?"

"It's nice to visit, it's just a shame I won't be staying long enough to explore."

"Of course. It's cold this time of year, but beautiful none the less. I'd recommend visiting in the spring if you ever get the chance, the lake comes alive with the warmth"

"I'd enjoy that."

"You should talk with your supervisors now you've been here once; they may be inclined to send you back."

"Perhaps, if I'm lucky." Harriet smiled politely, and swallowed down the urge to let him know that regardless of the beauty, she had absolutely no intention of travelling across Nazi occupied Europe ever again, at least not after she'd got back home. If she got back home. "Speaking of my supervisors, they gave me something for you..." She opened her purse and pulled out the small velvet bag containing the diamonds, and passed it across the table. He accepted it, then gently took her hand, making her tense with nervousness. He rolled her hand softly, and looked at the watch on her wrist. Cas' watch. She hadn't thought to take it off, she hadn't thought she'd need to. That is until he was holding her hand and looking at it closely, examining the men's pilot watch glinting in the beam of sunlight shining through the window, shimmering it's secret rainbow across the pearlescent face.

"Remarkable..." he gasped. "May I?" Harriet nodded, and he unfastened the strap, letting her pull her arm away while he marvelled at the watch. She sat in silence while he examined every detail, lifting his glasses and holding the watch close to his face. She didn't know what to think, and didn't have a thing to say. "May I ask, where did you get this watch?"

"It was a gift from a friend." Despite her discomfort and confusion at the situation, she was still able to feel the twinge of a knife turning in her heart as she remembered exactly who'd given it to her, and when. Her mind regressed to the moment Cas insisted she keep it, on long term loan, as she was now a proper pilot and needed it more than him. She smiled a little. They were much more innocent times, even in the midst of battle. The world had changed a lot since, and she felt sad that Cas was no longer part of it. Though a small part of her thought that may be a mercy, for him at least. Germany was stronger than ever, the Russians were falling back on every front, and America wasn't fairing that well despite being in the war almost a year. She'd often wondered if it was better to be out of it all, but that didn't make the pain of Cas' passing any less.

"Your friend has impeccable taste; you should thank them when you next see them." He smiled as he talked, hardly taking his eyes off the watch.

"I will..." Harriet replied, allowing herself to smile a little, as she wondered exactly when that would be. Knowing with increasing certainty that she'd be joining him soon. The battleship experience had left her under no illusions of that.

"This watch is unique, you know that?"

"He told me. Apparently, he bought it here in Geneva some time ago."

"A long time ago."

"Yes..."

"I know, because I'm the one that made it."

222

"Excuse me?" Harriet's eyes opened wide, and a chink in her contained and calm armour allowed a glimpse of emotion into her voice.

"I made it." He smiled, as he ran his thumb across the scratch on the glass. "I remember experimenting with the pearlescent face, and how I could make the sun catch the hidden colours."

"It's beautiful."

"It is. It's also the only one like it I ever made. I don't suppose you'd consider selling it back to me?"

"No..." Harriet replied, sharper than she expected. "No, sorry." She put on the best smile she could muster. "It's special to me, I couldn't..." She took it back from him and stared at it for a moment.

"I understand." He nodded, and gave a sigh of genuine resignation. "At least I've had the good fortune to meet its owner."

"I would if it were any other watch," Harriet continued, feeling a need to explain, worried that offending him could risk the whole mission. "It's just... My friend..."

"Forgive me for asking..." He looked at her with realisation and understanding, and gave her a warm smile. "When do you leave Geneva?"

"Tonight's flight."

"Then I hope you'll let me have the watch cleaned and serviced for you while you're in town? I'll put my best people on it, and have it finished before dinner." Harriet looked at the watch, and watched the colours as she rolled it in the sunbeam again. A part of her was scared to let it go, just in case. A thought was shouting that she'd never get it back, while another reminded her that she'd hardly ever been without it, and that it was the good luck charm that had got her through the many close scrapes that had killed many others. "I promise it'll be safe in my care, and you'll have it on your wrist again

223

before you leave Geneva," he added, sensing her reluctance. She smiled and nodded, and handed the watch to him again. If he was bluffing just to get the watch, her logic suggested it was safer to let him have it, than to antagonise him and risk the mission, or even her life. There was no escaping the fact that she was a spy in a foreign country. If the Germans got her, she'd be dead, if the Swiss authorities found out, she'd be in prison, at best, and she didn't fancy either. "Perhaps we can even replace the glass, so you don't have to look through the scratch to tell the time."

"Please don't," Harriet asked softly. "The scratch holds many memories."

"Of course... You have my word..." He smiled again at the watch. "Now, if you'll excuse me a moment?" He stood as Harriet nodded, then left the room, taking the diamonds and her watch with him, and leaving her to stare into space and fight with her thoughts. Whether or not she'd done the right thing with her watch was immaterial, she now just wanted to be home. It seemed like everything she'd done since arriving in Sweden was like three games of chess being played at the same time. She was used to puzzles, and problem solving, and even fighting in three dimensions when she was flying in combat. She even enjoyed the calculations most of the time, it made her think and exercise her brain. This was different, though. At least when she flew, she knew who the enemy was. When the watchmaker finally returned, dragging her from her thoughts, he was carrying a small box. "Your package will be delivered to your hotel this afternoon. It would be easier, I'm sure you'd agree, if you didn't have to carry it around with you until you leave. It is, after all, quite valuable."

"Of course," Harriet replied, smiling as brightly as she could, while starting to believe that she'd been had; and having been relieved of her watch and the diamonds, if she left with her life she'd be lucky.

"This is for you." He handed her a small box, which she took with a slight frown.

"For me?" She opened it to reveal a beautiful rose gold ladies dress watch.

"A gift. Something more befitting of a young lady travelling Europe." He gave her a wink, which she wasn't quite sure how to take. "I'll see you this afternoon."

"Thank you..." Harriet said, as he guided her to the door.

"My pleasure. I'd recommend visiting the cathedral if you have no other plans. The views are incredible." Harriet nodded and smiled, still not sure what was happening, and then was escorted out.

Harriet wandered around Geneva for the next few hours, visiting the cathedral as had been suggested, and enjoying the view of the city and the lake from the top of the tower. She wished she'd brought the camera Alastair had managed to source at her request, but tourism and sightseeing wasn't something she'd been expecting. She had a hot chocolate and croissant in an old cafe hidden away in the narrow streets as a rainstorm passed over, then had a slow walk along the lake, where she saw the most incredible and breathtaking rainbow arching from one side of the water to the other. She walked towards it, transfixed in the vibrance of the colours. Others walking along the lakeside path joined her in stopping and watching the beautiful display of colours. Couples, children, they all stood silent and appreciating the moment, until finally it faded, and they all went about their business. Harriet checked her new watch, then made her way to her hotel, where a large package containing a leather satchel had been left for her minutes earlier. She took it to her room and read the note that had arrived with it in a sealed envelope. A message from the watchmaker asking her to meet him at a given address on her way to the airport. She shrugged, then packed the narrow leather satchel in the false compartment of her suitcase, before getting herself ready for her meeting, all the time hoping this wasn't the last phase of an elaborate trap of some sort. She now had the watch tools, evidence of her espionage, and if she was caught with them no amount of acting would explain what she was doing with them. She was a banker, not a watchmaker. Her stomach turned, but once again she knew that she had no alternative, she was in it and had to keep going. At least if she was being set up, she'd be caught in Switzerland. That was her logic, having rationalised her fate while looking out over the city in the cathedral. A moment of serenity had washed over her there, and the worst of the worries that had been making her head spin eased a little. It was like being in combat after all. She just needed to accept her situation.

When the time came, she walked the short twenty minutes to the address she'd been given, having asked for directions from the hotel clerk while checking out, and arrived at what looked like a small cafe just as the sun was setting. She checked the note with the address to be sure she was in the right place, then walked up the street a little to check the street sign. She was where she needed to be, she just didn't expect to be at a cafe. She took a deep breath, then entered what quickly appeared to be a much larger restaurant than she'd imagined from the outside. Before the waiter could get to her, the watch maker stood and waved her over. She smiled and nodded, then joined him at his table, just as the waiter finally caught up with her and took her coat with a polite welcome.

"You made it," the watchmaker said.

"Yes... I wasn't sure, I thought I'd got the wrong place."

"Please, take a seat. Our food will be here in a moment."

"Thank you..."

"It's the best restaurant in Geneva. I thought it would be nice to say farewell properly, seeing as you've had such little time here. I also wanted to give you this." He opened a box and removed her watch, which he handed to her after smiling at it once again. "Repaired, cleaned, serviced, and returned complete with polished scratch." He looked at her hopefully, as she looked over her watch, then went to put it on her wrist. "Keep it in the box for your journey, perhaps?" He passed her the box and gave her a nod. "As I said, our gift is much more befitting a young lady travelling around Europe. Much more so than a gentleman's pilot watch." He gave her a knowing wink and a nod, and the penny finally dropped as his meaning sunk in. She blushed a little, and smiled. She'd been so wrapped up in the very real threats she'd faced that she'd struggled to see a friend right in front of her. He knew she was coming, and he knew who'd sent her. He also knew that young ladies didn't wear pilot's watches, especially not those that were thick with sweat, smoke, and cordite from so many missions. He was trying hard to save her, while all the time she was concerned he was trying to steal her watch or set her up. She felt foolish, but relieved. "I'm not entirely sure how you managed to get sand in the movement, it was a devil to clean," He laughed. "Usually this job would take weeks, but we broke it down and each of my people took a piece to clean and renovate, before it was reassembled and tested."

"It looks like new, thank you so much. For everything..."

"It's our pleasure. You'll have to make sure you come back and visit us again, in the spring when the weather changes.

"I'll make sure of it." She couldn't stop smiling at her watch, and at the conversation, though she was soon distracted by the sizzling steak that was delivered to her smothered in a hot foaming butter. A tray of golden French fries followed, and the waiter scooped them onto her plate. "How did you know I like steak?" she asked.

"It's the only thing they serve here," he replied. "The butter is a special secret recipe passed down from the owner's father. You won't taste anything like it in the world. Eat, enjoy it while it's hot!" He cut into his steak, and Harriet did the same, and felt her tastebuds explode with pleasure at the incredible flavours as she chewed a small piece. The steak was so tender it fell apart in her mouth, and the golden fries were wonderfully crisp. Both were perfectly cooked, but the butter was something else. It was like nothing she'd ever tasted, and while some of the flavours were almost recognisable, they were just far enough her way to stop her putting her finger on anything specific. All she knew was that she was eating the best thing she had in a long time, and the wine she'd been served was the perfect accompaniment. More fries were delivered whenever she ran low, and she welcomed them hungrily, stuffing herself as she used them to mop up every last drop of the butter. It was a meal she wished she could take home with her, or eat again before leaving, which she would certainly have tried if she hadn't been full to bursting. Given the stress she'd been under, the food at the finale of her trip made it all worthwhile, almost.

After finishing the meal, and enjoying a conversation with her new friend, her taxi arrived and whisked her away into the night, back to the airport, and to the waiting Swissair DC3. She was still smiling when the aeroplane took off, leaving her to look out of the window at the mountains, while leaving the glinting lights of Geneva far behind. It had been a whirlwind visit, and an experience she couldn't begin to fathom. She liked Geneva, there was something special about it, but she regretted not being able to fully relax and enjoy being there. She'd made some wonderful memories in her short visit, though. The rainbow was an image she knew would stay with her forever, as was the feeling that she wasn't alone, like there was something there making her feel welcome, like it was a place she wanted to be.

The flight was as smooth as that going the other way, and Harriet's nerves only started to fray again when she felt the aeroplane start to descend. She checked her watch, and knew without doubt exactly where they were. Berlin. She talked herself through what would happen next, she'd been through it so recently that every step of the process was still etched in her mind. When they bumped to the ground and taxied to a halt, she stood confidently and joined the others in leaving the aeroplane, saying thank you to the cabin crew as she left, before walking with all of the arrogance and swagger she could muster into the terminal building, where once again she joined a queue waiting to be checked by an official. She glanced around, the SS guards were as terrifying as they had been previously, though there was no sign of the officer that had almost given her a heart attack when she last passed through, much to her relief. His absence didn't make the experience any less tense, and even the official's politely formal greeting before checking her documents before waving her along didn't put her at ease. She still needed to visit the bathroom almost immediately, though there was no heaving or vomiting involved this time, just a nausea that threatened to floor her. To her relief, there wasn't a long wait for her flight north, and she soon joined other passengers in boarding the four engine German aeroplane due to take her to Sweden. Most appeared to be businessmen of some sort, though there weren't as many as had been going the other way. There were also some young men, loud and confident types who she suspected were military personnel of some sort, and as such she gave them a wide berth. There was also an odd looking man who'd made her feel quite uneasy since she'd first seen him in the terminal. He was odd because he was so nondescript. He could have been anyone, no remarkable features at all, which made him all the more remarkable. Everyone had something unique, something that made them who they were, everyone except him. He seemed to take an interest in her, glancing over when he thought she wasn't looking, then quickly checking his watch, or reading his newspaper when she looked in his direction. Much to her disappointment, he took the seat opposite her, having stopped at the top of the steps, and talked to the stewardess for a while. A move that made her all the more uncomfortable, especially as the aeroplane was only half full of passengers, and there were plenty of other seats in the cabin.

"How was Switzerland?" he asked in French, after the aeroplane had climbed into the darkness, and settled at cruising altitude for their relatively short trip north.

"Excuse me?" Harriet replied. Her heart raced a little, she wasn't expecting him to talk, or for his chosen topic of conversation to be her travels.

"Switzerland. How was it? It often rains in Geneva this time of year, sometimes quite heavily."

"Fine, thank you. No rain..." She was searching her memory, she hadn't seen him on the aeroplane from Geneva, she'd have remembered if she had, his absence of features would have stuck in her mind.

"It's a nice city. A wealthy city. Lots of gold goes in and out of there,"

"I wouldn't know..."

"No? I thought you were a banker?"

"How would you know that?" Harriet stared at him firmly. Her stomach was now spinning as fast as her heart was pounding, knowing she was on a German aeroplane and practically hostage, and any sign of weakness could be the start of her unravelling.

"I overheard you talking to the official in the terminal."

"I see..." She smiled politely, knowing full well that he hadn't heard anything of the sort in her brief conversation. The first she'd seen him was while she was at the official's desk, and he was a long way distant, out of earshot and watching her from the waiting area. "I'm sorry, it's not something I like to discuss. People think we Swiss are all bankers, and like nothing more to talk about gold. It's shallow, don't you think? An obsession over money and gold, that is?"

"Of course... Then what else should we talk about?"

"I'm quite tired, and if you wouldn't mind I'd rather not talk."

"Oh, come now. It can be lonely and boring flying alone; a conversation helps pass the time."

"I'd really rather not. I don't fly well, and it makes me sick."

"Then the conversation would be a distraction, don't you think?"

"I don't."

"If not gold, perhaps we could talk about something else? Horology maybe? That other great achievement of the Swiss..." He looked at the watch on her wrist, staring at it for a moment, before moving his eyes back to hers.

"It's not something I'm familiar with, I'm afraid."

"Yet you wear such an exquisite piece."

"I wouldn't know about that, I like it, that's all. It matches my clothes."

"Quite... So, what did you do in Switzerland?"

"I'd really rather not talk, if you don't mind. I'm tired, and feeling quite unwell from the flying."

230

"I'll go and talk to the stewardess for you, see if there's anything they can give you. A tonic perhaps, or a brandy." He stood and walked off down the aisle before Harriet could protest, leaving her to ponder nervously about what to do.

"Listen to me, and don't turn around," one of the confident young men she'd seen boarding the aeroplane said through the gap between the chairs and the window. "The man sitting opposite you is Gestapo. Be careful." A chill ran up Harriet's spine, and she was instantly filled with dread. She knew there was something not right with him, she'd sensed it just from his appearance, and had it confirmed by his conversation, as much as it could have been without the words actually being said; but now they had been, she was terrified once again, and the nausea became acutely genuine. She'd got all the way there and most of the way back, and now, almost within sight of Sweden, she was considering her options, the gun or the pill. Not for the first time she wished she was in battle; she'd know what to do then. She knew how to fight, and how to escape a difficult situation, but this was all new to her. She was lost. The aeroplane was over Germany, and any moment could be turned around. That's what he could have been doing while getting her a drink. Warning the cabin crew, and having them alert the pilot. She looked out of the window for landmarks, then tried to focus on feeling the flight, and trying to sense any turns, no matter how gradual. She pulled open her handbag and slipped her hand inside, feeling for her pistol and gripping it lightly. Then, before he returned, she closed her eyes and leant her head on the window. Hoping he'd leave her alone.

He coughed when he got back, several times. Making it obvious he wouldn't give up until she looked at him, which she eventually did through artificially heavy eyes. She grasped her pistol a little tighter as she sat up, and once again was engaged in conversation about Switzerland, which she continued to remain vague about, other than talking about the lake and the swans, and trying to appear as shallow and uninteresting as possible. It didn't work, though. He continued to ask questions, while trying to expertly steer her in any direction where she may trip herself up and give herself away. He was skilled, and patient, and each time she closed him down, he simply opened another line of questioning. It was exhausting. More tiring than any dogfight. She could feel herself getting tired, and started to worry even more that she'd contradict herself as his intricately planned questions spliced each other, darting in and out of different threads, going back to a conversation they'd already had, then looping back to the present. It's a game they played for the entire journey, until the lights of Sweden far below brought a huge sense of relief when finally, they started to descend into Stockholm. Harriet took her hand from her purse, releasing her pistol, and preparing herself for disembarking. As soon as the pilot put the aeroplane on the ground and brought it to a halt by the terminal, Harriet quickly stood and collected her things. Before the Gestapo man could join her, the loud young men bustled along the aisle, talking loudly and confidently, as they had before they boarded, and found a way of slowing him and generally being in the way. The member of their group who'd warned her gave her a wink and a nod, and allowed her to make her way quickly from the aeroplane while they made a nuisance of themselves. She nodded in response and forced a half smile, then quickly left the aeroplane, and made her way to the terminal at pace, while fighting the urge to burst in a sprint. She did walk past other passengers, though, knowing it was rude, and knowing that they were looking at her and rolling their eyes, but not really caring. She just wanted to get away. As she entered the terminal, she turned and glanced behind her to see the Gestapo man descending the stairs of the aeroplane. He looked straight at her, and fixed her in his stare. She headed inside and presented her passport to the official, and as soon as he'd stamped it, she made her way towards the doors again, keeping against the wall and out of sight until her pursuer had entered the building, then slipping outside and running fast to the line of aircraft, towards the Mosquito she'd seen parked up and waiting. It was hard running in heels and a skirt while carrying a heavy case, and despite her best efforts her progress was slow. She was becoming desperate, and pulled the pistol from her purse as she ran.

"Harry...?" AP said with a big smile, as she stepped down from the cockpit to greet Harriet. The smile was quickly replaced by a frown as she recognised the distress on Harriet's face, and then noticed the pistol in her hand. "Harry, what's wrong?"

"We've got to go," Harriet replied breathlessly. "Right now. AP, we've got to go!"

"What is it?"

"The Gestapo."

"Here?" AP's face drained of colour as Harriet nodded urgently. "We don't have clearance to take off yet, it's going to take a few minutes. She looked Harriet in the eyes, and saw the fear. She'd never seen her look so scared, and she knew her better than most, and had seen her I'm some of her worst states. "Wait here!" She turned and ran back up the steps into the cockpit, leaving Harriet standing and shaking nervously, looking around and expecting to see him any moment. She flicked off the safety catch as she waited. Determined to shoot if she had to. She jumped as she heard the Mosquito's batteries whir, and turned to look as the bomb bay opened, while AP jumped down out of the cockpit. "Come on!" AP took her arm and pulled her underneath the aeroplane, and helped her up into the bunk fitted in the bomb bay for passengers, the one used by the man they were transporting on their way out. "Get in and stay quiet!" Harriet nodded and climbed onto the bunk. AP threw her bag on top of her before disappearing again, and closing the bomb bay doors. Harriet lay shaking in the dark, pistol in hand.

"I'm looking for a young woman who came this way, my fiancé," the Gestapo man said in English as he stood by the aeroplane, almost within arm's reach. His voice was as clear as day, and for the first time since meeting him, Harriet's mind was empty, no thoughts, no nothing, she just lay silently, breathing as quietly as possible and preparing herself.

"I'm sorry, I haven't seen anyone," AP replied, her voice devoid of emotion, or interest.

"You must have seen her. She was wearing a brimmed hat and turquoise coat, she came this way just a few moments ago, she was carrying a large suitcase."

"Sorry..."

"Perhaps she got in your aeroplane?"

"Why would she do that?"

"Maybe she's lost, or confused. She doesn't like flying, and was feeling a little unwell."

"I assure you nobody's in my aeroplane! There are only two seats, and until a couple of minutes ago I was in one of them."

"Then you won't mind if I check? I'm very concerned about her."

"Be my guest, but don't touch anything."

"You're sure you didn't see her?" he asked a few moments later, after Harriet had heard creaking in the woodwork as he climbed the ladder to look in the cockpit.

"I'd tell you if I had; but as I said, I was in the cockpit so wasn't really paying much attention to what's going on out here."

"Thank you..." His footsteps clicked on the concrete as he ran away to search other aeroplanes.

"Knock on the fuselage if you can hear me," AP whispered, as she pretended to be doing her external pre flight checks. Harriet knocked twice in reply. "Sit tight. I'm going to get our clearance sorted, then I'll get us out of here. I won't be long. OK?" Harriet knocked twice again, and AP finished her checks before walking over the terminal. Every minute she was away felt like an hour for Harriet, hidden away in the darkness of the bomb bay beside a number of boxes she could only assume were the ball bearings she'd been told were so desperately needed from Sweden. The shaking wouldn't stop, no matter how hard she tried, though she no longer felt nauseous. She was beyond that. She was so tense that she doubted she'd go to the toilet for a week, if she ever got out of the mess she was currently in. Unless she was found, of course, in which case she was quite sure she'd go on the spot. Never in her life had she wished so hard to be in a Spitfire and surrounded by German fighters. After what felt like

234

several hours, but in reality was probably no more than a few minutes, Harriet heard footsteps approaching again, and then some more creaking and shuffling. "What are you doing?" AP said a few minutes later.

"Oh..." the Gestapo man replied. "Sorry. I couldn't find her, so thought I'd check she hadn't come back this way."

"And accidentally stumbled up the ladders into my aeroplane?"

"What? No, well, it could be possible."

"There's something not right about this. You shouldn't be climbing around aeroplanes; they're protected under law. Who are you, anyway, and what are you doing out here?"

"I told you, searching for my fiancé..."

"I don't believe you. You shouldn't be out here without an escort, where's your identification?"

"My identification?"

"Yes. Show it to me, or I'll call the guards."

"No need. I'll go back to the terminal and check in there, maybe she went back inside?"

"Maybe she did, and if she had any sense she'd keep going. There's something odd about you that I don't trust."

"I assure you..."

"I'm going to call the guards." AP cut him off and turned for the steps. Her bluff worked and he turned and walked quickly away. She climbed into the cockpit and pulled up the ladder, then after closing the hatch she started the engines, and as quickly as she could started to taxi to the runway. She did her checks as she went, and let the control tower know there as a suspicious man lurking about near the aircraft, giving the description of the Gestapo man, and telling how she thought he was messing with the aircraft as she'd found him in hers without permission. Thanks were received from the tower, and a few minutes later she was climbing into the night. "Harry!" AP's distant voice called into the darkness, as Harriet lay scared and shaking, and increasingly cold in the bomb bay of the Mosquito. "Harry, put the headset on!"

"Hello..." Harriet replied nervously, having followed AP's voice to the headset, and pulled it into place.

"Don't sound so startled to hear from me."

"Shut up! I'm not exactly at my best at the moment!" she blasted nervously in reply. "What's happening?"

"I had to take off quickly before he came back. Don't worry though, I'll have you home in no time."

"I don't exactly feel safe in here, and it's freezing!"

"There's a harness, and a lamp behind your head. Put them both on, and then get wrapped in the blanket. I'll let you know if we get into any trouble."

"Wait, I don't have a parachute..." Harriet panicked as she put the lamp on and looked around the bomb bay. Some small crates were secured to her left, and then there was her bunk, with her and her suitcase.

"Damn it!"

"What?"

"It's up here in the cockpit. I didn't think. Look, I'm sure it'll be fine. Don't worry about it."

"Do me a favour, don't tell me if something happens."

"Don't be ridiculous."

"I mean it. Don't tell me. Just get yourself out. I'd rather not know it's coming..."

Several hours of cold darkness later, and the bomb bay doors finally opened. Harriet peeked out from under her blanket to see AP smiling up at her. She couldn't do much but stare in return, she was frozen. She'd wrapped herself in the provided blanket as best she could, but her smart skirt suit just wasn't the best choice of clothing for laying in the belly of a wooden aeroplane for hours on end, especially not in December, and when there was absolutely no way of getting to the cockpit and the heating from the engines. Instead, she had to shiver, and keep herself focused by cursing the Gestapo man. If it wasn't for him she could be sitting up front in the cockpit, warm, and able to see what was coming. Instead of hoping the Mosquito wouldn't be caught out by a night fighter, or be a victim to engine failure, or any other bad luck which could have sent them crashing into the sea. She'd kept her pistol at the ready throughout, just in case. If they did crash, there'd be no escaping, and despite her first hand experiences in Hawaii, drowning still scared her more than anything else, and she had absolutely no intention of taking the 'L' pill that was still hidden in her hair bun.

"Well?" Carlyle asked, as Harriet closed the door to Alastair's office, having been collected from the dispersal and driven straight there, once AP had finally prized her from the bomb bay and given her a hug, in a brief yet vain attempt to warm her up while welcoming her back to safety. "Did you get them?"

"You didn't mention anything about going to Berlin!" Harriet replied angrily, while looking him firmly in the eyes and doing all she could not to pour his cup of tea over him.

"Berlin? What?" Alastair replied, frowning as he joined Harriet in looking at Carlyle for an explanation.

"There's no other way of getting to Switzerland from Sweden, it's a long old ride, and civil services are limited." He shook his head casually, as though he was talking about taking the long way around London. "Besides, if I mentioned having to stop and change planes in Berlin, you'd likely never have got on the plane in the first place."

"And never have had a run in with the bloody Gestapo, either!" She was so irritated she didn't even bother to correct his use of the term 'plane'.

"Harry, are you OK?" Alastair asked.

"Thanks to an out of uniform Luftwaffe pilot tipping me off, and AP's quick thinking. Otherwise, God knows what would have happened!"

"Carlyle, what's going on here? You said it was a simple courier job, in and out with limited risk."

"As I said, a simple matter of logistics. There's no direct flight to Geneva, you have to go via Berlin. I assume the passport worked OK?"

"Fortunately..." Harriet replied, seething but lowering her voice. Her emotions were a mess. She was still scared half to death from her experience, angry with Carlyle, and happy to be safe. She pushed the case across the desk to Carlyle, who stood and opened it, and after taking her things out and piling them neatly on Alastair's desk, he opened the false bottom and then the leather satchel, then took out a large wooden case with velvet insets, each one holding a precision tool used to make the highest quality of watch. His eyes lit up, just as much as they did when he opened the small boxes containing thousands of tiny watch parts.

"Fantastic. Absolutely fantastic!" He excitedly packed everything away in the leather satchel, beaming with a huge smile as he did. "I can't tell you how much you've helped, Harry. Really, your success is no less than heroic. These tools and parts will help us make thousands of timepieces and chronometers." He could hardly contain his excitement. "I never meant to risk you, Harry, not unnecessarily at least, you must believe that; and I'm genuinely sorry for any difficult situation you may have been put in as part of your mission. The Germans know how valuable this delivery is, and I'm not surprised they were watching. After all, it's why we sent you, remember? The least conspicuous of us."

"Is that it, am I done?"

"That's it. Unless I can convince you to come and work for us more permanently?"

"I'll stick to flying, thank you."

"Unfortunate..." His shoulders slumped a little, as though he'd genuinely thought she would say yes. "In that case, I'd better get these back to London." He tapped the satchel, then put it back in the case and snapped the lid closed. "You'd do well with us, if you ever feel like a career change."

"I doubt I'd last long enough to do well, but thanks anyway."

"Our loss." He walked around the desk and stood in front of her. "Just so you know, and I don't pretend to imagine whether this will make the risk of your mission worthwhile to you or not, the tides of war are changing. British and American forces landed in North Africa a few weeks ago, Vichy France surrendered almost immediately, and Rommel's finally on the run. What comes next requires unblemished precision and accuracy if we're going to make the most of the success and win this war. The watches that these tools and parts make will go onto the wrists of those who will change our fortunes. The tides of war really are changing, and you just made our success significantly more possible than it was." He smiled as he looked her in the eyes, and she could see that he meant every word he was saying. "Friends?" He held out his hand.

"Just don't ask me for any more favours, because the answer's no." She gave a half smile as she shook his hand. "If my bag's still here, I'll get changed out of these clothes and you can have them back. I won't be long"

"No time. Besides, they were made for you and likely wouldn't fit anyone else quite as well. May as well keep them, consider them our thanks for your help. Cheerio!" He gave her a wink and opened the door. "Thanks for everything, Alastair. I'll be in touch."

"Goodbye, Carlyle..." Alastair replied, rolling his eyes as he left, then gesturing Harriet to sit down. "Was it awful?" he asked, as he closed the door behind Carlyle.

"That's one word for it. Please, Alastair, never ask me to do anything like that again."

"My dear girl, they'll have to go over my dead body if they want you. You have my word."

"Thanks..." She gave him a smile, then opened the small cardboard box Carlyle had taken from the case and piled with her things, and offered it to Alastair.

"Macarons?" His eyes opened wide as he looked at the delicate and beautifully coloured treats inside.

"I've never seen so many bakeries and patisseries in one city than I did in Geneva. You can't walk down a street without passing one, and seeing things like this in the window. I haven't had them since France, so thought I'd bring some back."

"Gosh, it's been so long... Are you sure?" he asked almost nervously. Harriet nodded and smiled, and he took one and stared at it for a moment, before taking a bite and theatrically melting into his chair. "Heaven." Harriet took one herself and savoured it, trying not to rush it so the fine shell could melt on her tongue, and she could enjoy the refreshingly sharp taste of raspberry that cut through the bitter taste of fear she'd had in her mouth since Berlin. "As much as I'd love to sit here eating macarons with you, we should probably get you home. You must be exhausted," he said after finishing his treat.

"More than you'd imagine, but my nerves are so frayed I don't think I could sleep if I tried."

"Try you must, though! You've had an ordeal; you need the rest."

"I know..."

"Is there anything we need to do? Do you need to talk to somebody about it?"

"No... No, I don't think so. I'll be fine with a good sleep."

"I'm sure you will." He stood and helped her with her things. "Maybe have tomorrow off and get yourself together?" She nodded, not having the energy or inclination to argue. "Look at it this way, at least you got some new clothes out of it..." He smiled at her mischievously.

That night, after Alastair had dropped her at her cottage, she laid in bed with the curtains and blackouts open, staring out of the window and watching the moon, while she thought through her adventure. Of everything she'd done since the war started, in her life even, her Geneva trip was the most terrifying. Her hands were still shaking as her imagination ran away with itself, and created scenarios for what could have happened if she'd been found out, and fallen into the hands of the Germans. It wasn't something she wanted to think about, but she had no choice, and the increasingly creative and horrendous images her mind kept throwing up kept her awake for many hours, and made her thankful that Alastair had given her the following day off. The only respite she had was when she dragged herself out of bed to find her silver hip flask so she could have a brandy, hoping it would ease her nerves. She caught herself in the mirror as she passed, and the moonlight reflected off the diamond earrings she was still wearing. She looked at herself in the mirror, her dark silhouette looking back, with the precious stones in her ears almost lighting up her face. She took them off and looked at them in the silver moonlight. Carlyle had been in such a rush to get back to London that he'd never even asked for them. Or the pistol, or dreaded 'L' pill, but neither of those held her attention anywhere near as much as the diamonds. She wondered if he'd even noticed she was still wearing them, or if he'd simply assumed she'd used them to pay off the Gestapo. It made her smile. She put them on her bedside table, then sipped at the brandy. He knew where she was if he was missing them.

Chapter 12

It's a...

Harriet dropped the left wing of her Mosquito as she circled, searching the sea below for any sign of the convoy she'd expected to have raided twenty minutes earlier. There'd been reports of ships making a run south, but AP hadn't been able to find them, leaving Harriet to lead her Mosquitoes up and down the Norwegian coast searching for their targets, before climbing high and circling around the scattered clouds, while scouring the area for something to attack. She'd called the CO of the Beaufighters and suggested they hold off further out to sea and away from the coast until they were needed, but as Harriet's frustration grew, it seemed that they likely wouldn't be needed at all. It was the second time that week they'd been tipped off about a prize target heading south, and the second time that week they'd come up with nothing, and it was starting to grate on her nerves. The week before that had been one of patrols, between some horrendous weather that led to the station being practically grounded as snow squalls reduced visibility to nothing, making the weather so deadly that any idiot who did go up wouldn't get down again. It had been a difficult time for Harriet. She'd struggled emotionally after Geneva, and her already raw nerves had been stretched close to breaking point by the experience, making it even more difficult than it was to strap herself back into her Mosquito and go out looking for trouble again. She still hadn't got over the battleship experience. It felt like it had been one thing after another, and that she hadn't truly rested since America, meaning that it was taking more and more effort to put on a facade for those who looked to her to lead them, and give them the strength to keep doing their own jobs.

"What do you say, skipper?" Eskimo asked. "Should we head home?"

"I suppose so..." she sighed. "It doesn't look like our convoy's turning up."

"Another day."

242

"Another day... Viking leader to Claymore, no joy out here again, we're heading home." She banked tight and opened the throttles, and led the squadron west, picking up the Beaufighters on the way. She talked with Eskimo on the way home, needing to keep her mind occupied and away from the dark places it was drawn to. He mostly talked proudly about his family. They owned an accounting company, where he'd been training as an accountant when the war came. He was originally asked by his parents to stay home, it was the plan that he'd take over the company when he was older, and they needed his help running things while his elder brother, the tearaway of the family, had escaped to England to fly Spitfires. It didn't last. They knew he couldn't stay home knowing his brother was away fighting for his country, so they'd paid for him to be smuggled out of the country on a fishing trawler. It was a story that made Harriet smile, more so when he talked about his younger sister, who at the age of thirteen was furious she couldn't go to England and fight for her country too. She couldn't understand why it was OK for her brothers, but not for her, and her age didn't even come into her thinking. He explained how proud he was to be flying with a female pilot, and how he couldn't wait to tell his sister all about it, knowing she'd be both terribly annoyed and simultaneously inspired.

"How was it?" Ginny asked, as Harriet hung her flying jacket and Mae West on the hat stand.

"Another waste of time," Harriet sighed.

"Stood up twice in a row? You must be losing your charm..." Ginny smirked, then put a cup of tea in front of Harriet as she sat behind her desk.

"Honestly, I'd rather take on another battleship than this! All the anticipation and then nothing. It takes hours for me to come down."

"If that's what it's doing to you, trust me when I say you need to get out more."

"Shut up." Harriet rolled her eyes and blushed a little. "Well, I have to do something. Go get Chloe for me."

243

"Oh, leave the poor girl alone. You can't take it out on her."

"When have you ever known me take anything out on anyone?"

"Other than me?"

"Why are you still here, and she's not?"

"Charming..." Ginny smirked, then went to find Chloe, leaving Harriet to sip on her tea. "Here we are..."

"Ma'am," Chloe said, as she stood to attention in front of Harriet's desk.

"Close the door, please," Harriet said to Ginny, before turning back to Chloe. "How are you getting on?"

"OK, Ma'am. I think?"

"What are your thoughts?" Harriet asked Ginny, who was stood by the side of her desk, hiding a knowing smirk.

"She's done well since she's been with us. The admin side of things couldn't be better."

"Despite her moonlighting with Flying Officer Kaye, and disappearing off on reconnaissance flights when she thinks we're not watching?"

"Apparently so. I can't fault her work."

"Ma'am, I always ask permission before taking a flight, and I always make sure my work here is done. I stay late if things aren't finished, or get in early."

"It seems you like the flying side of things though?"

"I love it!"

"Good. I've put your name forward for training as an Observer, and the Station Commander has agreed. The next course starts in January, and you'll be on it."

"Ma'am?"

"Unless you'd rather not? I'm sure Section Officer Russel can find enough paperwork to keep you busy for the rest of the war."

"Oh yes," Ginny added. "Easily, there's mountains of the stuff, and it isn't going to get any less."

"No!" Chloe replied. Her eyes were wide open in shock, and she couldn't help smiling, despite her best efforts not to. "Ma'am. I mean, I want to. Please. Thank you."

"Don't thank me, it's Flying Officer Kaye who sold me on the idea, apparently she thinks you have potential."

"I won't let you down, Ma'am!"

"I know you won't, Sergeant. You'd better get those sewn on; you're improperly dressed." She threw the rank stripes on the desk and smirked at Chloe. "We're giving you two weeks annual leave over Christmas, so you can spend the time with your family before you report for your training in January. You can spend the time between now and then tidying up what work you have outstanding, and we'll try and get you a few flights so you can get some practice in ahead of your training."

"I don't know what to say, Ma'am."

"Don't say anything. You may as well finish work for the day, go get those stripes sewn on, and maybe have a celebratory drink tonight with your friends?"

"Yes, Ma'am!" Chloe saluted, then picked up the stripes and left quickly.

"I thought you were going to tell her nearer to Christmas?" Ginny asked after she left.

"I was, but I needed something to make me smile."

"My delightful company not enough for you?"

"I'm not sure..." Harriet smirked mischievously.

"I don't like to have to keep reminding you of this, but you're the one who brought me here. I was fine down south without all the rain and snow."

"Well, if you'd really like to go back to marching WAAFs up and down?"

"It's tempting..." The phone rang, and she grabbed it before Harriet could get to it, smirking as she did. "Your convoy's turned up!" she said after putting the phone down again.

"What?"

"Alastair's on his way over, you're to be on standby to go up again."

"Great..." Harriet slumped in her chair and put her hands over her eyes. "Go and let Eskimo know that he needs to get the met reports for this afternoon, would you?"

"I'll put it tactfully."

"He won't care, he'll love you if you tell him we're going up again."

"So, it's just you that's not thrilled by the prospect?"

"Honestly, I'd rather be finishing early and having a drink."

"No rest for the wicked..."

After a brief from Alastair over a light lunch, Harriet was leading the squadron east once again, and racing low across the North Sea towards their phantom convoy. Apparently, the Norwegian resistance had got a message through to give the exact location of the convoy, which had stopped in a fjord earlier in the day due to a submarine sighting, explaining why it wasn't where it was expected to be. It was the fifth time chasing one invisible convoy or another recently, always reported to be big, bristling with overladen merchant, ships and escorted by only a few flak ships, yet it never actually appeared, and it was starting to irritate Harriet. She'd briefed her squadron with the same professionalism and confidence as she always did, and put a positive face on what some pilots were starting to call the great wild goose chase, but it was starting to become a chore. Going through the briefing, the preparation, and all of the anxiety and adrenaline that came with approaching the target area, and then nothing. The only success they'd had since her return from Geneva, was when a patrol led by Pietersen stumbled on a lone merchant ship making a run for it. They'd made short work of it, and sent it to the bottom with their bombs and cannon fire, and all four Mosquitoes had returned without a scratch. It was a frustration to Harriet not being on the patrol herself, and missing the opportunity to offload some of the tension she was carrying, but she was happy for Pietersen. He'd grown over recent months, becoming a real leader, and the best second in command she could have asked for. The aircrews and ground crews alike respected him, and they appreciated his 'Viking warrior' aggressiveness, which inspired them to be fearless in battle. It was a different approach to Harriet's quiet confidence, but it complimented her style, and the squadron was better for it. She led, and he fired them up. It would have been difficult for anyone to imagine how cold their relationship was when they first met.

"Coming up on the target area," Eskimo said, breaking Harriet's daydreams. "We should be seeing their smoke any time."

"OK, Viking squadron, keep your eyes open," she said over the radio, while scanning the horizon for signs of the convoy as the Mosquitoes formed into their loose pairs, ready to break off and circle when the flak started, and await the gunners' reloading and Harriet's order to attack. "Can you see anything yet?" Harriet asked Eskimo a few minutes later. AP had already been tasked on another mission when the news came they'd be going up again, off taking photos

247

somewhere far to the north, and wasn't available to lead them in this time.

"Nothing..."

"You're sure we're in the right place?"

"Positive."

"I can't believe it!" she blustered. "Again!"

"It's impossible," Eskimo shrugged, trying to be supportive, but sharing the frustration.

"Five times in a bloody row! I've got better things to do with my time than chase ghosts. How do they hide a massive convoy of ships anyway? It's not like they can hide them behind some trees!"

"What should we do?"

"What we always do. Fly up and down a bit and look for them. What do you reckon, north or south?"

"They'd have to be going faster than they're capable of going to be ahead of us, more likely they've slowed, so I'd say north."

"OK, let's go and have a look." Harriet sighed and pulled the squadron around to head north and search for the convoy, keeping them low, as she knew that if they came on the ships head on, they'd be in a good position to surprise them. "You'd think they'd do the decent thing and turn to the fight, wouldn't you?" she asked, giving Eskimo a half smile to try and thaw the atmosphere she knew her mood was creating."

"Maybe we've scared them off. We've got pretty good at this."

"Maybe..."

"Next we can start attacking them in their ports, and kick them out of Norway altogether! They'll regret messing with us Norwegians and our Mosquitoes."

"Focke Wulfs!" One of the pilots shouted. Harriet instinctively pulled up, and searched the sky above and behind, seeing it filled small black crosses diving out of the broken cloud, swarming like gnats on a summer evening.

"Viking squadron, break, break, break!" Harriet shouted, as her heart started to pound while her mind spun, trying to work out the best response to being dropped on by deadly enemy fighters. She couldn't dive for speed, she was so low that she was a sneeze away from being in the water as it was, so all she could do was open her throttle and pull up hard, hoping to reduce the distance between her and her attackers, and in doing so shorten the angle of their dive and dodge the initial attack. The g force pulled her into her seat as she turned and lurched upwards, while the rest of the squadron broke formation and flew in every direction, trying desperately to make themselves difficult targets just as they'd been trained. Harriet climbed straight up, pushing the throttles fully forward to squeeze every last breath of power out of the pair of Merlin engines, which roared and screamed in reply. Her number two kept up, dropping slightly behind, but following as close as he could, matching her moves as she rolled out of the climb facing the first of the diving Focke Wulf 190s. She gave a blast of her cannons, missing and sending tracer between two aircraft, but not putting them off their stride. They were committed, and weren't going to be swayed from their attack, they couldn't get the angle to attack her anyway, so it was pointless trying, but they could get on one of the Mosquitoes that couldn't get away in time, and before Harriet could get around on them, they'd raked it with guns and cannons, igniting the fuel and blowing it to pieces. She just got the tail of the closest 190 in her sights and clipped it with a cannon shell, before having to rapidly change direction again, kicking the rudder hard and pulling tight on the controls to escape the rain of tracer now coming down on her from the rest of the diving 190s. She pushed the Mosquito to the limit, rolling, diving, climbing, and pulling the steepest turns, which punished her body mercilessly as she tried to avoid bullets, cannon shells, and falling aeroplanes, as the sky quickly filled with 190s.

There wasn't a gap to fly through without hitting something, and bullets rattled the fuselage like hail as she pulled up hard again, and climbed out of the raging battle taking place within reach of the waves. A pair of 190s followed her, chasing and closing as the altimeter quickly wound up. She rolled to avoid their tracer, then made herself dizzy as she eased and reversed the roll, trying to make herself a hard target, while maintaining her climb. The speed quickly started to drop, and the chasers came closer, then the stall came exactly as she'd planned, and she kicked the rudder bar and pushed on the controls as the Mosquito's tail flipped upwards, and her guns and cannons were lined up with her chasers. She gave a firm blast, rattling the leader's engine with sparks briefly, before it exploded and blew apart, sending the second 190 spinning to escape both the debris and Harriet's keen eyes. She clipped its wing as she flew through the glowing remnants of the exploded 190, then pulled back and around to try and get on the tail of the escapee, who was turning tight in an attempt to get away, and it was working, until inexplicably the pilot reversed his turn, and pulled the nose of his aircraft right through Harriet's sights. She clipped him again, this time leaving him smoking and running for home, while she turned back to the battle just as she was jumped by more 190s. They hit her in two flights, one to the left and one to the right, forcing her into a steep dive to avoid them, though some of their shots still found home. She looked around quickly, and saw a Mosquito right below, flying towards her and skidding and slipping with one engine smoking, desperately trying to avoid the long stream of fighters jockeying for position on its tail. She pushed the fire button and let go with guns and cannons, hitting the closest chaser and scattering the rest, giving the Mosquito a brief respite while she passed overhead and opened her throttles fully. More tracer passed the cockpit, sending her into another tight turn to run back into the scrap, but to her surprise the fight was starting to disperse into smaller skirmishes spread over a wide area. What seemed like hundreds of 190s had dispersed, with only the smoking Mosquito left circling and taking on three of them.

"It's Pietersen!" Eskimo said, as they saw the letters on the side of his Mosquito.

"Let's get in and help him!" Harriet said in reply, as she came in hard behind the chasers. "Pietersen, on three, pull up hard right."

"Got it," Pietersen replied breathlessly.

"One... Two... Three!" He pulled up and right, and dragged the chasers with him, presenting them perfectly at just about maximum distance, and Harriet pushed her fire button just before the leading 190 crossed her sights, sending a stream of tracer into its cockpit and knocking it out of the sky. The second and third split left and right, responding quickly to avoid sharing the fate of their leader.

"Got him!" Eskimo cheered, as Pietersen dropped to the waves and opened his throttles, despite having a smoking engine, and raced away. Before Harriet could say anything, or even respond, one of the 190s had come around almost impossibly, and was charging nose first at her. The flicker of fire was the only warning she had that it was firing, and less than a second later a wide hole opened in the windscreen, and a fine mist of blood filled the cockpit and splattered the right side of her face. She instinctively pulled up and hopped over the 190, not firing, just reacting, then she dropped low and opened the throttles, putting as much distance between her and the fighters as she could, desperate to give Eskimo a chance when she put down in the sea before she inevitably lost consciousness from her blood loss. She quickly checked her instruments and prepared for a ditching, she knew she didn't have long, the cockpit seemed to be sprayed with blood, and that meant she'd lost a lot already. Eskimo couldn't fly, so the best she could do for him would be to land on the sea and give him at least an opportunity to get out and into a life raft. Her mind was a blur of activity as she checked her instruments again, then looked over her left shoulder to check for chasers. She'd opened up a lot of distance, and seemingly the 190s weren't interested in chasing, at least not that she could see with a gentle pull around to the left to check her tail properly.

"OK, Eskimo. I don't have long. So I'm going to ditch shortly, and you need to get out before she goes down. You have to move fast. Get the emergency hatch open now, it's one less thing to do." She looked up and scoured the sky above to make sure nobody was about to knock them down before she had chance to put them down as safely as she could. "Eskimo!" She shouted, irritated he wasn't paying attention. She looked at him and froze. He had his mask off, and his

251

mouth was open as he was trying to say something to her but making no noise. She looked down and he had a bloody hole the size of a fist in the right side of his chest. A cannon shell had gone through the windscreen, through his harness and Mae West, and ripped through his body. "Oh God..." she gasped. "Eskimo, hold on." She moved her left hand from the throttles to the control column, and pushed her right first firmly against the hole, trying desperately to plug it and stop the bleeding. She looked in his eyes, then quickly scanned herself. She was sprayed with blood, but she couldn't see a wound, she couldn't feel any pain. "Eskimo, talk to me. You've got to stay alive, OK? You need to lift your hand and put it on the wound and stop the bleeding." He nodded and smiled, as a trickle of blood ran from the corner of his mouth. His right arm twitched, but there was no lifting it. "Eskimo. Eskimo!" He lifted his left arm and put his hand on hers as she kept it pushed into the hole in his chest, then he squeezed gently and nodded.

"I..."

"Don't try and talk. Just stay awake. We can do this. We can be back in no time. You've just got to fight."

"I've loved flying with you..." he gasped, then smiled again and stared at her for a moment, before coughing up a mouthful of blood which ran down his face and body, and covered Harriet's sleeve.

"No! Don't you dare!" Harriet shouted, while switching her attention furiously between flying the Mosquito, which was cruising at a little over four hundred miles per hour, and looking at Eskimo. He smiled and gave her hand another squeeze, then the life went from his eyes, and his head slumped to his chest. "No, no, no!" She repeated, as she pulled her hand from his chest and lifted his head. His face was already pale under the smoke and blood, and his eyes just gazed into the distance, lifeless. She felt a tear run down her cheek as she let his head slump again, and returned her bloody hand to the controls. He was gone, she knew he was. Even if he wasn't, she knew there was nothing she could have done to save him. She had an aeroplane to fly. She pulled up and away from the wave tops she'd come dangerously close to, and glanced up and behind to check she wasn't being pursued, before releasing her bombs and letting them fall into the sea. It was the first opportunity she'd had, and the Mosquito responded well for losing the added cargo. Once free of her load, she dropped to the waves again and focused her mind on her navigation, pulling the blood stained map from under Eskimo's thigh, and checking where she thought she was. She could see smudges of smoke in the distance, which she assumed to be others from her squadron, and warily headed in that direction while trying to calculate how much ammunition she had left, just in case she was heading towards trouble. Fortunately, she didn't need what she had left, if she had any left, as she soon caught up with the source of the smoke and pulled alongside Pietersen's stricken Mosquito. The left engine was out, but still smoking, and they were making slow progress. "What's your status?" she asked.

"I don't think we'll get back," he replied stoically. "You should probably get going, just in case they follow us."

"I don't think so. You're still flying, so keep an eye on your gauges and we'll see how far we get."

"You don't have to stay."

"Shut up and do as you're told. You're a good pilot, and you're going to need every bit of knowledge and skill to keep her in the air. That has to be your focus, OK?"

"Yes Ma'am!"

"How's Tommy?"

"Shaken, but OK."

"Good. If you feel like you can't old her, you need to ditch sooner rather than later. Get the emergency hatch open, and the pair of you need to get out quickly. She'll float for a while, but the engines will soon drag you down. Have you got rid of your bombs?"

"No. I daren't risk climbing to ditch them."

"OK, well it's going to be risky, so you'll have to do it properly if the time comes. Slow her down to just above stalling speed, and remember you're only on one engine, you'll stall sooner and faster, then drag your tail and ease the front end down."

"Understood... How are you and Eskimo?"

"Don't worry about us, just focus on keeping that crate in the air!" Harriet barked, then looked over at Eskimo again, thinking he'd look peaceful if he wasn't so shot up. "How's your fuel?"

"Lower than it should be."

"Keep straight and level, and I'll have a look around." She pulled back on her throttle and dropped back, looking along Pietersen's Mosquito as it passed. It was like a sieve, and she was amazed it was even in the air. She dropped behind, then came along the other side, which was no less damaged. "She should hold up..." she said with as much confidence as she could muster, and not believing a word she was saying. They flew side by side, with Harriet doing frequent turns to check around for the enemy, until on the distant horizon they saw the first signs of land.

"I'm losing power..." Pietersen said with desperation in his voice. "We're almost there! Come on!"

"What's happening?"

"Power is falling off... Wait, it's the fuel. We're almost out. We're not going to make it."

"You need to put her down before she falls down. You won't manage a stall."

"OK..."

"Remember what I said."

"Got it..." Seconds later, the emergency hatch on top of the cockpit flipped open, and the slowing Mosquito started to lower to the sea.

Harriet pulled up and away, not wanting to be an obstacle, and started a wide circuit above as she watched. Her stomach was tensing again, and her heart pounding. He was about to try one of the riskiest manoeuvres while flying a wreck, and she wasn't happy about his chances, or about having to watch another of her crews die.

"Power off. I'll put in a distress call. Good luck."

"Good luck, Ma'am, and thank you! Powering off now." He lowered the Mosquito to the sea as Harriet called control and gave them their position, while climbing and circling to make sure she was visible on radar. He trailed his rear wheel, cutting a fluffy white line across the dark green sea, then a huge plume of water jumped into the air as the propellers and engines caught the water and dragged the fuselage down. Harriet's heart was racing, and the seconds after impact felt like hours. Tommy appeared out of the hatch first, quickly followed by Pietersen, and after throwing the life raft into the water and inflating it, they were able to climb in from their Mosquito, which stayed afloat long enough for them to get to safety before the tail broke and the fuselage flooded, dragging the wooden wonder down below the waves and out of sight. The crew looked up and waved, and Harriet waggled her wings in reply, smiling with relief to see them survive. They just needed to get through the ordeal of the cold and increasingly choppy North Sea.

Harriet kept on station, circling slowly in a wide arc to conserve fuel while keeping her eye on Pietersen, determined not to let the current or wind blow the downed crew so far from their last point of contact that they'd never be found. The day's losses had been enough, and she wasn't prepared to accept any more. Finally, to her relief, the high speed launch appeared on the horizon, and she was able to guide them to Pietersen, staying only long enough to see the cold and wet airmen pulled onboard the boat, before turning west and heading for home. She couldn't smile, despite seeing them rescued. She knew they'd be frozen to the bone after spending so long in their life raft, and wouldn't be out of danger until they were on dry land and in a warm bed. Besides, other than knowing their chances of survival had improved, there wasn't a great deal to smile about. The squadron had been massacred, ambushed by enemy fighters hiding in the clouds, and waiting for her to lead the Mosquitoes into a trap.

It made her angry, and sad, emotions which threatened to flow over during her flight home to safety each time she looked to the seat next to her, and Eskimo's lifeless body. There wasn't even a smile when she crossed the coast and lowered to the runway. By that time there was nothing. She was numb. The only way to get back was to shut her emotions down before the anger and sadness confused her, and she gave in to the urge to turn back towards Norway and go shoot up the Luftwaffe airfield she knew the 190s must have come from. It was marked clearly on her map, and she was sure she had the fuel to get there at least, though there wouldn't have been enough for a return trip, and she knew it. Not that it was something that bothered her. She was more than happy to be as dead as Eskimo, though it was his lifeless body that helped her shut the thoughts down and go home. In her mind there had been enough pilots lost, never to be seen or heard of again, and while Eskimo was dead, a voice inside her insisted he should be taken back to safety where he could be buried with dignity. She also felt a need to write to his family and tell them how he lived, and died.

"Ma'am..." Ollie said, as he looked up through the open hatch. After taxiing to the dispersal, she'd stopped and shut down at the end of a much shortened line of mosquitoes. With hers, only seven of the twelve that had set off remained. She'd sat in the silence, not wanting to get out, not wanting to talk to anyone or look them in the eyes. The anger and sadness had been replaced by an overwhelming feeling of guilt and shame for leading them into a trap and getting her crews killed. "It's OK, Ma'am," he gave her a reassuring smile as she finally looked over to him. "We'll get him out." Ollie reached in and unfastened Eskimo's harness, then carefully pulled him out through the hatch, leaving Harriet to look around the shattered cockpit, stinking, and stained with smoke and blood. She unfastened her harness and shuffled in her seat, she wanted to get out before Ollie came back for her. Things were bad enough without having to be helped out of the cockpit, giving the impression to anyone watching that she was as weak in her body as she was in her mind. She slid across Eskimo's blood stained seat, and climbed out into the cold afternoon air, then descended the few steps down the ladder to the ground just in time to see the doors of the ambulance slammed closed before it was driven away. "Are you OK?" Ollie asked as he approached.

"Yes... Thank you," Harriet replied quietly, before walking away. She didn't look at a soul as she entered to dispersal hut, not at the crews outside smoking, or those inside collapsed on chairs and looking exhausted as they drank tea. Instead, she kept her eyes forward and went straight into her office, and closed the door behind her before dropping her kit and slumping against the door. She breathed deep and tried to compose herself as she waited for the inevitable footsteps and knock at the door. A normal enough routine which was filling her with dread. She waited, but to her surprise nobody came, which was just as anxiety inducing as any hammering at the door, and went some way to confirming her suspicions that nobody wanted to talk to her that much because of what had happened, what she'd done. It was nauseating at best. She took off her flying jacket and Mae West and threw them on the hat stand, then took her seat and pulled out her writing things. She needed to write to Eskimo's family, but try as she may, she couldn't think of a word to put on the paper, and instead sat staring blankly into space. The dreaded knock at the door finally came, startling her in the process. "What is it?" Harriet shouted.

"Tea," Ginny replied, as she came into the room carrying a tray of tea and biscuits.

"Thanks, you can leave them on the desk." Harriet forced a half smile, then looked down intently at the blank paper in front of her

"Leave them?"

"Yes..."

"Gone off my company?"

"What? No..."

"Good. Sorry it's late, I usually like to have a cup waiting for you when you land, but I had to run to the Mess to borrow some biscuits."

"Have we run out?"

"Not really, but I heard the chef had made fresh shortbread, and thought you'd appreciate some." She handed Harriet a mug of tea, then offered her a large triangular petticoat tail of shortbread.

"This tea has rum in it," Harriet said with a frown after taking a sip of the hot, sweet, and heavily laced tea.

"Yes, I know. Lots of the stuff, too. I thought you'd need it after what happened."

"You've heard, then?"

"I heard that you fought your way through over thirty enemy fighters, and bought time for the others to get away."

"What?"

"That's what the word is among the crews, anyway. Apparently you turned into them and started causing chaos."

"It was already chaos; it didn't need me. Anyway, that's not what happened."

"Then what did?"

"I led the squadron into an ambush, and as a result we lost five aircraft and nine men. With two more having to be fished out of the sea."

"Four..."

"Four what?"

"Four fished out of the sea. Hakon and Berg were picked up not far off the coast. It's why the launch was able to get out to Pietersen so quickly, they were already halfway there."

"I see... That doesn't change the facts."

"No, and it shouldn't. The fact remains that you did what you could, as you always do, and looked after your people. Their words, not mine, so stop feeling sorry for yourself and drink your tea." She took a sip of her own and had a bite of her shortbread. "Sweet and buttery, with just a hint of salt. Still warm, too. It'd be a shame to waste it."

"It's nice," Harriet replied, after washing down a large mouthful of shortbread with an even larger gulp of tea.

"Told you."

"Eskimo's dead..." Harriet said with as much control as she could.

"I know..." Ginny's voice softened a little. "He was nice, I liked him."

"Me too. I couldn't stop it. I tried, the cannon shell just came straight through the window and hit him in the chest. I tried to stop the bleeding. I..."

"Did your best."

"Did I?"

"Yes. A hundred times, yes. You'll question yourself forever, it's who you are, but you know as well as I do that you only ever do your best. You couldn't do any less, it's not in your nature."

"But what if I didn't do my best? What if I've got so tired and burned out that my reactions are slow? What if I could have avoided that shell and saved Eskimo?"

"You are tired, Harriet Cornwall, that much has been obvious since you picked me up in London, but being a pilot in the middle of a war I'd expect that. I must say though, even if you were as fresh as a Daisy, I can't imagine even the great Harriet Cornwall could dodge a bullet that had already been fired."

"I don't even think I have the energy to talk about it..." Harriet put her cup down and put her hands over her eyes. She know that Ginny was probably right, but she couldn't accept it. In her mind she'd let

259

people down, a lot of people, over twenty young men injured or killed since she'd taken over the squadron. Over twenty families back in Norway not knowing their sons were dead or maimed. She took another deep breath. Tears were coming, she knew it, but she was determined not to let them out in company. She'd already broken her rule of not being a disappointment, at least she could salvage something by not breaking the 'no crying in front of people' rule. "I'm sorry," she said, after composing herself and taking her hands from her face. "And thank you, I really appreciate what you've said, and the tea and biscuits. I should probably get on with writing this letter to Eskimo's family."

"I can help..." Ginny offered, but Harriet shook her head and forced a smile. "In that case, at least come outside with me and get some air, just for a few minutes?" Ginny finished her tea and stood to leave, looking hopefully at Harriet

"No... No, I'll be fine. You get on, there's lots to do." Harriet forced one last smile, then broke eye contact and picked up her pen again, deliberately ending the conversation and hoping Ginny would take the hint. There was no way she was ready to look her Norwegians in the eyes, they'd see the guilt in her as plain as day. Ginny nodded, getting the message, and leaving Harriet to her own company, and her writing.

As soon as Ginny left, the tears ran like rivers down Harriet's cheeks. She was so upset that she was shaking, and the only thing she could think of that would make it better was Cas. He'd helped her before, he'd supported her through the difficulties and taught her how to manage the adversities of her job, and process the responsibilities. He'd been by her side through the toughest times in her life, and prepared her the best he could, but now she needed him more than ever, he wasn't there. She was angry at him for a moment, for not being there, for getting her into it all in the first place. Then she remembered why he wasn't around anymore, and another wave of sadness hit her even harder than the last. She could hear his voice in her head, his advice, and his guidance, yet she still couldn't focus on writing the letter. Then she remembered the way he'd tease her and say the most ridiculous things that inevitably made her laugh, even when she was at her most upset; and from nowhere she let out a small giggle. It was the breakthrough she needed, though it was totally unexpected. In a moment of clarity, she remembered his advice about being a leader. 'Try and do the right thing by the people that depend on you. You may sometimes make mistakes, and you may get it wrong, but nobody can ever judge you as long as you've at least tried to do the right thing.' She could even remember herself telling him to 'shut up' after he'd said it, as he'd been so serious, and that embarrassed her. She put her pen down and stood, then walked across the room and looked at herself in the mirror on the back of the door. Her face was still smeared with smoke and blood, and her hair was a mess. She tidied it quickly, and after drying her eyes she pulled the door open and stepped into the main room before she could stop herself. The airmen immediately jumped to their feet, and to her amazement quickly came over and asked after her, and talked about the battle, and even thanked her for getting them out of trouble. Others came in from outside and joined in the conversation, and despite Harriet not being able to remember half of what she talked about, she started to relax. As she quickly realised, the Norwegians, like their counterparts in every other squadron she'd flown with, didn't mention the dead. There'd be time for that, and each would deal with in in their own way, but there and then they needed to be alive and remember that they'd got through another day; and Harriet knew she had to do the same. They drank tea and ate biscuits, and talked through the battle from different angles.

"At ease," Alastair said, as he waved his hands to try and relax the room that had been brought to attention when one of the pilots had seen him at the door. Harriet turned and looked at him, his face was like thunder, despite his softly spoken words. Unusually he was wearing flying kit. He hardly ever flew. "Harry, could I have a word in your office?"

"Yes, Sir," she replied. Something was wrong, she could sense it, and her stomach knotted as she followed him into her office and closed the door.

"I'm sorry I haven't been here to see you before now, Harry. There were a few things I needed to take care of."

"That's OK..."

"No, no it isn't. You and your squadron had a mauling today, and I should have been here to support you." He smiled a little, though the frown stayed. "How is everyone? How are you?"

"Holding up."

"Yes... Good... I just came from the Beaufighter boys, they send their thanks for holding those 190s off long enough for them to get away. A few beers will be coming the way of your chaps, I think."

"I'm sure they'll appreciate it."

"Look, Harry. I've just got off the blower with Coastal Command Headquarters, and I have something pretty horrible to say."

"Alastair, whatever you've got to say, just say it. I know I got it wrong today, but I did my best for the squadron, and I'm prepared to take full responsibility for what happened." She stood tall and squared her shoulders, even lifting her nose in the air a little as Nicole often did when standing her ground in a fight.

"Whatever are you talking about, old man?"

"I..." Her shoulders slumped a little.

"Let's talk about that later. The fact is, Harry, we've had word from a contact in Oslo. It turns out that the Resistance cell who have been feeding us information on the convoys were infiltrated by the Gestapo and wiped out. The Germans have been feeding us dud information for over a week, pretending to be our Resistance friends, and leading us along so they could set us up perfectly. A few practice runs over recent days to lure is in and test out our strategies, then today they sprung the trap. Frankly, it's a miracle any of you got out alive. They had three squadrons of 190s up waiting, apparently, with two more squadrons of 109s on their way from the south."

"So, it was an ambush..." Harriet's stomach squeezed tight, and a wave of nausea hit her.

"Yes, and a cleverly hatched one, too. It's going to change the way we do things for a while, that much is certain. We have you and your chaps to thank that things weren't much worse. If you hadn't put up a scrap and pulled the fight to the north, they'd have got among the Beaufighters and cut them to pieces."

"We still lost nine men."

"Which is why I'm here."

"I don't understand."

"We lost nine, but we could easily have lost a hell of a lot more, so we're going to go and give them a bloody nose and let the bastards know what we think of their little game."

"What?"

"If you and your crews are up to it, I want to go shoot up the airfield those 190s came from."

"When?"

"Now. What do you reckon?"

"OK..." She nodded and agreed instantly, knowing if she thought on it she'd find a million reasons not to go.

"Good. Let's get going."

"You're coming with us?"

"You try and stop me! Besides, I heard what had happened to your navigator, so I thought you'd fancy some company."

"You want to fly with me?"

"If I'm going to put my neck on the line, I want a better than average chance of getting out of trouble again. Come on, let's go brief the chaps. If we time it right we can get there for sunset!"

263

As the sun started to set over the German airfield on the Norwegian coast, Harriet led her squadron of nine Mosquitoes up over the cliffs to the southwest, and raced towards her target at treetop height. She led from the front, coming in low and out of the sun at the point of a Flying V, with four Mosquitoes lined either side in staggered pairs. Alastair had scraped together all the crews he could, including AP and Chloe, who'd volunteered to take one of the spare squadron aircraft into the fight, and there wasn't one among them who had to think twice about joining the entirely voluntary mission. As the airfield came into view, with its neat lines of 190s being inspected and serviced by the mechanics, there was no thought in Harriet's mind other than revenge. The nine Mosquitoes hit the airfield at the same time, some joining Harriet in strafing the lines of fighters with machine gun and cannon fire, while others shot up the buildings, hangars, and still silent anti aircraft guns that hadn't seen them coming. Enemy aircraft exploded, starting a chain reaction along the lines, and the whole airfield was in chaos by the time Harriet was coming back down and throwing her load of bombs at the main buildings. The anti aircraft guns hardly got a shot off, and those that did were quickly silenced by the circling Mosquitoes. Once Harriet's ammunition was fully expended, and almost every inch of the enemy airfield was burning, she called an end to the attack and led the squadron back out to sea, dropping over the cliffs and skimming the waves as the dying winter sun lit up the sky with beautiful oranges and pinks. Not a bullet was left unfired, and not a bomb left in their racks, the entire squadron had expended everything they had and destroyed the enemy airfield entirely. Not a fighter or building was left, and even the soldiers and ground crews had been gunned down as they fled. No quarter was given, and there wasn't a single guilty thought between the attackers. They got their revenge and paid back the enemy's trickery with interest, and not a word was said as the force of mosquitoes returned home. Each had their own thoughts, and that was enough. Harriet gave Alastair a nod, which was returned, and that's all that was needed. It had been a day of days, filled with disappointment, heartache, and rage, among other things, and it had been bloody.

Chapter 13

Enough

"I'm happy you came home for Christmas," Nicole said, as she and Harriet lay in bed drinking cocoa and watching the moon reflect off the snow outside. The house was cold in the summer, so the winter months meant a mountain of heavy blankets were needed to keep warm at night, even with a log on the fire for extra heat. It was cosy though, and Harriet was happy to be home and in her own bed, snuggling with her best friend.

"Where else would I be?"

"America? Malta? You haven't exactly been around much the last few years."

"Missed me?"

"Yes..."

"What?" Harriet looked at Nicole in surprise, having expected a casually dismissive comment in reply.

"What? It's true... We spent so much time together for so long, even when the war started we were in the same squadron. Then everything changed, and I don't see you much anymore. You're like my sister, closer even, and I miss you."

"I miss you too."

"You're just saying that because I said it."

"I mean it."

"You have AP with you in Scotland, and everywhere you go you have your new friends. Like Ginny and that American girl you talked about, Bunny was it?"

"You know it was, and you know that they're not you. None of them are."

"I know... It's just that I miss you. I miss our adventures." She lay her head on Harriet's shoulder. "Do you remember the last Christmas we had in France?"

"How could I forget it? We nearly got expelled from school!" Harriet smiled as she remembered how she and Nicole had dive bombed her school, dropping Coke bottles near their teachers, and laughing as the bottles whistled like bombs and sent them running and diving into snow filled ditches.

"It was fun, wasn't it?" Nicole laughed. "The Head's face was a picture."

"You always did get me into trouble."

"You don't need my help; you find trouble all by yourself. You're a magnet for it!"

"You're probably right."

"I know I am."

"I seem to have attracted you, after all." She smirked as Nicole nudged her.

"It's good of Alastair to give you a few days leave for Christmas."

"He's a good boss, I'm lucky to have him. He's kept half the squadron on patrols and sent the other half to London for Christmas leave, the other half get to go for New Year as soon as we're back to take over."

"I wish you didn't have to go back tomorrow. The days have passed so quickly."

"I know..." Harriet slumped back into the pillows stacked against the headboard. The few days at home had been exactly what she needed to recover from the recent horrors she'd lived through, not that she

266

mentioned them to Nicole or Aunt Mary. She'd even sworn Ginny and AP to secrecy on their flight south in AP's reconnaissance Mosquito, which all three had squeezed into the cockpit of, with Harriet spending the trip laid on the floor of the nose in the Observer's position, looking out of the Perspex9 and marvelling at the snow dusted scenery. Ginny and AP had stayed the night with Aunt Mary before heading off to their own homes on train, each carrying a bag full of freshly butchered venison from the carcass Alastair had presented the three of them as a Christmas present. They'd both returned the night before their trip back to the station, and gone with Harriet and Aunt Mary to the local pub, all dressed in uniform, and they hadn't needed to buy a single drink. Not that they stayed out too long though. Harriet wasn't really in the mood to get drunk, so after a few drinks she made her excuses, then headed home for cocoa and a last night in her bed before heading north. "I wish I didn't have to go back."

"I thought it was OK up there?" Nicole frowned as she lifted her head and looked at Harriet.

"It's alright."

"Alright good, or alright bad? I can never tell with you."

"Just alright."

"You don't like it?"

"Let's just say that I don't like sharing a cockpit with somebody else."

"I know..."

"Somebody's been talking," Harriet said with a raised eyebrow. It was her intention to leave Nicole none the wiser about how dangerous things had got in Scotland, not wanting to worry her.

"Yes, and it isn't you. Why didn't you tell me about your navigator?"

"He's dead, what's to tell?"

"You tell me..."

"Nothing..."

"You can't lie to me, Harriet Cornwall. I know you."

"Don't call me that!"

"What?"

"You know what. My name's Harry." She rolled her eyes and smiled a little.

"So?"

"So, I don't like the idea that I can't keep people safe."

"You're not God."

"I know that!"

"Do you?"

"Don't be ridiculous..."

"I'm not. You think you can save everyone, that's your problem."

"I'm quite sure I don't need you to tell me my problems. You don't have to live with me twenty four hours a day."

"I don't need to, I lived with you for years." Nicole gave her trademark casual shrug, while being dismissively French. "I know you better than most, and I know it tears you apart each time you lose somebody up there. I'm not saying it's a failing, it's a beautiful part of who you are, it's just a problem. Unchecked it'll drive you mad, because you can't stop fate. You're not God."

"I know..."

"So, what will you do?" Nicole laid her head on Harriet's shoulder again, relaxing after making her point.

"Shut up and get on with it. We're in a war, what else can I do? At least I'm alive."

"You could talk to Alastair."

"About what?"

"About how you feel."

"No."

"It wouldn't hurt."

"No! Shut up, let's change the subject." Harriet was beginning to squirm uncomfortably. She didn't even want to talk to Nicole about what she felt were her shortcomings, she had absolutely no plans to share them with her commanding officer.

"Think about it. For me."

"I'd rather think about other things."

"Like?"

"Like how you manage to talk so much, yet I still miss you when I'm away."

"Of course you do, I'm delightful." It took a moment, but she eventually let out a giggle, which made Harriet smile. "Promise me you'll think about it though."

"I'll think about how quiet it'll be when I go back to Scotland. Though apparently I'll be going north with somebody who can't keep their mouth shut. Which one of them was it?"

"I don't know what you mean."

"It was AP, wasn't it?"

"Shows how much you know, Squadron Leader..."

"Ginny... That girl's hard work."

"That girl's older than you."

"I don't know, I feel about fifty."

"You look it!" Nicole laughed, and Harriet put down her cocoa and pounced on her friend, and they both burst into giggles as Harriet tickled until Nicole howled. They giggled and laughed, until they collapsed in a heap and watched the moon and stars as they fell asleep.

The next morning, Nicole waved Harriet off as she joined AP and Ginny in heading over the snow covered hills and valleys on their way back north to Scotland. It was an uneasy moment for Harriet. She felt conflicted, and confused, she didn't want to go back, and at the same time couldn't wait to. Ultimately, she knew she had no choice, so logic suggested it was best to just get on with it, but deep down inside she wanted to be back in bed and looking out of her bedroom window. Talking with Nicole about how she felt had both helped, and hadn't. It was a relief to talk about how she felt with somebody she knew she could trust not to judge, but it was also a burden. Now she'd actually said the words out loud they were real, in her mind anyway. She stayed in her thoughts for the entire journey, laid on the cockpit floor and looking out of the nose at the passing scenery, while Ginny snoozed in the navigator's seat, totally unfazed by flying, as was normal for her. The only one that had to pay attention was AP, who expertly flew them home in comfort, without finding a single patch of bumpy air, or pulling a sharp manoeuvre; and in what felt like the blink of an eye they were landing in a Scotland as snowy as Yorkshire.

"Come in, Harry old man! How was the leave?" Alastair said, as Harriet knocked at his seemingly always open door.

"Good, thank you," Harriet replied with a smile. "It was nice to get away." There'd been a message left at the control tower asking if she'd call in and see the Station Commander on her return, so she took the opportunity to drop off a jar of Aunt Mary's homemade strawberry jam, something she knew had had a liking for. "I brought you this." She put the jar on his desk and his eyes lit up.

"Strawberry?" he asked in whispered excitement, as she closed the door and took a seat.

"Made from last summer's strawberries."

"Harry, you're wonderful to me. Thank you!"

"My pleasure... There was a message to come and see you...?"

"Yes... Yes! Yes, of course." He put the jar of jam back on the desk before leaning forward on his elbows and clasping his hands together, while looking Harriet in the eyes. "How are you doing?"

"Alright," Harriet shrugged casually, not sure where he was going with his questioning. He'd looked at her this way before, and she knew it was more than just a casual catch up, though she wasn't particularly stressed by it, and unusually she didn't feel unnerved.

"I mean, how are you really? You've been on continuous operations for almost all year, first in Malta and then with us. That sort of work can take its toll on a chap."

"Tired, I suppose..." Harriet blushed a little when she heard the words come out. She hadn't planned to say a thing.

"Yes, I thought as much. You know, the Air Ministry brought in a new policy some time ago, mostly to help us keep our good pilots from getting a little too tired, by rotating them out of operational units every now and then, subject to them meeting the criteria."

"What criteria?"

"Two hundred hours for scrappers in your trade." He raised an eyebrow, as she frowned at him while calculating her flying time. "You're well over, if you're counting. You were well over before you left Malta, and your work here's been icing on the cake, so to speak."

"I see... What does that mean?'

"Well, I know that things haven't been easy on you recently, and the SMO mentioned he's worried about just how tired you are, and how much it's taking to keep you going." His voice was soft and understanding, and for once there wasn't a thing that Harriet could do to argue the point. If anything, she had to fight to stop herself from saying 'if you only knew', so instead she just nodded and forced a half hearted smile. "So, I've pulled some strings and arranged for a posting. Somewhere away from operations for a while."

"When?"

"No time like the present, don't you think?"

"I suppose..." She paused for a moment. Despite her resignation, and the unavoidable feeling of relief she was unexpectedly feeling, there was a twist in her stomach. "Will you be honest with me if I ask you something?"

"I always have been, Harry, and always will; and before you ask, no, this isn't driven by your skill as a pilot or performance as a leader. You're exactly the pilot and squadron commander that I want on my team. You took a group of broken young men, and turned them into a formidable fighting force to be proud of, and I am very proud of them, and of you." He paused and gave her a warm smile. "The truth of the matter is, Harry, you're absolutely bloody exhausted. If we rest you now, we get to keep you around a little longer, and God willing, we'll get you through the war alive. You more than most have earned it."

"Thank you." She returned his smile as she felt the tension in her stomach dissipate. One of her biggest fears, bigger even than drowning, was letting people down. Especially those that had put their trust in her.

272

"If you need any further evidence of my congruence, you should know that the King of Norway himself has been paying close attention to your progress with the squadron, and I received a call from him on Christmas Day informing me that you've been awarded the Krigskorset med Sverd.

"The what?" Harriet frowned as she tried to work out what he'd said, patching together the sketchy but improving Norwegian she'd been learning while with the squadron.

"The War Cross with Sword, a respected Norwegian medal presented for gallantry in action. In particular for your dedication to duty in leading a Norwegian squadron against forces occupying Norway." He gave her a reassuring wink. "Very well done, Harry, you've made us all very proud."

"I'm not sure I deserve a medal… I was just doing my job." Her blush was intense, it wasn't what she'd expected to hear, and not something she was sure she'd wanted.

"Nonsense. You earned it, as did the others that have been decorated, including your navigator, who has received the medal posthumously. It'll be presented to his family in the future." He gave her a nod, and she smiled. "So, that's it. You made it, Harry. Time to sit back and take it easy for a while."

"You didn't tell me where..." She moved the conversation on quickly, not wanting to linger in the thoughts of Eskimo.

"Didn't I?"

"No..."

"I was sure I'd mentioned it. Not to worry, my mistake. You're going to Norfolk, of all places."

"Norfolk? In England?"

"Yes, I couldn't quite swing you a posting back to America I'm afraid, as nice as Norfolk in Virginia may be. Though I think I've managed to pull off the next best thing..." He smirked and Harriet looked at him curiously, not wanting to seem over excited, or even allow herself to get excited. She'd been on the receiving end of the RAF's erratic postings systems more than once, and she'd learned not to get her hopes up. "A new American fighter group are due to arrive from the states next week, and you're being posted to their headquarters as the RAF liaison officer."

"Liaison to the Americans?" Harriet's eyes opened wide.

"Yes. They've been sending B17 bombers over here for a while now, as you know. The east and southeast are littered with bases. They've also started sending fighters over to fly as escorts, and as they're the new kids on the block, the Air Ministry are posting in liaison officers to show them around and keep them out of trouble. That's your job."

"I..."

"My friend at the Air Ministry and I agreed that a decorated fighter ace with experience of working with the Americans would be a good fit."

"I don't know what to say."

"You don't need to say anything, Harry old man. I learned from the moment we first met that your actions speak louder than anyone's words ever could."

"Who will take over from me?"

"I'll be putting in a request for a new squadron commander in due course, I wanted to make sure you were on board with my plans before sending for your replacement. Could have been awkward otherwise."

"What happened to the man they were sending before me? Weren't they sending him on a conversion course?"

"They were, they did, and it didn't work out I'm afraid. Apparently he doesn't get on with two engines."

"Then if it would help, I'd recommend Pietersen for the job. He's got the skill, and the squadron would follow him anywhere."

"You think he's ready?"

"I've met much worse."

"I'll take it under advisement. So, happy?"

"Happy!" She smiled warmly, feeling a weight lifting from her shoulders, and feeling so relieved she could cry, if that wasn't breaking a cardinal rule about crying in front of people.

"Good, then go and get your things packed. I'll have you flown down to London tomorrow, so you can enjoy a few days off before reporting for duty, but tonight we're going to have a massive send off in the Mess!"

That night there was the biggest party in the Officers' Mess, bigger than any she'd been to since the old days back in the squadron, with all ranks invited. Alastair had given a speech, explaining Harriet's posting, and embarrassing her with the many accolades she'd received in her time with the squadron. He'd also announced her medal citation, along with the others in the squadron who'd been commended. Then it was over to Pietersen, who Alastair had briefed ahead of the gathering, and he gave a speech which had Harriet's face burning with embarrassment. He talked of his resistance to her when she'd first arrived, and how on their very first flight together she'd scared him pale with her flying, and her taking on an overwhelming enemy without a flinch; he also talked about how humble he'd learned to be when he recognised her skill, and what a wonderful leader she was. He'd learned a lot, and as a gesture of thanks from the squadron she was presented with a pair of solid silver Norwegian pilot's wings that had travelled all the way from Norway. It would have been an emotional moment if it hadn't been so rowdy, and she wasn't dragged up on a chair by Alastair to sink a pint while everyone sang and cheered. Something she did expertly, much to the pleasure of the Norwegians.

"I can't believe you're leaving me here with these savages," Ginny said, as they stood together at the end of the bar while a game involving a roll of newspaper, some matches, brief nudity, and lots of singing got underway.

"I'm sorry..." Harriet shrugged. "Posting order, I had nothing to do with it."

"If you say so…"

"I can have a word with Alastair, if you'd like? See if he can get you back to teaching WAAFs how to salute and march."

"Too late, I already talked with him."

"What?"

"He asked me this afternoon if I was happy where I am."

"And?"

"And she's staying. She's got used to the venison and whisky," AP said as she joined them.

"Ah, the other deserter," Ginny sighed, making Harriet frown in confusion.

"I feel I've missed something."

"I'm being sent back to Oxfordshire. Back to Spitfires, apparently."

"Lucky you..."

"Not as lucky as some. Liaison to the Americans? What does that even involve?"

"I've no idea," Harriet shrugged. "Showing them around and making them feel at home, or something like that." The three of them laughed, and topped up their drinks. "It's a shame, in a way. I've enjoyed being here with the two of you."

"Don't start getting sentimental."

"Shut up!" Harriet was happy. For the first time in as long as she could remember, she felt relieved, and happy that it was over. She'd survived a vicious tour of Malta, followed by a dangerous time in Scotland that had given her the taste of running a squadron in the RAF at home, while pushing her to the limit of her endurance. She knew she'd been close to breaking. She knew she was close before she even got to Scotland, flying headfirst into flak day after day had just made it all the more likely she'd flinch sooner or later and end up dead, or worse, get people killed. Being with AP again had been an unexpected bonus of Scotland, and working with Ginny every day had made the job more than tolerable, but there was no way she could repress the feeling of elation that came with leaving operations. What was to come was an unknown, but for once that was more reassuring than anxiety inducing. She'd made it.

Chapter 14

Very, Very Frightening

"OK, that's enough for now. Let's get back before they get really angry," Harriet said over the radio, as she rejoined the three American pilots she'd been flying a patrol with over the Channel. They hadn't long been in England, and all three were desperately keen to see France, so Harriet had agreed to take them almost close enough to touch, without getting so close that they'd come into range of the German anti aircraft guns on the coast. There'd been some debate at first, and the Americans had wanted to go and get stuck in, and have a go at the defences, that is until Harriet had left them to circle out of range, while she used the flak dodging skills she'd learned in Malta to test the coastal defences, and show her American friends the barrage of explosions that filled the sky in her wake. While the heavy scattering of small black clouds from the thundering explosions thrown up by the flak guns had been enough to silence most of their bravado, she'd been smart enough to stay out of range of the light stuff, and moved fast enough at changing altitudes to avoid the 88s, while still giving enough of a show to prove her point about how dangerous it was to approach the French coast unless you meant business. To an onlooker it could have looked reckless, but the experience made her smile, and had the desired effect of raising her heart rate enough to let her know she was still alive, and not a million miles from the war.

The Americans fell into position without hesitation, and Harriet led them back towards their airfield in the rolling flatlands of Norfolk. She smiled to herself as she opened the throttles of the twin engine single seat Lockheed P38 Lightning, and felt herself pulled into her seat as the fast and powerful all metal American fighter roared across the pale blue winter sky. It was a beast of a fighter, and unique looking with a pair of long booms extending backwards from the engines and forming the tail. It had taken a few weeks from arriving for her to get fully used to it, but in traditional American style, the Colonel who commanded the fighter group of three squadrons of Lightnings simply assigned one to her and told her to get to know it. Not having much else to do, the hours soon racked up, and she quickly became proficient in throwing the fast and agile fighter across the sky at over four hundred miles per hour, pushing it to its limits and getting a feel for the handling. It wasn't easy to fly, but it was a pussycat compared to the raw unrestrained power of the wooden Mosquito, an aeroplane that pushed even the best pilots to master it, which had been perfect preparation for the Lightning. With its 20mm auto cannon in the nose, along with four .50 calibre machine guns, it was certainly well armed, and she'd spent a lot of time shooting up the ranges when she wasn't looping and rolling, and half freezing to death in the winter cold. The only failings she'd found were that it could be complex to fly, especially when configuring the cockpit ahead of getting into a fight, and it was like flying in an ice bath. The cockpit heating was poor at best, and even at low levels she got cold quickly, but when she'd pushed up to the ceiling of almost forty four thousand feet, she'd almost frozen in just a couple of minutes, and could barely feel her fingers and toes for hours afterwards. She was happy with the rest, though. It was unashamedly American. Big, fast, and heavily armed, with a spacious cockpit, long range, and high service ceiling, and, making it unique to any other aeroplane she'd flown, it had a nose wheel instead of a tail wheel, meaning that taxiing, taking off, and landing were a dream, thanks to the clear vision that came with the aeroplane being level. The only thing not American about it was the relative quietness of the engines, compared to the noisemakers she'd flown before at least, certainly the big radial engine Harvards, SNJs, and SBDs.

"Well, Squadron Leader, that was one hell of a display you put on up there," one of the American pilots said, after they'd landed and gathered by her aeroplane. Clinton 'Clint' Edwards was the squadron commander of one of the fighter group's squadrons, and along with his two senior flight commanders they'd asked her for the grand tour as soon as they'd got settled in after their trip from America, and were ready to start preparing for operations.

"Sorry, I thought the best way to convey the dangers of straying too close to France was the show you," Harriet replied with a smirk. She'd been welcomed with open arms by the Americans, and made to feel like one of them as soon as they'd met. Tex, the commander of the group, had talked with Harriet's old friend in Washington, the General who'd hosted her on her trip across the states, and that was enough to make Harriet Tex's daughter for all intents and purposes. A very public brief to the gathered squadrons warning them on pain of a transfer to the infantry told them that she was an officer, a pilot, and an equal, no that was the first and last time anyone had even thought of her as anything else. The fact that she was female didn't even register, and if it did, it wasn't spoken about.

"Looks like the Jerries ain't that good at shooting, if you don't mind me saying, Ma'am," one of the flight commanders said confidently. He was a tall man, tanned and strong looking, with narrowed eyes that made him look like he was permanently squinting into the sun.

"You're welcome to test them for yourself," Harriet shrugged politely. She'd quickly learned that the pilots on an American fighter squadron were both very similar, and very different to her RAF colleagues. There was a lot of confidence and swagger amongst the Americans, something which could be considered arrogance to those that didn't know them. Harriet didn't take it that way though, in every one of them she saw Billy, the brother of her American friend, Bunny. The keen and confident young pilot who'd wanted to learn everything there was to know about fighting the enemy, and couldn't wait to get stuck into them. Unfortunately, he'd died at Pearl Harbour, but the pilots she was now surrounded by were no different to him. They just wanted to get stuck in and do their part.

"Don't be dumb," Clint gave him a firm but playful clip around the back of his head. "You'll get your chance, idiot, but you've gotta learn first. That's what the Squadron Leader's here for. Maybe listen to her, and save me having to write a letter to your parents, and let them know their only human son did something stupid. Ain't that right, Squadron Leader?"

"I'll do my best." Harriet smirked, then left them and headed back to her office in the HQ, a very nice old mansion house that had been requisitioned by the government on behalf of the Americans. It had been derelict before they'd arrived, a long neglected relic that had been left to crumble when the owners had moved to Australia, leaving a manager to run the land and collect the rent from the farmers who worked it. An American construction crew had turned up in early winter, in anticipation of the fighter group's arrival, and got to work building an airfield, control tower, barracks, and hangars, and even found time to renovate the mansion for use as headquarters. It made her smile. There never seemed to be any messing about with the Americans, somebody high up decided something was needed, and it was done. Money and materials were thrown at a problem until it was solved, and it was an approach that was leading to airfields popping up all over the south and east of England.

"How was it, Harry?" Tex, the CO of the Group asked, as he stood in her doorway smoking his cigar. He was lithe and tanned, with a pencil moustache, and a cigar almost permanently clenched between his teeth. He had a reputation for being a hard case who took no nonsense, and his officers knew where the line was in terms of his expectations. He wanted the best of his pilots, and expected them to train hard and play hard ready for their first combat against the Germans, something they were all desperately keen for, to the point of frustration. "Those boys behave themselves?" He tapped the pearlescent white handled revolver slung on his right hip, making Harriet think of him as a gunfighter from the books she'd read about the Wild West. She liked him, and to her relief he liked her too, and when they ate in the canteen he'd regularly suggest she should come visit him and his wife in Dallas when they'd won the war. A confident statement that despite her reservations had even Harriet believing it may be a reality. One Tex was confident would be much sooner if the 'damned brass got off their behinds and let us at the Luftwaffe!'

"They were fine. I took them to see the French coast."

"The Luftwaffe show up?" He asked eagerly.

"No..." She smiled warmly. "We stayed out of range of the flak guns. The Luftwaffe don't tend to come out and play over the Channel these days."

"Not like the old days, right?"

"Not quite."

"Tell me again what it was like..." His eyes twinkled as he talked. He'd had her tell stories of her past whenever he could twist her arm enough to share the details, and every time he got lost in them, his eyes drifting away as though he was there in the battles. "Hundreds, didn't you say?"

"Sometimes. Three, maybe four hundred or more would come at once. Bombers as far as the eye could see, and fighters stepped up almost every thousand feet around them."

"God damn! What a sight that must have been!"

"Yes..."

"And all the time we were sitting on our behinds back over in the States! We should've been here, Harry! We should've been fighting with you."

"Some of you were." She smiled as she remembered Max, her American friend who'd been with the British right from France.

"Yeah... Lucky sons of guns! Anyway, get out of your flight kit, we're going visiting."

"Visiting who?"

"An old friend of mine, the CO of a Bomber Group down the road. He's invited us to dinner."

"Us?"

"Yes, Ma'am. So, make sure you're in your best blues, he's gonna want to see those pretty medal ribbons of yours."

"I'll change right away."

"Thirty minutes, Harry. I'll meet you down on the flight line!" He puffed out a cloud of blue smoke from his cigar, then left and pulled the door closed behind him. She smiled to herself and shook her head. His irritation at having not being in the Battle of Britain

282

amused her a little, or at least his innocence did. Her heart had almost stopped each time she raced up to meet hundreds of enemy bombers and fighters, hopelessly outnumbered and without a clue where to even start; it was hardly something anybody who'd seen it wished they were part of, and if they did, they'd soon change their mind when they saw how many didn't come back, or how badly broken some of those that did make it were. She pulled off her flight kit and headed back to her accommodation, a small cottage on the edge of the airfield that had been put aside for her far away from the rowdiness of the men's accommodation. She quickly tidied herself and pulled on her best uniform, and straightened her hair in the mirror, she even gave herself a squirt of her favourite Chanel perfume. She smiled again. She was glowing. The permanent tan she'd picked up in Malta and the desert was still hanging around, her eyes were bright, and she was feeling the benefit of living with the Americans, who'd managed to bring their appetites with them across the Atlantic. Mealtimes on the American air station were exactly as they were back in America. They had the best food shipped over, and it was available in large quantities. Any other time Harriet would have felt uneasy knowing they had so much food, while the civilians in the local villages and towns were living on rations, but for once she was content to think of herself for a while. Finally, she'd accepted she needed rest, and with that came the need for good food to build her strength again. Much to her delight, pancakes with bacon and maple syrup were on the menu every breakfast, and she'd had them every day since she'd arrived.

Ten minutes after arriving at the flight line, Harriet and Tex were sitting in the comfortable leather seats of a small twin engine Beechcraft transport aeroplane imaginatively referred to as a 'Twin Beech', one of the eclectic collection of types, including a Spitfire, that the Group had on their communications flight. It was used mostly for moving senior officers around to attend meetings, but on weekends it was also used to ferry a lucky few to London for a night on the town. It was luxurious compared to most transports, and much more agile, and Harriet loved flying in it enough that Tex had taken her up a few times and taught her how to fly it herself. The trip they were taking wasn't one for driving though, and Harriet spent the short flight gazing out of the window and into the darkness outside, searching for the slightest glimmer of light, and briefly remembering seeing Geneva for the first time, as the C47 hopped over the snow capped mountains and revealed the black lake illuminated by the lights of the city. It was a memory that made her smile, and frown. As much as she'd liked it there, it was the scariest mission she'd ever been on. Much more so than the hundreds of bombers and fighters Tex was so desperate to see.

"Good to see you, Tex!" a Colonel with slick dark hair and piercing blue eyes said as he greeted them from the Twin Beech. He was film star good looking, with a brilliant white smile that lit up the darkness. "Ma'am!" He saluted Harriet, which made her blush a little, then he shook Tex's hand.

"Meet Harry Cornwall, Bob! Harry, Colonel Bob Carter. He's a damn Yankee, but don't hold that against him, he's a good man."

"I've heard a lot about you, Harry, welcome to my base. Let's get inside, dinner's waiting." He led them to a candle lit room with a long table, where other officers were waiting. They stood politely when Harriet entered, and her chair was pulled out for her before they all sat, and drinks were served. "These are my squadron commanders and my second in command, I thought they'd like to join us."

"Gentlemen," Tex said as he gave them a nod, which they politely returned.

"Colonel Tex Hunter and I go way back," Bob said as they all settled. "He's a fighter man, runs a P38 Fighter Group not far from here, and he and his boys could well be up there keeping the Luftwaffe off our back when they finally send us across the water."

"Sooner rather than later, Bob!" Tex laughed.

"You bet. Anyway, boys, Tex is in possession of something which may come in handy in our preparation for taking on the Luftwaffe." He looked at Harriet and smiled, which instantly made her nervous. "Squadron Leader Cornwall is on attachment, and as luck would have it, she's a true blue fighter ace." He gave Harriet a firm nod, which she smiled back at, while fighting the urge to get up and run from an uncomfortable situation which was rapidly unfolding around her.

"Better than that," Tex continued, much to Harriet's disappointment. "Our fighter ace flew against German bomber formations of hundreds over England a couple of years ago, and lived to tell the tale." It was enough to make Harriet pray for the ground to open up and swallow her. She was dying on the spot of embarrassment as every eye at the table was fixed on her, while her mind spun in wondering what on earth they wanted with her. "Anyway, Harry, Bob wondered if you wouldn't mind going up and chasing his boys around the sky for a while, and giving them some experience of fighting off somebody who knows what they're doing?"

"Sir?" Harriet replied, not able to think of anything else to say.

"Well, I can't make you, Harry. You're our liaison, and belong to the RAF. Bob's boys are mighty green, though, having just got here from the States. They're going into the line soon, and anything you can give them would be a help."

"No pressure at all, Ma'am," Bob added. "Tex is right though, our boys are as keen as hell, but there ain't one of them been up against the Luftwaffe yet. If there's anything at all you could offer, we'd take it with both hands. We can even fit gun cameras and use the footage for training."

"What do you say, Harry?"

"It'd be my pleasure," Harriet said with a composed smile, feeling totally ambushed, yet somehow flattered. She even felt a little excited at the prospect of playing at war for a while, without actually getting into danger. Faces around the table eased and broke into smiles, and as dinner was served, Harriet was subjected to a barrage of questions from the squadron commanders. She relaxed, eventually, and settled into the conversation as the good food went down, and the drinks flowed. It was a surprisingly enjoyable night, and one that she was a little disappointed to end. The company had been perfect, though the good food and drink had got to her, and when they finally got back to the airfield, she crashed into her bed and fell into a deep sleep.

The next morning, after a breakfast of pancakes, bacon, and maple syrup, accompanied by several mugs of coffee topped up with cream, Harriet was ready to go; and she made her way to her office to get into her flying kit. She was feeling good, the sleep had been deep, and she'd hardly moved all night, and she was feeling better for it. She was also looking forward to helping the bombers, and had spent every moment since she woke thinking of what she'd do and how she'd fly.

"Ready?" Tex asked, as he looked in through her door, his arrival being announced by a waft of cigar smoke.

"Ready," Harriet replied, as she pulled her blue and white silk scarf around her neck, and zipped up her sheepskin flying jacket. Tex had issued her a smart American black leather flying jacket, among other things, but the Lightning cockpit was cold, especially in the winter, so she much preferred to fly in her thick RAF issue Irvin jacket. She wore the issue flying overalls, though, as an extra layer, and under everything she wore the shirt and shorts she'd made from parachute silk brought home from her bed in Malta. It was wonderfully warm in the winter, and several times since being back in Britain she'd said a silent thanks to Lissy for forcing her to pack it. She followed Tex through the headquarters and out to the dispersal, where she was greeted by a sight she hadn't expected. "A Spitfire..."

"Yes, Ma'am! One of Bob's buddies up top heard what you were planning to do for his bomber boys, and pulled a few strings. This arrived for you first thing. She's fresh from the factory, a mark nine, I think they said." He shrugged as he guided her over to it. "I couldn't tell one from another if I'm honest, they all look the same to me. I hope it's OK."

"Better than!" Harriet replied excitedly. The mark nine was the latest Spitfire, and she'd heard good things about it. Fast, light, manoeuvrable, and heavily armed. Those that had flown them said they were even better than the mark fives she'd flown in Malta, and the thought of having one to play with was thrilling. The Mosquito had been a good aeroplane, but she'd missed the light agility of a pure fighter.

"Well, enjoy her. You'd better get going if you're going to meet Bob's boys. You've got the coordinates?"

"Yes, Sir."

"Good. I'll see you up there."

"You're coming too?"

"Sure am. Every day's a school day, so I thought I'd tag along and see what to expect. If I watch you in action, I can maybe figure out a strategy for my boys to counter it. I'm going in a Lightning, though, a proper fighter. You're welcome to have one if you change your mind?"

"I'll stick with the Spit" She smiled excitedly, almost bouncing on the spot with energy as she waited impatiently to climb into the cockpit. He nodded and smiled, and gestured to the Spitfire, letting her loose to walk quickly towards it, do a quick external check, then lightly and confidently leap up onto the wing and threw her parachute inside before climbing in after it. It smelled new. A hint of smoke, but none of the oil, sweat, cordite, and fear she'd got used to in every other Spitfire she'd ever flown. No rubbed or chipped paint, no bullet holes, no burn marks. It was as fresh as it could be, and that was enough to make Harriet giggle to herself excitedly as she went through her checks, trying hard not to rush them just to get into the air. Before that, though, she had the thrill of starting the powerful Merlin engine, and breathed in the blue petrol smoke as it hung in the air for a brief second, before the four bladed propeller spun into life and blasted it away. The engine vibrated the airframe in a way that made her feel like she was home, and soon she was taxiing at speed to the end of the runway Malta style, doing her checks as she went, swinging left and right so she could see around the long nose pointing up into the sky ahead of her. With the final checks done, she opened the throttle and let off the brakes, and almost let out a scream of delight as the Spitfire leapt forward into a sprint that pulled her back into her seat. A gentle push forward on the stick and the tail

287

came up into the airstream, and seconds later Harriet let out a sigh of delight as her tummy flipped a little, and the Spitfire eased into the air. Flaps up, wheels up, and she pointed the spitfire northwest, heading for the meeting point. The engine was smooth and purred with power, and the controls were clean and light, and incredibly responsive. It was a Spitfire, but it was new, and powerful, and she was so happy she couldn't help pulling up into a loop, before rolling out of it and continuing on her way. Having flown the Lightning in recent weeks, she'd been impressed with its power and speed, but it wasn't a Spitfire, it wasn't as agile and light, and while she'd enjoyed flying it, it didn't make her smile the way a Spitfire did. Nothing really could. She played a little more, checking her watch to make sure she had time, but not being able to resist the opportunity to see what all the fuss around the mark nine was, and she soon found out. It performed incredibly. Finally, after pushing the fun, and the service ceiling, and climbing up to forty thousand feet to confirm that it really was the Lighting that was cold, and not just her, she caught sight of Tex thousands of feet below and flipped into a dive down to join him, which she did mischievously, dropping in behind him as close as she could, and tailing him like a shadow.

"Lone Star Leader to Lone Star One, where are ya?" Tex called over the radio.

"Behind you..." Harriet whispered, then laughed to herself as his Lightning pulled up with a jump as he caught sight of her. "Sorry, Lone Star Leader, I didn't see you there," she said, trying hard not to laugh out loud.

"Behave yourself, Lone Star One, you'll be giving people heart attacks doing things like that."

"Understood, Lone Star Leader." She pulled alongside him and waved, and he smiled and nodded in reply.

"Yankee, this is Lone Star, is the date on?"

"Good morning, Lone Star. Sure thing, we're on the boardwalk and waiting," Bob replied.

"Roger, Yankee." Tex looked over to Harriet again, and gave her a nod. "All yours."

"Understood." She pushed the throttle forward and left him behind as she raced towards the bombers, which she could now see in the distance. Four of them, B17s, flying in a diamond formation and crossing her horizon left to right. She swung into a wide arc, heading for a cloud bank sitting between them and her, and used it to cover her tracks before swinging around and coming at them head on, startling them as she passed close enough to see the shocked looks on their faces as she rolled away, then climbed hard. They'd instinctively scattered, but came loosely back together just in time for her to dive on them, aiming at the rearmost bomber before dipping underneath them, and coming back up at the belly of the leader, before again rolling away. She was having more fun than she'd had in a long time as she attacked again and again, hitting them head on, diving, swooping, and hitting them in the quarter. Each time getting in close enough to score hits if she'd been firing, before rolling or flipping away. She flew aggressively as instinct took over, and memories of past battles flooded back, leading her to get in and split them up, until she'd isolated one of them and ran rings around the lone bomber, before heading back for the rest and having her fun with them. She hit them again and again, before disappearing into the clouds to recuperate ahead of another attack.

"OK, Lone Star One, that's us done for this morning," Tex said, after a long time of watching. "Let's say goodbye to our friends and head on home."

"Wilco, Lone Star Leader." Harriet pulled alongside the leading bomber and gave Bob a wave, then waggled her wings and pulled up and away, climbing to join Tex, who'd sat above and watched the whole show.

"Had your fun?"

"Yes, Sir!"

"Well, let's head home and debrief. Wanna race back?"

"Yes, Sir. I'll see you there." She flipped the Spitfire on its back, then pulled the stick into her stomach and dived away, opening the throttle as she did. She headed home at speed, racing over the rolling countryside below, and flying a couple of victory rolls before landing and shutting down several minutes ahead of Tex. She sat smiling for a while, enjoying being in a Spitfire again, feeling the close constraints of the cockpit wrapping around her. It was so much closer, and so much more intimate than the American aeroplanes. She felt part of the aeroplane, not like she was sitting on top and riding it into battle as she did with the Lightning, and everything else American she'd flown, with the possible exception of the Mustang.

The simulated attack had been analysed in depth by Bob and his squadron commanders, and in a post flight question and answer session with Harriet, they started to develop an understanding of what they were flying against. With Tex's agreement, she spent the following weeks chasing formations of B17 bombers through the sky, with the occasional one on one where bomber pilots would circle and dive to try and escape her, sometimes throwing the huge four engine bomber around like a fighter, and flying it in a way the German bomber pilots never had. It was a fascinating time for her, and she made some great friends among the bomber squadrons as she helped them prepare for the Luftwaffe. In thanks they'd taken her up in the B17 a few times, and because the bombers were fitted with dual controls and had two pilots, unlike the British bombers which almost always had just the one, she'd been able to take the co pilots seat and fly it. She was happy, she was relaxed, and she was content. After the increasing pressures of Malta, and then Scotland, had almost broken her, she was finally starting to recognise something of her old self again. The nightmares weren't as frequent, she was sleeping, she wasn't so exhausted, and at long last she didn't look like a sun blasted skeleton.

Chapter 15

Into the Fray

"Ok, everyone, time to keep your eyes open," Tex said over the radio, as he led the three squadrons of the Fighter Group over the French coast. Harriet looked out of her cockpit at the sprawling mass of bombers thousands of feet below, escorted by a swarm of P47 Thunderbolt fighters, who were there to escort the mass of heavy four engine B17 bombers over the coast, and past many of the German fighter bases that were likely to send 109s or 190s up to intercept the raid in the early stages of the mission. It was an incredible sight which kept Harriet's attention, over one hundred bombers flying in tight formations designed to keep the enemy out with interlocking fields of fire from the many gunners onboard each aeroplane, and all supported by five squadrons of Thunderbolts. It would be a brave Luftwaffe pilot that flew up through the much appreciated cloud cover to intercept them, though Harriet was well aware that there was plenty of those about. Fortunately, the cloud cover meant the anti aircraft guns on the coast would struggle to do anything more than irritate the formation with a few well guessed shots, but that in itself meant the formation would be a more tempting target for enemy fighters. The Luftwaffe weren't that keen on flying through their own flak, so not having that to worry about changed the situation a little.

Harriet scanned the sky, searching for the tell tale sign of fighters, while all the time holding station off to the right of Tex. She'd made a nuisance of herself as soon as she'd heard the Fighter Group had been made operational, and would be flying their first bomber escort mission to Germany and back. Officially, she wasn't allowed to go along, neither the Air Ministry nor the American high command would allow it. RAF liaison officers were there to liaise, not to fly combat missions, and the rules were set in stone. She didn't want to go into battle as such, she wasn't ready for that, but she did want to go along and see how the Lightnings worked in battle. Since she'd arrived she'd spent most of her time flying mock dogfights with her American friends, or attacking bomber formations to give them practice, and she'd become the local expert on aerial combat; which is exactly what she used in her repeated verbal assault which finally led Tex to break and agree that she could go along as an observer only, on the understanding that she stayed on his wing all the way there and back, so he didn't have to explain to the RAF why their Squadron Leader had gone missing over occupied Europe. Being allowed to join the Group on their first mission had meant a lot to Harriet, it made her feel like she was a full member of the unit, and not just some English girl there on sufferance, not that they'd been any less than charming since she'd been with them; but as always she'd overthought it to the point where, at times, she thought she may be more of a hindrance than a help. She was also simultaneously excited and nervous. Something deep inside stirred when she knew she'd be going back into harm's way, it felt like her natural environment, while at the same time she was full of the terrors of what had happened before. Her nine lives were running out, and flying high over occupied Europe was a whole new risk. There were no life rafts if things went wrong, and no crash landing and walking away. If she survived, she'd be a prisoner of war at best. She'd made her peace with the worries, though, and felt comfortable knowing there was safety in numbers. It was different to be part of a large force, and despite having seen exactly how a determined attacker can make a meal of a large bomber force when she used to attack the waves of Germans raiding over Kent, she felt relatively safe. Especially as she was sat up above forty thousand feet, where the 109s and 190s wouldn't be able to drop in unexpected. If the Luftwaffe wanted to attack the Lightnings, they'd have to find a way to encourage them down to fight. The only downside was that it was absolutely freezing. The Lightning's notoriously cold cockpit was hard work, even more so at forty thousand feet in late February, and Harriet was shaking with the cold after only thirty minutes, despite wearing all the warm clothing she owned.

"Bandits, three o'clock low," Harriet said over the radio, as she caught sight of two squadrons of fighters coming out of the cloud, and heading for the bomber formation in their usual formation of loose pairs. Her stomach squeezed and her heart raced, as she thought through her checks and tasks before engaging, while looking around for signs of trouble coming from other directions, but initially she couldn't see anything other than the small swarm of gnats heading for the bombers.

"Hold positions, Lone Star," Tex replied, then called up the leader of the Thunderbolts to warn him of the uninvited guests coming up to meet them. Harriet felt herself shaking with nervous energy. Instinct was screaming at her to dive and engage, and it was taking every drop of self control to hold her position and watch. Three squadrons of Thunderbolts turned away from the bombers, heading on a collision course to what Harriet was sure were 109s, and before long battle was joined and the two sides were all over each other. Harriet's nervous energy built, and for a moment she forgot how cold she was, while simultaneously watching the battle, and the bombers, and scanning for other enemies. The fight raged, but was quickly left behind, with not one of the enemy fighters managing to break through the screen of Thunderbolts, giving the bombers the time that they needed to continue on their journey unmolested.

Thirty minutes later another attack came up to meet the bombers, and once again it was beaten off by the Thunderbolts; though this was their last action, and the remaining escorts turned for home as they reached the extent of their fuel tanks, leaving the bombers in the hands of Tex's Lightnings who, with their long range fuel tanks, were intending to see the bombers all the way to their target and back. Tex brought them down to thirty thousand feet, so they were within reach of the bombers, but still keeping a safe distance so they didn't get in amongst them. Much to Harriet's concern, the cloud thinned out as they approached the German border, just as the meteorology report had suggested it would, meaning that the bombers would quickly become a target for the flak guns down below. Nothing happened as they crossed the border, but as they approached the target, a tank factory, the sky around the bombers erupted with thousands of tiny black dots which quickly expanded into fiery explosions. It was startling to watch, and Harriet felt her stomach squeezing as her subconscious started to throw up memories of diving through the flak thrown up by the ships she'd attacked. A bomber near the front of the formation took a direct hit, and exploded so fiercely as the cargo of bombs ignited, that it took off the wing of the bomber to its right, sending it spiralling down in a death dive that would pin the crew to their seats and stop them escaping. It was horrifying to watch, and Harriet felt her stomach grip tightly.

293

"Bandits, twelve o'clock high!" Harriet called, as she saw the sun glinting off the Focke Wulf 190s coming directly at them.

"Lone Star Leader to Lone Star Group, clean up and get ready to fight!" Tex said confidently. Harriet quickly went through her tasks, reaching to the out of sight fuel cocks and switching them to the main tanks, dropping the long range tanks, switching on the gun heater, switching on the gun sight, increasing the revolutions of the propeller, then opening the throttles. It was something she'd practiced for hours, often blindfold as Cas had insisted she do when she first learned to fly the Hurricane, until the routine was stuck in her mind, and she could do it without looking. Despite her practice and proficiency, she was still slower than she'd intended, frustratingly so, as it allowed the enemy fighters to close far more than was comfortable, but no matter how hard she tried, she couldn't make her frozen fingers work any quicker. She shouted out in anger when finally she'd done everything, while pulling back on the stick and taking aim at the leading 190, which was already in a shallow dive at the fighters. As she closed, she glanced briefly below, and saw other fighters racing in at the bombers. A stream of tracer passing her cockpit from above snapped her eyes forward again, and after lining up her sights she pushed the fire button, setting off the four heavy machine guns and single cannon with a roar, and shattering the lead 190's propeller before rattling the engine and immediately setting it on fire. It rolled right and she rolled the opposite way, avoiding a collision while firing snapshot without aiming at the next 190 in line, missing it, but making it flip to dodge her, and throwing both it and next off their attack. She continued her roll, flipping her Lightning on its back and pulling on the stick, diving and rolling to escape. She looked up as she dived, and watched as almost in slow motion the 190s ripped into the Lightnings. She couldn't believe what she was seeing. While many of the Lightnings were breaking and getting stuck into the fight, more than a few were still flying straight and level, not responding at all, and she watched as two were shot clean out of the sky, disappearing in fiery explosions while others were sent down smoking after taking direct hits. She had to drag her attention from the apparent massacre and focus on the 190s, as she pulled out of her dive and climbed back towards the fight. "Clint, get your boys down to the bombers and help them out, we'll hold these guys off and keep them off your backs!" Tex shouted, and almost immediately a dozen

Lightnings started their dives. Meanwhile, Harriet was back in the fight, and sitting behind a 190 that was chasing hard on Tex's tail and firing wildly, making Tex roll and flick so much that the streams of tracer seemed to somehow spiral around his aeroplane. Harriet came in close and fired a short burst. Bits flew off the 190, and it turned on its back before dropping away quickly. She didn't give chase, instead choosing to sit on Tex's tail and follow him back around into the fight. He gave a 190 a hard blast, and then had a go at another as they cut through the battle, which was starting to splinter into a number of one on one fights that were spreading out across the sky. More tracer sparked off Harriet's wing, and after looking over her shoulder she pulled up hard, pointing the spinner at the heavens and climbing straight up at maximum power. The 190 belatedly followed, having taken a shot at her from a distance, and by the time it was in a straight up climb, Harriet had pulled back on the throttle and was starting to feel the shake of a pending stall. As the wing dropped, she kicked the rudder bar and pointed the nose straight down in a perfect stall turn, facing the chasing 190 and giving it a blast. It immediately started smoking from under the engine cowling, and the pilot stared at Harriet in shock as she dived down past him, leaving him wondering what on earth had just happened while she raced away.

As the battle above her stretched out across the sky, Harriet's attention turned to the bombers, which were turning north and heading away from the burning firestorm on the ground below, having accurately dropped their bombs through the upcoming flak, which had resumed while Clint's Lightnings kept the attacking German fighters at bay some distance away. A few of the B17s had gone down over the target, having been blown apart by the deadly accurate flak, and others were smoking and burning while their crews fought to keep them in the sky, and with the main bomber force. One of the badly damaged stragglers had caught Harriet's eye, with two engines out and trailing thick black smoke; it was a long way behind the others and being stalked by a 109 that had somehow slipped past the Lightnings, and was closing to finish off the wrecked bomber. Harriet dived at full speed, determined to get to the 109 before it got to the bomber. Her heart was racing, and she was sucking in the oxygen as she closed, but her eyes were as steady as always, and her aim perfect. Having calculated her speed and angle of attack, the speed and drop of her bullets and cannon shells, and the speed of the 109, she fired, sending a stream of tracer towards the piece of sky she knew the enemy pilot would almost certainly fly into. As the 109 fired its first rounds at the stricken bomber, Harriet's shots hit home, cutting along the right wing, and almost immediately it caught fire as it rolled away. She chased it down and gave another burst, sending it into an uncontrollable spin before she pulled back up and searched the sky, but there were no more enemy fighters to be seen, so she pulled alongside the bomber. She was amazed it was still flying, there were holes in the airframe, some as big as a man, and she could see the injured crew inside. The pilot gave her a nod and a thumbs up, which she returned before pulling up and away, and taking station above and behind, then throttled back to lower her speed to conserve fuel and keep with their slow pace. The main body of bombers were nowhere to seen, neither were the fighters, all being swallowed up by the large patches of broken cloud, though they did find another shot up B17 which joined with them on their journey west.

Harriet checked her watch frequently as they made their way through the increasingly cloud strewn sky, they were making reasonable time, despite being slow, and her fuel was holding well enough to get her back safely. She just had to hope that the Germans didn't show up again. She'd calculated the best she could how much ammunition she had left, and she didn't think it would be much. If fighters came at them again she'd have enough for two or three burst at the most, and she knew full well that wouldn't be enough to protect the bombers. Her entire reason for staying close was in the hope that the sight of her presence would be enough to put an opportunist off from having a go at the bombers, which were sitting ducks for even the most inexperienced Luftwaffe pilot. The sight of an escort fighter would be enough to suggest that more were lurking around, maybe in the clouds above, and that may plant the seed that two already shot up bombers weren't worth the risk. Every now and then she'd drop to the bombers and come alongside, waving and reassuring them she was still around, before going back up and flying a circuit to check their tails. While it was reassuring for them, it was also helpful for her. It kept her awake, and kept her thinking, despite the intense cold returning again now her adrenaline was easing a little. Looking at her map and checking her timings, with adjustments made for the slower speed, she calculated that they should be close to the coast at any time, though the thick grey cloud they were surfing made it difficult to know for sure, not without leaving the bombers to go and have a look down below, which she was reluctant to do. She became irritable after a while, wanting to be back, and not knowing just how much longer her nerves would hold as she scanned the sky relentlessly for signs of fighters. Then, at almost exactly the time she calculated they should be crossing the English coast, the bombers started to descend. She followed them through the cloud, staying close and keeping them in sight as they dropped, then felt herself smile as they broke through the cloud base, and she saw England. They'd made it, much to her relief. She escorted them to their airfield, and gave them a wave before circling and watching them in, then headed home.

The debrief from the raid was uncomfortable. Harriet was the last to return home, much to the relief of her American friends, who'd thought she was one of the many of their comrades they'd seen go down. The operation had cost them seven Lightnings shot down, and another thirteen shot up quite badly, three so bad they were total write offs. The overwhelming theme of the reports of those who made it back was the combination of the freezing cold and complexity of preparing to fight had been the reason they'd suffered such losses. The consensus among the pilots was that those Harriet had seen shot down while flying straight and level had just been too slow to respond. Whether their hands were so cold they couldn't turn the fuel cocks, or they'd forgotten to increase the propeller revolutions before increasing the power and unintentionally caused their engines to fail, they just hadn't been able to get themselves and their aeroplanes into the fight before they were knocked down. The reason that this was agreed to be the explanation for the devastation was that those who'd been shot up pretty badly had been slow themselves for the same reasons, though just a fraction of a second quicker than their unlucky comrades. The Lightning had actually done quite well when it got into the fight. It was fast and powerful, and gave as good as it got, and only one of the losses happened after they'd engaged in battle, and even then it was only because it had been swarmed by 109s hitting it from every direction. The Americans had done remarkably well in their first battle, they'd just been failed by the complexity of their aeroplane and its lack of warmth. Tex's report to the top of the United States Army Air Force said as much, and he'd been summoned to headquarters almost immediately to explain his comments. He'd wanted to take Harriet with him to put her expert opinion forward, but as she wasn't even supposed to have been in the fight, he had to make do with her contribution to the reports.

It was a solemn time in the Group at first, until they quickly learned the British way of dealing with their losses, and closed ranks so they could move forward. A night off in London helped, and a couple of days later the pilots were back to themselves, something helped by a party arranged in the Officers' Club to celebrate the awarding of Distinguished Flying Crosses to a number of pilots that had taken part in the escort, Tex included. Much to his embarrassment he hadn't been able to formally recognise Harriet's efforts, in being the first to respond to the attack, breaking up the diving fighters, and escorting the broken bombers home, because she wasn't officially there. Instead, he'd written a commendation to both his headquarters and the Air Ministry, citing her dedication to duty, and invaluable support in helping her American pilots prepare for combat. Not that she'd wanted any recognition, though. If anything, she was frustrated that she hadn't been able to do enough to prepare the pilots for combat, and while she knew she couldn't change the Lightning, she was kept awake thinking of how she could have maybe got another 190, or maybe broken up the attack earlier, and given the boys who were shot down a few more seconds to react. There was no stopping the thoughts, it was who she was, and they continued for a good few days until she received an unexpected visit from the pilots of the two B17s she'd escorted home. They were taken aback when Tex presented a lithe young English rose as their saviour, and they weren't sure at first whether or not he was messing with them, but when they were reassured of who she was, and her provenance as a pilot, she was thanked warmly and presented with gifts and warm handshakes from grateful pilots, in addition to a barrel of beer they'd donated with their compliments, which Harriet immediately passed on to Tex to be shared with the pilots in yet another night of drinking.

It had been an unexpected end to winter, and after a few months of being away from combat, the brief yet intense escort mission had brought back a lot of memories. Not to her recent posting in Scotland, apart from the brief moments she'd seen the flak filling the distant sky, but to Malta and Kent. Back to the days when she'd flown into raids made up of hundreds of bombers and fighters, and flown out of her skin, living on instinct to get her through swarms of aeroplanes shooting at her from every direction. She couldn't comprehend how she'd survived. Getting through France was chance enough, getting through the Battle of Britain alive had been miraculous. To add two tours of Malta on top of that, with little in the way of rest in between, she was able to accept why she'd been so exhausted that Alastair had found a way to get her somewhere peaceful for a while. It was a thought that made her smile at herself. She'd missed her fighters, but she knew that Alastair would be beside himself with distress if he knew she'd found the first opportunity to take one into battle just two months after he'd tried to send her to safety. Something inside her just couldn't help herself. She seemed drawn to danger, especially the type of danger that had wings, and there was nothing she could do, consciously or otherwise, to pull herself away. It was like she was supposed to be in an aeroplane, it's where she felt alive. Despite the smiles, the thought led her to another much darker assertion, one she'd had since the war had started for her. While she felt alive in an aeroplane, she couldn't shake the thought that she'd die in one too. It was a thought that led to others, to the people she'd lost. The American faces she'd got to know all too recently, some of whom hadn't come back from the escort mission, and those in her past that she'd known much better. Sully, Flash, Barnes, all were such strong and influential characters in her life, and all of them were dead. Their fires burning brightest right before they met their ends while in their beloved fighters. There were lots of others, faces she'd laughed with and drank with, and others she'd done her best to try and keep alive, despite knowing their inexperience would see them dead before she got to know them. She remembered every one of them, their faces, their voices, the way every one of them spoke with such passion about flying, even those that were terrified of what was to come. Then there was Cas. Her favourite and most treasured memory, and the one that hurt her the most. It had been six months since he'd died, and she still couldn't make her peace with it. Not being able to say goodbye pained her daily, though that in itself gave her a great deal of conflict. She didn't want to say goodbye, and didn't have a clue how she would have even if she'd had the chance, despite thinking of it a hundred and one times. She often thought of what it would have been like had she been on the Sunderland with him when it went down in the

Mediterranean. Would she have been able to save him? Would she have managed to save herself? She liked to think she'd have tried. It's why she'd swam so hard to rescue AP when she found her in the North Sea. She couldn't lose another friend, not like that, and while she knew it was AP she was swimming to save, there was a competing thought that she was battling to save Cas from the Mediterranean. They were hard thoughts to have, but being with the Americans had given her time to actually think them and explore them.

"I've got an announcement to make," Tex said, as he stood on a table in front of a hangar packed full of every member of the Group. An impromptu meeting had been called a few hours earlier, and all ranks were summoned after Tex had returned from a briefing at headquarters. Harriet had stood with the senior officers and listened as bets were placed on the news. The favourite was that the invasion of Europe was about to start, and they were being put on notice to cover the ships carrying the troops over to France. While it was a favourite for many, the theory didn't hold much water with Harriet. The Allied forces had tried and failed to put boots on European soil only the previous August, and it had been a massacre when thousands of Canadians were killed or captured at Dieppe. Nothing much had changed in Europe since, and anyone that had been around long enough knew all too well that the Germans were as confident and competent as ever, and they weren't about to let anyone walk in the front door. Despite knowing this in her heart, it didn't stop her hoping a little. Invasion would mean the war was almost over, and nobody else needed to die. It was an exciting thought to have. "I'll cut to the chase," Tex continued, as the hangar fell silent. "We're being redeployed. Ground crews need to pack up and be ready to move the day after tomorrow, pilots will need to be ready to fly in the morning. Long range tanks will be fitted, and you can take what you can carry, everything else can come with the ground party. Oh, and don't forget your sunglasses, we're heading to North Africa." The hangar erupted in mumbled chatter as those gathered nudged and whispered to each other. "Alright, settle down and let me finish." He waited a moment until the mutters died away, then continued. "It seems Rommel, the notorious Desert Fox, has bitten off more than he can chew this time, and with a couple of hundred thousand German and Italian soldiers he's currently stuck in Tunisia between the Brits to the east, and our boys in the west, and we've been called to go help kick his behind right across the Mediterranean!" The hangar burst into a cheer, making Tex smile and nod his head encouragingly. "Right, get to it. The sooner you're squared away, the sooner we can stand down and have a couple of drinks. Don't get carried away though, tomorrow's a busy day!" The hangar quickly emptied, noisily, leaving Harriet standing with a few of the other officers as Tex walked over to join them. "Sorry for the short notice, fellas, command only just told me. Better get the admin sorted. We'll take the Twin Beech with us; it can carry some of the HQ staff. We have a couple of C47 Skytrains coming over to carry the priority staff over, too. Crew chiefs and a few of the senior ground crew need to be out there with us, make sure they're briefed." They saluted and left Harriet facing him. "Walk with me, Harry." She nodded, and walked slowly by his side.

"What does that mean for me?" she asked. Her heart was squeezing. She'd got used to her new posting, and wasn't ready for it to end. In the few minutes since he'd announced the news, she'd already started to imagine where she'd end up next. She'd missed her fighters, but she wasn't ready to go back to them full time. Not yet.

"Well, my boss talked with your boss, and they can guarantee you a job back in London at the Air Ministry, if you want it?"

"Oh..." Harriet felt the life sucked from her body as she imagined the depression of a desk job, surrounded by stuffy officers who'd no doubt think of her as no more than a glorified secretary. As much as she was still exhausted from operational flying, the fear of flying a desk for the rest of her career was the one thing guaranteed to send her into despair.

"Or they're happy for you to come over with us, if you like?" He smirked, having watched her face turn from disappointment, to disgust, then confusion and hope.

"You're serious?"

"We'll be working closely with the RAF over there under a combined Allied Air Force, and it's thought you may be able to help us settle in. I mean, if you want to?"

301

"Yes!" Harriet replied, almost as soon as the words had left his mouth.

"It's the same deal as here. You come across as liaison, and help us talk to your guys out in the desert. No getting in harm's way, and no matter how much you nag me this time, no more missions. Got it?"

"Yes, Sir!"

"Alright then. Better get yourself packed. You can take that Lightning you've been borrowing since you've been here, unless you'd rather go in the back of a transport?"

"The Lightning will be fine, thank you." She gave him a smirk, which was replied to with a nod and a wink, before Harriet marched quickly away, heading to her cottage to pack.

After choosing what she'd take with her, and packing the rest to go with the bulk of the Group's kit, apart from the bits and pieces she was sending home to Aunt Mary's, she sat down and wrote a few letters. First was to Nicole, letting her know how she was doing, and that she was going out of town for a while. She hadn't seen her since Christmas, and letters had been as infrequent as ever. She'd much rather have gone to say goodbye in person, but the tight schedule meant that was out of question, so a letter was the next best thing. She wrote to Aunt Mary, too, and to a few friends, Alastair, AP, and Ginny included, then, when she was done, she headed to the Officers' Club to join them for a farewell meal and drink. Tex had shared in confidence with her and his senior officers that command had been worried by his report on the Lightning's performance in combat over Europe. It hadn't been the first damning the aeroplane's unsuitability escorting bombers in the cold northern skies that were defended by swarms of experienced Luftwaffe fighters, though it was accepted that command needed to do something to try and make sure it was the last. The Lightning had been performing well elsewhere, places where the enemy fighters weren't quite so overwhelming, and the atmosphere wasn't quite so cold, so Tex and his group were being sent to the Mediterranean, while a new group of much more suitable Thunderbolts were coming to England to replace them. The

Thunderbolt didn't have the same range, but it was hardy, easier to fly, and the cockpit had heat. The revelation wasn't something Tex wanted to share with the pilots, he wanted them to be confident with their Lightnings. He knew that once they were, they'd be unstoppable in combat. Assuming that combat wasn't escorting slow moving bombers over Europe in winter.

Tex sent his officers to bed after only a couple of drinks, wanting them fresh for the following day, and Harriet made her way back to her cottage, ready for her last sleep in a cold bedroom and a comfortable bed, knowing all too well that whatever she found in North Africa, it wouldn't be anywhere near the same. She remembered her last visit to North Africa, and how uncomfortable everything about it was, with the exception of Cairo, and for a moment she questioned her decision to join the trip. She liked being in England, but if she stayed she risked a desk job which could end her flying altogether. More than a few combat tired pilots had found themselves flying a desk at the Air Ministry, before being moved on to other administrative roles which kept them firmly on the ground, and no matter how tired she was, she couldn't do that. Almost as bad was the worry that if she asked for a flying posting instead, she could well be sent back to Mosquitoes, or worse, Beaufighters, or even Blenheims. Either way, she'd be stuck in the machinery of the RAF's day to day grind, the pomposity, the ridiculous rules, and the almost certain fights she'd have to face just because she was a woman. She enjoyed being with the Americans, she was left alone, the officers were pleasant, and from day one nobody had even mentioned she was female. They hadn't dared. Tex had laid down the law, and that was good enough for everyone concerned, she was just Harry, one of the guys. Better the desert with them than the alternatives.

Chapter 16

Here Comes The Sun

"Squadron Leader Cornwall, Ma'am," the young officer said, having stood at the back of the terrace coughing politely and trying to get her attention.

"What is it?" Harriet asked, as his voice woke her from the light sleep she'd slipped into while relaxing and enjoying the midday sun. She hadn't had much to do since arriving in Algeria, other than fly a few patrols to have a look around the area, while the ground crews got the Group's fleet up to standard for air operations, and the pilots got settled into their new environment. So, she spent much of her time sunbathing on the upper terrace of the villa where Tex had set up his headquarters. The weather was perfect, like early summer in England, not too hot, but warm enough to enjoy, and it was a welcome relief from the cold she'd got used to since Scotland.

"Ma'am, the Colonel would like to see you in the briefing room."

"OK," she sighed, then stood from her deck chair and straightened her sand coloured shirt and shorts, which she hadn't imagined she'd wear again after her last trip to Malta. The young man looked at her and blushed a little, making her check herself nervously to make sure her clothing hadn't come open in some way, but nothing was out of place. "Well?" she asked irritably.

"Ma'am?"

"If I'm going to walk through that door, you're going to need to move."

"Yes, Ma'am!" He blushed again and jumped out of her way, leaving her to walk past while rolling her eyes. He was new with the Group, having joined them in Algeria direct from America, and he seemed to blush at the mere sight of her. She left him in her wake and headed into the villa, finding Tex in the briefing room with his second in command and a few others.

"Harry, thanks for joining us," Tex said as he saw her, and immediately handed her a bottle of Coke, which despite the warmth in the room was still ice cold. It made her smile as she took a mouthful, the Americans were nothing if not resourceful, and despite being thousands of miles from home, they made sure they had their comforts. They made sure she had hers, too, which reaffirmed her happiness to be with them. She looked around the room at the other faces, the squadron commanders, the second in command and intelligence officer, and a few she hadn't met before. RAF officers, including a lean and well tanned Air Vice Marshal. "Sir, this is our liaison officer, Squadron Leader Harry Cornwall," Tex continued, as he introduced Harriet to the AVM.

"Of Malta fame?" the AVM asked with a soft New Zealand accent.

"Maybe... Sir," Harriet replied, standing smartly to attention, and almost dropping the bottle of Coke at the same time. "I mean, I didn't meet anyone else called Cornwall while I was there, so I could be." She felt her cheeks start to burn with a blush as the words fell out of her mouth.

"How come you're here with our American friends, Cornwall?"

"I was posted in after finishing my operational tour on Mosquitoes with Coastal Command, Sir."

"Mosquitoes... Anti shipping raids?"

"Yes, Sir."

"I see... Well, if I'd known you were on the market, I'd have snapped you up myself. I could do with somebody like you on my staff." He gave her a nod, then turned back to the planning table. "Right, now you're operational, this is where I want your chaps patrolling," he continued, while tapping the map. "We've got the Germans cornered in Tunisia with their backs to the wall. It's a crucial moment, and if we get this right, they're finished. We've got a big push in the pipeline, which should see us kick them and their Italian friends out of North Africa once and for all, but to do that we've got to shut down

305

the Luftwaffe. Their fighters and light bombers are still causing us headaches, and we need rid of them. On top of that, they're stepping up their resupply efforts, sending transports across the Mediterranean loaded with fuel and ammunition." He looked around the table for a moment. "Think you can get stuck into them?"

"We'll get to it right away, Sir. You can rely on us," Tex said confidently.

"I don't doubt it, Colonel. You need to be a visible presence over Tunisia and the Mediterranean. Let them see you're there, and make a nuisance of yourselves enough to make them think twice about hanging around." He gave a nod and stood straight. "That's everything. We'll call you if we need anything else, and I'll expect a report on operations at the end of each day, including any losses and significant damages you experience. There are more aircraft on their way over to you, and I'll make sure you have enough pilots to fly them, just as long as you're doing your job. Right, I need to get back to headquarters. Good luck, gentlemen. Make us proud." Tex and the others jumped to attention and saluted smartly. The AOC returned the salute, then turned to leave with his small entourage. "Cornwall, join me outside, would you?"

"Yes, Sir." She walked at his side as they headed out into the daylight, and he sent his staff off to prepare his aircraft for their flight.

"So, what are they like? As a fighting force, I mean."

"They're good pilots, Sir. The Lightning isn't really suited for bomber escort over Northern Europe, but the pilots still made a good go of things. Given the right environment, I'm sure they'll perform well."

"We'll soon see, I suppose. What about you? How do you find flying with them in combat?"

"I don't, Sir."

"Excuse me?"

"I'm not allowed. Apparently, being a liaison officer means I don't fly with them. I stay on the ground and liaise. Sir."

"Who on earth made that rule up?"

"The Air Ministry, I suppose?"

"Well, out here you come under my command, and I'm happy for you to fly with them. So long as you don't go doing anything stupid like getting yourself killed. It'll help you get a better appraisal of their skills, and let me know how they're getting on. Besides, I can't imagine you're much use sitting around building sandcastles down here."

"Thank you, Sir." She couldn't keep the smile from her face as they arrived at his transport aircraft, which had arrived with an escort of Spitfires. She wasn't in a rush to go into combat again, but having permission to fly made it easier to get away from the boredom and jealousy she was starting to feel at being left on the ground. His aide met them, and the AOC took a piece of paper and wrote his authorisation for her to fly. After signing it he held it out to her, then pulled it away just out of reach as she moved to take it.

"Remember, nothing stupid. I fully intend to have you moved to my staff sooner or later, and I need you alive for that."

"Yes, Sir." She smirked, then took the paper.

"Good luck, Cornwall. I want you at the briefings with your CO, and I expect an honest report from you each week on their performance. Understood?"

"Understood." She tried not to smile too much as he gave her a nod, then climbed into the aeroplane as the engines started to rumble into life. She quickly moved away as the propellers started swinging, and the sand and dust swirled.

"Well?" Tex asked, as he joined her at the edge of the runway.

"Well, what?" Harriet replied casually.

"He tell you to keep an eye on us?"

"A close eye," she replied with a sly smile, then handed him the note.

"Authority to fly, huh?"

"For now. Apparently, he's going to move me to his staff..."

"How'd you feel about that."

"I like where I am for the moment."

"In that case, you'd better give him a good report, otherwise I'll ask him to take you sooner rather than later."

"We'll see." She gave him a mischievous wink, which made him sigh and shake his head.

"What do you say we get to work on the Air Vice Marshall's orders, and get a patrol up to see what the Germans are up to?"

"Yes, Sir!"

An hour after the AOC had left, Tex was leading the three squadrons over the nearby Tunisian border, eager to get on with the war and face the Germans again. He'd been angry, and keen for retribution since their first escort mission over England, to the point of being driven by a need to get into another fight. Harriet stayed in her position on his wing, with two squadrons behind her, one left and one right, and the third keeping watch from a few thousand feet above. Looking down at the endless miles of desert reactivated memories she'd long tried to repress, and instantly made her mouth dry. It had been less than a year since she'd walked across the mountainous dunes of sand that rubbed and irritated incessantly, while the baking summer sun burned her skin mercilessly. For a moment she started to regret her choices, both returning to North Africa, and accepting the invite to fly. She could have stayed home in England, flying a desk in the relative safety of London, or even if she hadn't, she could have kept her mouth shut and not got permission to fly. Life on the ground with the Americans was more than comfortable. The food was good, they had ice cold Coke almost on tap, her bed was comfortable, and nobody really bothered her. Instead, she was facing her fears, either deliberately or subconsciously, and doing the very thing she had absolutely no intention of ever doing again. She shook her head to rid herself of the cringing feeling that was starting to consume her, and instead focused on the distant greenery lining the coast, as Tex turned them northeast and towards the sea. It was a welcome sight. A sign of civilisation and relative safety, just in case, and it was enough to keep her settled until finally they crossed the rugged brown and green cliffs and headed out over the Mediterranean. Something that brought another wave of memories, this time of Malta, and all that went with it.

"Aircraft, ten o'clock low," a voice said over the radio, some twenty minutes after crossing the coast, instantly breaking through Harriet's circling memories as her eyes fixed on the scattering of black dots far in the distance. "Bombers!"

"Alright boys, here we go!" Tex said, as he swung the Group around to face the enemy.

"Fighters up above," Harriet said, as she caught a glimpse of the sun glinting off the 109s. Her senses were instantly sharpened as the memories quickly faded and she started to plan her attack.

"Got them. Clint! You and your boys up there keep those fighters off us, while we go say hello to the bombers," Tex said to the squadron above. "Alright, everyone, prepare yourselves for a fight." Harriet had already switched on her gunsight, heated her guns, and increased her propeller revolutions before he gave his instructions, leaving just the throttle to push forward when the others were ready. The Americans had learned their lessons in Europe, and wherever possible they prepared their aircraft before getting stuck into battle, to save the valuable seconds that had cost them so dearly in the past. It seemed easy out over the Mediterranean when there was time to think, much easier than trying to work through the tasks with hands so cold they wouldn't move, while German fighters were falling out of the clouds above, bearing down with guns blazing.

"They're not bombers," Harriet said as they came closer, approaching the German formation from the side and recognising the unique looking three engine transport aircraft. "They're Ju52 transports. Be careful, and look out for the gunners on the top, and others firing from the side of the fuselage." She opened her throttle and kept on Tex's wing, while calculating the angle and drop of her shots. The German gunners reacted almost instantly, and lines of glowing tracer bullets lashed through the air like giant fiery whips, making Harriet nudge her rudder left and right to keep out of their way as she continued to move closer. Tex let rip with guns and cannon as soon as they were in range, sending a stream of bullets and cannon shells into the third engine on the nose of the Ju52, which immediately started it smoking and spraying oil up over the windscreens. He pulled up and over as the transport dived away, but not before Harriet had put a burst into the wing for good measure, rattling the starboard engine and sending pieces of debris flying into the air. She followed after Tex, staying with him while spinning her head in search of the escort fighters, and being reassured that Clint's squadron were holding them off comfortably. Tex led them in a wide arc to come back at the scattered line of transports that the two squadrons of Lightnings were chasing all over the sky, and knocking down with ease. Harriet's stomach twinged a little as they came in for another attack, and Tex ran his guns along the fuselage of another Ju52, ripping the side open and sending bloodied bodies tumbling out into the sky. She held her fire as she passed, leaving it to trail smoke into a dive towards the coast, and as Tex swooped around to go on the attack again, joined by one of the other Lightnings, Harriet peeled away and followed the Ju52 that had just been ripped open. The dorsal gunner was still firing desperately from his post at the top of the aeroplane, though his aim was being thrown off by the pilot's efforts to keep the transport in the air, and it was easy for Harriet to avoid his bullets by slipping left and right. The feeling in her stomach continued. She could see the shot up bodies inside, and even the terror in the eyes of the survivors, and while they were the enemy, she couldn't bring herself to finish them off. It felt wrong. After all the destruction she'd seen, and all the times she'd been on the receiving end of a massacre by overwhelming numbers of enemy aircraft, she couldn't understand why she couldn't push the fire button. Instead, she just watched and followed. The gunner eventually stopped firing when the ammunition ran out, but instead of ducking inside and hoping for the best, he stood his post and watched her, no doubt giving instructions to the pilot and letting him know where their pursuer was. As the coast came into view she pulled alongside the transport and looked over to the terrified looking pilot, who was fighting his badly damaged aeroplane to keep it going just a few more miles. Harriet gave him a nod and a wave, which he responded to in kind, and she flew alongside him until they came within range of any anti aircraft artillery that could be hanging around on the cliffs. Once she was sure they were likely to make landfall, she waved, then pulled up and away, and headed back towards the fight had been.

The sky was full of vapour trails and smoke, but the fight was over. A scattering of black dots had made it to the coast, and the water was littered with wreckage, life rafts, and parachutes. It had been a massacre. There was no other word for it. The feeling in her stomach didn't go away as she circled the area, looking down at the sea for signs of downed Americans whose positions she needed to report. She had no idea how many transport aircraft there had been, but she couldn't get the image out of her mind of the men falling from the ripped open aeroplane, and those left crammed inside, bleeding and shot up, and desperately scared. Not one of them was wearing a parachute, not even the poor souls that had fallen through the hole in the fuselage. It was war, and the men in the aeroplanes were the enemy, bound no doubt for the front lines where they'd fight British, American, or Commonwealth soldiers, but it just didn't feel right to shoot them up while they couldn't fight back. Despite holding her fire and not putting them into the sea, she felt guilty. It was the first time she'd felt it so strongly, and she didn't like it. It was confusing. She finished her sweep of the area, then quickly remembered that there may be more German fighters around, and there was nothing to say they'd have any guilt at all about putting her in the sea, so she opened her throttle and headed off in the direction she'd came, where in the distance she could make out Lightnings heading for home.

"Damn, what a turkey shoot that was!" Tex said confidently, as he stood in the garden of the headquarters villa, and puffed out a cloud of blue smoke from his ever present cigar. He was surrounded by his senior officers, the intelligence officer, and the squadron commanders, all of whom were charged with excitement after the

311

patrol. All except Harriet, who stood quietly, unable to rid herself of the feeling of sadness mixed with disgust that had sat heavy on her since she saw the Germans fall from their transport. "We must've knocked down twenty or more of those Nazi transports. They were easier to hit than a barn door. How'd your boys get on with their escorts, Clint, the 109s put up much of a fight?"

"No, Sir. There weren't more than eight of them, and two Ju87 dive bombers. They didn't stand a chance. We knocked three down, and the rest made a run for it when they realised what they were up against."

"Losses?"

"Just the one, though we saw him in his parachute, so he'll be good. One of the other boys got shot up, but he made it back home and we've sent him off to the hospital."

"Boys, I can't tell you how proud I am. Twenty three for two is a pretty good outing. Get yourselves back to your squadrons, and get the aeroplanes ready for the next time we go up. The intelligence officer will be around to debrief shortly." The squadron commanders stood to attention and nodded smartly. "Tell your pilots we've just hit back for what happened over in Europe, and we're only just getting started." They left, leaving Harriet with Tex, his second in command, and the intelligence officer. "Thanks, boys. I'll see you inside." He gave them a nod, sending them away and leaving him with Harriet, who despite her best efforts could only force a half smile. "Penny for 'em."

"What?" Harriet replied, a little startled. "Sorry, nothing, I'm fine."

"The hell you are. We've just had our biggest success since we got into this war, and you're looking like somebody just shot your dog. What's up?" He sucked on his cigar and frowned considerately. Harriet looked at him for a moment, she trusted him and knew that no matter what she said, he'd take it the right way, and while he was right that she couldn't be happy even if she tried, for once she was aware that despite the awkwardness of the situation she wasn't blushing. "Well? You gonna make me force it out of you?"

"No..."

"You can speak freely, Harry. You know that."

"I do..." She nodded as she composed herself. "I'm genuinely happy for the Group's success. You've all worked hard and trained hard, and you deserved it after England."

"But?"

"But today was like shooting up buses."

"You're saying we shouldn't be happy with what we achieved?"

"No..."

"Then what?"

"I'm saying that eight older model 109s and two slow moving dive bombers trying to protect a string of transports against almost forty heavily armed Lightnings were never going to give the best account of themselves. Your pilots did a good job, but if they let a turkey shoot define them, they risk becoming complacent, and you'll lose more than two when you go head to head with equal numbers of fighters. They may have taken a beating recently, but the Luftwaffe are a dangerous enemy, and even when you have the upper hand you can't be complacent. If you are, you're dead." She shrugged almost defiantly as she finished talking. He'd asked, and she'd answered. At least she'd answered as diplomatically as she could. She didn't dare tell him she'd held fire and not shot down the wrecked German transport, neither did she tell him about the confusing and conflicting feelings she was experiencing.

"Message received and understood," he replied as he nodded slowly in acceptance of what she'd said. "You know, after what happened in Europe, many of the boys were scared. They rightly thought they were going to get their behinds kicked every time they flew in combat. Today changed that, broke the curse so to speak, but I've heard ya, Harry, and you're right. I'll give 'em tonight, and tomorrow I'll give them a reality check. Focus them on what's to come." He gave Harriet a nod and a smile, and she felt herself blush a little. "Why don't you get yourself a drink and take it easy? You flew well up there today, you've earned it."

"Thank you." She forced another smile, then headed into the villa, grabbing an ice cold Coke as she passed through, listening to the excitement of almost everyone talking about the success of the patrol as she made her way through the building to her room. She threw her flying kit by the door, then headed out onto the terrace and slumped back into her chair. As she relaxed and enjoyed the cold drink, she couldn't pull her mind away from what had happened. It was the first time she'd held back in battle. Every other fight, wherever the fight, she'd been in the thick of it and fighting hard. It's all she knew how to do, or so she thought. She was confused and a little upset, and she didn't have a soul to talk about it with, not that she was one for talking about her feelings at the best of times, but more than ever it was what she needed. She genuinely didn't know what to think, or do. The Americans had adopted Harriet and treated her like family, but there wasn't one of them she'd feel comfortable talking to about such things. It made her feel more alone than she had in a long time. Worse even than her time stranded in the desert, at least then she was genuinely alone. Not surrounded by people and not having a soul to talk to. Scotland had been hard, it had frayed her nerves and pushed her to the edge, but at least she had AP to talk to, and Ginny. She missed them both, and she missed Nicole, and as her mind wandered around her sadness, she started to think of Cas again. He was one of the few she'd opened up to, and felt comfortable around enough to be herself, and be vulnerable. It somehow seemed OK with him. Everyone else, even Nicole at times, was wanting something from her, even if only subconsciously. They wanted a leader, or a friend, or somebody they could rely on to be rational and composed, and hold it together when things got tough. As she thought back, she realised that had been her entire life, and why she'd created her strict rules about not crying in front of people, and not showing weakness. She'd even created a narrative for herself that she had a heart of stone and nothing much bothered her, and she let herself believe it at times, especially since she'd become a fighter pilot. A series of incidents and accidents, and desperate seat of the pants flying, had painted a picture that she was somehow this

314

renowned ace, and it's what everyone expected. Whether she was a good pilot or not wasn't what was going through her mind though. She'd been exhausted and on the edge before being sent to America, and she'd been exhausted on the edge when she came back. She'd felt the changes in herself. Her snappiness and irritability, feeling as tired when she woke in the morning as when she'd gone to bed, her increasing inability to form friendships, which only served to deepen her loneliness and her longing for the people she cared about. She'd also recognised the more serious signs, the blurred and patchy memories of combat in Scotland, where she'd get back from a mission with hardly any memory of what had happened. When she looked back it seemed obvious that sooner or later she'd hold fire in a battle. She'd started second guessing herself and overthinking during combat. She'd heard the stories, and she knew that the next stop was being killed because she'd stopped to think. It had happened to lots of pilots before her.

The weeks passed, and the Group were thrown into battle with increasing frequency as the allied armies launched their assault on Tunisia, squeezing the remaining German and Italian armies between them, and forcing them into an ever more desperate position. The desperation quickly put the reality to Harriet's words, and the Group were soon coming up against swarms of Messerschmitt 109s with their blood up for a fight. It took the Lightning pilots a while to compose themselves and react, and in that time they lost more than a few good pilots across the squadrons. They soon adapted though, and once they'd learned to respect the Luftwaffe, they were giving as good as they got in pitch battles over Tunisia. They'd also flown bomber escort missions, taking B25 Mitchell medium bombers to raid German defences. These missions were significantly different to Europe, much to the relief of the pilots. Being based relatively close to the target, the Lightnings didn't need long range tanks, their guns and cockpits were warm, and they could fly ready for a fight, just needing to switch on their gunsight and increase speed when the enemy appeared, which wasn't as frequent as they'd expected.

Harriet had flown with the Group every now and then, having been allowed to pick and choose when she flew and when she didn't. Most of the time she'd engaged herself in training duties, and liaising with the RAF, who they'd flown with frequently. It was a conscious choice to stay away from combat, something she'd needed to do after reminding herself of how tired she was, and that the posting was supposed to be non operational. She'd also been 'borrowed' by the AOC a few times, and sent on errands after reporting on the good performance of her Americans. These were often liaison missions with the former Vichy French landlords in Algeria who, despite the collapse of the Nazi sympathising Vichy rule in the area, still had a great deal of control and influence. These colonialists were largely warm and welcoming to a young European woman who spoke fluent French, and Harriet was often able to communicate with them on behalf of her British or American commanders in a way that they couldn't, which in turn smoothed communications and relationships. She enjoyed the work, and while the only flying she did was as a passenger in a transport aircraft of some sort, it was enough to satisfy her need, and keep her away from further intercept missions, of which there'd been a few, so she wasn't forced to hold her fire when attacking poorly armed transports again. Despite being kept busy, the loneliness didn't go away as time moved on and the North African offensive continued, and she still had more and more questions about herself as a pilot and what her future would be.

Chapter 17

Alright...

"Alright, everyone, this is the big one. Eyes open and let's do our jobs, and let the boys on the ground finish this thing!" Tex said over the airwaves, as the Group flew over the Tunisian border. Harriet looked around at the scene surrounding her. Lightnings and Spitfires were stretched out high up, keeping watch over the swarms of B25 Mitchells, Hurricanes, and Curtis P40 fighter bombers that were hurrying towards the German front lines, which were bracing themselves to receive what seemed liked hundreds of allied tanks that were racing towards them, and kicking up clouds of sand so big it looked like a sandstorm. It was the start of the major offensive designed to break the Germans and Italians once and for all, and finish their presence in North Africa. Their supply ships and aircraft had been savaged with alarming frequency for weeks on end, leaving them so desperate for fuel and ammunition that Allied commanders were sure that they couldn't continue to put up a fight. Every aircraft and pilot available, Harriet included, had been summoned to soften the enemy positions ahead of the arrival of the Allied tanks, and hopefully give them an easier ride. Both British and American bombers would hit the bigger installations, the headquarters, and large formations, while the P40s and Hurricanes would attack gun positions and tanks, and generally make a nuisance of themselves. All the time they would be covered by the Lightnings and Spitfires that were briefed to provide an umbrella of protection, so the bombers could do their vital work before the tanks arrived just minutes later. It was perfectly timed, and it was crucial the combined airforces did their job to protects the tanks, and the truckloads of infantry that rolled along behind them. Harriet was almost overwhelmed as she switched on her gunsight and scanned the sky ahead for signs of the Luftwaffe. She'd never been part of something so big. There must have been hundreds of aircraft all heading in the same direction, and it was awesome. She thought back to the Luftwaffe raids that had rolled over Kent, and wondered how they must have felt flying in formations three or four hundred strong. She imagined they felt invincible, right up until they'd been thrown back, when they must have wondered how they lost.

"Bandits, eleven o'clock low!" Harriet called, as she caught sight of several pencil thin lines of 109s snaking through the hot blue sky towards a wave of B25s below, looking like black arrows darting towards the bombers, contrasted starkly against the sand below.

"Got them!" Tex replied. "OK, Lone Star Group, let's go say hello. Tally Ho!" He pushed the nose of his Lightning down, and everyone followed, almost as if the three squadrons of Lightnings were tied together. Harriet picked her target, then scanned upwards, looking left and right to see if there were any unwelcome guests planning on coming down on top of them. To her relief the sky was clear, so she went back to her target, and just a few seconds later she was pushing her fire button and joining the others in sending a stream of glowing tracer at the 109s. The firepower was awesome, and while the 109s returned fire, the first squadron was quickly overwhelmed. German fighters went down in smoke in every direction, while others erupted in balls of flame, as the Lightnings cut into them. Harriet's target tried to pull up to avoid her, and timed it perfectly to show her the belly of his aeroplane, which she ripped apart with a stream of cannon fire, almost cutting it in two. She picked the next and gave chase, but it was hit and sent down smoking by another Lightning, which crossed in front of her perilously close and almost hitting her. She pulled up and over it, and aimed for the next line of fighters closing on the already busy sky. A 109 came in close and hit a Lightning in the fuel tank, making it burn for a few seconds before it exploded in mid air right above Harriet, sending shrapnel in every direction, rattling Harriet's aeroplane so hard it sounded like rain on a tin roof, even above the engine noise. The aeroplane shook violently, and it took an effort to keep it upright, but she quickly passed through the firestorm and into a blue sky crisscrossed with trails of black and white smoke, as fighters from both sides clashed. It was a bitter battle, with so many aircraft in such a small space the risk of crashing was as high as being shot down, and it took expert skill for Harriet to weave her way between rolling and diving fighters without hitting any, having only fractions of a second to push her fire button and take shots as targets passed in front of her gunsights. She was sweating, and her mouth was as dry as a bone, and the battle quickly became an uncoordinated game of chance as more 109s came up to join the fight, and more Spitfires came down. Bullets and cannon shells crisscrossed the sky, forming an ever tightening mesh which closed in around the heart of the battle, hitting and clipping aircraft from both sides, Harriet included. As she rolled to avoid a stream of cannon shells that narrowly missed, bullets rattled her port engine and sent a stream of sparks firing in all directions, and for a moment she caught sight of the bombers wreaking havoc below. The ground was obscured with black smoke and flaming red explosions, mixed with a sandstorm created by all the action. In the mess she saw a trio of 109s circling a pair of P40s that were swooping and rolling, and stirring up the smoke and dust as they tried to escape the enemy fighters. The P40 was a workhorse, a tough aeroplane that could take a lot of punishment, and it had become a great ground attack fighter bomber, but it was no match for a 109, let alone three of them, and it wouldn't be long before both were knocked out of the sky by their stalking hunters. Harriet pushed her stick forward, and the nose of her Lightning dropped steeper, while at the same time she opened her throttle fully and lined up her sights. The calculations streamed through her head effortlessly as she positioned herself and pushed the gun button, sending a stream of fire into the closest 109, and sending it diving into the smoke almost instantly. One of the others pulled up, breaking its attack on the badly smoking P40 it had already riddled with bullets, and firing directly at Harriet. Her starboard engine was hit, and the propeller shattered. She immediately levelled out and half rolled, while adjusting the throttle and the fuel, and praying to any god listening that the port engine would keep going. The 109 pulled up and over, turning tight to get on her tail, and in doing so leaving his friend to deal with the two P40s. The Lightning became much less fun to handle with only one engine, and it was a fight to get it to do what she wanted, as she wanted. Everything was laboured and slow, so much so that she was sure the control surfaces had been damaged at the same time as the engine, though she had no time to look around and check. The 109 had come back at her quicker than she'd hoped, and was already launching streams of tracer at her, all of which was getting closer and closer, until she felt thuds on the armour plating behind her seat hard enough to make her feel like she was being kicked, as the enemy pilot found his mark. There was nothing for it. She had to act, or she'd be dead. After levelling out she pulled back on the throttle then dropped her flaps. The rapid deceleration threw her against her harness and twisted her stomach as she pulled back tight on the stick. Before she knew it, the Lightning was spiralling out of control and entirely unresponsive to anything she tried, and in a brief second of looking around she saw the twin tail booms of her aeroplane falling away into the distance, after the 109 had flown right through them, severing them, and causing itself irrecoverable damage in the process. It had been closer than she'd expected, and her rapid slowing had put it on an unavoidable collision course with her tail. She cursed herself briefly as she looked around in horror, trying to think how she could bring the spinning aeroplane under control, until her survival instinct kicked in and she released the canopy and unfastened her harness. A push against the floor and she was fired out of the cockpit by the airstream, and found herself tumbling through the sky.

The sound of the wind rushing past her ears was interspersed with the thud and buzz of guns, as she tumbled through the sky, acutely aware of the fact that the thick cloud of smoke obscuring the ground below was rushing up quickly to meet her. She reached across her chest and grabbed the ripcord handle, then pulled hard, releasing the parachute which jerked her back and stopped her tumbling with a violent snap as it filled with air and slowed her descent. She fought to get her breath and compose herself, then looked around, and almost passed out in fear as one of the engines and half the wing from her Lightning rocketed past her like a steam train, having been torn away as the stricken aircraft spun out of control. The debris half collapsed the canopy of her parachute, instantly increasing the speed of her descent again as she dropped into the cloud of smoke. She pulled at the riser lines trying to stabilise the parachute, while her lungs filled with foul tasting acrid smoke that stung her eyes and burned her throat. She looked down through the murk and saw the sand dunes fast approaching. German gun positions were scattered around the area, some burning, others still firing, and the ground in between was littered with bodies and wrecked vehicles around the fortified positions and trenches. If she wasn't already scared about hurtling downwards with increasing speed, the knowledge that she was dropping down in the middle of an enemy position was enough to do the job. Before she had too long to think, she hit the top of a shallow dune and collapsed into the sand, which mercifully took some of the impact out of her landing. Her knees folded and collided with her chest, winding her, and knocking the air from her lungs, and making her gasp as her face hit the sand, which quickly filled her mouth. She coughed and choked as the parachute canopy billowed gently, she was disorientated and desperate to get her breath and take stock of her situation. As she rubbed the sand from her eyes with her blue and white silk scarf, a machine gun spluttered into life not far away, and sand jumped into the air in a fast moving neat line which cut up the dune and sped towards her. She dived in the opposite direction, and slid down the shallow slope and pressed herself into the sand, just seconds before the stream of bullets ripped through where she'd been sitting. Tracer passed overhead, and between the bursts she heard angry German voices shouting obscenities towards the 'American flyer', leaving her shaking with fear. She laid still for a moment, gasping, and trying to think what to do. There were dunes all around, none particularly big, no higher than waist height at the most, and to get away she'd have to go over the top of one of them, which would make her the perfect target for the German machine gunners. She also knew she couldn't stay. All she had was the Walther pistol that Carlyle had given her, which she'd decided to keep on her at all times in North Africa, especially after her last experience in the desert; and if the Germans came for her, that wasn't going to be enough to fight them off, and it didn't sound like they were in the mood to take prisoners. The machine gun continued in bursts, almost trimming the top of the dune each time, and filling the air with choking sand. She pulled her scarf over her mouth and shielded her eyes with her hands, while listening to the bursts and shouts. They weren't giving up on her, and as the minutes passed, every German in the area seemed to be using the dunes around her for target practice. Not able to fight back against the aircraft still swooping and roaring somewhere above the thick black smoke, it was clear that they were going to take out their frustrations on her.

After laying at the bottom of the dip between the sand dunes for a while, and realising the shooting wasn't stopping anytime soon, Harriet started to involuntarily scrape at the sand beneath her in a desperate attempt to dig herself lower. Then the voices got louder, and she picked out the distant barking of orders to 'go and bring back the American dog'. The words sent shivers up her spine, and made her pray to for anyone or anything to get her out of the situation. In the brief seconds of praying, she thought through the scrapes she'd been in, and started counting her lives, and how many she had left. Her eyes opened wide as the machine guns and rifles stopped, signalling the approach of the German soldiers. She unfastened her parachute harness, then rolled onto her knees and took the deepest breath she could, before dusting off her Walther and standing, ready to shoot anything in the way as she jumped over the dune and ran in the opposite direction. As she jumped, she was knocked flat by the sight of a P40 skimming the dunes and flying right towards her. She hit the sand again and took another mouthful as it rocketed overhead with guns blazing. It was so low that sand was whipped up into the air as it passed, turning the dark smog of smoke into night. Instinctively, Harriet jumped to her feet and ran as hard as she could up and down dunes, then dropped and crawled to the side, trying to leave the Germans guessing as to where she was. Her heart was pounding, and she laid against the wall of a dune for a minute to catch her breath, while trying to think her way out of danger. The P40 had answered her prayers and given her temporary respite, but it was soon gone, and as the engine noise faded, she was left with the sound of screams coming from the direction of the German positions. It had obviously hit home, but while it had saved her skin, she couldn't imagine the Germans would be in any better mood after being shot up again. They were already angry, being shot up and seeing more of their comrades dead and injured would just make them all the more determined to find her and make her pay. A reality that was soon realised when German voices started shouting at her again. Phrases such as 'come here, American, we won't hurt you,' and 'we're going to skin you alive' made her feel cold, despite the almost choking heat. She was out of options. In her desperate need to escape she'd run down a dead end of dunes, which became shallower the further they stretched. An idea popped into her head as she was jolted by the German machine gun buzzing into action again, and she remembered Cas telling her how in the last war he'd spent a night between the British and German trenches in no man's land, injured and hiding in a half flooded shell crater, while German patrols crawled around cutting barbed wire and planting mines in the mud. Out of desperation, she started to burrow against the wall of the dune she was hiding behind, collapsing it, and trying to smooth the excavated sand over her, knowing that the only hope she had was to hide until nightfall, and pray they Germans didn't look too closely.

Time passed slowly as Harriet laid entombed in sand, except for her mouth and eyes, baking in the heat and flinching at every noise.

She'd packed herself in the sand as well as she could, but it was so light and dry that even the slightest movement threatened to start a small avalanche that would uncover her. She couldn't even move to scratch the hundreds of itches irritating almost every part of her body as the fine sand found its way under her clothes. The voices came closer, and her heart almost stopped as they stopped in the next ditch between the dunes, almost on top of her, and well within reach. They were quickly followed by another pair, and more voices joined them as the Germans talked to each other, frustrated as they searched. Competing voices shouted inside her head, one telling her to stand up and surrender, and hope for the best. She'd met honourable Germans, like the pilots she'd shot down. One German had even saved her life when a mad French General had tried to bayonet her for being a spy. Maybe they'd be forgiving if she gave herself up and stopped messing them about. At least that's what the voice said. The other voice shouted at her to not be an idiot, and reminded her of the Gestapo man who was going to take her to Berlin to be interrogated, and who was going to have his own countrymen shot for trying to protect her. The voices were soon silenced by a sound she couldn't quite place. Something mechanical, clanking and squeaking, and driven by a heavy rumbling engine. The Germans panicked and started shouting, but some were quickly silenced by heavy machine gun fire, while the others ran. The clanking and rumbling intensified, and was amplified and repeated in almost every direction. The ground started to shake, and Harriet instinctively rolled from the sand she'd packed around her, and jumped to her feet, just as a British Sherman tank crested the dune, crushing the sand under its weight as it came to a halt. The main gun fired, launching fire and smoke from the muzzle, and making Harriet's ears ring loud, while its heavy machine gun continued to rattle away.

"I say down there, you haven't by any chance seen a downed yank pilot around these parts, have you?" A remarkably well spoken English voice shouted from above. Harriet staggered back and looked up to the officer standing out of the commander's cupola of the Sherman tank. She stared at him in amazement, and slowly rubbed her eyes, not sure whether the hulk of a tank in front of her was a mirage. "It's just that we're in something of a hurry to get moving again, sitting around tends to make us a magnet for unwanted attention." As if on cue, a large projectile, something much bigger than a bullet, ricocheted off the tank's front armour, and shot off at an angle with a high pitched whizzing sound. "As you can see!" he continued, almost casually, before turning his attention to the distance and speaking into his microphone. Seconds late the main gun blasted into life again, shaking Harriet from her daze. She quickly climbed the dune and reached up to the officer's outstretched hand, and was pulled up the side of the metal beast. "My God, you're a girl..." he said as she stood beside the turret.

"And British," she replied, with a smile that was fighting to spread across her face. "Sorry to disappoint."

"Not at all, old girl. Monty's taxi service welcomes all passengers." He gave her a wink and a smile, and nodded to the rear of the tank. "Better pop yourself behind the turret and keep out of the way, it seems we're in a rough neighbourhood."

"Anything you say."

"Oh, here, you'd better take this." He pulled a Thompson machine gun from the turret and handed it to her. "Just in case the locals get rowdy. Right, hold on." He shouted into his radio as Harriet slipped behind the turret and onto the rear deck, bracing herself against the kit bags and camouflage nets secured to the rear. It was hot and smelly, but the whole turret sat between her and the Germans ahead, who were quickly retreating as the Sherman continued shelling and shooting them, while rocking into life. Other Shermans raced forward to join them, then together they rolled onwards towards the German positions with guns blazing. Harriet pulled her silk scarf back up around her mouth to filter out the sand and smoke, and held her machine gun at the ready as she looked over the side of the tank at the destroyed German positions. The ground was littered with destruction. Bodies and machinery broken and ripped apart, and the sand was stained with blood, and in other places burned black. With the heat and the smell, it was like hell on earth, and even though she'd been rescued from certain death, she felt sick to the pit of her stomach at the destruction. She'd seen the aftermath of a battle the last time she was in the desert, but that wasn't even in the same league. What she was experiencing while rocking and rolling on the back of the tank was the tip of the spear, the armoured thrust at the point of the battle, and it was horrifying. Infantry came out of the smoke behind the tanks, and ran up to clear the remnants of the German gun positions, as the armour continued to push forward towards a ridge climbing out of the smoke that was drifting west on the strengthening breeze. The tank came to a halt before cresting the ridge, as did the others, which stopped left and right, and the officer jumped from the cupola holding a flask. He knelt beside her and poured a cup of lukewarm tea, which she took gratefully and tried not to gulp as she tried to take the glass like scratching dryness from her throat. "Take it steady," he said. "Little bit at a time is best, swill it around your mouth and you'll feel better for it."

"Thank you," Harriet gasped, as the black liquid soothed her vocal cords.

"Not at all. We're not stopping for long, just a couple of minutes to consolidate before we push on over the ridge." Harriet nodded as he talked. "You should probably jump off and hang around here for the supply tucks. They're following behind, and shouldn't be too long."

"No thanks," Harriet replied, after swallowing down more of the tea. "If you don't mind, I'd rather stick with you for now."

"It's hardly safe."

"I've been on my own in the desert before, and I'd rather take my chances with you, if you don't mind?"

"Well, I can't guarantee your safety, but it's your choice."

"Can I keep the gun?"

"I don't see why not. You'd better keep a hold of this flask too." He handed it over to her, and she took it gratefully.

"Thank you, again," she gasped with a smile, which was replied to with a nod. "And for coming to my rescue."

"Our pleasure. We saw you shot down, and thought we'd better try to help before the other side got to you."

"I can't tell you how happy I am that you did that. It was a close thing."

"We're the cavalry, we're supposed to arrive in the nick of time. Arriving ahead of schedule would be bad form." He stood and looked around as the other tanks started revving their engines. "Time to go, be safe and hold on; and remember what I said about the tea. Sip and swill."

"Got it."

"Alexander Charles." He held out his hand

"Harry Cornwall." She shook his hand firmly, then he was gone, climbing up the turret and slipping back inside. She smiled for a moment, and slumped back into the camouflage net again as the tank rocked forward, and joined the other two in cresting the ridge in a stretched out line. The tanks rolled at speed down the slope at the other side, and raced across the rock strewn sandy plain, pushing on to their next objective. Harriet sat on the hot decking and bounced back and forth as the tracks rolled over rocks on the ground, crushing everything that stood in the way of the huge metal beast. The adrenaline was still flowing from her run in with the Germans, and her imagination ran wild with what could have happened if the tanks hadn't come. They weren't pleasant thoughts, and part of her wondered whether she should start carrying the cyanide pill she'd been left with after her trip to Geneva. It was a better option than being captured by enraged soldiers. She retreated into her thoughts as the journey continued, getting lost in how close she'd come yet again, and how the thought of a desk job was becoming more and more appealing. She couldn't keep doing it. She was supposed to be resting in Norfolk, not riding a tank into battle against the German Afrika Corps in deepest Tunisia. She questioned herself, and criticised herself, and couldn't understand why she had to keep putting herself at risk. She'd had plenty of opportunities to stay safe, but she fought them and did everything she could not to be part of them. One thought came back again and again, and quickly became inescapable, maybe she was trying to get herself killed. It was the only reason for it. At first she was trying to do her best, trying to fight the war and do her part, but since leaving Malta she'd been so overwhelmed with such a darkness that the thought of not coming back was the only thing that dominated her mind. She'd stopped making plans for the future, she couldn't even see her future, all she could see was the next day. It's why she didn't find a way to talk to Alastair about leaving Scotland, instead waiting for him to do the deed, and it's why she hadn't said no to going to Geneva, despite the obvious risks that come with any mission that sees a person issued with a cyanide capsule to kill themselves with. Then there was the desert. She wasn't supposed to be flying operationally, she wasn't supposed to be in harm's way, yet she'd flown more than a few combat missions that had eventually led to her being on the back of a tank in the middle of Tunisia, having narrowly escaped being skinned alive by blood thirsty enemy soldiers. The sudden slowing of the tank shook her from her darkening thoughts, and shortly after they'd stopped, Charles looked back to her and shouted.

"Don't suppose you speak Italian, do you?" he asked, almost embarrassed that he had to ask at all.

"A few words, why?" she replied.

"Really? What a stroke of luck. Would you mind awfully giving me a hand talking to this chap?" He pointed ahead of the tank, encouraging Harriet to drag herself up and stand against the turret. Ahead was a wide pass between rocky hills, and in the middle of the track stood an Italian officer waving a white flag. Behind him was a trail of destruction, with burning vehicles winding along the pass, and sending plumes of black smoke swirling into the clear blue sky. The officer was shouting something in Italian, but it was hardly audible above the noise of the tank's engine. "Any thoughts" Charles asked with a shrug.

"I can't hear him properly, but I think he wants to surrender."

"Yes... I assumed as much from the white flag..." He frowned a little, not impolitely, but suggesting he'd expected a different answer. Harriet frowned too, a little irritated and embarrassed at her reply, then she jumped off the tank and walked forward towards the Italian officer, keeping her finger on the trigger of the Thompson machine gun as it hung by her side. He started babbling quickly as she approached. He looked scared, his face was blackened from oil and smoke, and his uniform was shredded, and while he tried hard to stand tall, it was clear to see that he was broken.

"Slow," Harriet said in Italian. "Slow words." He nodded, but still spoke too fast for her to grasp much more than aeroplanes and death. She shook her head, and in desperation asked if he spoke in German or French, which had him nodding excitedly.

"Speak slowly," she said in French. "Speak slowly or I can't understand you."

"We surrender!" He nodded excitedly, and pointed at the flag. "We surrender. No more fighting, no more war. We surrender."

"What's going on?" Charles shouted.

"They're surrendering!" Harriet shouted in reply. Charles rolled his eyes and continued watching as Harriet went back to their conversation. "Tell your soldiers to come out here with their hands up."

"I can't," the Italian shrugged. "Our convoy was attacked by aircraft, and many were injured or killed. We surrender to you. Please. My men need help, yours too."

"Ours?"

"Yes, we were moving prisoners ahead of the advance, and joined with the convoy for safety."

"You know that there's a whole army following behind our tanks? If you're lying, and you attack us, there'll be no surrendering to them."

"You have my word. Please, we don't want to fight anymore."

"OK, come with me." Harriet led him back to the tank and gestured for him to climb on the front with her, so he could stand facing Charles in the turret.

"We're not a bus, you know," Charles said.

"Their convoy was hit by aircraft, and most of his men are injured or dead. He said they were escorting prisoners, and some of ours are hurt too. They want to surrender to us." Harriet explained. "I've warned him there's an entire army behind us, and made it clear any funny business won't end well. He gives his word."

"Very well. Tell him that he's going to stay standing on the front of the tank as we move forward. If his friends get any silly ideas, he'll be the first to get it." Harriet nodded and explained, and the Italian officer nodded and smiled eagerly, as though he'd just been offered a cold beer. "You did tell him he'd be the first to die if anything goes wrong?" Charles asked, raising his eyebrow at the Italian's apparent happiness.

"Exactly as you said."

"Well, he's either genuine or stupid. Better get yourself behind the turret again, no point you making a target of yourself. Just in case stupid wins."

"I won't argue with that!" She climbed around the turret and stood on the rear deck, leaving the Italian officer to hold on tight as the tank jerked forward, after Charles told the other two tanks of the Troop to hold their position, and come in shooting if anything went wrong. They rolled forward slowly, with the turret sweeping the gun barrel left and right as they entered the shallow pass and approached the first of the wrecked vehicles. Harriet stood behind the turret with the machine gun pulled tight into her shoulder as she watched for anything suspicious. It was a nervous moment, she'd heard of traps being set by enemy soldiers pretending to surrender, but these were stories attributed to the most hardcore Germans of the SS, fanatical Nazis who'd fight to the death by fair means or foul. It wasn't the Italian way, though, at least not that she knew of. The Italians were good fighters, but poorly equipped and supplied, and they didn't really have the stomach for war against the allies. Their crazed fascist leader, Mussolini, was hated as much by Italians as he was by anyone else, and they hadn't thanked him for dragging their country into war. Knowing this made Harriet slightly less apprehensive as they rolled forward, though her stomach was still flipping as she wished she was back in an aeroplane. The first smouldering truck wreck was still loaded with bodies, all burned black where they sat, apart from the few broken souls that had made it a few paces in their desperate attempts to escape. The smell was gut wrenching, and Harriet pulled her silk scarf tight around her nose and mouth to try and filter some of the stench of burning flesh. Trucks were scattered all along the pass, some burned out, some damaged, and the ground was scorched and holed by bombs, and raked with bullet holes. To Harriet it was an extension of the hell she'd been in before being rescued by the tank, though she couldn't imagine what it must have been like for those trapped in their burning trucks with nowhere to hide, hemmed in by the steep walled hills either side of the pass. She found herself thinking it was a miracle anyone survived at all.

Travelling through the pass was an assault on the senses in every way. The smell, the sight, the furnace like heat, all were almost too much to bear, and Harriet was relieved when the tank rolled out the other side, to where canvas from the roofs of the trucks that hadn't burned entirely had been used to make shelters for the many wounded. The tank came to a halt, and Charles climbed from the cupola onto the top of the tank, looking around and surveying the destruction. One of his crew followed him out and handed him the flare pistol, which he fired into the sky, sending a burning green light up to signal for the others to follow.

"Wait here," Charles said, as he jumped down from the tank and stood beside the Italian officer. "Keep your eyes open. If they start playing silly buggers, shoot the lot of them." His crewman nodded, and Charles started walking towards the makeshift tents. "I feel sure that I said to wait with the tank..." he said quietly, as Harriet appeared by his side.

"You did, and they are," she replied, deliberately ignoring his intent as she pulled her scarf from her nose and mouth. The Italians that could, stood as they approached, and put their weapons on the ground while raising their hands in the air.

"Tell them to put their weapons over by the tank, would you?" Charles said. Harriet nodded and translated, and the Italian officer gave the instruction. The soldiers hurriedly collected every weapon and took them to the tank, keen to show compliance and avoid even the question of irritating the crew, who they knew could use their machine guns and main gun to cut them apart in seconds if they chose.

"English," the Italian officer said, as he showed Charles and Harriet to a Captain laid under one of the tents.

"Australian, you bloody ignorant Italian!" the captain replied in a gnarled and pained voice. He had what looked like a bullet wound in his thigh, which was bleeding through the dirty tourniquet made from a shirt.

"Lieutenant Charles," Charles said in reply. "We're the spearhead, and the army's following right behind us. If you can hold on, our ambulances will likely be up this way within the hour. The infantry are just mopping up a few miles back."

"Captain Cain, and I'll do my best... Though I'm not sure how much blood I've lost already, because I'm pretty sure I'm hallucinating. Unless that really is a Sheila standing next to you, Charles."

"What?" Charles looked around, then at Harriet. "Oh, no. No, this is a friend from the RAF."

"Squadron Leader Harry Cornwall," Harriet said with a half smile.

"Well, at least I'm not dead yet," Cain said with a wince. "Though we could have done to see you hours ago, when the Luftwaffe started shooting up the convoy."

"The Luftwaffe attacked you?" Harriet asked.

"Yeah, Stukas and 109s. The Italians waved flags and tried everything they could, but we were shot to pieces, as you can see."

331

"Is this all that survived?" Charles asked, as he looked around the tent at the different uniforms and skin tones. Australians, Africans, Indians, and a few British lay around in varying conditions.

"No, we're just the ones waiting to die. Those that could walk set off under armed escort hours ago. The Italian officer leading them is one of those fascist nuts, and was determined to take his prisoners north as ordered. They took what was left of the water."

"Which direction?"

"North..." Cain pointed weakly, then gasped again. "Can't have got too far."

"We'd better go have a look... There's next to nothing out there, and they'll die of thirst before they get anywhere near civilisation," Charles said, as he looked to Harriet. "Tell the Italian to come with us." The three walked back to the tank, as the other two other Shermans of the section arrived through the pass and came to a halt. "There's a number of our wounded mixed with the Italians over there," he said to the commander of the second tank, a short and wiry looking Sergeant with a shock of red hair. "This is the Italian officer in charge here, he'll keep his men under control. Make sure everyone has some water and cigarettes, Italians included, but keep your eyes on them just in case. Do what you can for the wounded, and get on the radio and let headquarters know where we are."

"Yes, Sir," the Sergeant replied. "What about you, Sir? If you don't mind me asking?"

"We're going to have a quick drive up the road to see if we can find the rest of the survivors. Follow on as soon as relief arrives, and if we're not back in a couple of hours, assume the worst. Oh, and you'd better keep your eyes open for Jerry aircraft, apparently this little lot is their handiwork."

"Sir."

"I don't suppose it makes any sense to ask you if you want to stay?" he asked Harriet.

"Have you learned Italian or French since we met?"

"Better get yourself onboard in that case, and pray the Luftwaffe don't come back."

The tank crews were already taking a jerrycan of water and carton of cigarettes to the wounded when Charles' tank rolled into life again, and started following the trail of boot prints heading north, and away from the scene of the massacre. Harriet pulled her scarf up around her mouth and nose again, and leaned against the turret, half shielded by the cupola cover, just in case bullets started flying from in front, though that wasn't the direction that concerned her most. It was difficult for her not to scan the skies repeatedly, searching every direction for signs of aircraft, knowing what an easy target the tank would make for a prowling Stuka. Even a 109 could cause problems for a lone tank.

As the scene of destruction passed into the distance, the ground flattened out into a plain of sand and rock which stretched as far as the eye could see, with heat haze shimmering in the distance. The heat was rising, and the air was dry, and despite the adrenaline that had been keeping Harriet on edge since she'd entered the fight thousands of feet above, she was starting to fade. Her mouth and throat were dry, and her skin was tingling with the relentless heat of the desert, and her mind started to wander to her last trip to North Africa. She felt for the wounded they'd left behind. The other tanks had given them water, but she knew that laying there for hours on end wounded and thirsty must have been horrendous. The heat was also making her tired, and the vibrations of the tank's engine combined with the gentle bumps and rocks as the tracks rolled through dips and over humps made her wish she could just slump down and go to sleep. To make it worse, she knew that she probably could. She was there of her own volition. Had she been brave enough, or patient enough, she could have waited for the following army, or even waited with the wounded. Either would have allowed her to rest and compose herself after the trauma she'd been through. She knew, though, that as much as she wanted to, she couldn't have stayed. She couldn't have waited for the army, as she was genuinely terrified of being missed, and left alone in the desert again; and she couldn't have waited with the wounded, as she had the irritating, demanding, and dangerous driving urge to do the right thing, and she knew her linguistic skills could be the difference in keeping people alive. Or at least she hoped as much. As polite and pleasant as Charles was, he was a killer, and she didn't doubt that he'd shoot first and ask questions later if it looked like the enemy were even thinking of not cooperating. He had his crew to protect, so it was understandable, at least that's how she rationalised it.

Finally, a column of men came into view, marching north towards what looked like a lake, and sending up a light cloud of dust which made them easy to spot. They were like ants at first, tiny brown specks under a smoky haze that hung above them like a beacon, but as the tank continued on its journey, it was possible to pick out the shapes of bodies among the murk, trudging ever onwards at a painfully slow pace, and they were highlighted by a trick of the intense desert light which turned the lake they were marching towards a bright glowing pink. Harriet smiled to herself, it would have been a beautiful scene if they weren't in the middle of a war, and she wished she could capture it somehow before the light changed, and it became just another memory among many.

"Aircraft, twelve o'clock high!" she shouted, as she noticed the column of men, now only a mile away and practically on the shore of the mesmerising lake, scatter in response to a black dot diving down at them. Her daydreams were instantly shattered, and the adrenaline started flowing once again as she slapped Charles hard on the shoulder, and pointed at the growing black dot. "Aircraft!"

"Bloody hell!" he shouted, and after yelling at his driver through the intercom, the tank lurched forward and increased speed, forcing Harriet to cling on as it raced forward. She looked around desperately, there was nowhere to hide. The closest hills were back where they came, not that they'd done much to protect the Italian convoy, but they were better than the vast nothing of the plain. "Hold on, this is going to get a bit interesting!"

"Wait!" Harriet said. "Wait, look! It's a P40!"

"A what?"

"It's an American. It's one of ours!" She felt herself smiling with relief as she shouted, and the stars of the United States Army Air Force painted boldly on the wings came into view, as another dot appeared in the sky behind it, following close behind.

"Oh, thank God!" Charles gasped, turning to smile at her in relief. In an instant he disappeared, and seconds later she was flying through the air and surrounded by a flickering darkness. She couldn't think as she spun in slow motion, only imagining it had all been a dream, and she was still falling from her stricken Lightning. Instinctively, she reached for the ripcord of her parachute, but there was nothing there, and then, without warning, she hit the ground so hard that she felt her brain rattle in her head. Her ears rang with a high pitched scream she couldn't shake, and her eyes burned as she stared up as the darkness lifted to reveal the still blue sky above. It's then she realised that she couldn't breathe, her lungs were burning, and it felt like there was an elephant sitting on her chest, and she desperately kicked at the ground while trying to sit up, fighting to find some air as a wave of heat ran over her. As she rolled onto her knees, a sudden rush of air breezed past her face, and she was able to gasp it in, before coughing and choking as dust and sand scratched her throat. After gasping a few more breaths and reassuring herself she was alive, she lifted to her knees and sat back on her feet before looking around. The tank was burning fiercely and throwing a plume of thick black smoke high into the sky, having received a direct hit by one of the P40's bombs. It took effort to break her gaze away from the inferno, but when she did, she caught sight of a pair of P40s rolling victoriously, before heading away into the distance. After watching them leave, she grabbed the Thompson machine gun, which was lying beside her, and used it to lever herself from the ground. Her left forearm was burned, and she'd been hit by a long slither of shrapnel which stung the left side of her waist, but miraculously she was otherwise unhurt, except for being sore to the touch from being blasted through the air, and having her brain rattled around the inside of her skull. Her ears were ringing, but she could hear the remaining ammunition in the tank cooking off, and the machine gun bullets pinging around the inside as the heat ignited them. She didn't get too close, not wanting to be hit by bullets, or the rounds for the main gun if there were any left to blow, but she was close enough to see Charles' remains slumped in the cupola, and the driver burned into his position. Not one of the crew had stood a chance, and the only reason she was still breathing was because she'd been standing on the rear deck, and was blown away by the shockwave of the explosion. The only other thing to survive was the flask of tea she'd stuffed under the camouflage net and forgotten about. She picked it up and took a sip to relieve the burning in her throat, then slung the machine gun over her shoulder and pulled her scarf up around her mouth and nose again, once more trying to filter out the sickening smell of burning fuel and bodies. There was nothing else to do but head towards the Italians and their prisoners. It was too far to head back to the other two tanks, and once again the spectre of her last trip to the desert returned to remind her that she was better with others than alone. Besides, they'd be missed soon, and the other tanks would come looking for them. At least that's what she told herself.

The lake had become more vivid in its colour as she came closer, despite being shrouded in a fog of smoke, and the pink and turquoise water was framed with brilliant white shores, making the colours stand bright against the starkness of the surroundings. It was beautiful, or at least it would have been if it hadn't been sullied by the death and destruction that faced Harriet as she walked slowly and silently past the contorted and butchered bodies that littered the ground, staining it red with blood that ran in channels through the salt encrusted sand and into the pink lake. There were moans and cries, and those that had survived called to each other as they tried to help the dying, too busy to notice her, or even care that she was there. The P40s had literally cut them to pieces. She stood and looked at the hell that surrounded her, as the smell of death invaded her senses, and made her so sick that she knew the only thing she could do to improve the situation was to leave. She couldn't help those that were dying, nobody could. She turned to leave and froze in her tracks, eyes wide open as she stared at the vision staring back. Standing before her, unshaven and wearing a scruffy and dirty Italian uniform, was a ghost that took her breath away. Any other time she'd question herself, but she knew those eyes anywhere.

"Is it you...?" Cas asked. His voice was coarse and weak, yet instantly recognisable. "Harry?"

"Alright?" Harriet replied, as she pulled the scarf from her mouth and nose, and fought to stop her heart exploding out of her chest. Her mind was empty, the competing thoughts and questions had spun out of control, and left her with nothing but silence for the first time in as long as she could remember. She always had a thought, an answer, something to dominate her attention, except when she was faced with a spirit long lost.

"I don't know... Am I dead?"

"I thought you were..."

"I don't understand..." For the first time in all the time she'd known him, she saw tears in his eyes as he tried to comprehend the situation, while her own tears ran down her cheeks in torrents. "How can you be here?"

"I told you I'd find you."

The End.

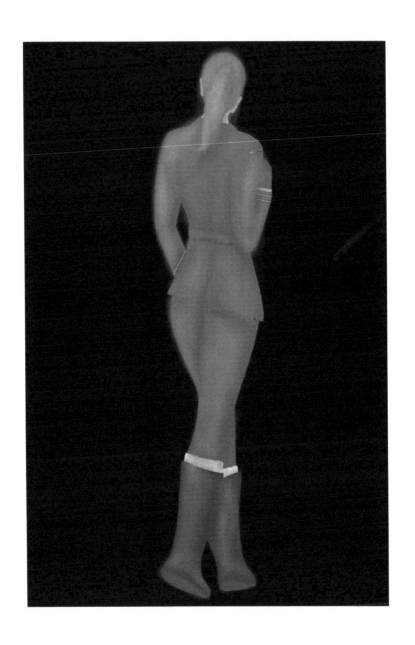

Titles in the Harry's Game Series

Harry's Game – First Of The Few

Published in November 2019

Harry's Game – Hell's Corner

Published in February 2020

Harry's Game – Shadows and Dust

Published in May 2020

Harry's Game – Sleeping Giants

Published in January 2021

Harry's Game – Blue Skies and Tailwinds

Published in July 2021

Harry's Game – Sands of Time

Published in November 2021

Printed in Great Britain
by Amazon

68996020R00201